THE TROUBLE WITH WIZARDS AND OLD ENEMIES

A CARY REDMOND NOVEL, BOOK 6

KAT SIMONS

Published 2022 by T&D Publishing
Cover design: © 2021 Evernight Designs
Interior book design © 2021 T&D Publishing
ISBN-13: 978-1-944600-46-4 (Trade Paperback Edition)
ISBN-13: 978-1-944600-47-1 (Large Print Edition)

First printing T&D Publishing edition: January 2022
For information, contact T&D Publishing: https://www.tanddpublishing.com

To my whole family.
Who made these last few years not just bearable but full of love.
Even occasionally fun. Thank you for standing by me on this journey.

Cary looked up at the ceiling of the dojo and groaned. She really ought to be used to this view by now. That faint water spot that Lucy had never gotten around to getting painted. The inset lights that felt entirely too bright in her face. The white textured panels that made up the ceiling.

She'd stared up at that ceiling from her back so frequently over the last ten months it was like looking out her living room window into her backyard. Very very familiar.

"You're still overthinking," Lucy said from somewhere off to Cary's right.

She rolled onto her side and looked up at her best friend and current worst enemy.

The petite redhead had her hands on her hips, her mouth turned down in a disapproving scowl. For their training sessions, Lucy wore a simple white gi, the top crossed over her stomach, with an ordinary black belt wrapped around her waist, the uniform flexible and easy for any contingency. She looked like a cute, harmless woman with her smattering of freckles across her nose, her curly red hair pulled up on top of her head in a loose bun. She even sounded a bit like a child with her high-pitched voice.

But after more than thirty years of training, Lucy was *not* harmless. She had multiple black belts in more than one martial arts discipline, and Cary had personally seen her kick the ass of men twice her size, more than once.

"I don't know how to not think," Cary grumbled as she pushed herself back up to her knees, working to catch her breath.

Lucy kept her dojo spotless, which ensured it almost always smelled like pine cleaner and faintly of incense. Right now, all Cary could smell was her own sweat—which was significantly less pleasant than Lucy's lovely frankincense sticks burning near the front desk by a miniature brass statue of the Buddha.

At least the dark blue mats beneath her hid the blood.

Not that Lucy had made her bleed. In fact, Lucy was a superb teacher and had never once actually hurt Cary during training. But given how often Cary ended up flat out on her ass, or in some sort of bound position, she kept expecting blood. A nose bleed at the very least.

"You have to let the muscle memory take over if you want to handle shifters who can move significantly faster than you can," Lucy said. "You can't pause and *think* about what you're doing. You just have to do it."

"I did manage to do that once, you know," Cary said defensively.

Okay, it had been while she was protecting and she would have been safe anyway. Still, she'd reacted exactly the way Lucy had trained her to and managed to disarm someone with a knife! She'd done it on her own without the magic her bosses gave her. She'd considered it a big deal.

Lucy had congratulated her. And then increased her training sessions by an extra hour a week.

"Besides," Cary said as she climbed to her feet, slowly, trying not to groan aloud, "it's not shifters out to kill me." Right now, anyway. "It's a wizard. And he's vanished. Since that vampire incident, he hasn't made another attempt. Maybe the vampires killed him." The previous Master of Portland wouldn't have hesitated if he thought it expedient.

"His protégé, who you thought was dead but who isn't dead, is still out there," Lucy reminded her without missing a beat.

Cary scowled. "Yes, but apparently I drained him of all his magic."

All this mess with the wizard out to kill her—she still didn't know his fucking name—had started with Sheldon, a teenage wizard who'd been killing shifters in an attempt to steal their bodies.

Sheldon—and her former mentor Jaxer—were responsible for Cary meeting her mate, boyfriend, future king of the leopard shifters, Deacon Jones. So she supposed she should thank Sheldon for that. She had grown to love having Deacon in her life. Even if their future was filled with potential...difficulties.

She'd thought Sheldon had died during her confrontation with him, but turned out he hadn't. And thanks to his enraged mentor, she'd discovered she absorbed magic and wasn't the ordinary human woman she'd thought she was before being tricked into becoming a magical Protector.

The last few years had been really complicated.

"Magic or no, he killed shifters and he can kill you," Lucy said. "He knows what you are. His mentor knows what you are. You can't rely on your Protector magic to protect *you*."

When Cary had become a Protector years ago, she'd been an ordinary human woman rethinking her career goals. Her bosses, the North American Fae who made Protectors—whom she'd dubbed the Nags because they were—and her faery mentor Jaxer had sort of tricked her into the job. The Nags had imbued her with the ability to channel their magic and keep good guys safe from bad guys. And that had been her job ever since. They even paid her for it.

The problem was that when she wasn't channeling that magic, she was still an ordinary woman who could be killed as easily as any other. Unless she was protecting someone, she was vulnerable. All a bad guy had to do to kill her was want to kill her and only her, and not be any danger to anyone else.

That last part could be tricky, though. Bad guys by their very definition were usually dangerous to *someone* else besides her. It was all in the intentions of the moment, which made it more difficult to kill her than some bad guys thought because…well, they were bad and intended bad things.

But if a bad guy *knew* how to kill her, knew what she was, they could manage it.

Sheldon's mentor had come close to killing her a couple of times before siccing the vampires on her. He'd figured out that trick. If he could do it, others could as well.

And now that she was in the last part of her seventh year as a Protector—a test year she had to either pass and come into her full powers (whatever that meant), or she'd die and her family would be compensated—she felt even more vulnerable to these issues. Too many people now knew what she was, despite her best efforts. She'd made a lot of enemies in her time as a Protector. Turned out, bad guys hated the person who stopped them doing whatever the hell they wanted.

Who knew.

"You have to learn the stuff I'm teaching you," Lucy continued emphatically. "And you have to have it in your bones. You have to be able to react. *Not* think."

"I swear, this is the first time in my life I've been accused of *thinking* too much."

"Ha! Want me to list the other times."

"No." Cary lowered her chin and gave Lucy a look.

Lucy returned it with a grin. "I have a surprise for you."

Cary groaned. "I'm going to hate it, aren't I?"

"Depends on if you can stop thinking or not."

Cary watched Lucy's back as she disappeared into one of the two back rooms the students used for changing. She came back out followed by a man large enough Cary had to crane her neck back to look up at him.

He was six foot nine if he was an inch, wide and thickly muscled, dark brown complexion, clean shaven, his dark curly hair cut close and tight to his head. He wore a navy blue gi with a black belt circling his waist, the two colors blending together so well it was hard to tell the belt's color unless she looked close. His expression when he stepped onto the mat was serious and fierce.

And Cary's pulse kicked hard.

"Cary," Lucy said, smiling up at the man who was two and half times her size, "this is Brandon Hawthorne. He's a bear shifter." Lucy met Cary's wide-eyed gaze. "And your new sparring partner."

Brandon grinned.

Oh boy.

ONE HOUR LATER. THE CEILING AGAIN.

That water spot was spreading. She'd better warn Lucy to have the landlord look into it.

"Can you breathe?" Brandon asked, his grinning face coming into Cary's view overhead.

She took a test breath just to make sure. "Give me a minute. Just a minute."

Brandon, as it turned out, was a delightful man. Happy and friendly and easy with a joke. And he did not pull his punches even a little bit. Or well, he did in that he kept them to human tolerable levels. But he didn't give her a break from tossing her around on her ass.

"I am never going to keep up with you, you know?" she said, still prone on the mat. It seemed safer down here. The minute she stood up, Brandon and Lucy came at her again.

They'd been tag teaming her for the last hour. And while Cary could *see* Lucy when she moved, she couldn't seem to avoid the hits. Brandon, she couldn't even see most of the time. She'd blink, he'd be in front of her, he'd flip her onto her back. And she'd stare up at the ceiling for a few minutes catching her breath.

"Lucy's right," he said, offering a hand to help her to her feet.

She took the offer gratefully, groaning as he easily lifted her to a standing position—without her having to put much effort into the process. Which was good because she was exhausted and only stubborn will kept her from tumbling back onto her face onto the mat once Brandon released his hold. She straightened her gi top in a bid to delay the inevitable next attack.

"I'm always right," Lucy said, her little girl's voice smug.

Cary snorted.

Brandon's smile widened. To be fair to the bear who kept knocking her on her ass, the man had a really charming smile. Broad and open. He was one of the most laidback shifters Cary had ever met. His movements, when he wasn't tossing her around the dojo, were all easygoing grace, almost lazy and slow. And he laughed easily.

He was extremely careful of his strength, too, gentle with her fragile human body, despite flipping her onto the mats repeatedly. She knew without having to be told he could break her in half with his pinky finger. Even if he wasn't a bear shifter, he'd likely be able to do that. But he didn't seem inclined to exert any of that power. Given all the shifter power plays Cary had witnessed—and been the focus of— over her years as a Protector, his seeming uninterest in showing off that strength struck her as extremely refreshing.

"Sensai's arrogance aside," Brandon said, winking at Lucy. She rolled her eyes at him. "She is right about your overthinking. You're trying to see me. But you will never see a shifter move. You have to act on instinct and stop relying on your ordinary senses."

Actually, she *could* see shifters move when she was protecting someone. But she took his point. "I don't know how to stop relying on my ordinary senses," she said with a sigh. "I don't know how to stop trying to see you."

"Instincts take time to develop," Lucy said, rubbing Cary's sore shoulder. "That's why I asked Brandon to help us. You need to get used to acting, just moving, without worrying about everything else. And you need to learn how to do that with someone like Brandon."

"I'm here for you," he said with a friendly nod. "Don't worry, we'll get you there."

Cary finally let out a long sigh and smiled. "Okay. If you're willing to put in the work with me, I'll try my damnedest to stop thinking so much."

"Good girl," Lucy said.

Cary was about to comment on the condescension when a new voice called from the front of the dojo.

"You two done yet?" Marianne said. She stood at the edge of the mat, hands on her hips, shaking her head at them. "Angie's expecting us soon. The restaurant won't hold our reservation all night."

Marianne was a seamstress extraordinaire and a magical weaver. She created most of Cary's clothes now—all with magic pockets that kept Cary from losing her keys and wallet all the time—and she was one of Cary's best friends.

Dressed in a casual, sexy pearl gray pants suit she'd made to fit her curvy form perfectly and complement her dark skin, Marianne looked almost her old self. She'd returned to the short, soft afro she'd kept for most of the years Cary had known her, after a brief stint with long braids. Her makeup was understated except for a bright plum lipstick which was a powerful pop of color. She looked both indulgent and annoyed that they weren't ready to go. And her smirk and raised brows said clearly she wasn't waiting long if they didn't move their asses. That was Marianne in every way.

Which made Cary's heart happy to see.

Marianne had gone through a very rough breakup a few months back with her longtime girlfriend, and Cary was still worried about her. Marianne had decided not to move back to New York City, which was frankly a relief, but she hadn't really returned to her pre-breakup self yet. And maybe she never would. But Cary, Lucy, and Angie had been making an effort to keep her busy and distracted so she could at least try to get back to some level of peace.

She waved at them. "Move it, ladies. We don't have all night."

Cary grinned. "You've just saved my poor, sorry self from another ass-kicking and I will be forever in your debt."

"I will take you up on that debt later when you buy the wine."

"Deal."

Marianne's gaze flicked to Brandon and she raised her brows again at Lucy, the question clear.

"Sorry," Lucy said. "Brandon Hawthorne, this is Marianne Johnson. Marianne, Brandon. He's helping me train Cary now."

"Nice to meet you," Marianne said. "Try not to hurt our girl too much."

"It's an absolute pleasure to meet you too, Marianne Johnson," he said.

Cary gave him a look. His voice had dropped at least half an octave, to a pretty sexy base rumble. And he was staring at Marianne with an intensity that could have been intimidating if he weren't offsetting the look with his most charming smile.

Marianne blinked and frowned a little at the bear shifter. But she didn't dismiss him or scowl at his obvious attention.

Which was…good?

Well. Now they had some serious things to discuss over dinner.

"Same time tomorrow?" Lucy asked Brandon, her gaze moving between him and Marianne, too.

"Absolutely." He gave them each a nod goodbye, his last for Marianne. "See you again soon."

He ambled back to the dressing room, and all three of them watched him go.

"Hm," Lucy said.

"Hm indeed," Cary said.

Marianne did scowl at them and opened her mouth to retort, but Cary shook her head, cutting her gaze to the locker room. She mouthed, "shifter hearing," and tapped her ears.

Marianne nodded in understanding but her scowl didn't drop.

Yeah, they definitely had a conversation ahead of them. Dinner at this new restaurant suddenly seemed the least interesting part of the night.

At least, it did until the Nags materialized at the back of the dojo to give her a new job.

2

ary dropped her head back, staring at the water stain from a standing position this time. "Now?" she whined, without any regrets. "I'm exhausted, sore, and really hungry." She glanced down at Marianne. "And we have things to discuss."

"No, we don't," Marianne said.

"Yes, we do," Lucy said.

Marianne gave Lucy a look. Lucy returned it completely unrepentant.

"You are needed, Protector," Liruk said. "You have a job to do."

Cary nodded toward the locker rooms and mouthed, "shifter," at them. Geez, as if there weren't enough people in this town who'd figured out what she was. She didn't need her new sparring partner to know all as well. Even if she did like the man.

"We are aware of the bear shifter," Liruk said as if annoyed Cary would think otherwise.

"It was a good decision to bring him in for Cary's training," Wisat said to Lucy.

Lucy grinned.

Cary's bosses, the North American Fae who imbued her with her Protector powers, were…well, a complicated part of Cary's life. A lot of real love-hate between them. Okay, hate was maybe a strong word. Most of the time they just annoyed her. Hate only happened occasionally, depending on the circumstances.

Though, this might just be one of those circumstances since she was sore and really really hungry. Brandon no doubt heard her stomach growling all the way in the locker rooms.

"What do you want?" Cary asked, rolling her shoulders to try and speed up her healing. Everything ached now. Even with Protector magic, she was going to have a hard time moving fast.

"A simple job," Liruk said, her tone softening.

Cary narrowed her eyes. Liruk had, until very very recently, been the most critical of Cary's two bosses, the one most difficult for Cary to get along with. The most disapproving of Cary's attitude toward her job. Liruk was all gold and white, gold skin, white hair, gold horns sticking out of her hair, white robe and pants—which seemed to be their uniform. The only non-gold or white thing on her were her outrageously green eyes, eyes so green it was like nature on steroids. She was a stunning being, a creature most definitely of the Fae.

And she did not understand why Cary resisted so many aspects of her job as a Protector.

Liruk didn't understand Cary's fears. That she wasn't good enough. That she wasn't cut out for this job. That she was going to get people killed.

Something had changed in their relationship recently, though. Liruk still put on the impatient face and disapproving tone when she first appeared on the scene, but her sour attitude softened quicker these days. And she dealt more…gently with Cary.

That shift had Cary on high alert for whatever other shoe they intended to drop on her.

"You are needed to protect a woman from a passing band of angry sprites," Wisat said.

He had always been the more traditionally patient boss, the one who had some vague sympathy for Cary's fears and hesitancies. He was all black and red to Liruk's white and gold. His robe and pants were black, his skin red, his hair black, the velvet-covered antler-like halos that circled his head red. But like Liruk, he had green green eyes.

Cary had never found out if that was coincidence, if Liruk and Wisat were related, or if it was a common trait among their people. The Nags were not inclined to tell her much about themselves or their particular group of Fae. And she'd never been able to uncover *any* information about them beyond some of the names given to them and legends told about them by Native Americans and First Peoples. Even those stories gave them different attributes and quirks. For all Cary could find, Liruk and Wisat might as well be the only two of their type of Fae out there.

"Sprites?" Cary asked, her brows quirked. "You mean the tiny Fae who usually don't do more than cause mischief?"

"They're very angry about some things happening in Faery," Liruk said.

"And will take it out on an innocent human if you don't get there in time," Wisat finished.

"Shit. Okay. Where?"

Wisat gave her an address not far from Lucy's dojo, but she'd still have to drive to get there fast enough.

Cary sighed. "How much time do I have?"

"Not much," Liruk said. And then did something that made everything in Cary freeze. "I am sorry for the last-minute notice."

Cary blinked. Hard. Several times.

Sorry? Liruk had just *apologized*? For something they did to Cary all the time?

"Uh." She didn't know what else to say. Liruk never apologized. Certainly not for popping in and sending Cary on missions willy-nilly. They usually refrained from doing so in front of other people. The fact that they were here in Lucy's dojo, doing this in front of Lucy and Marianne, was a testament to the need for Cary to hurry to this job.

But apologize for...anything?

Now Cary really was worried. She narrowed her eyes at Liruk. "After I've saved this woman from rampaging sprites and then had a nice, conversation-filled dinner with my friends, you and I are going to have a talk."

Liruk lifted her chin, but didn't argue the point with Cary.

That didn't bode well either.

Cary turned to Lucy and Marianne. "I'll meet you at the restaurant. Don't wait to order food but get me something gooey and with a lot of carbohydrates involved. Thanks!"

She hugged them both, gently since she'd been sweating, and hurried to the locker room for a quick change. She'd have to do a better clean up after she'd saved the poor human woman from the sprites.

And she'd have to worry about her bosses later, too.

But worried, she definitely was.

3

----

ary pushed into her one-story cottage-style house, covered in green slime and very very ready for a bath.

Why did so many of the Fae have to pelt things like slime and glitter and stuff that *stuck*?

She sighed. To be fair, the slime was harmless, like that slime kids used. It was just sticky. And at least the human woman who'd shared the slime bath with her had been pragmatic about it. She had kids so sliming wasn't new to her.

Sprites trying to kill her because she happened to be in the wrong place at the wrong time... That had been new. And the woman, Elise, had handled that pretty well too, all things considered.

Cary waved to her little dog pack as they strolled into the living room to greet her. "Better wait on hugs, guys. I'm a bit messy here." She showed them her slimmed t-shirt. "And I missed dinner with the girls because of this. I'm very unhappy about that." She couldn't show up at a fancy restaurant covered in goop, even if the stuff did smell unusually mild for Fae slime. A bit like cotton candy but a little tarter. Not the worst thing she'd been hit with.

Pickles, her foo lion disguised as a basset hound, and the only other girl in the pack, flopped onto the floor on her stomach and looked up at

Cary with a baleful expression that was only possible with a basset hound's heavy jowls and loose skin.

"Yeah, you get it, huh, Pickles?"

Pickles let out a low woof in reply.

Fred, the mundane terrier-collie cross, jumped up and down, trying to bounce as close to Cary as possible without touching her. He wasn't very successful, despite his efforts, and she ended up with some of his pale brown fur mixed with the slime on her jeans.

"At least you tried," she said to him.

He yapped and dropped hard onto his butt, thick tail thumping on the carpet.

Buck, her golden Labrador who was actually a demon dog—never to be referred to as a hellhound or he got mad—sat next to Pickles looking as laid back and pragmatic as Elise had been while being attacked by sprites. For all that Buck could rip holes between this realm and demon realms without much effort, and when his true nature came out, he had three heads and a *lot* of teeth, he mostly just hung out in his Labrador form and went with the flow of things, happy just to be part of the pack.

"Ah, guys," she said with a sigh, looking at her little band of happy animals. "It's good to be home. Even if I did miss dinner."

Her stomach growled loudly at the reminder.

"Bath first," she told it. "Then food."

She carefully removed her leather coat and hung it on the door handle of her front closet. Fortunately, because the jacket was Marianne-made, it not only had magic pockets, it was self-cleaning. Which meant it would be back to its old battered self by the time she got out of the shower.

How Cary had survived any time as a Protector without Marianne-made clothing, she'd never know. The woman was a genius. And magic pockets were the best thing ever. Second only to coffee and pizza.

As if she'd conjured them by the sheer force of her hunger, when Cary emerged from the shower and headed back into the living room, she caught the distinct scent of both coffee and pizza.

Her stomach growled loudly and happily.

Her heart did a giddy little flip of happiness all its own.

And a moment later, Deacon stepped out of the kitchen. "Angie, Lucy, and Marianne all texted me that you got called away on a job," he said, his deep voice rumbling with his amusement.

She shivered a little. His voice did very wicked things to her, without him even having to try. "All three of them? Did they think you'd ignore one text?"

"They know I worry," he said with a shrug. "More now than ever."

She winced. Yeah. Ever since she'd died that one time recently, he'd been extra worried about her. It wasn't like she'd been dead for very long. She didn't even remember much of it anymore. Not really. At least not the during.

But he remembered everything. And he hadn't gotten over the moment yet.

Because she needed it, and got the feeling he did too, she went into his arms. He was warm and solid and she always felt remarkably settled when surrounded by his scent. She knew some of this was their mate bond, a bond she'd taken a long time to accept. But some of this was just Deacon.

"I love you," she said.

She'd been working hard to make sure those words came out more often now, in moments when she wasn't in danger. It had taken her months to get them out, to say what she was feeling out loud. And then she'd gone and done it for the first time just before dying. She felt like she needed to make up for that by saying the words in non-life-threatening situations as often as possible.

To be fair, he'd said the words the first time to her after she'd almost been killed—by one of his exes no less!—so he didn't have a lot of moral ground to stand on here. Still, he'd managed the words a lot sooner than she had, so she felt it important to balance the scales a little.

She wasn't sure if that was a healthy attitude or not. But it did mean she told him how she felt about him regularly, and that had to be a good thing.

"I love you, too," he murmured into her hair. "Want to tell me about the sprite adventure or just eat pizza and talk about nonsense?"

"Pizza and nonsense first. Coffee and sprites after."

It wasn't dinner with her best friends, but it was equally as good.

"How did training with Brandon go, by the way?" he asked as he led her into the kitchen.

She almost missed the question as the scent of pizza, coffee, and Deacon filled her with so much pleasure she hummed.

Then she blinked. "How did you know about that?"

"Lucy felt the need to warn me ahead of time," he said with a little chuckle. "She didn't want me to get all growly jealous of you working out with another shifter."

"Smart woman."

She didn't even wait for a plate to take her first bite of pizza. She was too hungry. Fortunately, she never felt self-conscious eating around Deacon. He ate more food than three full grown human men thanks to his metabolism and was used to shifters, all of whom ate a lot to keep up with their metabolisms. Cary did not have that fast shifter metabolism to offset all the pizza, but screw it. You only lived once.

Well, in her case, she supposed this was technically twice.

All the more reason for pizza.

"The session went well," she said, setting the rest of her slice on the plate he offered and scooping up a second for good measure. "I ended up on my ass even more than when it's just me and Lucy. And I never once saw him move. So yeah, great session."

Deacon's chuckle danced along her spine, distracting her momentarily from her food. The man could rule the world with his smile and the sound of that chuckle alone.

"I'm sorry you ended up on your ass so much, but I'm glad Lucy thought of this. You spend a lot of time around shifters. Learning how to defend against our speed is important."

Since he was the future king of the area's leopard shifters, and as his mate she'd be considered a leader of them too—which she was still really freaked out about—she knew he wasn't just talking about her job. If nothing went wrong between them, and neither of them died, she'd be spending the rest of her life surrounded by shifters. Knowing how to *not* get her throat ripped out seemed like a very wise idea.

"Does it bug you at all, me training with a bear shifter? Who, I might add, is huge, but super charming and adorably handsome, and I think he likes Marianne, but the Nags interrupted before we could dig into that topic."

"Brandon and Marianne, huh? Is she ready for that?"

"No. But if he's patient, she might be someday. You know him?"

"I do. Pretty well actually. He's volunteered at the shelters before."

Deacon's family business was animal rescue. She'd known she was doomed the minute she'd learned that.

"And he's done some fundraising work for us. He's a professional fundraiser. Did he tell you?"

"No. He was too busy tossing me around the dojo. Is he worthy of Marianne?" After the heartbreak Marianne had gone through when Gina cheated on her, Cary was very protective of her now. They all were. Brandon couldn't be just any ordinary prospect if he intended to pursue her best friend.

"No," Deacon said without even hesitating. "But if anyone can aspire to be, he can."

She grinned. "Good enough."

The way Deacon and her friends had taken to each other had been a huge relief. Mate or not, she would have dropped kicked Deacon to the curb if he hadn't gotten along with her friends. Fortunately for all involved, she hadn't had to do that.

They settled on her couch and ate at the coffee table, as was her habit, with Fred nearby begging for scraps, and Pickles and Buck snoozing under the big bay window in her living room that looked out on the backyard. Both Pickles and Buck were interested in any spare food going, they were just a lot more subtle about that interest than Fred. Fred bounced off Deacon's leg once in his enthusiasm and then proceeded to pound his long tail against the floor until Deacon fed him a slice of pepperoni. Which earned Deacon some bonus points with Fred, she was sure.

They talked about nonsense for a while, and she ate until her stomach finally felt full and happy. Then she ate about a half slice past that because…pizza. Her night might not have gone exactly as she'd intended, but this was definitely a wonderful alternative.

Until her doorbell started to buzz. And not just someone ringing the bell once. No, the ass on the other side of the door set his finger to the buzzer and let it ring in a steady, irritating drone.

"Why does he do that?" Deacon said scowling at the door.

"Because he's Jaxer," she huffed, and went to answer.

4

$\mathcal{C}$ary's former mentor stood on her front stoop, grinning at her scowl. He looked as gorgeous as ever, blond hair pulled back from his face in a low tail—he'd let it go a little longer in the last month—his blue-green eyes sparking with mischief, dressed in his usual silk shirt, opened enough at the neck to show off his perfectly muscled chest.

For a long time, she'd wondered what Jaxer looked like when he wasn't using his glamour to present himself to the world with a more human façade. He was too vain not to appear gorgeous, but she'd always suspected under the glamour he'd be even more stunning, that he used his glamour—his strongest magic—to actually tone down his look because most of the high Fae she'd met over the years were almost too…overwhelming to look at. Her bosses included.

Turned out, she was right.

He'd been toning down his ethereal gorgeousness for years. And now that she'd seen him in all his Fae glory, sometimes that glow, that underlying Faeness seemed to superimpose itself over the image she was used to. She had to blink a few times to ensure she was looking at the man she'd known all these years, her former mentor, her—she hoped still—friend.

A friend who had really bad timing and liked nothing better than to irritate the hell out of her.

"What?" she asked, with as much bite as she could manage when she wasn't actually mad at him. Just annoyed he'd interrupted her quiet evening—and the kiss she'd been leaning in to start with Deacon.

Jaxer's grin widened. "I didn't interrupt you mid-pizza, did I? I'll leave and come back."

"Shut up." She opened the door wider and let him in.

He and Deacon exchanged a grunt of greeting. Not super friendly. But not hostile. Which was a serious change in their dynamic from just a few months ago. She liked the change. It cut the tension in the room down a lot when the two of them weren't at each other's throats.

Especially because they'd been at odds over her, and she really really hadn't enjoyed being in the middle of that jealousy nonsense.

But since they'd all returned from their adventures in Faery six weeks ago, Deacon and Jaxer had settled into a kind of truce. Not quite friends again. But…closer.

And Jaxer had bigger relationship issues than her to deal with now. Which, if she were being perfectly honest with herself, she found delightfully fun to watch.

She settled on the couch next to Deacon, leaning into him when he put his arm around her shoulder. Jaxer sprawled elegantly on one of the two chairs that bracketed the coffee table. He didn't scowl at Deacon's arm around her. That was also a change. Yay for the truce!

"What's up?" she asked, more friendly this time because relief had a way of dampening her irritation. And now that she was in a test year, Jaxer wasn't her mentor anymore, so he wasn't here with job-related news.

At least, she hoped he wasn't.

He'd been dropping in to check on her more without it having anything to do with work. She had a feeling, although he wouldn't admit it, that he'd been as shaken by her death and recovery as Deacon.

To add to Jaxer's trauma, he'd also lost his father in that same battle. He refused to talk about it, though, so she wasn't sure how much of his visits were tied to that. And she didn't push. When he wanted to talk, she was here to listen. But everything that had happened in Faery had changed things for all of them.

And they were still adjusting.

"So, I was in The Bookstore yesterday…" Jaxer started.

Cary sat up a little straighter. "Renee is good?"

"Great as always. She says Hi."

Cary grinned. The Bookstore was this wonderful place full of books on all things supernatural and preternatural. A neutral haven for every species and talent. And not *exactly* connected to time and space. Renee was the current proprietor. She'd been super helpful to Cary over the years. Also, she gave Cary a friends-and-family discount because of that one incident early on. To be fair, Pickles had sorted out the problem, but Cary had helped, and Renee had been grateful enough to give her the good discount.

The Bookstore was where Cary had gone to learn the full extent of —or at least what little was known about—her ability to absorb magic. Learning she absorbed magic in the first place had been a pretty big shock. Especially because she'd learned the fact from the wizard who wanted her dead. He thought she'd stolen his protégé Sheldon's magic on purpose, magic the old wizard wanted for himself. And one of the only reasons they knew Sheldon was still alive and hadn't been killed when she'd drained him of his magic was because he'd shown up at The Bookstore.

And Renee had promised to let them know if he appeared there again.

Cary narrowed her eyes at Jaxer. "Is this about Sheldon?"

Jaxer smiled a little, and nodded as if she'd done something clever. She rolled her eyes at his condescension but didn't want to throw the conversation off track by making a big deal of it.

"Sheldon has been back to the store a few times in the last couple of months," he confirmed. "Renee was finally able to get more than a word or two from him. She still doesn't know if he's working with his master or not, but he told her he's learning spellcraft. And he makes no claims of being a wizard. He told Renee he was a novice witch."

The fact that Sheldon was still trying to wield magic wasn't good news. He'd done very very bad things with magic before.

"We knew I'd accidentally drained a lot, if not all, of his magic. On accident," she felt the need to emphasize. "But does that mean he's *not* a wizard anymore? I mean, does that happen? I haven't been able to find anything in the literature."

Wizards came with innate powers that they fueled and augmented with rituals and a sort of magical chemistry—a cousin to alchemy, but no wizard would deign to admit to studying alchemy nowadays. Their power was different to a witch's, tapped different magical "stuff". And they tended to work with things like energy bolts and brute force powers and chemically-created potions, where witches worked more with elemental magic and herbal potions and divinations and the like. Witches and wizards felt there was a very distinct line between their different magics and skill sets. Most of the time, Cary could see their point of view. But occasionally, it all just looked like magic to her.

"The literature is pretty sparse on anything to do with your abilities," Jaxer said. "A wizard having his powers drained that way probably doesn't come up a lot."

She made a face. "So what do we do about him? I kind of feel like I should confront him. Because his master did try to kill me more than once—including getting me on the bad side of the Master of Portland," she added with a scowl. She typically tried *not* to get on the bad side of Master vampires because they were scary as all hell.

"I think you were already on Gabriel's potential-problem list before the wizard," Jaxer said.

"But he never summoned me or tried to make contact with me before that. We could have just continued on ignoring each other, and we would have both been perfectly happy."

"And he wouldn't be dead," Deacon added. "Or, you know, permanently dead."

She nodded. "I still wonder if the vampires didn't go after the wizard for his part in all that."

After that mess, the new Master of Portland, James—an unaccountably ordinary name for a vampire Master—had come to an agreement with Cary that ensured the vampires didn't bother her and they continued the rule of not feeding off the unwilling in Portland. There were more than enough willing to go around. The rule had been set in place two Master vampires back, when Ariel ruled, because she had agreed with Cary that vampires should not feed off defenseless kitten blood. Though probably for different reasons.

Gabriel, the next Master, had upheld that rule after he'd killed Ariel and taken over. But he'd pushed it when the whole wizard mess happened, forcing a confrontation with her.

She hadn't actually killed him on purpose. More like *channeled* the being who had. Who hadn't even technically been a full being yet as she was still a fetus in the womb at the time. But baby gods had different rules to humans, and even vampires for that matter. From the outside, the actual process of what had killed Gabriel hardly matter. Cary had seemingly killed the Master of Portland. And the Master who took over ensured his people believed that. She got the impression James knew better, though. The vampires had been quiet ever since.

But the wizard going to the vampires had catalyzed that whole situation. That couldn't have made most of them happy. Except maybe James. But even if he was pleased with what the wizard had started, that wouldn't stop him from killing the man just to tie up all the loose ends.

"We haven't seen Sheldon's mentor since all that," she said. "No signs of him even though Sheldon keeps showing up."

"Well, you did come across as pretty indestructible then," Deacon pointed out.

Fortunately, no one had known *why* she was indestructible while facing Gabriel. Still… "The wizard was really angry, and he thought killing me would give him back Sheldon's power. He wouldn't just give up, right? He didn't strike me as the 'give up' type. If he's not dead, he's in hiding from the vampires."

"Or formulating a better plan," Jaxer pointed out.

She winced. That didn't bode well. "So do I confront Sheldon or not? The Bookstore would be safe enough for both of us to talk."

"Renee won't let either of you hurt the other," Jaxer said.

She scowled at him. "I'm not going to hurt Sheldon unless the little shit attacks me again. I didn't hurt him on purpose the first time."

Jaxer's mouth twitched. "I was thinking of Sheldon hurting you, but…" He shrugged elegantly, and her huff made his grin widen.

"Would Renee facilitate that meeting, do you think?" she asked.

"Maybe. But only if you guarantee no fireworks."

"I can't do fireworks."

Jaxer raised his brows.

She made a face. "I can't do them on purpose," she corrected.

She actually had unleashed a few big storms of magic over the last year. Mostly on accident. She still didn't know how to do it deliberately and with any kind of control.

But the good news was that she was training that skill with a dragon now. An actual, honest-to-god—not-a-shifter version, but an honest-to-god—ancient dragon. Who was friends with a hero named Joan.

A golden dragon.

A dragon Joan had named Rory—because he roared.

The whole thing was wild and a little surreal. Even for her life. She'd helped Joan and Rory just recently, and now Rory was helping her. She still couldn't consistently unleash any of the magic she absorbed, but she had managed to let out the dragon magic she'd taken in while helping Joan and Rory, so she wouldn't die. Again. And that was always good.

"How's your training with the dragon going?" Jaxer asked as if reading her thoughts.

"Good. I get the theory better now. And the mechanics of the process. I think. But putting it into practice and controlling the release are the real issues."

"You haven't absorbed any big outlays of magic since the dragon thing," Deacon said. "I assume the sprite issue tonight didn't add too much to the mix?"

"Sprite issue?" Jaxer asked.

She waved that away. "Just work. And no, I don't think I picked up too much sprite magic. A little of course, but nothing I can't live with."

Deacon's arm tightened on her shoulder, and she regretted her phrasing. "Anyway," she said, "I can guarantee I don't have enough magic filling my human cells to cause any issues. Or fireworks. So long as Sheldon doesn't attack me on sight, we can manage." She hoped.

She needed this wizard issue—lurking in the background like the other shoe waiting to drop—taken care of soon. She only had two and a half more months left in her test year. A couple more months to survive. Then she found out what her bosses meant when they said she'd come into her full powers. And she'd hopefully get some help and backup again.

Though, to be fair, she'd had a lot of backup this year. Her friends. Deacon. Even Jaxer at times, though he wasn't supposed to be helping her—there was always an excuse the Nags accepted. She hadn't been nearly as alone this year as she'd feared when learning about it.

Huh. That was…nice.

"Will you talk to Renee for me?" she asked Jaxer. Then because she *was* still in her test year, "Can you? This isn't technically work, but…" She shook her head. "Never mind. I'll just go in and talk to her. I haven't given her a Pickles update in a few months. It'll be better if I do this."

Jaxer tilted his head to one side, his look speculative. She couldn't read his expression or the emotion behind it, but for some reason the look left her feeling a little irritated. She could practically feel his condescending pride.

Or maybe she was just grumpy.

"I'll go with you," Deacon murmured.

"Oh, no. You can't see Sheldon again. He tried to steal your body. Even if he doesn't still have nefarious intentions, you want to kill him. And I need to *talk* to him not *kill* him. I hate when I have to protect bad guys from good guys, especially when the good guy is you. So, please, do not come with me."

He held her gaze for a long moment. "I won't try to kill him for your sake and because I doubt Renee will let me. But I will have your back. Don't ask me not to do that."

She let out a long breath. "Fine. But you mind your manners. I don't want Renee to have to ban you from The Bookstore. It's one of my favorite places, and I will be very mad if I can't go back."

His mouth lifted in a faint smile.

That would have to do. "Any other news?" she asked Jaxer. "Or is this the reason for the visit?"

"I can't just want your company?"

"Ha! No." She narrowed her eyes. "How's Eriana doing? Settling into her training as a future mentor for Protectors? That...tough, you training an ex?"

"Who said I was training her?" he asked, leaning back in the chair like this conversational turn didn't bother him.

She was not fooled. "The Nags," she lied, just to see what he'd do.

"They don't talk about that with Protectors."

"If you say so. Must be hard, though. Given yours and Eriana's history. Working together now." She shrugged. Waited.

Jaxer narrowed his eyes. Glanced at Deacon.

Deacon's expression was blank, at least as far as Cary could tell. Jaxer had known Deacon longer, but Cary had been studying his face for months now. And she couldn't see any outer expression or reaction to the fact that she was lying through her teeth, though she had no doubt he smelled it.

Jaxer faced her again. "The Nags wouldn't have told you."

"Sure, sure. Want some pizza? Coffee?"

Jaxer's frown probably shouldn't have amused her so much. But she never got to needle him this way. And she had to admit, she was enjoying it.

"I don't drink coffee," he said, still frowning at her.

"That's right. Tea, then? I could put the kettle on." She made a move to stand.

"The Nags would not talk to you about this," he said, more firmly.

"You said that already. Tea or not? I'm not boiling water if you're not interested."

"Nothing. Thanks," he muttered absently.

She settled on the couch.

"They wouldn't have," Jaxer said.

She smiled. "Sure."

"You're trying to get me to admit something."

"Why would I do that? Where are you with the pizza? Want some? Deacon brought two large so there's a slice or two left."

Fred lifted his head from his spot by the window at that news and thumped his tail twice.

Cary shook her head. "No more for you. You've had enough pepperoni. You'll make yourself sick."

Fred whined a little but put his head back down and closed his eyes, his tail still thumping against the floor a few more times. Fred would eat as much as Deacon if she let him. It wouldn't be good for him, but he would do his best.

"Pickles," Cary called, "you want to come with me to visit Renee?"

"Woof," Pickles said and then flattened herself further onto the floor, closing her eyes.

Cary took that as a no. Which was fair enough. Pickles hadn't been back to The Bookstore since she'd adopted Cary and left with her. Since she'd gone to the store to retire after losing her mate, Cary figured Pickles preferred not to revisit the place she'd been in mourning.

Or it could just be Pickles was lazy about getting into the car if the trip didn't end at the park.

"They wouldn't have told you," Jaxer said.

"Who told me what?" Cary asked, pretending she didn't know what he was talking about.

"The Nags." He gritted his teeth. "About me training Eriana."

"You're training Eriana? That must be awkward, what with your history and all." Her lips twitched, though she tried to contain her grin.

"That's not what I said."

"So it's not awkward? You're getting along well?"

"That's—" He cut himself off and scowled at her. "You're doing this on purpose."

"What?" she said, hand to her chest, all false innocence.

"I'm leaving." He stood.

"So no pizza then?" She rose to follow him to the door.

Deacon cleared his throat in a way that sounded suspiciously like a chuckle.

Jaxer spun to face her at the door. "They wouldn't have told you," he insisted, pointing a finger at her.

"About pizza?"

He growled a little and walked out, leaving the door hanging open.

She watched him stomp to the nearest tree, one of the larger ones lining the sidewalk, and walk right into it, and into Faery, without pause. Without even trying to be subtle.

"Wow." She shut the door. "That conversation really got under his skin." She chuckled. "That was fun."

"So," Deacon said when she settled next to him. "Bookstore tomorrow?"

"Bookstore tomorrow."

5

The Bookstore was one of the most charming places Cary had ever been. From the outside, the shop didn't even look open. The name was etched in white on the large front window, but looking inside, boxes were piled haphazardly, a layer of dust covered everything, and the lights were off. It looked like a place that had gone out of business and some leftover stock had been abandoned. Try to push open the door and it would feel locked…

Unless you were allowed in.

Cary moved into the soft light and busy bustle of The Bookstore with a sigh. This never got old.

Book-stuffed shelves lined the walls, tables and self-standing shelves made a maze of the central floor, recessed lights gave the place a cozy feel, and patrons of every known preternatural nature wandered the stacks.

A vampire stood several shelves away from a being with horns that may or may not have been from Faery, who stood just behind a large hairy creature Cary was convinced was a Yeti but she'd never been brave enough to introduce herself, who stood two tables away from a diminutive woman wearing a prominent pentagram around her neck, who stood beside a large, handsomely dressed man with a pointed tail curling up over his shoulder, who gave a passing nod to a lion strolling between tables toward the back of the room, who moved to one side to let a sentient plant-like being made of shivering vines and leaves shuffle through a narrow space between shelves.

Cary wasn't entirely sure some of the people who came into the store were even from Earth or any of the realms with connections to Earth. The store wasn't linked to space and time in the usual way. People came in from different places, different times, different realms. Everyone was welcome and everyone knew the rules. No fighting, no causing trouble. This was a neutral, safe place.

And that safety was strictly enforced.

Though by magic or alien science or something even more Cary had never been sure. And Renee wasn't telling.

With all that coming and going from other realms, Cary had wondered early on how everyone got back to where they'd come in from. But apparently the front door took care of that by DNA scans linking a being to its time and place for exit. This ensured everyone got back to their own homes without hassle, and that no one tried to use The Bookstore as a gateway to invade other realms.

All very well organized and peaceful.

For beings in the world of witches and wizards and demons and shifters, a place like this, a haven to be oneself without having to worry about attack… This was priceless.

Cary spotted Renee at the far end of the store, helping a willowy thin, very pale being pick out a book. She had to stare at Renee's customer a moment to reassure herself the being was corporeal. Cary was terrified of ghosts. Facing a vengeful wraith in Faery had only made that fear worse. But the being with Renee wasn't a ghost. Cary wasn't sure what kind of being they were, but they were very much corporeal. And they had a lovely smile when Renee handed them three different volumes to consider.

"Do you want me to make myself scarce while you talk with Renee?" Deacon asked.

He'd stuck to her shoulder as they'd taken in the lay of the land. She was sure he'd been hunting for danger and found the place satisfactorily safe or he wouldn't have offered to leave her side. That sort of overprotectiveness was sometimes a pain in the ass, but she'd gotten used to it over the last few months. Plus, she had to give him a little leeway with it after Faery.

And honestly, she kind of liked it now. After Faery, she was still shaky sometimes too.

Renee spotted them, waving as she moved around the stacks toward them.

Cary said to Deacon, "Stay. I'll just end up telling you everything later anyway. This saves a step."

His hand brushed the small of her back, a gentle caress that made her smile.

"Cary," Renee greeted when she reached them. "Deacon. It's good to see you both. What can I do for you today? More research I assume."

Renee was a lovely woman of indeterminant age who Cary suspected might be a god of some kind but no one would confirm that. She'd been favoring a 70s hippy look for the last couple of years and today was no exception. Bellbottom jeans, a paisley shirt in swirling purples and oranges that complimented her dark complexion. Her dark brown hair was pulled up into two fluffy puff balls on top of her head. And if you didn't look into her eyes, you might mistake her for human.

But her eyes… Black with pinpoints of sparkling light like stars. As fathomless as the universe itself.

Sometimes Cary wondered if, like Jaxer, Renee presented a different look to different people. Or if she looked like this to everyone who came into the store. Deacon saw what Cary did. So maybe she didn't bother. She had the perfect balance of attentiveness and distance required of a good bookstore owner, and all her customers seemed happy and content. So whatever they saw when they looked at Renee, it was reassuring and business-like.

"I have a question," Cary started. "And I might need some help."

Renee's thin eyebrows rose. "What's happening?"

"Sheldon. The wizard who claimed to be a witch to you."

"Jaxer told you he'd been back?"

"And I think I need to talk to him."

"I can't allow fights in here." Her mouth quirked. "Not even for you. The Bookstore won't allow it."

"I don't want a fight." She winced. "I'm still not very good at them anyway. I just need to talk to Sheldon, find out what happened to his mentor… I don't know, try to put an end to this thing with the wizard. It's hanging out there, waiting to bite me in the ass. I need to do something, even if it's just confronting Sheldon." She raised her hands when Renee opened her mouth. "In a non-violent-I-just-want-to-talk sort of way. I promise."

"What if Sheldon gets violent?"

"I can protect the store from him."

"He'll be aiming at you, not my store or my customers."

Always the wrench in any of Cary's plans. If she didn't have someone to protect, she was vulnerable. And screwed.

"I'd rather it didn't come to any kind of fight," Cary said, avoiding Renee's point. "I just want to talk. I don't want to ambush him or put him into a position where he feels like he has to attack."

"He's very jumpy and paranoid, Cary. He's going to feel ambushed no matter what."

"Even if we organize the meeting here ahead of time? Even if, say, someone he's sure is neutral presents the idea?" She raised her brows hopefully at Renee.

"Neutral I am," Renee allowed. "But that's the very reason I can't arrange the meeting. Not and still be neutral. I don't get my store involved in the conflicts of other people or species or…anyone for that matter." Her smile was gentle but firm. "No matter how much I like them and see their point. This is a neutral place. And I'm a neutral proprietor who enforces that neutrality on my property. I have to," she finished more quietly.

Cary nodded and let out a long breath that fluttered some of the short hairs on her forehead that had escaped her ponytail. "Fair enough," she said. "It was worth a try."

"How goes the training?" Renee asked, changing the subject.

"With Lucy? Great. She brought in a shifter to toss me around the dojo now instead of just doing it herself."

Renee chuckled.

"With the dragon…" She tipped her head to one side, frowning slightly. "I get the theory. It all makes sense logically. But the doing. That's been the tricky part."

"Probably because you don't have enough magic built up. You keep instinctively releasing it."

"Well, Rory did help with the dragon magic," she said.

"But without absorbing more and practicing that way, you won't be able to learn the 'how'." Renee motioned her to follow. "I have a book that might help a little."

"Of course you do."

Renee grinned over her shoulder.

She didn't lead Cary and Deacon into the backroom, the place with books that weren't allowed to leave the store. Books either too dangerous or too rare to be sold. That room was where Cary had learned about her own strange and rare gift—only, gift seemed like the wrong word. And talent implied she had some control over it. Trait maybe? Her trait was rare, this ability to absorb magic right into her cells. There wasn't much know about it or written about it. Mostly, because almost everyone who had the trait ended up dead. Sometimes before they even knew what they could do.

The single slim volume on the subject that Renee owned was kept in the back room. And while it had at least given Cary an idea of what she could do. The author hadn't had any useful information on how to survive. Absorb too much magic without releasing it, her cells explode. Simple as that. But how to release it so as not to kill people… The author had no good insights.

Instead of leading them to the back room and that one little book, however, Renee took them to a shelf against the wall, near the middle of the store. A little black sign, hand lettered in white, listed the subject of the books on the shelf. This one read: Alchemy.

"Alchemy? I'm not sure that'll help," Cary said dubiously.

Alchemy had been a forerunner of chemistry and medicine, but with a lot of extra magical and religious undertones that the modern sciences had dispensed with. And while there were still some people practicing alchemy, as far as Cary could tell—between her own readings, and talks with Angie whose main interest outside witchcraft was astronomy—one of alchemy's main goals, turning base metals into so-called noble metals, had been made irrelevant by modern chemistry and physics.

"Smart people studying suns already figured out how gold is made," she said aloud.

Deacon raised his brows at her.

"Supernovas," she told him.

"Supernovas?"

"Apparently. The heat and pressure of supernovas is nature's way of making gold. Impossible to replicate that on Earth, though."

"How do you know that?"

"Angie told me. I'm not sure I understood all of it, and I think there's more to it than just supernovas, but that was the gist. You know Angie would have been an astronomer if magic hadn't called, right?"

"I thought she studied psychology."

The fact that Deacon knew that, that he paid attention when she talked about her friends, made her smile. "She did. But that was after magic called and she had a vague idea of what she'd be doing with her life. Astronomy was just a hobby after that."

"Huh. She and Dylan would have a lot to talk about."

"Yeah they would." Dylan was Deacon's youngest brother who actually was an astronomer studying suns. The fact that she'd just told Deacon something his brother probably already knew gave away how little Deacon spoke about astronomy to Dylan.

"Believe it or not," Renee said as she scanned the shelf, "there are still some things in these old tomes that chemistry and physics and your modern medicine haven't cracked. Yet. Ah, here it is." She pulled a book off one of the lower shelves, a thick, brown-leather hardback. The leather was cracked and stained darker brown in patches. The lettering on the front was punched in using black ink which made the title hard to read.

Cary squinted at it when Renee handed her the book. "*Alistair Reginald Bleak's Collected Essays on the Subject of Alchemical Processes and the Human Anatomy. Volume Two.*" She looked up at Renee. "Not volume one?"

"It's…not here," Renee said.

"Someone bought it?"

"No."

"What happened to it?"

"Long story," Renee said. "Needless to say, it'll find its way back to this reality eventually."

Cary raised her brows. Okay.

"But what you need is in this volume. Bleak was considered the authority on the subject at the time of this writing. He's still considered a genius today, despite the more eccentric habits he adopted in his declining years."

"Do I want to know?"

"Probably not until after you've read the book. It might color your opinion of his information."

"Uh huh."

"Chapter fifty-three will have what you're looking for. It's not an answer, per se, but it'll help I think."

"There are more than fifty-three chapters in here?"

"It starts at chapter forty-one. The first forty are in volume one. Wherever it is." Renee nodded to another customer trying to get her attention, then said, "Let me know if you need anything else. Good luck."

When Cary opened the book, she expected the spine to crack and crinkle, the leather to protest in some way. The book looked old, and used, and then not used for a long time. To her surprise, it flipped open easily. The pages weren't yellowing and brittle but white and supple. And while it did emit a mildly chemical smell, it didn't overwhelm her with the stench of a chemistry lab.

She opened to the title page. The ordinary black ink print in an easy-to-read script stated title and author again. No magic symbols or runes or even a publisher's stamp. Which seemed kind of strange for an alchemist's book, given their obsession with secrecy and cryptic symbols.

"I'm always amazed at how many of these old books are so ordinary," she murmured. "I mean, some of them look the way you expect, with aging pages and crinkling spines. Some of them smell like old paper decaying. Some of them you have to be really really gentle with. But so many more are just…books."

She flipped slowly to chapter fifty-three, trying not to get caught up in reading earlier chapters, despite her curiosity. There were a lot of images and pictures that were hard to pass, though. She'd have to go back and look at those later.

The chapter she needed was titled *On the Movement of Magical Energies Through The Human Humors.*

Okay. That sort of sounded right.

She skimmed through the first few paragraphs, which were mostly about people who had innate magic, like wizards and witches, humans who possessed this "extra humor" at birth and therefore had a unique physiology, different to humans without magic. Bleak believed these differences extended to the smallest levels of material that made up the human body. In his time, he didn't know what cells were, or DNA, or really any of the modern understanding of physiology. So his ideas of the "smallest components" that made up the human body were vague, but sort of danced around the idea of individual particles. And among those particles in people possessing magic was this extra piece. That extra piece wove through every part of them, and altered their "ordinary humors" in certain ways—ways he didn't precisely define, to Cary's irritation.

As she continued skimming the chapter, she wondered if maybe this was just more theory, like Rory was giving her. Though, to be fair, Rory had a full understanding of modern science, so was able to use terms more in keeping with contemporary knowledge. And Rory actually knew some of those things science hadn't figured out yet—at least according to Rory. Since he was a multi-millennia-old dragon, she tended to believe him. Plus, Rory wasn't trying to hide knowledge using cryptic language and references.

Bleak, on the other hand, had written a few passages that made absolutely no sense. She assumed he was either being vague on purpose, using a cypher of some kind, which alchemists were notorious for, or the man was a little crazy.

Given what she *could* read, chances were good the answer was all of the above.

"Anything interesting?" Deacon asked. He hovered near her, without hovering over her, and kept his attention on the rest of the store. He wasn't exactly looming and glowering at the other customers, but a slight change in his mouth or brow would turn his stare into a dangerous warning.

She considered scolding him and telling him to relax, but since that never worked, she decided not to waste her breath. "All interesting," she said. "What I can read. But mostly just theory. The same stuff Rory, and Angie for that matter, has been teaching me."

She was close to putting the book back on the shelf when she reached a paragraph about two-thirds of the way through the chapter. And stopped. She slowed and read the paragraph very very carefully.

Then she read the paragraph again.

Huh.

6

"**Y**our scent has changed," Deacon murmured. "You've found something?"

Cary kept her gaze on the book, on the paragraph that had caught her attention. "Stop reading my scent," she replied absently, automatically.

"Can't," he answered, also absently. "What is it?"

She looked up, staring at nothing for a moment as the quiet murmur of bookstore sounds hummed in the background. Then she read the paragraph again. Bleak might have been crazy, but she was starting to understand why people thought he might also be a genius. A crazy genius.

"Okay," she said, "according to this… He's been talking about how magic changes the 'four humors' of the body. How having this additional 'humor' affects everything. To attempt to remove one of the humors would severely affect the human, likely even kill them because the rest of the structures would collapse. He likens it to building an arch, where each stone must be placed properly and line up exactly or the arch won't hold together."

Deacon grunted so she knew he was listening even though he was still watching the rest of the bookstore and the various preternatural beings wandering the stacks.

"So if you try to remove magic from a human born to it, a lot of other things will fall apart, and they won't survive."

Deacon finally glanced down at her. "Sheldon survived having his magic drained. By you."

"Right. Now here's where we get to the interesting part." She skimmed the paragraph again. "It says that, while this was the accepted wisdom of the most learned natural philosophers of his time and through history, he had been doing some experiments and discovered something that might, in future, alter this perception." She looked up. "Lot of this is his words, not mine."

"I get it. Keep going."

"He says he wanted to learn how to remove magical humors without sacrificing the life of the subject, but he did this study because he was trying to...reverse engineer it, though that's not what he called it obviously. He was really attempting to learn how to get that magic into a person previous born without it."

"He was trying to do through experiment what you do naturally?"

"Apparently." She read a little further. "He argues that if he could find a way to take magic out, he could find a way to put it in, and that might be a more powerful tool than even the discovery of the philosopher's stone."

"He wanted magic more than gold?"

"Hard to tell, but that seems to be the undertone here. That it would enable a perfecting of the human body. It would be the 'universal panacea.'" She paused, let out a long breath. "Well...he killed a lot of people during his experiments. He calls them subjects and doesn't say it so bluntly, but sounds like anyone dumb enough to volunteer themselves for his experiments didn't do well."

"Do I want to know how many?"

"There aren't exact numbers. I'm pretty sure I'm grateful for that."

Without taking his gaze from the store, he reached out and squeezed her hand. She smiled a little before continuing.

"So after a lot of not successful experiments, he..." She reread the section. Bleak was kind of a wordy bastard even when he wasn't using archaic language and nonsensical cyphers. "He claims he managed to extract a solution of mixed humors—he specifically mentions phlegm and black bile—without killing the subject, and the mixture contained this fifth humor of magic. And then he… Oh gross. He drank it." She gaged.

"That doesn't sound even a little appetizing," Deacon said, a slight hiss in his voice.

Even his leopard didn't like the sound of that drink.

When she could choke back her response to someone drinking phlegm and "black bile" whatever the hell that was, she continued reading.

"So the icky drink made him sick for a week—no surprise there—but when he recovered, he managed to…" She shook her head. "Okay, I'm not sure whether to take this guy seriously or not. He claims he could light a candle taper with his fingertip, no other source, and that this ability to call fire from his own body lasted about a week before it faded and he could no longer perform the feat."

She looked up. "He's not doing what I do, but…can you really *drink* someone else's magic and have it for a period of time before it fades? That sounds pretty farfetched."

"He drank something with phlegm and bile in it. I'm not certain he was in his right mind."

"Then why would Renee point out this book to me except as a historical oddity?"

"Keep reading. Maybe there's more."

"Vampires don't take in other people's magic when they drink their blood, right?"

That wasn't anywhere in the literature she'd read over the years. She wasn't sure she wanted to ask a real vampire. Her comment had drawn the attention of the one vampire in the store standing several shelves away, but after a quick look, the vampire went back to the book she was reading, and Cary didn't want to disturb her further since she was a stranger. But if something like that were possible, she was sure someone would have mentioned it somewhere.

Vampires *liked* the taste of magical beings—wizards, witches, shifters, the Fae—but they didn't get anything from them besides a kind of high. They didn't get any of their magic. The only time drinking blood gave a vampire anything permanent was when they were turned into a vampire through blood exchange. And even then, the process was tricky and not something just any vampire could do.

Or so the accepted wisdom said.

"Did Bleak keep experimenting after that one incident?" Deacon asked.

She noticed he didn't call it a success. "He and the subject who hadn't died did try again." She paused. "Still didn't kill the subject. Bleak still got sick. Still lit fires for a week before it faded." She winced. "Bit of a glutton for punishment, doing that a second time for something so little."

"Old school alchemists were…dedicated," Deacon said, his tone still a bit growly. "Does it say *how* he extracted these magic humors? Maybe that's what Renee was talking about."

Cary kept reading. "Not a lot of detail on the exact process yet. Typical alchemist, lots of cryptic language. Some references to stuff I don't understand. Wait, here we go." She ran her finger over the passage. "He tried the experiment a few more times, trying to perfect the process. Finally says he did, though the transfer was still temporary and faded away."

"Magic doesn't fade away for you, does it?" He sounded hopeful.

She snorted. "Got me. I'm only just figuring out what it feels like when I absorb magic beyond that tingling sensation. Can't feel it once it's part of me at all. And I wouldn't know if it trickled out and faded away or not. But according to the other book on the subject of my specific skill, it doesn't. I just keep storing it up until I release it, or it overwhelms and kills me."

He let out a sigh.

"You knew it wouldn't be that easy," she said.

"I know. But a man can hope."

She patted his arm, got momentarily distracted by the flex of his muscles, pulled her mind back to the task at hand, and returned to reading.

"Okay, Bleak says the process required the subject to…" She lifted her lip. "Gross. To throw up after drinking a concoction of Bleak's devising, but he doesn't describe the drink in words I can read or understand." She showed the book to Deacon.

He grunted. "No clue."

"More cyphers," she muttered and took the book back. "Anyway, since the drink was probably toxic, I'm not sure I want to know."

"If it made a magic person throw up some of their magic, maybe that's what Renee thought would be useful to you?"

"If I have to drink toxin and throw up to get rid of the magic, I'll just keep the magic." She shivered. "Can't be any more deadly."

"This subject didn't die," Deacon pointed out.

"Not right away. Who knows what kind of cancers or terminal stuff the poor bastard ended up with."

"Keep reading," Deacon said.

She glanced up to see his brow furrowed, his gaze turned inward. Though he wasn't looking at anyone in particular, his expression must have been fierce enough to scare the vampire standing nearby away because she put her book back and hurried to a different part of the store.

"So, the subject would throw up. Sounds like a rough bout of sickness too. Lots of sweating and barf and some blood." She swallowed hard. "Do I really need to keep reading?"

"Yes. Skim the bad stuff."

"It's not the being sick so much as the fact that Bleak mixed this together with another tonic he only describes in the cypher, and then drank the whole thing. I mean… How could he get that shit past his gag reflex? I want to throw up just thinking about it."

"You're not trying to get magic in, you're trying to get it out. You don't have to drink someone's vomit."

"Wouldn't even if that was the answer," she muttered. She couldn't even imagine wanting magic that badly—especially temporary magic that just let you light a few candles. Get a pack of matches and be done with it.

She forced herself to finish reading the chapter, though. Renee hadn't promised an answer, just more information. Maybe this would all figure into a way for her to dispel magic eventually.

"Huh," she said after a few more paragraphs. "Bleak seems to think he found the 'universal panacea' with this concoction. That he was on the verge of solving human disease and illness. He claims that for months following the experiment, even after the magic faded, he was in the best health of his life, able to do things physically he hadn't been able to before the experiments." She snorted. "But his subject died about six months after they stopped trying to pull magic out of him." She looked up at Deacon. "Told you that stuff was toxic."

"He could have died of something else. War. Plague. Burned at the stake for having magic. Run over by a horse."

"Bleak says he died of a bleeding disease." She met Deacon's gaze, her chin lowered.

"Might have been a pre-existing condition." Even he sounded dubious of that explanation.

"He drank poison, he died of poisoning," she said firmly, not willing to brook any arguments on that. "I will not be drinking poison." She skimmed the last couple of paragraphs. "Once the subject died, Bleak couldn't find another subject who he could successfully extract magic from."

"Because no one would participate in his experiments or because everyone else died?"

"He doesn't say. Just that after that one subject, he was unable to recreate the success with anyone else. He still feels he found this universal panacea, though, and that it was just a matter of time before he uncovered what was unique about the successful subject." She grunted and closed the book. "And that's where he ends the chapter. He moves on to another subject in the next."

"That all seems less useful than I was hoping," Deacon said, looking down at her.

Cary mulled over the chapter, considering it from a few angles, trying not to get hung up on the grossness of drinking barf mixed with poison. "I think... I think the fact that Bleak stumbled on a way to extract magic by a mechanical process, a physical process, might be what Renee wanted me to see." She looked at Deacon, her brows furrowed. "I should talk to Rory."

"You should talk to the dragon," he said.

"What do we do about Sheldon?"

"Renee won't arrange a meeting here. Short of stalking the place and hoping to intercept him, I'm not sure there's much we can do yet. We'll have to catch him somewhere else."

"We haven't managed that in months."

"We'll up our efforts. Time to put this mess to an end."

His gruff, deep tone gave her a little shiver.

She really really didn't envy Sheldon if Deacon ever got near him again.

7

Cary met with Rory in her backyard, though how the huge golden dragon managed to fit into her backyard was a mystery to her. Her yard wasn't that big.

As per usual, he arrived in the dark. Though he could fly during the day and his scales reflected light in a way that providing a kind of cloaking against detection, he preferred moving around at night when chance sightings were unlikely and avoiding airport control radar was a little easier.

They arranged these lessons during Rory and his hero Joan's down nights, when Joan didn't have to go stop a monster or rescue the world from some ancient threat or something. Turned out, while they didn't have Protectors like Cary in Europe—yet—they still had a few heroes knocking about. Joan was one of them. And from what Cary had witnessed, she was one impressive hero. Her home country of Ireland was in good hands.

Rory landed gracefully, soundlessly on the grass, his large shape shrinking enough so he could lay down, his wings tucked tight to his back, his spike-tipped tail wrapped around his back legs. As always, Fred charged out barking at the "invader." When Rory didn't fly away, Fred plopped down on the grass next to him and wagged his tail. Fred never really had any idea what to do with the things he chased if they didn't run.

Rory rumbled a greeting to the dog, and Fred wagged his tail faster.

Although Cary *heard* the greeting out loud, and Fred obviously heard it as well, Rory actually spoke in their heads. He could manage it with several people—or animals—at once if necessary, or direct it to a single person, and he could create the illusion that he was speaking aloud. But turned out, dragons didn't have vocal cords that would make sounds like human language. And dragon language was…not good on human ears.

Rory was an honest-to-god real dragon. Not a shapeshifter dragon, one that moved between human form and dragon form. Cary had fought one of those before, a young one who'd gotten in with a bad crowd and didn't last long. The shifters were rare. They existed and were out and about in the world. But you didn't encounter a dragon shifter every day.

Real dragons…

Well, frankly, outside of other realms like Faery, you just didn't see real dragons these days. There were, according to Rory, barely enough in the world at large for Cary to need all her fingers and toes to count them. Most were currently asleep and had been for centuries. Some for several millennia. In fact, most modern scholars assumed all tales of dragons were referring to dragon shifters and that real dragons had died off a long time ago.

They hadn't. But most didn't move in the world these days.

Rory was one of the exceptions.

"You've learned something new, Protector," Rory stated as Fred settled in for a nap in the grass next to Rory's large front leg.

"How did you know?" She sat on her small wooden porch, at the top of the short set of stairs that led down to the grass. Buck settled on one side of her, snoozing in the cooling night air as if there wasn't a dragon in the yard. Pickles took a moment to exchange a nod of greeting with Rory before also flopping down on the porch, on Cary's other side, her loose jowls spreading out around her face as she laid her head down between her paws.

Pickles, being a foo lion who'd retired and taken the form of a basset hound for her retirement, was familiar with dragons— apparently. When Rory had first come to ask for Cary's help, it was Pickles who'd assured Cary she could trust the dragon. In her Pickles way. Which involved a few deep woofs and nudging Cary's leg with her head.

"You look perplexed and like you have questions," Rory said, answering her question. Resting his own head on his forepaws in a remarkable mirror of her dogs, he said, "Please, feel free to ask what you need to. It may help our process."

"Why do you have an Irish accent sometimes and a more formal tone other times?" she asked, even though that wasn't her real question.

His breath chuffed out in a small puff of smoke with his chuckle. "The Irish accent is for Joan. The more formal tone, a fallback for when I'm teaching. Habit," he said, as if that explained everything and didn't leave her with a ton more questions.

But she wanted to talk about Bleak's experiments so she put the diverting, but less important, conversation to the side and got to the point.

She told him about the book, what Bleak had managed—trying her best not to gag too much through the description of what the crazy bastard had ingested—and how it had only worked with the single subject.

"Do you know anything about Bleak and his experiments? What he was doing? And...does this help me at all?"

A slight ripple went through Rory's neck spikes where he had them safely tucked against his long, thin neck. Pickles lifted her head at Rory's gesture, then flopped back onto the porch again, closing her eyes.

"Bleak was interesting, even for an alchemist," Rory said. "Most were interesting. Watching their efforts over the years proved both entertaining and enlightening."

"Said the dragon who wasn't part of their experiments," Cary said.

Rory's chuckle released another huff of sulfur-scented breath.

Which was less unpleasant than Cary would have expected. The sulfur was so mild, it was almost more like the scent of a campfire.

"Actually, alchemists did get involved in dragon hunts, hoping dragons might be the key to gold transmutation."

Cary raised her brows and nodded to Rory's scales.

"They didn't know about me specifically," he said. "But the myths of us sitting on gold gave them the idea that we could perhaps make gold."

"First, you do have a gold and jewel hoard. You told me that part is true."

"But I don't make it," Rory said as if that was obvious.

"Second, I have a friend who can weave gold from straw."

"The weaver. She and her sisters are very talented."

"You know her? They don't know you." Marianne would definitely have mentioned knowing a golden dragon before now.

"They don't. I do tend to know more than others."

Cary rolled her eyes. "Anyway… You don't make gold, but there are magical beings like weavers who can. If you don't want to tackle the natural way of making gold by supernova."

Rory dipped his head.

"And alchemists at least suspected that there were some beings in the world that might be able to make gold, which is why they went dragon hunting?"

Another slight dip. Rory's way of letting her know she was on the right track.

So she continued. "But Bleak didn't create gold with the magic he managed to extract. He made fire. And then only a small spark for a short term."

"Bleak was more concerned with eternal life than making gold," Rory said. "He was well known for his genius, and he focused that genius on anatomy. His goals were all about perfecting the human body so that it never had to die."

"Okay. I kind of picked that up in the one chapter I read. He thought magic would get him there. But he only succeeded with that one person. Why? Do you know? Because he didn't seem to."

"I read about the results of his experiments after he'd concluded them, so I didn't know the successful subject before he died."

"Poisoned by Bleak's experiments, though, right?"

"Likely. They really didn't know what they were mixing together in those days. But then, history is riddled with natural philosophers, and later scientists, making major breakthroughs in knowledge while at the same time killing themselves with the effects of those efforts."

Cary immediately thought of Marie Curie and had to agree with Rory. She let out a sigh. "So this information, interesting as it is, doesn't really help me?"

"Oh, I wouldn't say that." Rory adjusted his position a little, a slight ripple of muscles that drew Fred's attention this time. The collie-terrier hopped to his feet, wagged his tail a few times as if expecting Rory to stand. When the dragon didn't, Fred spun in a few quick, tight circles and settled down for another nap.

"Meaning?" Cary asked.

"We know from his experiments that magic can be extracted, physically through mundane processes."

"I'm not drinking poison and throwing up the magic I absorb," Cary said. "I hate throwing up."

Rory let out another soft chuckle. "I wasn't proposing you try, Protector. Especially since that would kill you and our efforts here are centered on keeping you alive."

"True," she said. "So…?"

"So. You mentioned a wizard trying to kill you."

"Yeah, his student is still out there somewhere. In fact, that was why we were even in The Bookstore. Hoping to arrange a meeting with Sheldon so I can get the stupid wizard off my back."

"He has been quiet, this enemy wizard, for many months now."

"Maybe dead?" She sounded way too hopeful for another person's death. Granted, that person had tried, more than once, to kill her. Still. She felt a bit ghoulish for *hoping* someone was dead.

"Maybe. Or maybe hunting for alternatives to retrieving the magic he believes you have stolen."

She was a little afraid of that. And if the wizard thought Bleak's method for retrieving that magic from her was possible…

She shivered. "But Renee didn't get me Bleak's book as a warning," she pointed out. "She thought it could help me in my efforts to release magic on command. If she wanted to warn me about something, she would have."

"The Bookstore, and its proprietor, are interesting entities," Rory said, his tone philosophical. "Like reincarnated heroes, they don't always *know* the underlying reason they do things."

Reincarnated heroes? That was a turn of phrase she wanted to know more about. She was pretty sure he wasn't referring to Renee. Cary suspected Renee was an alien. Or a god. Maybe he was referring to Joan?

She opened her mouth to ask more, then decided that was a rabbit hole that would lead her too far off topic. "So what you're saying is that the wizard may be looking for ways of getting magic out of me without me…participating in the process?"

"And with the same level of concern Bleak had about whether his subjects die or not."

Cary made a face. Not a farfetched option. The wizard certainly didn't care if she died. What was a little poisoning and barf between enemies?

"I'm not drinking anything the wizard gives me," she said bluntly.

Rory's chuckle was almost a snort this time. "I doubt he'd use that particular method—it only worked that one time for Bleak, and genius though he may have been, even he didn't figure out why it worked with the single subject, or why it didn't last."

"And you don't know either," Cary said with a sigh.

"Still, it's not so much the method Bleak used, or the results of his experiment. The point is that it is possible. And perhaps that's why the wizard has been quiet. He's been looking for an alternate way. Since killing you with his own powers, and then attempting to kill you by putting you on the bad side of vampires, has all failed so far."

"Just to be fair, I was already on the bad side of most vampires," she allowed, with a shrug. "But I get what you're saying. The only problem with all this is that I don't *have* his apprentice's magic any more. I released all that accumulated magic in my fight against a demon's army." And leveled much of Oliver Holland's army while she was at it.

"You have absorbed, released, and absorbed a lot of magic since then. Much of it from very powerful sources. A demon god. A developing future god. Faery. Shadow dragons."

She winced. When he put it that way…

"But I released all of that as well," she said. Even if she hadn't known what she was doing.

She frowned a little as she thought back to the demon god's magic. She hadn't released that right away. Or, well, maybe she had a little? She wasn't sure after so many months. At the time, she hadn't had a clue she could absorbed magic, so she couldn't remember what she'd done, if she'd done anything, to release any of it from that encounter.

By the time she'd been protecting the little fetal god, she'd learned what she was able to do and knew what was happening when she got tingles after encountering magic. She still hadn't known how to release it on cue, but she'd managed to release the baby god's magic after absorbing it. Hadn't she? Or had she just channeled more of baby god's powers?

She'd definitely released all the magic she'd absorbed in Faery. That's what had killed her.

And Rory had helped her release the shadow dragon magic.

She shouldn't still have any magic at all lurking in her cells because she hadn't absorbed any since the dragon fight. Unless you count the sprites from a few days ago.

She rubbed her temples as she thought back over the last year, all the magic. And all the magic before that. Everything she'd done since becoming a Protector.

Her very job required her to channel magic regularly. Her bosses' magic flowed through her every time she'd protected someone over the last six, almost seven years.

If the alchemist was right, magic changed those born with it at a fundamental level, the level of DNA in today's understanding. Their physiology was different in a way that was so much a part of their being, that extracting the magic part of them killed them most of the time.

Had all that magic she'd been absorbing changed her?

Was she now a permanently different being?

And if she was, what happened if the wizard found a way to take out the magic she still had stored in her cells?

That last question was at least easy to answer. Whatever the wizard tried to do to her, she was sure of one thing—he wanted her dead, and he didn't care what killed her. Only that she died.

Oh boy.

8

"Can you tell if I still have magic in my cells?" she asked Rory, even as the conversation, and all the unknowns, made her want to hide under the blankets and not think about any of this.

Rory was silent for long enough she started to worry.

She pulled her jacket tighter around her as a cool night breeze blew through her hair. Lights from around the neighborhood and spilling out her back door kept her backyard from being gloomy. But the subject of whether or not she still had magic stored in her body, and what the wizard would do to get that magic out of her, wasn't a topic that filled her with a lot of cheery vibes.

Finally, Rory said, "You smell of magic, Protector. But you have always smelled that way to me. The scent changes with the magic you absorb—for example, with the shadow dragons."

"You smelled a change and that's how you knew I had taken in magic I needed to discharge?"

"Part of the reason I knew," Rory said. "Also, after Faery, everyone knows you 'eat' magic." He made the word eat sound like a joke.

Since Cary had been combatting an entity that *did* in fact eat magic —destroying it as it ate—and was in the process of eating Faery into oblivion, she wasn't sure the comparison was accurate. But she let it go. Mostly because Rory had a strange sense of humor. Whether that was age, or Joan's Irish influence, she'd never been sure.

"And you are a Protector," Rory added. "Protectors channel magic regularly. It would be strange if you didn't smell of magic."

"Yes, but no other Protectors absorb that magic. They just channel it. And usually have magic of their own. To actually use. I can't use the stuff I take in." According to the leading authorities on the subject.

Who didn't actually know all that much about the subject.

Which meant they could be wrong about that part.

Could she use the magic? Had she used it?

Not in any purposeful, controlled way, she hadn't. She knew that much. She'd leveled Oliver Holland's army in what, at the time, she'd thought was a use of her Protector magic. Just exploded out what she'd assumed was her Protector shield, and it barreled over the army. They only learned later she'd likely just released all the magic she'd been taking in during the attack.

There'd been that moment during the fight with the demon god when she'd stopped a stream of lava from reaching Deacon. But that could have been her Protector magic because she was trying to protect him. And whatever she'd done hadn't worked for long. Just seconds really. But still, it wasn't how her Protector magic usually worked. Could that have been her *using* the demon god's magic?

And then there was the incident with the vampires and the baby god who was, by that point, gestating in someone else. She was pretty sure the potential god—her human parents had named her Jewel in homage to her first surrogate, Mila Juhl—had just channeled magic *through* Cary, the way Cary channeled her bosses' magic to protect people. So while that might have also helped release a lot of the magic Cary had absorbed up to that point, it wasn't her releasing it on purpose. And she hadn't used it.

Could she use it?

Bleak used the magic he took from his subject. But it faded away. Because he used it? Because he…released it by using it.

She straightened her shoulders. "If I *could* use what I take in," she said slowly, her gaze focused on the air in front of her, not the dragon, as she worked her way through the idea, "if I could use it, the way Bleak did to light a candle, not just release it in one big chunk like I've been trying to do, but use it like any other magic wielder, would it fade away? Would that drain the magic down to safe levels? Is that what Renee was thinking when she handed me Bleak's book?" She looked back at Rory. "Could that be the answer?"

Rory tilted his head to one side, another ripple of movement flowing through his big body. The spikes around his neck rose and fell in a wave.

"Magic drains when used," Rory said, his voice sounding distant and more "in her head" than usual. "For all magic wielders there is an ebb and flow to the strength of their innate powers. Usually replaced by simple rest. For them, it's like using a muscle. And the muscle can be strained, even damaged, by overuse. Because it's a part of them in the same way as their muscle and bones. You do not have magic that is innate to you. You channel and take in everything you have, but…" Another ripple of his neck spikes. "The channeling, which you do so well because you have no innate magic to interfere, *is* a use of magic. That process has been training your body to use magic."

"But that's not in my control at all," Cary said, quietly because she didn't want to disrupt Rory's thinking, but this was a point that needed emphasizing. "I don't control when and how the Protector magic moves through me. I rely on it to work, but I can't make it work. I'm talking about controlling the release of what I absorb. The books— well, the one book—says that's not possible. That I can't use what I take in. But also, most people like me end up dead before anyone can really test what we can do. Maybe… If Bleak could use the magic he took in, and he wasn't innately magical at all, then maybe I can since I'm also not technically magical. Maybe if I use it, like Bleak did, the magic will drain away."

Although, if she wanted to drain the magic from say a demon god, she'd probably have to light a shit ton of candles to do it.

"It is possible, Protector," Rory said after another quiet moment. "It is possible. But, if so, it means we must train you differently." Another moment of silence. Another ripple of muscle that made his golden scales glitter in the light leaking out from her back door. "We've been working to have you release the magic. To…push it back out. And that hasn't been working."

"It worked with the shadow dragon magic," Cary felt obliged to say. "You were able to talk me through releasing that."

"Since then, we have failed."

"But I also haven't absorbed much magic since then. There isn't much to push out."

"All things we knew. All things we assumed were the issue. But in the months you worked with your witch friend, she also couldn't help you master just releasing magic, even when you had magic in your cells."

"There's a difference between the way you've both been trying to get me to release the magic, and the process of actually using the magic, though, isn't there?"

Cary felt like they were edging up on the answer, that it was just right there. But she didn't have several millennia of experience to draw on. She was also afraid she was fooling herself, or there were flaws in her thinking she hadn't spotted.

"It is a release—for you—to use the magic," Rory said, his huge eyes narrowed. "You are not like an ordinary magic wielder, one born to it." He nodded very slowly. "You are, in fact, more like Bleak." His mouth tilted up at the corners and opened a little, revealing teeth.

It had taken Cary weeks to realize that was Rory's way of smiling —on a dragon the smile looked like a terrifying threat.

"The Bookstore and its proprietor are, indeed, geniuses," Rory said with another nod. "Whether they realize it or not."

"So you're saying we are on to something here? That this makes sense." She'd been afraid to hope, afraid he'd just tell her she couldn't use magic and she was clutching at straws. The fact that Rory thought the idea feasible made her heartbeat thump harder.

"We shall try," Rory said. "An experiment of our own." A little huff of smoke came from his mouth with his chuckle. "One that doesn't involve…poison and barf."

"Thank the universe for that! Because I'm not drinking poison." She could not emphasize that point enough.

"I need to consult with someone before we can begin," Rory said. "But I feel this experiment will be worth our time."

"If it keeps me from dying again, then absolutely it will be worth the time."

Rory unfurled his body, slowly, giving Fred time to jump up and trot up to the porch. Fred flopped down next to Pickles, his tail thumping happily on the wooden deck. He barked once, a high-pitched goodbye, as Rory rose to his full height—still smaller than his actual size to accommodate the fenced in yard.

"I will return in a few days," he said. "Unless Joan and I are required for something. But I promise to return as quickly as possible." He launched into the air with a few downbeats of his massive wings.

Cary covered her eyes as the wind from the dragon's take off stirred up dirt and leaves. When she looked up, there was no sign of the dragon. Rory was gone.

And she had a possible answer to one of her biggest problems.

Now, if she could just sort out the wizard issue…

9

*C*ary had barely gotten back into the house when her bosses appeared in her living room.

She wasn't sure why she hadn't been expecting them. They popped in and out of her living room all the time, no matter the time of day or night. But she supposed she'd hoped for at least a little more time to mull over what she and Rory had discussed. Deacon wasn't due to arrive for another hour—he went back to his own (rarely used these days) home so she had privacy whenever she worked with Rory—and she'd intended to use that hour to think about all this mess.

All well. Protecting waited for no woman. Even a woman in the midst of a series of never-ending crises.

"What now?" she asked with a sigh. Then winced. "Sorry, that came out ruder than I intended. Who needs saving, and where do I have to go?"

Wisat raised his brows at her apology. Liruk tilted her head to one side and frowned a little.

What? Like she never apologized for being rude. She considered that a moment. Huh. Maybe she didn't?

Too late to take it back now.

When they didn't immediately say anything, she pretended to

looked around herself for their source of distraction and then gave them the "well?" expression. Because, really, if they had a job for her, it was almost always something she needed to get to quickly. Why the holdup?

"Protector…" Liruk started and then fell quiet.

"Okay, wow. You guys are really freaking me out. What's happening? Is someone that shouldn't be dead dead? Is this going to send me into hysterics? What? What?" Her voice rose with each sentence.

Wisat raised his hands. "No, Cary, please calm yourself. It's nothing like that."

She let out a breath. No one being dead was a good thing. Still, there was a lot of hesitance and silence coming from her bosses and that didn't bode well.

"You two really have to let me know what's happening right now? You're making me extremely nervous."

"We have a job for you," Wisat said. He exchanged a look with Liruk.

"It involves magic at levels bigger than a sprite attack, doesn't it?" she guessed.

Liruk sighed. "It is important. But… We require you to protect—" She cut herself off and shook her head. "This may be too much. And yet it is important, Protector. The signs point to this being very very important."

"Who the hell do I have to protect? Why is it too much? You've never once worried about that before."

Well, okay, to be fair they had worried about just that thing when they'd asked her to temporarily serve as incubator to a fetal god. They'd been very good about letting that be her choice. And even Liruk had softened her normally stringent attitude during that job.

But outside of that, especially this year, they hadn't given a lot of thought to her comfort with any particular assignment.

"We need you to protect the former wizard Sheldon," Wisat said.

"No," Cary said. "I don't protect bad guys." If she could *at all* help it. "He killed shifters for the stupidly selfish reason of wanting to steal their bodies. He almost killed Deacon. No. I can't." She realized she'd been shaking her head ever since Wisat spoke and she made an effort to stop the knee-jerk denial. But the effort wasn't easy.

"We understand," Liruk said. "Believe it or not, we almost ignored these portends. Sheldon is young, but old enough to be held accountable for his actions. And his actions were evil."

She narrowed her eyes. "Why didn't you guys ever send me to protect the shifters he was hurting? Why was that something Jaxer was working on outside of his job for you?"

It hadn't occurred to her before to ask that question. To be honest, a lot of bad things happened, even in her own territory, that she couldn't stop or her bosses didn't send her in to stop. Bad things happened all the time, the world over, and there were only so many Protectors. There was also only so much her bosses could do. They worked in premonitions and educated guesses and sometimes dumb luck. None of which was one hundred percent reliable. Sometimes evil happened so suddenly, so spontaneously, there was nothing anyone could do.

But Jaxer had been aware of Sheldon, had actively been trying to uncover his nefarious plot. Why had Jaxer asked her to go rescue Deacon, but her bosses hadn't asked her to protect any of the other shifters Sheldon had killed? There was enough time for them to have figured it out. Jaxer knew. They had to know.

Why hadn't they been on top of that?

She considered what had happened right after—the fight with the demon, Oliver Holland, and his army of supernatural bad guys, all trying to invade a powerfully magical Naga city for reasons Cary still didn't fully understand.

"You were otherwise occupied with Holland's activities, weren't you?" she asked, answering her own question.

If they'd been getting portends of that, they'd have considered that a larger issue and focused on it. Which she couldn't blame them for. The Nagas lived in cities separated from the human realm but linked to it at one single point. They had to remain linked at that single point or their cities were lost to this realm—and the life it fed into them— forever. To relink a city to a new entrance took time and a lot of magic.

Holland had been closing in on the city for a month, at least, before Cary had gone to rescue Deacon from Sheldon.

If Holland had managed to invade the city before the Nagas could move the entrance, there was no telling what he could have done with that level of power.

So, of course, her bosses had been more focused on that. It made sense. She was just a little surprised she hadn't worked it out before. Or even thought about it.

Liruk and Wisat exchanged another look. Wisat was smiling when they looked back at her.

"You have come a long way, Cary," he said.

"And learned a lot," Liruk added. "It is good to see you applying that knowledge and reasoning."

Cary narrowed her eyes. "I can hear the 'finally' at the end of that sentence, Liruk. And I can do without the condescension right now when you're asking me to protect a bad guy. You might as well be asking me to protect Oliver Holland."

Wisat raised his brows. "I think, perhaps, Sheldon is not quite so… bad." He didn't sound entirely certain, though.

"Ha! You don't believe that either. Listen, you two need to explain *why* I should protect that little shit or I'm not doing it." She paused as she realized… "Also, Deacon is going to object strongly to this. I need to be able to explain the why better than 'cause the Nags said so.'"

Liruk flattened her lips at Cary's nickname for them and that made Cary want to grin. She did like annoying Liruk, but only because Liruk so often annoyed her.

Wisat sighed loudly, a way to get both their attention, and said, "Your mate cannot prevent you from doing your job."

"Of course not," Cary said. "The problem is, if he gets near Sheldon, I might have to protect them from each other, and I hate getting in the middle of those fights, especially if it means I'm protecting a bad guy from a good guy because the good guy wants to kill the bad guy. Especially if the bad guy maybe deserves it a little." She made a face at those rambling sentences. Shook her head. "Just explain what's happening. You guys didn't want to ask this of me any more than I want to do it. But something's got you worried enough that you're here asking me to protect an enemy. What spooked you?"

"The usual," Liruk said dryly. "The end of the world."

"Well." Cary shrugged. "Not like I haven't faced that before. Several times just in the last year in fact. What's gonna end the world this time?"

"Sheldon's master," Wisat said.

"How?"

They exchanged another look. That couldn't be good.

When Liruk faced her, her grave expression made Cary's instincts hum in warning.

Liruk let out a slow breath before saying, "He is attempting to find, and release, Oliver Holland."

10

*C*ary had never actually experienced that sensation of having her knees give out in shock. Her knees had wobbled for various reasons, usually to do with fear. With Deacon the wobble was lust. She'd experienced enough shock she'd wanted to curl in on herself into a tight little ball—especially when she'd heard the banshee scream. She'd been so scared, so terrified, she'd wanted to collapse, had worried her legs wouldn't hold her up.

But she'd never actually had her body just drop out from under her in shock.

She only realized it had happened this time when she blinked and noticed she was sitting on her own couch, Wisat next to her, his arm around her shoulders.

That startled her back to the moment. They didn't touch her very often. She wasn't sure they touched much of anything in this realm that often. And when they did touch her, it was usually to a purpose, like to teleport—or whatever it was they did—her to a new location.

She couldn't remember either of them touching her in such an extended and comforting way before this. But Wisat was holding her securely and steadily, his brows furrowed as he studied her face. It struck her that he was quite warm, but not too hot. And he smelled faintly of the forest and woodsmoke. Had she ever noticed that before?

"Cary?" he asked quietly.

She pulled in a deep breath, let it out very slowly. "I'm okay. I think." She looked between Wisat and Liruk. "Has he found Holland? The new entrance for the Naga city?" The fact that they'd confirmed that the wizard was still alive settled over her only after the shock started to ease.

The wizard who wanted to kill her was alive. He was trying to release the demon who hated her into the world. And she still had two and a half more months of her seventh year test to go.

Shit.

"Shit," she said aloud, because it helped.

"He hasn't found the Naga city yet," Liruk said quietly. "If it were that easy, Holland would have succeeded."

"Holland almost did succeed," Cary reminded them. And Holland had killed to get that far.

"But it took more resources than the wizard has," Wisat said.

"So he can't find the city? Even if he tries?" She doubted that very much or they wouldn't be here.

"The problem is not so much him finding the city," Liruk said.

"The Nagas are very good at protecting their cities from intruders," Wisat added quietly.

"The problem is what the wizard will do in his attempt," Liruk finished.

Cary noticed Liruk hadn't actually answered her question. "Can he find the city's entrance or not?"

Liruk's mouth flattened. "The possibility exists. But it isn't as important as the dangers he poses on his journey toward that end."

"You're mincing words into quite the hamburger, Liruk. Just say what you mean."

"He can find the city," she said. "But his method involves a process of sacrifice and magic that will call down doom on this world."

Okay. That didn't sound good at all.

"Why didn't Holland do this?" she asked. Holland hadn't cared even a little for who had to be sacrificed and what magic he had to use. "If there was a way to find the entrance to the Naga city through a simple ceremony," she said, "he would have done it."

"He would have had to sacrifice himself," Wisat said. "That would have defeated his purpose."

"Wait, what?"

"The ceremony the wizard has uncovered, it requires the person who conducts the ceremony to sacrifice themselves. They must die for the answer to be revealed."

"Holland could have made someone do that," she pointed out. She wasn't sure how, but she was sure if anyone could manage that level of manipulation or compulsion, the demon son of a demon god could.

"The sacrifice can't be compelled. Can't be forced or manipulated. It must be a true sacrifice, willingly entered into."

She narrowed her eyes. "Then…why would anyone do it? If they're looking for an entrance to the city of the Nagas, and the only way to find it is to die, they never get to the city and… Why bother?"

"Exactly," Wisat said with a shrug. He finally let go of Cary's shoulders and sat back from her, but he didn't get up from the couch. "That's why this particular ceremony is never used. Very few would want to die to uncover a secret they then can gain no benefit from."

"The wizard's found a way round this, then? A loophole in the process?"

"He has," Liruk said.

"What?"

"That," Wisat said quietly, "is what we don't know."

They so rarely admitted to not knowing something, Cary blinked a few times. They hated not knowing. They hated getting something wrong even more. The admission that they didn't actually know something was…a very good indication of how seriously they viewed this situation.

"We only know that it has something to do with his apprentice, with Sheldon," Liruk said. "And that the only way to stop a disaster is to keep Sheldon safe from the wizard."

"Oh, this is so not good," Cary said, staring at nothing for a long moment as her mind churned.

A slight bump against her leg had her looking down to see Buck sitting next to her staring up. She set a hand on his head, absently scratching him behind his floppy Labrador ears. More demons, she thought. Or at least a wizard trying to free an old demon enemy. If that happened, would it affect Buck? Would it throw him back to his demon dog form, like the presence of Holland's demon father had done? Ho'Lud was a demon god. Buck hadn't turned demon dog in the presence of Holland, only during Lud's attempt to enter this realm. Maybe Buck wouldn't be affected at all, even if Holland did get out.

She really didn't want to have to test that, though.

"Sheldon might not let me protect him," she muttered, still staring down at Buck as she scratched his soft blond fur, the gesture helping ease her hammering heartbeat.

"That is…always a possibility," Liruk allowed. "But it is your job. And we need you to do it."

"Without help," she said, still not looking at them.

"You have managed to find help all year in ways that did not violate your test year rules," Wisat said, his tone a mix of mild amusement and annoyance.

She finally looked up and met his gaze, his eyes so brightly green they looked lit from within.

"We cannot help directly without endangering your test year," he said, more quietly and seriously now. "We cannot do anything that we don't normally do."

"Give you jobs and what information we have," Liruk added.

Though why she'd felt the need to say that out loud Cary wasn't sure. She knew what they gave her normally. Which most of the time wasn't much. Maybe Liruk needed the reminder herself.

"Jaxer cannot help you with this," Wisat said. "Not anymore, though we know he's been looking for the wizard for you."

"With the excuse that the wizard was a problem from before your test year," Liruk said, her lips flattening in disapproval.

"But this is now a current job, part of your test year trial, and no longer simply a personal issue from the past," Wisat said. "He will not be allowed to help you this time, without risking the results of your trial."

It occurred to Cary, slowly but eventually, that they were referencing her trial as if *they* didn't have anything to do with judging the outcome. As if some other body was in charge of determining whether she'd cheated or not. Could that be true? Were others among their people the ones to say if she passed this year or not? She'd assumed this whole time that pass or fail would be determined by Wisat and Liruk. But could she have been wrong about that?

Or was she just hearing undertones that didn't exist because her brain had gone on a hiatus a few minutes ago and hadn't fully returned from that break yet?

"But your mate is not part of this restriction obviously," Liruk said, almost too casually.

"Nor your friends," Wisat added, also too casually.

"Or even your dogs," Liruk said.

"The dragon cannot be seen as help from those who previously trained you," Wisat said, "as he has only just come into your life, and his training is nothing to do with your Protector magic or duties."

"In fact, any training to do with your ability to absorb magic is well outside the confines of your seventh year trial," Liruk said.

Cary narrowed her eyes at her bosses. Were they... Were they *helping* her? Without helping in a way that might get her into trouble, they were giving her an awful lot of hints. Either they were really worried about her, or they thought she was too dense to figure any of this out herself.

Probably both.

"So where do I find Sheldon to protect him," she said, giving in to the inevitable.

The last thing she wanted was any risk that Holland could be released back into this realm. Outside of the risk the demon posed all on his own, having him here could potentially attract the attention his super dangerous demon god father. Cary still wasn't entirely sure where Buck had taken Ho'Lud when he'd forced him back into the demon realms, but they hadn't had any trouble from the demon god since. She really didn't want to risk rocking that particular boat.

And to prevent all these disasters, she had to keep the wizard who wanted her dead away from his apprentice…who also likely wanted her dead.

She let out a long, resigned sigh.

This was not going to be fun.

11

ary stared up at the apartment building through her front windshield, shading her eyes and trying to slow her racing heartbeat. Liruk and Wisat had assured her that she didn't need to get to Sheldon immediately. So she'd been able to sleep—fitfully—and explain everything to Deacon—with some difficulty—last night. But now, in the bright mid-morning, mid-September sunshine, the reality of what she was about to do really sank in.

And she was not happy about it, even a little bit.

The apartment building itself was ordinary enough. Almost square shaped, five floors, mostly brick exterior, so on the older side. The door leading into the building was glass, giving a view into the black and white linoleum-floored lobby. She knew from the last time she'd been here there was a row of mailboxes to the right of that door, and a single elevator to the left, with a staircase door next to the elevator.

The last time she'd been here, she'd been retrieving her car, because she'd left it in the parking lot after rescuing Deacon and getting some ribs cracked in the process. He'd driven her to the hospital. She'd taken a taxi home from there. And she'd forgotten all about her car until she needed it a couple of days later.

"I hate this," Deacon said from the passenger seat of her Prius. "I hate this more than I can express."

She couldn't blame him. The last time *he'd* been here—well, the time before helping her collect her car—he'd been chained to a bed, waiting to be sacrificed by the little shit they were here to protect.

"I hate it too," she said. "I swore I wouldn't protect him because he was going to hurt a cat." She made a face. "Even if that cat's other form was…" She gestured at her mate, encompassing his full, extremely sexy other form.

"Liruk and Wisat are sure this is necessary? World-ending necessary?"

The growl in his voice didn't bode well for Sheldon. And Cary had seriously debated leaving Deacon out of this, at least for now. What he didn't know would make her life a lot easier. But when he'd returned last night, and she'd looked him in the eyes, she knew she couldn't lie to him. Not about this.

And when he'd insisted on coming with her to guard her back, well… Even the Nags had said they couldn't expect her mate not to help her.

"They were sure," she said. "And very very reluctant about this job. They understood what they were asking of me." Which didn't make it any less repulsive, but somehow it was a lot less irritating.

Well, okay, she was still irritated. But at the moment, she was more repulsed. Sheldon was not her favorite person in the city. And yes, she'd wanted to meet with him and talk about getting his master off her ass. But doing that didn't require her to *protect* him, just talk to him.

"You wanted to confront him," Deacon said, echoing her thoughts. "I guess this is as good a way as any."

"Unless he tries to kill us before we can explain why we're here."

"If he does, I will rip his throat out and the problem will be solved."

Cary narrowed her eyes at him. Yup, his eyes were glowing yellow. His leopard was definitely too close to the surface.

His control of his animal side had mostly returned in recent months, but not fully. Not as completely as it had been before they'd met. And whenever she was in danger, that control slipped a little more. It was both kind of romantic, and also very very inconvenient most of the time.

"No killing him," she ordered, waiting for him to look at her. The yellow glow in his eyes didn't dim. "I mean it, Deacon. No killing him unless absolutely necessary. That's not why we're here. Not why my bosses gave us his location."

"And why didn't they give you his location before this? We've been trying to track this shit down for months. And he's been here the whole time? While his mentor has been trying to kill you. Why didn't Jaxer know? Why didn't your bosses deign to mention it before now?"

She gestured at his face, at his glowing eyes. "Because you'd have just come here and killed him. And really, I'd rather you didn't do that. Please. I know it feels like you'd be justified. I can't blame you wanting him dead. But..."

She had to work to put this into words. "Right now, he's not the threat. He's being threatened. And he's so damned young. And... I don't know. I don't like him any better than you do, but I also don't want you killing him in cold blood, because that feels wrong and maybe like we wouldn't be any better than him if we did that." She made a face and ducked her chin so she was no longer meeting his gaze directly. "I don't know," she muttered. "Just, please don't kill him in cold blood. Okay?"

His lips twitched and the glow in his eyes faded just a little. "If he tries to hurt you, I will protect you. But... I won't kill him unless he forces my hand. Because you've asked. Nicely even."

She snorted and rolled her eyes to hide her pleasure and relief. Protecting Sheldon was skeevy enough. Having to protect him from her mate just made her stomach roll.

"Thank you," she said without looking at Deacon. She twinned her fingers with his, though, when he took her hand.

"How has he been getting in and out without anyone seeing him?" Deacon asked, sounding less growly and ready-to-shift than he had a moment ago.

Jaxer had said he had people watching this building. Or at least he had for the months following the night she'd rescued Deacon. When Sheldon's supposedly dead body hadn't been where she and Deacon had left it, Jaxer had put the apartment under surveillance. None of them had known at the time that Sheldon had a master, or that that master was the wizard trying to kill her.

Sheldon had been spotted once going into the apartment—the first time they were certain he was still alive. The person Jaxer had watching, though, hadn't seen Sheldon leave, and when he'd checked the apartment later, no Sheldon.

"He's a wizard," Cary said. "Maybe he's got a teleportation spell?"

"You stole all his magic, and he's been studying witchcraft to make up for that lack of innate magic. I doubt he's got a teleportation spell."

"His master could have given him one. Or… I don't know. A witch? He could have bought one. Angie had one from a witch friend on her keychain at one point."

"On her keychain?"

"Sure. You never know when you might need a teleportation spell, and you almost always have your house keys on you, right?"

He shrugged. "I suppose. When was this?"

"Few years back. She had to use it when we went to rescue Marianne's sisters from the goblin king." She waved her free hand. "Long story. Anyway, I just remembered, Angie told me her spell was a one shot deal. So if that's the kind of thing Sheldon is using, he'd have to have a bunch of them on hand. That seems like a lot of magic for someone without magic anymore, and if he bought the spells, they'd probably cost a fortune. Is Sheldon rich?"

She gave his apartment building a suspicious look. It wasn't the sort of place rich people usually lived, but sometimes you couldn't tell about these things. Deacon's "house" had turned out to be an apartment building. His family had converted the house that had been there to apartments years ago to better blend with their section of the changing Nob Hill neighborhood.

He lived on the top floor—the entire top floor—in a penthouse substantially bigger than her whole house. His younger sister Caitlin had most of the second floor to herself. The rest of the building was made up of apartments for other leopard shifters, visiting or permanent, and offices for the family business. Which was protecting animals and Cary approved of that career in a big way.

But because Deacon still remembered the house that had been in that location for years, he called the place his "house." She'd been there a few times now, but they didn't stay the night there hardly ever. She had the dogs to worry about and didn't like leaving them alone overnight very often. Sure, Buck was a demon dog and Pickles was a foo lion, and they could take care of themselves, and Fred if needs be. They were used to her occasionally being out all night for work, too. Still, she preferred not to stay away from them for too long if she could help it.

And frankly, she and Deacon both preferred her cozy little cottage house, to his very large, balcony-circled penthouse apartment. While his place was beautifully modern and had all the good technology, it was…colder than her home. Bare and sparse, just like his rooms in his mother and father's mansion. She liked her smaller, more lived in home, even without all the cool gadgets. It never ceased to amaze her that Deacon did as well.

"Jaxer hasn't ever mentioned it," Deacon said, answering her question and pulling her back to the topic at hand. "I didn't do a credit check on him before letting him kidnap me, though."

There was just enough sarcasm in his tone, she snorted.

"We should go in," Cary said. "Staring at the apartment building isn't going to get this done."

"I'm waiting on you to be ready."

"I'm never going to be ready," she said, and opened her car door, releasing Deacon's hand reluctantly to get out.

The lobby was as she remembered it from that last visit. The floor was clean, but there was a layer of dust on the shelf next to the wall of mailboxes, and the little paper recycling bin under the shelf was overflowing. The space had a very slightly damp scent to it, with just the faintest faintest hint of mold. Her nose twitched. Their footsteps sounded loud in the open space, squeaking a little on the well-worn black and white checked floor.

The elevator was resting at the lobby level, door closed, the little red light above the door displaying an L. She contemplated using the stairs. Elevators could be tricky and tight if something went wrong. But they had to go all the way up to the fifth floor and her Protector powers weren't working yet, which meant she'd have to face those stairs with just her normal level of fitness. Granted, that was better now after all the training with Lucy, but not something she wanted to test on stairs.

Elevator it was.

"The building is really quiet," Deacon murmured as the door opened. "Not a lot of people live here."

"It's the middle of the morning," she said, trying to be reasonable. "They're all probably at work or something."

Sheldon's place had been surrounded by empty apartments last October—who the hell wanted to live next to a mean and vicious wizard—but there had been other people in the building then. Just on different floors. And maybe not the apartment beneath his.

Had more people left? How much of this building did Sheldon have to himself? It seemed almost inconceivable that so many apartments would go empty in the middle of Portland. Somebody was losing money on that. Was it all down to Sheldon or was something else wrong with this place?

She listened to the sounds of the elevator as it rose, her unease at being back here growing with each floor.

Deacon took a step closer but stayed just behind her. She smiled a little. It had taken some effort for him to overcome his instincts to get in front of her to keep her safe, to learn that if he stayed behind her and let her protect him—let her magic get triggered by the danger to him— she'd be safer. That to guard her, he had to let her stand in front of him. The fact that he'd made the effort, and moved behind her now without hesitating, made her heart happy.

The elevator dinged. The silver doors slid open.

The fifth floor hallway lights were mostly out, only a single bulb halfway down the hall flickered, on the edge of burning out as well. The silence was eerie and oppressive, like her ears had been stuffed with cotton without her permission. She checked the hall carefully before stepping out of the elevator, glad of Deacon's presence at her back.

She reminded herself she was here to protect Sheldon, even as all her instincts went on high alert. Sweat slicked down her back, and her pulse hammered as they moved down the hall in that irritating, flickering light.

"Could this place be any creepier?" she murmured.

"Twin kids could suddenly appear at the end of the hall and stare at us," Deacon whispered back.

"Stop or I'm going to screech." She hated ghosts. More than almost anything else in her life, she was absolutely terrified of ghosts. And the fact that Deacon referenced a ghost moment in a movie—and the book she supposed—made her want to thump him. "That's not helping."

"Sorry," he said, and rubbed his big warm palm down her spine.

Now *that* helped.

Every apartment door they passed was closed, of course. She told herself that was normal. People didn't tend to leave their apartment doors wide open in the middle of the day. Still, as they crept down the hall past each door, she kept expecting one of them to open suddenly. The tension of waiting for something to jump out at her had a scream hovering at the base of her throat, waiting to erupt.

She had to clench her jaw when Deacon touched her lower back again, nearly startling the scream free. She frowned back at him. He nodded down the hall to the fourth door on the right. That wasn't the apartment Sheldon had been living in. His was the third on the right. But the door just after his was wide open, a gaping black maw beyond.

No one was standing there looking out. No one stepped into the hall. No light came from inside. No sound.

Just an open door in a silent, dark hallway with a single flickering lightbulb overhead.

Yeah, this wasn't scary at all.

12

Cary suppressed a shiver of apprehension, knowing Deacon would feel it since his hand was still on her back, and straightened her shoulders. She was here to protect Sheldon, she reminded herself as she stared at the open doorway, trying to ignore the flickering overhead light. She was here to keep Sheldon safe from his mentor. She was here to do her job.

And she was pretty sure she'd never hated her job quite this much ever before.

Which was saying a *lot*.

She cleared her throat and the noise sounded like an explosion in the quiet. She scowled. Damn it, she'd faced bigger and badder things than an evil former wizard. She could face Sheldon now. This was probably all just a show to creep people out and scare them off. Some sort of spell maybe, just to make the atmosphere feel more oppressive and potentially dangerous. But Sheldon didn't have his wizard magic anymore. He couldn't fire a wizard bolt from that dark doorway now. He didn't have the power.

Granted, that didn't mean he couldn't just shoot them with a perfectly ordinary gun. But as Deacon's mother liked to point out, most supernatural beings—even former ones—forgot that mundane weapons were an option. They always defaulted to their innate powers.

Sheldon didn't have those anymore. And he'd had time to consider his options. He could have considered mundane weapons at this point.

He'd been studying witchcraft at The Bookstore, though. Not guns. Did The Bookstore even have books on mundane weapons?

Shaking her head, she took a step closer to the door, ensuring Deacon was safely behind her, and cleared her throat again.

"Sheldon," she said, heard the rough, breathlessness in her voice and scowled. Firmer this time, she repeated, "Sheldon. It's Cary Redmond, and I'm here to talk." She let out a long, irritated breath. "And to protect you."

Something moved in the darkness of the open doorway. A shifting of shadows. Cary held her breath, waiting for whatever would step through that gaping hole.

A door on her left opened suddenly, banging loud against the corridor wall, and Cary finally let loose the screech she'd been suppressing.

She put a hand to her heart and her scowl deepened as Sheldon stepped through the newly opened door.

"That was rude," she snapped at him. "We're here to help you."

She blinked away her fear—and her irritation at being afraid—to take in Sheldon's appearance. She hadn't seen him since last Halloween when he'd tried to kill Deacon. The time hadn't been kind to him. Already skinny and gangly, he looked hollow now, wasted away to bone. His cheeks were sunken, his dark eyes wide in his pale face. His acne seemed to have healed a little, so that was something. But his dark hair was lank and longer than it had been, but no less greasy.

He was dressed differently this time. No black leather to emphasize his painful thinness. He wore ripped jeans and a plane gray sweatshirt that hung loosely on his wide shoulders. His tennis shoes were unlaced, flopping a little as he took another step into the hallway. His hands were empty—much to her relief, although that didn't mean much with someone used to using magic—and there were some unhealed cuts along his knuckles.

She sighed as she studied him. "You really need to take better care of yourself," she said, without thinking. He looked even younger than he had last time. Last time, there'd been an evil twinkle in his eyes that had dampened some of her sympathies for his age. Now… No twinkle, evil or otherwise. Barely any light of life in his expression at all. He looked as dead as a living human could look and still be walking around. And it was heartbreaking in a way she hadn't expected.

This asshole had tried to kill Deacon. He'd killed a lot of shifters trying to steal their bodies. He wasn't a good guy. He wasn't an innocent victim.

Still, her stupid sympathy reacted to the way he looked now. And she hated that she felt sorry for him even a little bit. Stupid sympathy.

From the way he lifted his lip in a faint snarl, he hated her sympathy, too. "Why are you here? Haven't you stolen enough from me?" Despite the snarl, there was no emotion in his tone.

"Hey, I'm not the one who kidnapped shifters and killed them. Don't bitch at me about theft. You tried to steal their bodies."

He flicked at glance at Deacon behind her. "You kept him, huh?"

"Why do people keep saying things like that? Like he's a pet I took home? He's not, and he has a say in where he goes. I didn't *keep* him." Technically, he followed her home and then never left, but she wasn't going to say that out loud because it kind of defeated her point.

"Would you have wanted me if I looked like him?" Sheldon asked.

"Ew. You're a kid, first of all." He was nineteen at the oldest. "Second, reminding me that you once tried to kill my mate is not helping this situation."

"He is your mate? I thought he just said that."

"Yeah, so did I. Apparently, I was wrong."

Sheldon's lip twitched, but she couldn't tell if it was a tic or amusement.

"Why are you here?" Sheldon asked. "How did you find me?"

"You're in the same place I left you," she pointed out. Though, to be fair, that hadn't helped them find him in months, so she supposed his question had some justification. "And I told you already, I'm here to protect you. From your master. Or mentor. Or whoever that asshole is to you."

Another twitch of his lips, though still without any real sign of what the twitch meant. "He is an asshole. He always has been."

"Then why did you let him mentor you?"

"Power. He knew how to teach me to use mine. Before it killed me."

"There were better options for teachers. Or did you want to be an evil shit so his methods appealed to you?"

"Why would you protect me? You stole my powers."

Not on purpose, but she didn't think she'd better say that out loud. "It's a long story. Should we just stand here in the hall, risking a seizure from the flickering light, or should we sit somewhere?" Not that she thought Deacon would sit around this shit. But she was getting tired of the flickering lightbulb. It was starting to make her eye twitch.

He gestured back into the apartment he'd come from. "I live in here. The whole floor is mine, though, so we could go into any apartment."

"How'd you manage that?" she asked. "It was that way before, when you had magic. How'd you keep it this way? Empty and all to yourself?"

He shrugged. "People get creeped out when they come to look at an apartment and leave."

"Good trick. Real illusion spell, or just old-fashioned smoke and mirrors?"

"None of your business," he said, his voice flat.

Even throwing out accusations, his voice had been flat and emotionless. None of the anger or rage she'd seen in him last Halloween. Just a kind of hollow shell, going through the motions.

She was starting to see why Renee felt sorry for him. Without having seen the evil-shit side of him, it would be easy to assume this was a damaged young man who just needed a little help.

But Cary still saw the evil-shit who'd broken his own apartment door because it was flashy, and kidnapped and killed shifters just because he wanted a new look. The two images of the two versions of Sheldon superimposed themselves on top of each other, splitting her mind further on this mission.

She gestured to the apartment at his back. "We'll go in there. But any tricks and Deacon will rip your throat out."

"Thought you said you were here to protect me."

"I did, and I am. But I don't trust you. Any more than you trust us, or you would have turned off the creepy-hallway spell by now."

He blinked. "I…" Then he pressed his lips together as if rethinking what he'd intended to say. "Come on in if you dare." He moved inside without waiting for them, but he did leave the door open.

Cary rolled her eyes at his underlying threat, though she did step very carefully into the room, keeping Deacon at her back so she could protect him from any nasty spells Sheldon might have in place. While she might have *accidentally* sucked out all his powers—and then only because he'd *thrown* them at Deacon—it was blatantly obvious he was still using magic of some kind, likely spells he'd learned studying witchcraft. Some witchcraft could be done without any innate inner power. Wizardry required inner magic. Witchcraft was helped along by inner magic. But a lot of witches just studied a lot, learned a lot, and knew a lot. They could do magic, sometimes create powerful spells, without any innate magic at all. Yet another big difference between witches and wizards.

The inside of the apartment was a lot more subdued than she'd been expecting based on Sheldon's last apartment. To be fair, she hadn't had a chance to study the décor in the last living room and kitchen much as she'd been too busy dodging fireballs and lightning strikes, but his bedroom had wedged an indelible image in her head. Red carpet, chains covering the overhead light, animal prints and leather everywhere. And a giant bed with a magic headboard to which a very naked Deacon had been chained.

That part in particular had been hard to forget.

Sheldon's current living space was significantly less animal-print and leather strewn. The floor was bare wood, scrapped and nicked, in need of a good sweep. The couch at the center of the room was gray microfiber with a few rips revealing the inner stuffing. There was a flatscreen TV on a low stand, but it was small and there was a crack in the lower left corner of the screen. A stack of books piled up in front of the couch and more stacks of books littered the otherwise spare space. There wasn't a coffee table or side tables. A single stand lamp arched over the couch. A few takeaway cartons were kicked to the side of the couch.

She couldn't see a kitchen so she assumed it was behind one of the three doors leading off the living room to the left. Thick curtains of an indeterminant dark color covered the windows opposite the door, making the room gloomy and dim. And the whole place smelled of stale food and sweat. Her nose wrinkled.

Perfectly broody, and something she might have expected, but still sad to witness.

"This place could do with an open window," she commented. "Air it out a bit."

Sheldon shrugged. "Why? Not like I get a lot of company."

She sighed. "I don't know. Self respect?"

He didn't comment as he flopped onto the couch, sprawling out in a way that left no room for anyone else to sit. Not that she particularly wanted to sit on that couch. She didn't even want to guess what substances stained that couch.

She took up a spot near the window, Deacon still safely just behind her shoulder, and crossed her arms as she stared down at Sheldon.

"So talk," he said, still sounding absolutely uninterested in… anything at all.

"Do you care that your master is likely trying to kill you?" Cary asked. "Because it's gonna be hard to protect you if you don't care." People with death wishes tended to walk into the danger she was trying to protect them from, which made her job a lot harder.

"I care." Though, from his tone, he certainly didn't sound like he did. "I wouldn't be here if I wanted to die."

"Yeah, you're gonna need to explain that."

"I would have killed myself. Or let him kill me. Months ago."

"Not to push any buttons or anything, but you don't look to be in a particularly good place. Why didn't you…?"

"Revenge."

"Ah. Of course." That wasn't helping his cause with her. But it was more in keeping with the person she'd thought he was. "Against me?"

He shrugged. "At first. He blamed you and made me think you were the source of all my trouble. He claimed that if he killed you, my powers would come back and I'd be healed."

"He tried. Why didn't you?"

"With what? My bare hands?" He held up the hands in question. "My super human strength?" He snorted and it was the most emotion she'd heard from him this whole time, a bitter irony laced with disgust.

"You could have helped him."

"I told him what you were so he'd know how to kill you."

"Gee, thanks."

He shrugged again. "I wanted my powers back."

"You aren't getting them. Not from me. Whatever I took, I also released in that fight with Oliver Holland's army." She'd thought she'd seen Sheldon there, but in the moment, she'd been otherwise occupied, so she'd never been entirely sure if she'd been seeing things. Even after they'd confirmed he was alive, she'd never been certain he'd really been there.

Sheldon didn't confirm or deny his presence at that fight, though, much to her frustration.

"I know my powers aren't coming back now," he said. "I read the book on what you are, beyond a Protector. My master…former master suspected and sent me to The Bookstore. To confirm it all." He stared at Cary when he said, "I didn't tell him everything I learned, though. I know when you release the magic, most of it's gone. But I also know some of it becomes a permanent part of you. Killing you won't release it. It just dies with you, like with any other magician."

"Wait, I didn't even know that last part. Where did you learn that?" She realized she'd given away too much of her knowledge in that admission, but why did Sheldon know something that she didn't? She'd read the book, too.

"I tore out a few pages," he admitted. "To study."

"Oh, Renee is not going to be happy about that. She finds out, you're banned from The Bookstore."

Something like emotion flickered in his eyes but the spark died quickly and he shrugged again, as if that didn't matter.

But what he'd revealed made her mind whirl. She kept some of the magic. It became a part of her. This crystalized an idea she'd considered during her conversation with Rory. She'd wondered if all the magic she'd absorbed over the years might be changing her in some way. Sheldon had just confirmed it likely did.

And that was terrifying. All that magic, even after she released it, had been changing her, making her…

She had no idea. But different than she'd been.

Did that mean she *could* use it? And if she did, did that mean she *couldn't* drain it all the way Bleak had?

Shit.

She forced down the worry because she had a job to do, but when she could think about this more, she was probably going to freak out a little.

Or a lot.

"So you knew you weren't getting your magic back from me. After that you wanted me killed just because. Normal, old-fashioned revenge."

"Initially, I was all for that. You and *him*." He nodded at Deacon without looking at him. "And that other guy, the blond one, whatever he is. I wanted him dead, too. He was responsible for…that night."

"You didn't have to kidnap Deacon, or any other shifter for that matter. You were the one responsible for all of that. Don't blame the blond guy." If Sheldon didn't know Jaxer's name, or nature, she'd avoid sharing it. "That's what gets you into trouble, you know." She pointed a finger at him, channeling her mother's scolding energy. "Not taking responsibility for your own damned self and your own damned actions."

Sheldon didn't respond to that.

"So why aren't you still trying to kill me?" she asked when the silence stretched out too long for her nerves. "Assuming you have stopped?"

He nodded faintly in answer to her question. It wasn't a resounding confirmation that he wasn't trying to kill her anymore, but it would do for now.

"So you don't want me dead. Your master still does."

"Former," he said, firmly. "Former master."

"Why former and not current? What caused the falling out, since you were still on his side after you initially lost your magic?"

"I finally figured out what he wanted from me. What he'd been… grooming me for."

That didn't sound good. "What did he want from you?"

"To steal my powers."

She knew that much from the wizard himself.

"By taking over my body."

13

For a long moment, Cary stared at Sheldon, sprawled and still looking entirely emotionless on his ugly gray couch, as the irony of his master's ultimate goal sank in. "So..." she said, "your master wanted to do to you exactly what you were trying to do with a shifter?"

Sheldon didn't answer. Which was fine. The answer was obvious.

"Not so much fun when it's *your* body getting stolen is it," she said.

He still didn't respond.

"Wow, so not even a little remorse for trying to steal Deacon's body, huh? Okay." Why was she here trying to protect this little shit again?

"World-ending disaster," Deacon murmured as if he'd read her thoughts.

When she glanced at him, he tapped his nose and she scowled. "Stop that."

"No," he said, fondly.

She didn't have time for that argument so she faced Sheldon again. He was watching them closely, his eyes narrowed.

"What?" she snapped.

"You two are strange," Sheldon said.

"That's the most pot-black kettle comment I've ever heard."

"What does that mean?"

"You're too young, and I love my father." The pot-calling-the-kettle-black saying was one of her father's favorites.

"Huh?"

"Just…" She rubbed the bridge of her nose. "Never mind. Tell me more about this body switch thing your master—"

"Former master," Sheldon interrupted.

"Former master intended."

"He's done it before. A lot apparently."

"Really? Why? More power?"

"Eternal life," Sheldon said.

She groaned. "That doesn't sound good."

"He finds a young, impressionable wizard with a lot of power, promises to train them, uses the training as an excuse to practice body swaps, and when he's ready, he takes over the new body and kills the old one." Sheldon's gaze was hollow as he looked into Cary's eyes. "How do you think I learned what to do with the shifters?"

"But you failed with the shifters," Deacon said, the first words he uttered to Sheldon.

"Shifters are different," Sheldon said with a shrug. "Not like human hosts. I couldn't control the shift and would get…thrown back into my own body."

"Leaving the shifter in mid-shift and dying," Deacon said, his voice a very deep growl.

"That's why I cut their throats," Sheldon said. "Thought it would be an easier death." He shrugged. "If it had worked, I would have killed this body with them in it anyway, so they were always going to die."

"You are *so* not helping your cause here," Cary said, moving just a little more in front of Deacon so he wouldn't lunge at Sheldon. "Back to the wizard." They'd deal with what Sheldon had done to all those shifters later.

But boy, she really really didn't want to be here protecting someone this awful. It grated against every nerve she had. If this hadn't been a world-ending disaster waiting to happen, if his former master wasn't such a monumental prick looking to unleash hell on earth, she'd have walked away from this. Actually, she'd never have walked into it in the first place.

"How often has your…" She made a face. "What the hell is his name? He wouldn't tell me so I called him Sheldon's Guy to his face. Mostly to irritate him—"

"You're good at that," Sheldon interrupted.

"Thank you. Anyway, calling him that here is a waste, and I'm getting tired of 'former master' all the time. What the hell is his name?"

"I called him Zorianthus."

"Zorianthus? No wonder he didn't want to say that out loud. What a mouthful."

"It isn't his real name. I don't know his real name. I'm not even sure he remembers after all these centuries."

That brought her up short. "Centuries?" Holy hell. "How many times has he body-swapped permanently?"

She thought back to her few encounters with Zorianthus. She'd only seen him once briefly in a parking lot after he'd tried to kill her, and once in the underground hive of the Portland vampires. Neither place had allowed for a rigorous study of his appearance, but she'd seen enough to know he wasn't a young man. Gray-white hair, blue eyes, creases around his mouth and across his forehead, bags under his eyes. But his movements had been spry and showed a level of fitness belied by the signs of age. He looked older, but he hadn't carried himself as if he was.

Knowing he was *centuries* old made her reevaluate her limited impression.

"I don't know the exact number," Sheldon said. "Just that he's done it multiple times. And once the new body starts to age beyond his ability to slow the process, he finds a new protégé and trains them up so he can use their bodies and their powers to keep extending his life."

"That's a pretty sick process. Why not just… I don't know get a vampire to turn him? He'd get to stay perpetually young in his own body and still have lots of power."

"Not lots of magic, though. And he'd be stuck living on blood and being weak in the daylight. He wanted something else. He wanted the magic as much as the body." Sheldon tilted his head to one side. "And he couldn't do what you do. If he could, he wouldn't have had to worry about body swaps."

"Why not? He'd still die eventually." She'd done that already. She knew her brand of skill did not bring immortality with it. It was much more likely to bring about the end of her mortality.

"With enough magic, he always felt he could find a way to resist death."

"Not a single wizard in the history of wizards has managed that, though. Not with just magic." She added the last because she realized Zorianthus had managed to delay death, for a long time. He just hadn't done it solely with magic. He'd needed new, young bodies.

And wasn't that just a creepy thought.

Sheldon shrugged. "I don't really know what he was ultimately capable of. He didn't let me see the extent of his powers. For all I know, he was getting weak magically as well as physically. And that's why he needed the new bodies."

She considered the energy bolts Zorianthus had thrown at her. If that was his magic faded, she shuddered to think what his powers might have been like before.

"How did you find out all this in the end?" Cary asked.

"I found some of his books, remembered some of the things he'd taught me and told me, discovered a journal of dates and plans… A lot of stuff fell into place and I figured it out."

"Did you confront him?"

"And get killed? No. How would I confront him now anyway?" He gestured at his body as if it were useless, as if without the magic he was useless.

"Boy, you have a lot of issues," she murmured. But she wasn't here to be a counselor, and she wouldn't want to be one to Sheldon anyway. She was here to keep Zorianthus from breaking her world. "So since you can't fight him anymore, how have you managed to hide from him?"

"I have a few tricks left. But he doesn't need me. So he hasn't put much effort into finding me yet. He's got bigger things to worry about."

"Like what?"

"Like dying before he can find a new host body. It takes him time and training to prep a new host. And he needs someone with a lot of innate power. When I lost all mine, I became useless to him, but he's still decaying, dying. He needs to abandon his current body soon or he'll die with it."

"Then why the hell isn't he looking for a new protégé? Why is he wasting time trying to kill me?"

"Revenge after you ruined his years of work."

Years? "How long was he your mentor?" She frowned.

"He found me when I was twelve. He trained me for seven years to get me ready."

She had to suppress a gag at the phrasing. It all felt so…well, molesty and gross. "It takes him seven years to ready a new host?" Gag, gross, ew! "No wonder he's panicked."

"Seven years for me. I'm not sure with others. I just know it takes time."

"Why?" Deacon asked, his voice deep but less growly than it had been when they'd been discussing shifter deaths.

"He picks strong wizards, for their magic, but because of that, they can kick him back out again, fight the permanent change, if he hasn't prepared them properly. Even as young as I was the first time we swapped bodies, I still instinctively kicked him out and returned to myself within seconds. He needs his new host body to adjust to having him in it, and he needs his protégé to relax enough to stay in the borrowed body for a while. All that takes time. You'd be surprised how long."

"Not really," Cary muttered. She couldn't imagine ever being relaxed enough to stay in someone else's body. For all its foibles and weaknesses, she liked her body. At least she did now. She wouldn't have wanted to answer that question when she was a teenager.

A thought that reminded her Sheldon was little more than a teenager himself. An asshole, but a young one. Who'd been groomed —ew—by a very evil master wizard for seven years.

She flinched as that number seven showed up in her life again. Not just her own seventh year test, but every so often the number showed up in ways that complicated her life. The fact that Zorianthus had needed seven years to train Sheldon felt a little foreboding. If she was the superstitious sort. Which, as it turned out, she was.

"*Is* he looking for another body?" Cary asked. He should be, even with the diversion of trying to kill her for revenge. But if he was busy doing that, why was she here protecting Sheldon? Why was the wizard wasting time trying to find Oliver Holland and free him? Seemed like he should focus on his new body first and then worry about revenge and all the other stuff later. Right?

"He'd have to be, wouldn't he," Sheldon said.

"You aren't sure?"

"I'm sure. But he doesn't consult me on it, if that's what you're asking."

She automatically scowled at his tone, but she was too busy trying to work all this out to put much effort into the expression.

Zorianthus needed a new body and that should be his top priority, since he was dying and he needed time to ready his new host—ew. But her bosses had sent her here to protect Sheldon from him. Which meant he was searching for Sheldon. Now. Even if he hadn't been before. To what end…no clue yet except that it probably had something to do with Zorianthus's attempt to free Oliver Holland. Zorianthus wanted something from his former protégé. And he must want it soon or Cary wouldn't need to be here.

So how hadn't he found Sheldon yet? Sheldon's hiding place wasn't very hidden. How had Zorianthus *not* caught up to him by now?

"I still don't understand how he hasn't found you," she said aloud. "How are you still in the same apartment building you lived in before you went into hiding? That doesn't seem like…well, hiding."

"Hiding in plain sight," Sheldon said.

"Not really. Try again. You have spells, at least on this floor to creep people out so they leave." Zorianthus probably wouldn't fall for that, but it indicated Sheldon was using magic somehow to keep anyone—including his former master—from finding him. Maybe he had more spells set up around here. "Did you buy the spells, by the way, or is your witchcraft study coming along?" She bit her lip as she said that last out loud. Shit. He'd know Renee had talked to her now.

His eyes did narrow a little but he let the revelation roll past without comment and said, "Most are bought. Witchcraft is…not natural to me, and it's taking me time to learn."

"Can you?" she asked. "Will you be able to do magic that way?"

"A different kind. Maybe." He shrugged.

"Where did you get the money to buy spells?" Deacon asked.

Sheldon's gaze went to him. "Stole some. Some came from my parents."

"They have money?" Cary asked.

"Dad's a preacher with a loyal following who donates lots to his church." Sheldon's lip lifted in another faint snarl. The emotion carried to the rest of his face this time, a spark of anger finally glinting deep in his dull brown eyes. "He and my mom are fanatics, and their 'flock' are stupid fucks. But they give my parents tons of money, and my parents think they can save my soul or some shit by sending me what I ask for."

"Do they know you're a wizard?" She winced inwardly. "Or used to be anyway."

"I showed them. They claimed I was possessed by the devil."

Cary sighed. Of course they had. "How did you take that?"

"None of your business."

"Fair enough." She didn't want to learn more anyway. She didn't want to feel any sympathy for Sheldon at all. "I still don't understand how your master hasn't found you, even with spells protecting this place, though." She couldn't get past this point. Sheldon was in the same damned place he'd been in when he broke with Zorianthus. A wizard who'd been around for *centuries* would surely be able to see through bought spells and illusions.

"You never found me before, despite looking for months," Sheldon pointed out. "I bought good spells. I knew what it would take. I might be low priority on my former master's list, but he'd come to kill me eventually."

"You must have spent a fortune," she muttered. "Why stay here? Why not go into hiding…somewhere else?"

"Where?" he asked simply. "Where could I hide?"

"I don't know. The Amazon? A quiet island in the South Pacific? You had money from your parents and a powerful motivation to avoid the enemies you'd made here." Not just Zorianthus. "Why stay here and risk being spotted by one?"

"I know this place. I don't know the Amazon or an island in the South Pacific. Why would I leave territory I know well?"

She supposed the made some kind of weird sense. Still, if she went on the run, she'd take herself off to someplace quiet and possibly tropical and definitely not remain in the same place she'd been living for the last seven years. But that was her.

She started to ask another question, curious how he got in and out of the building, but a faint tingling along her spine quieted her. She paused to study the sensation. Magic absorption? Her Protector instincts? The sense was kind of faint and not filled with the usual urgency that came when her brand of help was needed. Yet it wasn't the bugs crawling over her skin sensation she got when she was taking in magic.

Strange.

Deacon leaned down to her ear. "You okay?"

"Not sure," she murmured. "Something…" She narrowed her eyes and stared at the front door. "I think someone is watching the building," she said. "And I think they're a threat, but… Not an immediate one. I can't tell. Just…" She grunted in frustration.

"I'd know if we were being watched," Sheldon said. "Triggers an alarm spell I have set up around the building."

Well, that explained a lot. "You sure? Cause…" The feeling of unease intensified slightly, but still not strong, still not enough for her to pinpoint a source for the feeling.

Wow, this was strange. She sensed danger all the time as part of her job, but this was so...so mild. It was there. There was a threat somewhere outside this building, but she just couldn't place it.

"Maybe we should go somewhere else," Deacon said.

"Where?" she asked. "I'm not bringing this shit to my place. Or yours," she said before he could suggest it.

"You keep calling me a shit, but you don't really know me," Sheldon said.

"I know enough to know you're a shit. Don't interrupt."

"We're safer here than anywhere else," Sheldon said, ignoring her admonishment. "I've made sure of that."

"Yeah, yeah, okay. Not to doubt your bought magic, but..." She frowned again. Something just at the edge of her awareness. What the hell was it?

Without conscious thought, she edged Deacon farther behind her, then moved closer to Sheldon. Since she couldn't sense the direction of the threat, she couldn't put herself *between* Sheldon and the danger yet. But if she got close enough, and he didn't go wandering off outside her protection, she should still be able to keep him safe.

The feeling of being watched intensified. The hair on her arms rose. She could feel the threat from everywhere and yet it still felt really distant. Like someone far away was still somehow looking at them. But that didn't make even a little sense.

What the hell?

She looked down at Sheldon, back at Deacon, then for reasons she couldn't understand, she looked up. Nothing on the ceiling, no holes for someone to be spying into Sheldon's apartment. No little cameras. That she could see.

"No one has bugged your place, right?" she asked. "With all the magic precautions, you thought about mundane stuff, too." She faced him again. "Right?"

Sheldon scowled. But he didn't comment.

"You didn't think of that, did you?" She sighed. "Maria Jones was right."

Deacon's mother taught him that most supernatural and preternatural beings didn't think about using mundane weapons, because they were too focused on their supernatural gifts, and so bringing mundane weapons against them could be a good strategy. Seemed not just mundane weapons got forgotten.

"No one could have been in here to place a bug," Sheldon said. "I would have known. Anyone gets onto this floor, I know about it. In any of the apartments." He added the last before she could ask.

"Above and below?" she said, both to irritate and to see if he'd thought of that. "You're not here all the time. We both know you've been at The Bookstore." She gestured to the piles of books as if it hadn't already been obvious since he'd read the book on her magic and torn pages from it.

She was still annoyed by that.

"And," she added, "you didn't consider Zorianthus a threat right away. You still thought he was on your side. Are you sure he didn't rig something here before you started sealing the place off with spells?"

"He never came here," Sheldon said, his tone slightly more emotional than it had been, though only barely. "I met him. He didn't deign to set foot in my home."

"Bitter about that? You should be relieved."

"It was what it was." But he didn't meet her gaze.

She let it go. She wasn't here for his feelings. To Deacon, she said, "I don't suppose that super sniffer of yours could smell a mechanical bug?"

"A tiny one among all the other electronic equipment in an average apartment? No. The scent of the person who placed the bug, yes, if it was done recently enough."

The feeling of being watched strengthened again, but briefly. She scowled at the apartment, trying to hunt up a likely place to hide a nanny cam or something similar.

And then, like a bubble popping, the feeling of being watched vanished. The sense of threat, even if distant, went with it, and she felt normal again. Nothing to worry about. No one watching. No tingling of imminent danger.

"Dammit," she muttered aloud. "The feeling went away. If it was a camera or mic or something, they've just turned it all off."

"Zorianthus wouldn't use something as ordinary as a spy camera," Sheldon said. He hadn't budged from his sprawled position on the couch, even when Cary and Deacon had moved closer. "He'd consider it demeaning."

"You worried about it a minute ago, though," she pointed out. "When you realized you hadn't considered it. You thought he could have." She gestured at Deacon. "Can he hunt through the place and check for signs of a camera?"

"You're asking my permission?" Sheldon sounded surprised, or as surprised as a person could sound when not displaying much emotion.

"Of course. It's your place. You want to live with a camera, that's your business. We're not here to do anything but protect you."

"You keep saying that." He waved his hand in a little circle. "Feel free to do what you like."

"Any nasty spells I should know about before I trigger them?" Deacon asked, the growl back in his voice.

Sheldon shook his head, not rising to Deacon's show of anger. "Sniff away," he said. "Whatever."

Deacon made a quick circuit of the apartment, moving at shifter speeds that blurred his movements. He paused here and there, at the three doors leading out of the main room, in the corners, by the front door. His nostrils flared and then he'd move around the room again. He flashed through two doors, one that led to a bedroom, the other to the kitchen, pausing for only a moment on each threshold to get his bearings. And then he vanished into the rooms for a few seconds before returning to the main living room.

He was back at her side within minutes, the search so quick she wondered if he could possibly have scented anything.

She raised her brows at him in silent question.

"Magic, and Sheldon, and neglect." His nose twitched. "Your bathroom is disgusting," he said to Sheldon.

"The maid is due tomorrow." The faint sarcasm in Sheldon's tone gave some emotion to his otherwise flat voice.

"Any hint of the wizard?" Cary asked Deacon. Deacon had been with her when the wizard had confronted them in the vampire hive. Even with the stink of all those vampires around him, he'd still gotten the wizard's scent. He would know if Zorianthus had been in this apartment.

"Nothing. Just Sheldon. No other person has been here in months as far as I can tell."

"When did you realize what Zorianthus was after? How long ago?" Cary asked.

Sheldon shrugged. "March I guess. I've been in hiding for a while."

March. That was when Zorianthus had sicced the vampires on her. Or at least encouraged their interest. Did the two things have anything to do with each other or just a timing coincidence?

She'd probably have to ask the wizard to find out. But she didn't believe in coincidences.

"Okay, so no physical spy equipment. And no one's been here in ages. But we were still being watched so it must have been magic." She paused to consider if her skin was tingling. It wasn't. That didn't mean magic hadn't been involved, just that no one had thrown magic at her.

"I've got spells up to prevent that," Sheldon said. "Remember. In hiding."

"Well maybe the spells aren't as good as you thought," Cary said. She put her hands on her hips and grunted a curse. "We have to move him somewhere safer."

"Not your house," Deacon said.

"I don't want to, but…"

"No. You don't want him there. I don't want you to bring him there. The dogs won't like him."

"What makes you say that?" Sheldon asked. "Maybe animals love me."

"You killed shifters," Cary said. "Animals will know you don't have concern for life. At least mine would."

Well, Fred might not. He pretty much liked everyone. But Pickles and Buck would definitely smell Sheldon's nature. To be honest, she wasn't sure how they'd react to him either. She didn't bring bad guys into her house. And while she was supposed to protect Sheldon, she had definitely not moved him out of the bad guy category yet.

"I might know of a place," Deacon murmured. He pulled out his phone and texted someone while Cary looked at him, her brows raised. "Not my house," he said without looking up at her. "I promise."

"Not any of the family, either," she said. "Or any of your people. I don't want him near shifters."

"I can't do that anymore, you know," Sheldon said. "You stole all the power I needed to make the swap."

"Gee, I'm so sorry about that," she hissed, heavy on the sarcasm. "I still don't want you near innocent shifters. Or…well, anyone else really."

She scowled. This was the worst sort of assignment. She'd thought protecting a necromancer had rubbed her wrong—mostly because that brushed against her fear of ghosts but also because the necromancer and her brother had been working for the bad guy and their own status as good guy or bad guy had been very nebulous at first. They'd ended up in the good guy category, but there had been moments when she wasn't entirely sure.

This time, however, there was no nebulous to it. Sheldon was firmly in her bad guy category, even if he did need her help. She was giving him help only to prevent the world from ending. If not for that, she wasn't sure she could bring herself to protect him—even if she did feel a little *tiny* inkling of sympathy for him which she intended to squash at her earliest convenience because she didn't want to feel any sympathy for the little shit.

"Don't worry," Deacon said, "this place will be…safe."

She narrowed her eyes at him. "That's gonna need an explanation."

"Yup," he said, his gaze still on his phone. His thumbs moved swiftly over the screen, paused, another flurry of typing, another pause.

He grunted once, typed in a final reply, and finally looked up from the screen. "We've got a place. A few miles outside town. Isolated. We should be safe there."

"Safer here," Sheldon said. "If the old bastard is looking for us, won't have the spells you need on this other place to keep him from finding us."

"Actually," Deacon said, "there are."

14

Despite Deacon's claims that they were going just a few miles outside town, they were halfway to Astoria before he finally directed Cary off the highway and onto a series of sideroads winding through sections of dense forest interspersed with farmlands.

Cary drove while Deacon sat in the back seat next to Sheldon, keeping an eye on him. Sheldon slouched in his seat, staring out the window, pretending to ignore Deacon's stare. Cary flicked her gaze to the rearview mirror regularly to check on the two of them, her tension levels high with worry. But despite the obvious animosity between them, the two men didn't say more than a few words the entire trip, and they stayed on their respective sides of the backseat.

Which was something at least.

"The next turn on the right," Deacon said as they wound around another curve in the road. "Take that. The house is at the bottom of the hill, end of the road."

He hadn't elaborated on whose house this was, or who they'd find here, or how the wizard wouldn't find the place, so Cary was itching to ask questions. She'd been antsy and curious the entire drive. But since Deacon wasn't offering up information yet, she kept her mouth shut.

She had to assume he had reasons for keeping silent and those reasons likely had to do with Sheldon.

She'd grill Deacon later, when they had some privacy, if he didn't reveal all soon.

The drive along the dirt and gravel lane was bracketed by trees and views into a pasture filled with sheep, the setting bucolic in the early afternoon sunlight. The area had a lovely, relaxed, peaceful energy to it, like she could literally see contentment in the breezes, smell it in the air. Her windows were up, she couldn't smell anything outside, or feel the breeze for that matter, but the energy of the place felt so peaceful, she actually sighed and her shoulders relaxed the farther down the road they drove.

Wow. Whatever this was, if they could bottle it, they'd make a fortune.

"Magic?" Cary asked, without clarifying. If she, a mundane human—or, well, mostly mundane anyway; maybe formerly mundane?—could feel this, she was certain Deacon could. Maybe even Sheldon.

"A kind of magic," Deacon said. "Yes."

"Am I going to be…you know, while I'm here?" Not that she'd mind soaking in peace magic. She could use some peace and contentment magic.

"You might," Deacon said. "Let me know if it starts to feel too much and we'll leave."

"Should be okay in the short term."

And then she'd ask Rory to help her release what she'd pulled in—or at least try it. This would probably be a good test, actually having some additional magic to release so she could practice. See if her failures lately were just the lack of new magic in her system. If she couldn't release it, maybe they could try the process of draining the magic by her using it. She wasn't sure how to use peace magic, but it would be worth a try.

Plus, "Whatever this is, it feels good, so I won't complain."

Deacon's chuckle tickled her spine. That man's laugh… Even in the most serious of situations, listening to him chuckle made her toes curl. The mate thing was weird. But she wasn't complaining about that anymore either.

At the bottom of the dirt lane sat the house, just as Deacon had said. A small, cozy wood cabin with a wraparound porch and natural wood accents. The porch overflowed with potted plants, some herbs and some flowers, a few with what looked like lettuce to Cary's inexpert eye. The front door stood open, letting the cool autumn afternoon air in through a closed screen that keep bugs out.

As soon as she stepped out of the car, the scents of grass, trees, sheep, and herbs wrapped around her like a delicious perfume, and she breathed in deeply.

Whoever lived here had carved out a pretty idyllic home. Almost too perfect and ideal. She suddenly felt awful for bringing a murdering former wizard into this lovely atmosphere to escape his murdering master.

"Maybe we should have gone somewhere else?" she murmured as Deacon closed the car door.

She glanced up at him. He was frowning slightly, but in a contemplative way, not an angry or upset way. Sheldon stood on the opposite side of the car, slouching against the still open door, taking in the beautiful setting without showing any signs of interest or curiosity. Either he was dead inside or he'd perfected the "disinterested" look as a defense.

She was betting on a little of both.

"It's the only place I could think of where Zorianthus wouldn't be able to follow us or track us if he's keeping an eyes on Sheldon," Deacon said. "And you didn't want him at your place or mine—which I agree with," he added before she could justify that choice. "We don't have to stay long. Long enough to talk and confuse the wizard. Make him think we've taken Sheldon into hiding. Then we can go."

She let out a huff of a laugh at the thought of leaving soon. "I could live here. I haven't felt this at ease in…"

She considered. She felt easy and comfortable in her own home, but always with the knowledge that her bosses could show up at any time and give her a new assignment. Here, she didn't feel any of that.

Here, felt like nothing that might disturb the peace would ever venture close, even invited disturbances. Here, everything was ease and comfort and a long roll of time with no hurry.

"I'm not sure I've ever felt this at ease," she finally admitted.

"It's an illusion," a voice from just inside the screen door said. "You'll get used to it."

The screen door opened and the owner of the voice stepped outside. Cary's eyes widened.

"Cary," Deacon said quietly, "I'd like you to meet my great grandfather, Keith Ferguson. Gramps, this is my mate, Cary Redmond."

"Well," the man said with a wide smile. "It's about time."

CARY WAS STILL STARING AT KEITH LONG AFTER THEY'D GONE INSIDE and settled at a huge wooden table with cups of steaming coffee for her and Keith, milk for Deacon, and a cold soda for a disinterested Sheldon.

The resemblance was…strangely precise. It was like looking at Deacon in another… Well, since he was a shifter, she supposed it would take him another hundred years or so to get to this "age," but still. It was like a fast forward to what Deacon would look like in his older years. Right down to the golden eyes.

And that was really strange.

Deacon looked a lot like his mother, who also had those golden eyes. But that was a different side of the family. He shared his mother's tan complexion and black hair, getting his height and some of his facial structure from his father. His parents were very obviously his parents. There was no mistaking the familial resemblances. But she hadn't felt like she'd been looking *at* Deacon when she'd looked at them. Even his twin brother who looked so much like him it was a little scary had had their father's blue eyes and slightly different coloring.

But this man…

He *was* Deacon. At least, Deacon in a few years. The build, the facial structure, the hair and eyes. The only *only* difference between them, besides the age, was that Keith appeared tanned by the sun, whereas Deacon's skin tone was natural.

And yet, if she understood the familial relationship correctly, Keith was Deacon's father's maternal father, his grandmother's father on his father's side. From the Scottish line that married into a Welsh family that produced Deacon's father, Evan Jones. Keith was the man whose daughter had given birth to Evan.

She blinked a few times as she tried to work it all out from as many different angles as possible. She probably needed a chart. Or a picture or something.

"So, your daughter was the Scottish grandmother who taught Deacon how to use a Celtic brooch and sword fight and all that?" Cary asked, hoping she had this all straight now. The thought that they were sitting not with Deacon's grandfather or grandmother but his *great* grandfather was pretty amazing.

"Aye, you've the right of it," Keith said. Then chuckled and slipped out of the deep Scottish brogue into a more American accent which still rang with hints of Scotland. "That's my Belle. She was always one for ensuring the old ways continued on. Said you never knew when such things might come in handy." He glanced at Deacon. "Belle loved the way your mother embraced the new ways, though. Clever one, your old mum."

Deacon grinned at his great grandfather, and Cary had to blink again. The smile was so relaxed, almost boyish. Deacon was *never* this relaxed around other leopards. There were reasons, most of which had to do with the fact that, if he wanted to, he could kill another leopard with just a thought. Deacon was a rarity, the first born of firstborn parents tracing back seven generations. It was an almost unprecedented occurrence and it meant he possessed magic and powers that the average leopard shifter did not.

She'd seen some of those powers in action once. It had been pretty damned terrifying. His abilities scared him, too, so he never used them, never used his magic even when he probably should, even though his mother nagged him to learn and train that magic. He thought he was better off always suppressing that part of his nature, and he refused to hear any other arguments.

But the abilities were still there, and he had to manage them by being very controlled around his people.

He showed no signs at all of the icy, nearly emotionless, controlled man he forced himself to be around other leopards here, though. He was as relaxed, as free as she'd ever seen him.

And she wondered if that was the magic of this place, or something specific to do with his great grandfather.

Deacon's smiling gaze settled on her and he shrugged. "A little of both the place and the person," he murmured, proving yet again how irritatingly well he could read her mind through her scent.

"Stop that," she muttered. Then, "How?"

She wasn't sure how much to say in front of Sheldon, and actually, it was probably best if they didn't discuss this in front of him. When he'd tried to steal Deacon's body, he'd assumed he'd captured an ordinary leopard shifter. Had Sheldon succeeded, Cary realized suddenly, he'd have had access to the power to control *all* leopard shifters.

And Zorianthus would have taken over that body.

A sharp, quick, adrenaline-spiked jab of fear for what could have happened went through her. She'd never really considered all the repercussions of that night beyond how it had changed her own personal life. Beyond the fact that Deacon could have been killed. She hadn't thought about all the other horrible things that might have been.

She glared at Sheldon, and he raised a brow back in question. Well, she certainly wasn't going to explain, but she was even more horrified now by what had almost happened and that didn't help her sympathy for him. Even if he hadn't known. Hadn't realized what he'd have been handing to Zorianthus on a silver platter.

Deacon, of course, seemed to understand the undercurrents. He squeezed her hand and said, "Later."

She banked her curiosity about his relationship with his great grandfather for now because her interest, for once, didn't outweigh her better judgement. This was not something they should discuss in front of Sheldon.

"So what's brought you all here," Keith said, "though I've a fair guess it's something to do with the lad."

Sheldon nodded a little at Keith, but didn't comment.

Deacon filled his great grandfather in on the basic outline of the situation. "We needed a place where the wizard wouldn't be able to find us, at least long enough to figure out how to keep him from reclaiming Sheldon."

"You still think he wants my body?" Sheldon asked. "Why? I'm useless to him without my powers."

"If that were the case, I wouldn't be here protecting you," Cary said. "He still needs something from you. Whatever it is, if he gets it, it'll do a lot of damage to the world. My job is to prevent that. Thus, you're here."

Sheldon shrugged and slouched farther into his seat. "Can't imagine what he might want now except to kill me. Tie up the loose end."

Maybe, except she couldn't see how that led to the end of the world. Zorianthus had to want something more. Her bosses wouldn't have asked her to protect the little shit if all the wizard wanted was just to kill him. There was something else going on here. And she was pretty sure it had to do with Zorianthus's attempts to free Oliver Holland.

"He needs a new protégé," Sheldon said. "He wouldn't waste time trying to kill me yet. He'll be hunting for a new…body."

"He's hunting for something else," Cary said.

Keith's gaze, so like Deacon's, narrowed at her. She sighed. They hadn't mentioned Oliver Holland yet—to Keith or Sheldon. But if she was going to talk about the demon, this was probably the place to do it.

First, though, "This place… No one can spy on us here?"

Keith laughed. "We're cut off from the real world. A little bubble of peace."

"Like, we're not in our ordinary realm anymore?"

She'd experienced what was often called a bubble realm before.

There used to be one under Portland, called the Morgin, an area linked to but not part of the ordinary human realm. That had been destroyed in the fight with Holland's demon god father, though. And it was the only time she'd been inside something like that.

"More like this area has been covered by a shield," Keith said. "Not so much a separate realm, but this piece of our realm has been sectioned off."

Okay, her curiosity couldn't resist. "By you?"

Keith just smiled.

Which wasn't an answer.

"We won't stay too long, Gramps," Deacon said. "We just need a place to ask a few more questions and come up with a plan, a place where we're not in danger of being overheard."

"Stay as long as you need," Keith said. "Don't get to see you near as much these days, my boy. Stay as long as you like." He glanced at Sheldon still slouched in his chair, his gaze in his glass of soda.

"You've a choice ahead of you, lad," he said to the former wizard who was trying to ignore him.

Sheldon glanced up without moving his head.

"A choice that could redeem you if you wished."

"And if I don't wish?"

Keith shrugged. "I'm not one to argue with a man who wants to wallow in his mistakes and evils. And I wouldn't tell any man which path to take. Choices are what got you here and they're what will carry you forward. But know, they are all choices. Your choices. Even when they feel like someone else is forcing them on you."

Sheldon snorted and glanced back into his cup.

Cary scowled at his rudeness, although what did she expect from a murdering former wizard.

Keith patted her hand and stood, taking his mug to the large country sink in his spacious, open kitchen. The cottage's main room was all open, the light wood and yellow accented kitchen blending into more light wood around the table, melding into the woven rug strewn floors of a living room area with a large blue couch in front of a huge stone fireplace over which hung a big flat screen tv. The tv was the only real sign of technology in the cottage, and it looked a little out of place.

A narrow stairs near the fireplace led up a level to a loft where Cary assumed Keith had his bedroom. Windows in the front and back of the cabin flooded the place with light, most of it coming from the back windows at this time of the afternoon. And with his front door open, the scents of grass, trees, and the musky hint of sheep filled the cabin, accenting rather than competing with the scent of coffee wafting up from Cary's mug.

As she watched Keith rinse his cup and turn off his coffee maker, she considered how peaceful and quiet the place was. Sheep bleated occasionally from the field, but otherwise, there were no sounds of cars or people, no distant hum of a highway. They did truly feel like they were cut off from the rest of the world, but in a good way that made her sigh in contentment. Even her worries about Sheldon seemed less of an issue here.

What a lovely place to live. She wondered at Deacon not coming here more often. She'd spend weeks out of the year visiting her grandfather if his home was this much of a retreat from reality. To be fair, her grandparents had all passed away, so she didn't have them to visit anymore. And she'd never known any of her great grandparents.

Great grandparent. She took a sip of her strong, hot coffee as she tried to wrap her mind around that. There were human families with great grandparents of course. Families where people had children young and the generations managed to live long enough to see their great grandchildren. It wasn't that unusual, she supposed. But the thought of it still blew her mind, given how long shifters often lived. How old must Keith be?

"You three have a chat," Keith said as he turned back from tidying the kitchen. "I have some sheep to tend. Gotta keep an eye out for any wolves." He winked at Deacon, then ambled out the door.

Cary marveled. For a man in his hundreds, he moved with a kind of easy grace and comfort in his skin she could only aspire to.

"Does he actually have to worry about wolves here?" she asked Deacon when she turned back to the table.

"Not unless he's in the mood for a challenge," he said with a smile. Well that was…interesting.

"So what was the point of all this?" Sheldon asked, still slouched.

"Buying time to work out a plan," Cary said. Again. "And if you don't stop being rude to Keith, I'm going to box your ears."

"You sound like an old lady sometimes, you know?"

"Shut up." Fine, she did occasionally channel her mother. What could she say, she was her mother's daughter, like it or not. Still, it was rude to point it out. To Deacon, she said, "We can't stay here forever, so what do we do? Lure Zorianthus out and…stop him?"

She kind of sucked at strategy. She was the action person in most cases—run in, keep someone from dying by throwing herself between them and danger, once everyone was safe, she went home. Protecting people from threats over longer periods of time wasn't her forte even if she did have to do it occasionally. Actually solving the problem and getting rid of the bad guy… Yeah, she was really bad at that part. In fact, trying to do that was one of the things that had gotten her into trouble with Oliver Holland.

"Should we explain what the wizard is looking for?" Deacon said nodding at Sheldon. "He might know what the man wants from him then."

"He's looking for a new protégé," Sheldon said, slowly as if talking to idiots. "How many times do I have to tell you that?"

"You can stop now," Cary said. "We know what you think. But the fact is, he's *also* looking for someone else. Someone who couldn't ever be his new body."

"Why not?"

"Because," she said, slowly and distinctly, "the person he's looking for is a demon."

15

"Oliver Holland?" Sheldon said, staring between Cary and Deacon, his dark gaze narrowed. He'd set his glass of soda down and was leaning forward, his arms on the big wooden table, looking more involved in what was happening than at any other time that day.

He'd listened to the very beginning of their story with the same disinterest he'd shown all along, but when they specified that the demon was Oliver Holland, Sheldon perked up.

"The Oliver Holland who is currently a captive of the Nagas in a city with a hidden entrance somewhere in this world?" Sheldon said slowly, as if not really believing them.

"Yes, yes, that Oliver Holland," Cary repeated. For the fifth time. "That one. You were there that night? I saw you."

Sheldon frowned down at the table, not looking at her when he nodded. "My former master sent me out to the woods to watch and learn and see what happened. I stayed beyond the army until the fighting ended though and only snuck close enough to see the Nagas taking Holland's body into their city. I wasn't sure he was still alive."

"He was," Cary confirmed. "And I'm pretty sure the Nagas were angry enough to have…plans for him once he came to."

Sheldon shivered a little, proving he wasn't immune to some horrors. Not that Cary blamed the Nagas. Holland was a demon and the worst sort of evil. He'd killed one of their people. She couldn't blame the snake shifters for anything they did to him as punishment for that. But she was absolutely certain she didn't want to know the details.

"You killed most of the ones who didn't run," Sheldon said.

"I released all that magic I'd been storing up," she said.

"Including mine."

"Well, I hadn't known it at the time. But yeah."

"Are you sorry you killed so many people?"

"I consider it more that they committed suicide," she said, though inside she winced.

She didn't really think of it that way in her inner most thoughts. She knew *she'd* killed them even if that hadn't been her plan or what she'd intended. She knew she'd used powers and magic and had flattened an army of living beings—even if every single one of them was at that very moment trying to kill her. Still, the reality of what she'd done sometimes came back to haunt her, at unexpected moments, and it left her breathless with the horror of it. And the guilt.

So she tried very hard not to think about it. And when she did, she told herself the story that they'd brought on their own destruction by attacking the Nagas, and throwing all that magic at her. If they hadn't done that, they wouldn't be dead. That story let her sleep at night and live with what had happened.

Most of the time.

She pushed the guilt peeking through her fiction away again. No time for that now. "They wouldn't have died if they hadn't been there trying to kill me and invade a city and maybe even kill other people, so, yeah, they brought that on themselves," she said aloud, as much to continue convincing herself of the story as to justify the deaths to Sheldon.

"It didn't give you a…a surge? A jolt? Make you feel…powerful?"

"Not even a little bit," she said, scowling at him. "I felt exhausted and sad. Like a feeling, caring person with empathy." That was a dig at Sheldon, but she couldn't help it. He'd killed for purely selfish, ridiculous reasons. And there was no comparing what she'd done and what he'd done. Especially if he'd felt powerful because of what he'd done.

"I didn't feel powerful either," Sheldon said.

Surprising her.

"Zorianthus said I should have, that death would feed my powers and make me feel stronger. It did. But I was failing to do what I intended. It wasn't satisfying."

"Boy, killing isn't supposed to be satisfying and the fact that you think it should be is gross."

"I'm not a boy."

"You know what, you're right. You are a grown ass man. And a grown ass man should know killing isn't supposed to be satisfying."

"I didn't say the killing was supposed to be satisfying. Failing in the spells was what bothered me, what wasn't satisfying."

"I still have no sympathy. You were killing people because you didn't like your zits. Nowhere in that is there room for my sympathy."

"I wasn't looking for your sympathy."

"Good. Because you don't have it. Why did Zorianthus want you to spy on Holland and his army?"

"He never said. I assumed it was so we could see what you did, figure out a way to kill you and get my powers back."

"Could have been," Cary murmured, but she was staring into her now empty coffee mug wondering if the old bastard had had more than one reason for sending his protégé there.

"Why do you think he's going after Holland now?" Deacon asked. There was a faint growl in his voice.

Apparently, he wasn't enjoying the reminders of Sheldon killing shifters or that she'd had to level an army to survive that night. She wasn't the only one who'd come away from that battle with a few emotional scars. Though, she imagined he probably had deeper ones from when she'd died in Faery, ones that surpassed what he'd picked up that night of the Naga battle.

Wow, she was giving the poor man a lot of emotional scarring thanks to her job. That didn't seem like a good thing at all. Or even a little fair.

Sheldon shrugged. "I'd be guessing. I don't really know."

"Give us your best guess," Cary said. "Just revenge? Cause he'd be wasting a lot of time for something that's not going to get him a new body."

"He'd want more than just revenge," Sheldon said. "He'd be pleased revenge was part of it all, but he's got something more than just revenge in mind to put time into finding Holland before he finds a new body."

"He dies if he uses the spell to find the city," Deacon said. "He can't get around that."

"Unless he does a body swap and jumps out of the dying body at the last minute."

Every part of Cary froze, even her breathing. For long enough she had to gasp in a breath. The implications of what Sheldon had said washed over her.

"Shit," she murmured. She glanced at Deacon. "That's what he wants. That's why I'm here."

They both looked at Sheldon. Sheldon frowned back, his skin going even paler as the implications of what he'd said sank in for him, too.

"No," Sheldon said. "No. He wouldn't want to stay in my body with no powers. He'd be stuck. Without any magic, he couldn't do the body swap again. He'd be trapped in my body until it died. There'd be no point using me."

"You're assuming he'd trigger the spell in his body and then jump to yours to survive," Cary said. "But what if he does it the other way around? What if he jumps into yours to conduct the search spell, kills your body doing that, and moves back to his own before yours dies?"

"He's got you adapted to the change," Deacon said. "He can swap bodies with you a lot easier than with anyone else."

"He'd be relying on me to allow him back into his own body, though. The point of the training we did was that I wouldn't just instinctively jump back to my own body. I have control of his when

I'm there. I can stay there, without that instinctive kick back. I have to consciously make the switch now. Why the hell would I switch back to a body about to die?"

Cary took in a deep breath and let it out. "Maybe… He might have been counting on you not knowing the spell was a death sentence. Which we've now fortunately ruined for him."

"That sounds like him," Sheldon said, his mouth twisting in a scowl. "Hiding the truth until it's too late to stop him."

Sheldon's bitterness was sharp but at least it was emotion. His disinterest in what was happening to him, what his former master intended, had vanished. He'd take the situation seriously now.

"So we can all agree that letting Zorianthus talk Sheldon into helping him find the Naga city would be bad. That releasing Holland would be bad. And that I need to protect Sheldon from Zorianthus so that none of that happens. Right?" She stared directly at Sheldon as she said this last.

He looked away without answering.

"Right?" she said again, her teeth clenched. The last thing she needed was Sheldon not letting her protect him.

Grudgingly, Sheldon nodded. "Yes," he said. "I don't want to die. I wouldn't have spent so much on spells and learning witchcraft if I wanted to die."

"Speaking of which," she said, "how much witchcraft have you learned? Can you do anything yet or still working on it?"

She knew from Angie that the process took years, learning, studying, practice. It was like anything else. Even if a person had innate magic, training that magic took time and study. A witch who actually wanted to do magic but didn't have any innate magic of their own, well, that took even longer because those witches had to rely on the magic of the potions they mixed and the spells they memorized. And the results weren't anything like what someone with actual innate magic could get.

Still, Sheldon had been studying wizardry so he might have a leg up on the witchcraft study. At least the theory part of it.

"I can't do much yet. It's…awkward. Not like wizardry. I *was* a wizard, I knew how that felt, learned how to control it, but always instinctively knew how it worked. I'm learning something that isn't part of my nature, and it doesn't always…work."

"You keep trying to do witchcraft with wizard techniques, huh?"

"Exactly," Sheldon said with a nod, his expression, though exasperated, took on a little bit of light. Like being understood in his struggle with witchcraft made him feel better.

She wasn't here to make the little shit feel better, but if she were honest with herself, it was good to see him expressing emotion. Frankly, it was a lot harder to anticipate a person's actions if she couldn't read them. And Sheldon had been doing a dandy job of showing her only resignation and hollowness. Which hadn't told her much at all.

"So what now?" Sheldon asked.

The million dollar question. They had a good guess at what Zorianthus wanted. At least, what he wanted from Sheldon. But there was still the issue of him needing a new body soon. Killing Sheldon in the process of finding the Naga city, getting into the Naga city, and releasing Holland… None of that solved Zorianthus's dying body problem.

Cary exchanged a look with Deacon. "We take Sheldon back to his place, and we might lure Zorianthus out. We might even survive that confrontation because he needs Sheldon, so I have someone to protect even if the bastard wants me dead and knows how to do it. But…" And here was the crux of all her Protector problems. "But I can't make him leave Sheldon alone, so even if we confront him, that won't make Sheldon safe or end Zorianthus's efforts to free Holland."

"You could kill him," Sheldon said matter-of-factly.

"No."

"Why not? He wants to kill you. You have killed before. You thought you'd killed me."

"I thought *you'd* killed you with the ricochet of your powers off my shield. If you hadn't attacked Deacon, you wouldn't have been caught in your own damned magic."

"So let Zorianthus kill himself on your shields. His body is really old now. He can only slow the aging process for so long and then the inevitability of biology gets in his way. The body is breaking down. Once that starts, it goes fast because it's not his natural body and because he's been spelling it for so long to slow the process."

"How long does he have?" she asked. The less time he had, the more desperate he'd be, and that changed the equation. She still didn't know what to do about him, but if he was going to die soon, all she might have to do is wait him out.

"I don't know," Sheldon said. "Months maybe. A year at most. I really am surprised he's wasting time on this demon thing. With fresh powers and a younger body to work in, he'd be able to go after the demon, you, me… He'd have all the time in the world to carry out his revenge. Seems stupid to go after Holland now."

Yeah, Cary thought. It did. Which was why the Holland thing had to be about more than just revenge. "You said training a new body takes time. Maybe since he doesn't have much time left, he's looking for a shortcut. Maybe he thinks Holland can be that shortcut. He gets both revenge and an answer to his own problem in one fell swoop."

"But only if he gets to Sheldon," Deacon said, "and gets Sheldon to body switch with him while they do the spell."

"So we just don't let him get to Sheldon. That I can do. I'm good at that part."

Deacon's mouth quirked with a little smile. But the expression dropped away when he said, "But where?"

She sighed. That was the issue. She didn't want to live on Sheldon's creepy apartment floor inside his neglected apartment just waiting on Zorianthus to show up. But that might well be what she had to do. She wasn't taking him back to her place. She didn't want him in her house, near her dogs, contaminating her private and safe home. She didn't want him at Deacon's house because other people lived in that building, including his sister. They couldn't stay with Deacon's great grandfather forever. Fascinated as she was, and with the full intention of coming back here soon to get all the good stories from Keith, they couldn't risk his bubble of peace by hiding here long.

They'd needed a place to talk and figure out Zorianthus's likely objective. They got that. Now it was time to return to the world outside this peaceful bubble and somehow stop Zorianthus.

Keith walked back into the house, stomping his boots off on a rubber mat just outside the door before strolling inside. "I'm making fajitas and nachos for dinner," he said. "I have enough for a feast. Would you all like to stay for dinner?"

"You make Mexican food?"

A Scottish, leopard shifter, sheep farmer who cooked Mexican food? She wasn't sure why that combination of things surprised her, but it did.

"I've a good neighbor a few farms down taught me the basics." He chuckled. "I know my way around a tasty salsa now. What do you say, lads? In the mood for some nachos?"

Cary exchanged a look with Deacon. Her stomach gurgled in anticipation. He grinned.

"Looks like we're staying for dinner, Gramps," Deacon said.

Cary sighed happily. "I'm always in the mood for nachos." Second only to pizza.

16

After a spectacular and filling dinner that even Sheldon grudgingly enjoyed, Cary stepped out into the deepening night to call Angie.

"Is Marianne going to date Brandon?" she asked as soon as her friend answered.

"She says she's not ready to even consider dating yet," Angie replied without missing a beat. "And she won't be swayed. But she did say she thought Brandon was handsome, so there's at least that."

Cary sighed. "I suppose it is too soon for anything serious. Still, it would be really nice to see her happy again." Marianne hadn't been quite herself since her breakup with Gina. And it hurt Cary to see her friend so hurt.

"Is that the only reason you're calling?" Angie asked.

"Nope. Though it was the most important reason." She outlined her newest job for Angie briefly. "So I need to know how much witchcraft a former wizard can wield. I believe Sheldon when he says its awkward for him, but I don't trust him to tell me the truth about what he can do."

"I can't believe your bosses are making you protect that shit," Angie said.

"Yeah, well, if protecting him means stopping his asshole master from freeing Holland, I'll manage."

"Still. He almost killed Deacon."

Cary nodded, even though Angie couldn't see her. "It's one of my more complicated jobs."

"Okay, so because he's familiar with the basics of magic, even from a different angle, he could, with training and a lot of practice learn a few spells and actually make the ones that require some touch of magic work. Eventually. The ones that don't require actual innate magic, the stuff a kitchen or hedge witch could conjure with the right ingredients, he can learn those now. Again, he'd need practice to keep from accidentally blowing himself up or poisoning himself. Did you see into his kitchen at all?"

"No. I have no idea what kind of witchcraft he's attempting. I know he bought some spells to keep his apartment safe. I think mostly illusion ones, and possibly a transport one? Anyway, he bought some to keep Zorianthus from finding him."

"Did he protect against scrying? Most wizards don't think about it. It's a real witchy trick. But there are wizards capable of doing it."

"I thought scrying just gave you a location?"

"It does. In images. And with enough practice, a witch—or in this case wizard—can hold the images and watch them for longer than it takes to find their target. Especially if they already know where their target is. Then it's really just like spying on someone by watching them in the bowl."

"Can you do that?"

"Not very well. I get a picture and a location and then it all fades. I can't hold it for long. But you said Zorianthus is old, this isn't his first go around? So he's probably picked up more than the usual wizard tricks over the years. I'd lay money he's been practicing scrying."

"Shit," Cary muttered and rubbed her hand over her face. "Maybe that's what I was sensing, why my Protector instincts went into low-level alert but I couldn't pinpoint any directional danger. We thought maybe Zorianthus had bugged Sheldon's place with ordinary cameras or hearing equipment, and then shut them off when he realized we were looking for something like that? But I could have been feeling a scrying if the someone watching was a threat."

"Where are you now that he can't find you?"

"You'll never believe." Cary lowered her voice and glanced around just to make sure no one was nearby. She'd walked a few yards away from the house, leaving Sheldon, Deacon and Keith inside. The two leopards had excellent hearing and would probably still pick up some of what she said, but she tried to whisper anyway. "I'm at Deacon's great grandfather's house. With his great grandfather. Who looks exactly like Deacon but older. And he has a Scottish accent."

"A silver fox version of Deacon with a Scottish accent? Damn."

"Right? Actually, the resemblance is really amazing. Like we're visiting with Deacon himself only from the future."

"Has he told you any good Deacon-childhood stories yet?"

She raised her brows. "I haven't asked. I've been caught up with the Sheldon thing."

"When you get time, ask. There are going to be some good stories there."

Cary chuckled. Then she got serious again. "I can't stay here long, though, and I can't leave Sheldon alone. But I don't want to bring him to my house. I have no idea how the dogs will take him. Would you be free to check on my pack tonight?"

"Ah, sorry, I can't. I have a friend in town visiting for the week. We don't get to see each other as often as we'd like, so when they're in town, I try to dedicate the entire time to their visit."

"That's great. Why didn't you tell me? Of course you have to spend all the time with your friend. I'll see if maybe Marianne or Lucy can swing by. If they can't… I'll figure something out. Deacon's sister loves dogs. She might help."

Of all Deacon's siblings, Cary got along the best with his twin brother Michael and his younger sister Caitlin who worked in Portland with him. She'd never had to ask Caitlin for a favor before, but since it was for the dogs, she felt a little less guilty about it.

"Good luck with the wizard," Angie said. "Call if you need backup."

"I don't want to interrupt your time with your friend. We'll manage."

"It's okay if it's an emergency. Especially a magically related one. My friend will understand. Mind your back and take care of yourself."

"You too. Thanks!"

She stared off into the nearby pasture for a moment, the little lumps of white fluff that were the sheep growing more difficult to see as the last of the daylight faded behind the hills, painting the sky a spectacular red and purple.

"Scrying," she murmured. If that was what had happened, and Zorianthus was responsible, it meant he could watch them no matter where they were, so long as he could find them.

That was both creepy and…possibly useful. Though she wasn't entirely sure how to use the information yet.

She rang Lucy first and got her voicemail, then tried Marianne, who was free and able to check on the dogs. Marianne loved all animals—they'd first met when she'd been a volunteer at the veterinary clinic where Cary worked before becoming a Protector—but until recently, until her breakup with Gina, she'd had to be careful about being around dogs as Gina had animal dander allergies. Even when she'd been volunteering, Marianne had had to be careful about her clothes, changing at her shop so she didn't bring home anything that could trigger Gina's allergies.

Because of that, Cary had rarely asked her to dog sit before. She realized as Marianne enthusiastically agreed to hang out with the dogs that she didn't have that issue anymore. And maybe Marianne could do with a little more time with the dogs. Maybe she even needed to get a pet of her own.

Cary filed that away for later discussion, but she was excited about the idea. A pet would give Marianne some companionship and maybe help her with her healing. Her birthday was coming up in the middle of October. Maybe Cary could get Lucy and Angie to go in with her and they could surprise Marianne with a puppy. From one of Deacon's clinics.

Satisfied with the plan, she turned back toward the cabin. And realized she'd accidentally solved the wrong problem. Though one just as important since it involved the happiness of one of her best friends. But she still had the issue of Sheldon. And Zorianthus. And the possible end of the world. Again.

She stared at the front door a moment. Then changed directions slightly and sat on one of the low-slung Adirondack chairs on the porch. She wasn't quite ready to face Sheldon yet because she still didn't know what to do with him tonight or how she'd deal with Zorianthus. She needed a plan.

And she was so very bad at planning.

She ran her hands over the top of her head, smoothing the little hairs that had escaped her ponytail, and stared at the darkening sky. How the hell was she going to stop Zorianthus?

She could stop him from getting Sheldon. She could stand between him and Sheldon for as long as it took and he wouldn't get past her, even knowing how to kill her, because she had to keep Sheldon safe. That was her job right now. Keep Sheldon safe. It wasn't to actually stop Zorianthus from freeing Holland. Just stop him from using Sheldon to do that.

Except, she really didn't want Zorianthus to find another way to free Holland. Her bosses had said the *process* of freeing Holland would be the disaster for the world. Not Holland himself getting out, but the process Zorianthus would go through to free him. They'd said protecting Sheldon would stop that, but... What if Zorianthus found another option?

She wanted him stopped and no longer a threat. That wasn't technically her job at the moment. But it would be a great bonus to her life.

She just didn't know how to accomplish that.

The screen door opened on slightly squeaky hinges and Keith stepped out onto the porch carrying two bottles of beer. He lifted one. "Thought you could do with a little tipple as you're contemplating the stars."

She smiled and gratefully took the cold bottle. She glanced at the label, a Dutch lager, and raised her brows. "I would have pegged you for something a little more…Scottish."

Keith eased down into the chair next to her and chuckled. "I'd take a good Guinness over anything, to be honest with you, but I do like the occasional Irn-Bru."

"Is that a beer?"

"No. A Scottish…I suppose you could call it an orange soda. I wouldn't recommend it without a little practice first, though."

She tipped her bottle at him before taking a drink. "Thanks for this. Thanks for everything."

"You're looking a bit lost, Cary."

"I don't know what to do." She shrugged. "That happens a lot, though, so it's fine. I need to keep that… I need to keep Sheldon safe, but I don't have a plan for it, and I'm pretty bad at plans."

"You're all welcome to stay here for the night, if that helps."

"Thank you. Really. But I don't want this to disturb your lovely peace." She looked out over the darkening fields, the breeze gently ruffling her hair. "It really is lovely here."

"Aye. I don't leave often anymore. Reached an age where I'm happy to let the rest of the world roll by while I sit on my porch, drinking beer, and contemplating the sleeping sheep."

It was impossible to miss that Keith was here alone, but she didn't want to ask what had happened to his mate. Or any of the other too-personal questions that sparked her curiosity. Actually, she wanted to ask all those things very much, but she didn't think this was the time.

"You won't be disturbing my peace to stay the night," Keith said. "The great grandkids used to come camping here decades ago, bringing a lot of noise and chaos to the place. But they're all grown now. It's good to have a *little* noise again."

She chuckled. "Tell me about this neighbor who taught you to make fajitas."

They rolled into a conversation about food and his neighbor, an older woman who'd grown up in the southwest, become a world-renowned chef, and then retired quietly to her farm after her husband died. She and Keith got together weekly to trade food—she had an extensive garden; he had the sheep and chickens—and recipes and gossip. And listening to Keith tell stories in his mild brogue as they finished their beers was just the moment of reprieve Cary needed.

By the time he lifted away her bottle and went inside to set up the camping beds, she felt a lot less overwhelmed by her lack of a plan. She still didn't have one. But she didn't have to think about what to do tonight. She could spend the night planning, and know her charge was safe as she did.

Deacon came onto the porch a few minutes later, taking the seat his great grandfather had abandoned. "You two are getting along well. That's good."

She grinned. "I really like your Gramps. Did you help him with the camping beds?"

"Of course," he said, looking at her like she'd said something truly offensive.

She raised her hands. "Sorry. Just checking. Are you okay with us staying here overnight?"

"I'm good with having the extra time to plan."

"Do you have one? Because I don't. And we really could do with one." She shook her head. "I wish Wisat and Liruk would stop giving me *planning* jobs. I'm better at the jump-between-bad-guys-and-good-guys-in-the-moment kind of jobs."

Deacon's chuckle brushed warmly along her skin and she closed her eyes to savor the sound. The man's chuckle should be outlawed.

He wrapped his fingers around hers and squeezed. "We have a plan. Tonight, we stay here where Zorianthus can't find us."

"And tomorrow?"

"We'll figure out tomorrow by tomorrow. What did Angie say when you called her?"

She told him about the possibility that Zorianthus had been scrying and that's why she'd felt like someone had been watching them at Sheldon's place. "I'll have to ask Sheldon if he's seen Zorianthus do that, but it seems as good an answer as any."

"Something we can use," Deacon said, echoing her earlier thought.

"We could even set him up to come out of the shadows and try to get at Sheldon."

"Then what?" She turned a little in her chair to face him, still holding his hand. "The biggest problem with Zorianthus is that he knows what I am."

"You're protecting Sheldon. He can't kill you now."

"No, it's not that. Although him not being able to kill me is a bonus. No, it's that he's not likely to try coming up against my shields directly. He knows he can't. He knows what I'm capable of. So why bother trying to get through me to Sheldon? It would be pointless. Plus, he knows I might suck up some of his magic during that kind of a standoff, and until he kills me, he wouldn't get it back. Or at least he'd assume that he would only get it back by killing me. Whatever. He needs his magic right now. He's not going to risk losing it to me."

Deacon grunted an acknowledgement of that.

"Because he knows what I can do, his best bet is to just stay away until I think Sheldon is safe and leave."

"He doesn't have time to wait you out, though. Not if Sheldon is right about how much time he has left. He either has to abandon Sheldon as part of his plan. Or he has to try and lure Sheldon away from your protection."

"I'm betting he'll try that last one before he abandons anything. He's in a corner with time. He may well be running out of alternative options." At least she hoped. She wasn't so certain about that.

"There must be more he wants from Holland and the Naga city," Deacon said. "This really isn't a good plan on his part otherwise."

Cary agreed. "What do you think he really wants from the city, from Holland?"

"Got me. I'm not a wizard."

She squeezed his hand. "You're doing good, not attacking Sheldon. I appreciate that. I'd hate to have to protect him from you."

"That's the only reason I haven't gone for his throat. I don't care how old he is. He's a murderer. Not some innocent teenager that needs rehabilitation."

"He can't be both?"

She wasn't sure herself that he could be both, but she wanted to ask the question. This particular job was hard, no matter what way she looked at it, because Sheldon was both very young but had done some very evil things. He hadn't even shown any regret for those evil things. Just sat around pouting because he wasn't an all-powerful wizard anymore, and his master had betrayed him.

"Innocent, no." Deacon didn't even hesitate. "Rehabilitated? That's up to him and not my job."

True. It wasn't her job either.

"But he'd have a lot of atonement he'd have to undertake to make up for all the evil he's committed." Deacon held her gaze. "And I'm not sure he'd want to do that. He doesn't smell like he's sorry for what he did. Only sorry he failed."

She let out a long sigh. This was the reason she hated having to protect bad guys. Unless they were sorry for their actions and wanted to do better, they were still bad guys. Helping bad guys who would turn around and do bad things after they'd survived whatever trouble they were in seemed wrong.

And yet…

Cary kept coming back to how young Sheldon was. He was a teenager, barely legal age. Sure, he could join the army and fight in a war. He could vote. Legally, she supposed he was a grownup. But he was as young as a "grownup" could get. And he'd been groomed—she wanted to throw up a little at that word—by a very bad man. He hadn't had the chance to be a good guy.

Or maybe he had. Maybe he'd simply decided he didn't want to be one?

She scrubbed her free hand over her eyes and shook her head. She hated this. She preferred protecting good guys. No complicated moral dilemmas there.

"If this didn't have world-ending potential, I'd leave Sheldon to duke it out with Zorianthus on his own," she muttered. "Let the bad guys sort this out amongst themselves." She met Deacon's gaze. "But I don't feel particularly good about that attitude."

"Sometimes, my love," Deacon said, brushing her cheek with a gentle touch, "you really are too tenderhearted."

"Yeah, yeah. It sucks."

"He's safe for the night," Deacon said. "No world ending today. Tomorrow, we'll find somewhere else to hole up with him. We might just have to wait out Zorianthus. He'll either die in his attempts to find Holland, or he'll attack out of desperation. And die then."

"Only if he drains too much magic in the attack," she said.

"No." Deacon lowered his voice but didn't flinch from her direct gaze. "If this man attacks you, I will kill him, and this will be done. He's been trying to kill you for months. If he gets within my reach, I won't hesitate to end his threat to you."

She swallowed, hard. Because she wasn't sure how to feel about that declaration. "I… I don't want you…" She raised a hand when he opened his mouth to interrupt her. "I don't want you to take that hit to your soul," she finished. "Killing in self defense is one thing."

"This would be self defense," he said.

"No. No, if you attack him on sight, it will be…" She didn't want to call it murder. That was on the tip of her tongue, though. And she didn't want Deacon to do that, even for her. "It'll be different from self defense, from…saving me from him. It'll put a mark on you, inside, and you'll have to live with that."

"I can."

"But I don't want you to. I don't want you to have to."

"There's a lot I'm willing to live with for you," Deacon said. "Nothing I wouldn't do to keep you safe."

"I feel the same," she said. "Which is why I don't want you to murder Zorianthus on sight."

His nostrils flared as he looked away from her. He kept hold of her hand, but he stared out over the now dark fields, his eyes glowing faintly yellow.

"There's no court of law for Zorianthus," he murmured quietly. "There's no justice here. Not in our world. The only way to stop his evil is for him to die."

"Yeah," she said with a sigh. "I know. I know the world would be a better place without him. And I know we can't let him finish whatever plan he's put into motion. I'd prefer if he killed himself on my shields and we didn't have to worry about this anymore." She turned to look out over the fields too. "I'd just prefer you didn't have to take the hit in the name of justice."

He was quiet for a long moment, then, haltingly, said, "In the leopard world, when I take over for my mother, I will be the judge and jury for my people. And I'll have to issue the punishments. It will be my job to keep the peace and punish those who break our laws."

"But you'll have choices on which punishments to give out, and you have a jail in your mother's home to lock up criminals. That's different to what we're talking about here."

"How?"

"Cause here, this isn't your responsibility, your job. And you're not talking about just locking the old wizard up."

"How have you survived in this life, this world, for all these years with that soft heart of yours?"

She snorted. "Got me. Why the hell do you think I was so worried going into this year?"

He faced her again, cupping her cheek in one large palm. "For you, I will do anything. Even curb my need to kill to end a threat to you. But…" He brought her face closer to his, resting his forehead against hers. "I will not hesitate to kill this wizard if he comes close to hurting you. I will defend you and kill to do it."

She sighed. "Since I'd do the same for you, I can't tell you not to." She smiled faintly. "It is nice to know you have my back."

"Always, love." He kissed her gently. "Always."

17

Deacon shifted back to his human form on the front porch, silently slipping into the clothes he'd left on one of the Adirondack chairs while he went for a midnight run. He could hear Cary's deep, peaceful breathing inside, a sound that settled him like no other. Sheldon's snoring indicated he was still sound asleep too.

All around the sounds of sleep and peace—the chirp and chitter of night bugs and creatures, the snortles and bleats of sheep, the hush of wind blowing through the high treetops at the rear of the house. And the scents… Nothing in Deacon's life had ever smelled quite like his great grandfather's place. He wasn't entirely sure what was so unique about it because it was just a sheep farm in the middle of the countryside. But the combination of pines, grass, maple trees, soil, the neighbor's gardens, the sheep… All of it combined to tell Deacon he was on his great grandfather's property and nowhere else in the world.

"Did you scare the sheep?" Keith asked, as he moved into view from around the side of the house where he'd been sitting on a different part of the porch.

"I stayed downwind," Deacon assured with a faint smile.

"Worries have you up late." Keith settled onto one of the chairs, easing down carefully.

Deacon watched him closely, alert to the slower, careful way he moved now.

"Ye'll move slower when you get to be my age, too," Keith said with a quiet chuckle.

"You're okay, though? Still… Okay?"

Another chuckle. "Aye, as good as can be expected. Now, what has you up so late?"

"What else?" He nodded to the house before sitting down next to Keith.

"Your mate seems like a fine woman."

"She is. But her job…" He let out a long sigh.

"Puts her in harm's way a lot, I take it?"

He didn't answer. He didn't have to. Keith no doubt picked up all he needed to in Deacon's scent. This was one of the few places where he didn't feel the need to control his scent from another leopard. Usually, even that had to be controlled, regulated, carefully adjusted so that the others couldn't read him. Until Cary, control had been everything in his life, a part of his life he'd needed just to avoid hurting his people. Since her, his control had slipped. A lot. And while he'd regained most of it, enough to be less dangerous, he still slipped. Especially because her job put her in so damned much danger.

But here, Deacon didn't ever have to worry about his control. About it slipping. About accidentally hurting anyone. Here, he could relax as fully and completely as he ever did. He loved it. The peace and freedom here were addictive.

Which was one of the reasons he didn't come back very often. He was afraid one of these days, he'd show up on his great grandfather's doorstep and never leave.

"She seems well able for the job," Keith said, but there was a question in his voice.

"She is. That's also the problem. She's great at her job. Which means she never hesitates, even when she should."

They'd been vague about her job title, because Cary tried to keep the number of people who knew what she actually did down to a minimum. His mother knew Cary was a Protector, and what that meant, but the rest of his family and the leopards were vague on the specifics. Deacon had a feeling Keith was old enough to know what Protectors were, and he'd probably figure it out eventually. But for Cary's safety, Deacon kept things vague when discussing her job.

For what that was worth.

"You're afraid she'll get killed," Keith said, his tone full of understanding.

"She already has once." He ran a hand through his hair. "She wasn't… It didn't last long. A Fae healer saved her. But for a moment, she was dead. Gone. I felt the loss, felt the break, and… Gramps, I was going with her. If she died, I had every intention of following."

"Aye. I've felt that one, too," he said quietly.

Deacon glanced at him, but his gaze was turned inward as he stared out over the fields.

"How did you survive losing your mate?" Deacon asked quietly. It wasn't something he'd ever asked. Before Cary, he hadn't thought to ask. Since… He hadn't dared broach a subject he didn't want to contemplate.

"It was a difficult time," Keith said quietly. "A difficult time. I had the consolation of a long life with my Iona. Though in some ways that might have made it harder. So many years together, I hardly knew myself without her." He pulled in a deep breath. "I had the kids and grandkids to help me. They weren't ready to be done with me. And your grandmother, my Belle, insisted I stay if I could." He gestured at the lands around them. "Gave me some peace. But it was a very difficult time. I still miss my love every day."

He finally faced Deacon and there was a sadness mixed with acceptance in his scent, in his expression.

"You manage," he said quietly. "You even get on with living eventually. But I won't lie and say it's easy. And if you followed your mate… Well, not a one of us would blame you."

Deacon nodded, glancing away from his gramps. "I'm not sure we'll have kids, that we'll be able to since she's human. I may not have that to keep me here when she goes."

Even if they had a long life together, Cary was still human and she would die before he did. He might not live as long as Keith, but he still had a longer life expectancy than Cary, even without her job.

"But I'll have the responsibility of our people," he continued. "I…" He swallowed hard. "I'm afraid of what I'll do if— When she dies. What I might do to the others."

"Aye. Well." Keith sighed and patted his arm. "When such a day comes, if you think you might want to stay with us a bit longer, you can come here. You'll be able to grieve in peace."

"And if I don't want to leave again once I'm here?" It was a very serious question. He was supposed to lead his people after his mother. He couldn't lead from here. But he'd already had a taste of what he'd feel losing his mate, and he wouldn't be fit to be around other leopards.

"Then someone else will come along to fill the hole you leave. Your brother or sister. They're capable leaders. Jocelyn in particular would make a fine leader."

Deacon's lips twitched. "Not Michael, huh?"

Keith chuckled. "Too tenderhearted that one. He'd spend too much time trying to heal all the wounds instead of leading."

That was true enough. Michael was much better suited to his job as a vet. But Keith was right. Jocelyn would make a fine leader.

If she survived her own mate issues.

He let out a long breath. "I never realized how…complicated it would be, Gramps. Finding my mate. Loving her so damned much."

"It's a ride," Keith said. "But a worthwhile one."

"She's too tenderhearted for this world, too, though," Deacon said.

"Oh aye, that she is. But it's also her strength. Don't let her lose that. The softness and compassion. It's her strength." Keith smiled a little. "Just like it was my Iona's."

Deacon let those words sink in as he gently patted his great grandfather's arm. "Thanks, Gramps. For listening. And for giving us a place to rest."

"Here whenever you need me, lad. Now, take yourself off to sleep. I've a feeling you've a big day ahead of you."

Deacon snorted. That felt like an understatement. He pushed to his feet, but before going inside, he rested his hand on Keith's shoulder for a long moment, then bent over to give him a kiss on the top of the head. Keith kept his gaze on the field, patting Deacon's hand without comment. Everything they needed to say to each other was in their scents.

Inside, Deacon stretched out on the camping bed, the aluminum frame groaning a little under his weight, and faced his mate. She was sound asleep, her lips slightly parted as she breathed deeply, her eyes moved behind her lids as she dreamed. He let her scent fill him, reaching across the narrow space between their individual beds to brush his fingers over her cheek.

Then he let himself sleep. Let the worry for tomorrow, and the future, go. At least for now he could rest.

And tomorrow…

Tomorrow, he'd guard her back. And they'd face whatever happened together.

18

*C*ary woke feeling a lot less rested than she might have expected from such a bucolic setting. The camping beds were fine, though the mattresses were thin. Keith had arrayed them in his main room, near the fireplace, moving the couch to one side as a kind of barrier between Cary and Deacon's beds and Sheldon's bed. It hadn't exactly provided privacy, but at least they weren't sleeping right on top of each other.

Unfortunately, both Keith and Sheldon snored. And even when there wasn't a nasal orchestra playing in the background, she'd still had trouble sleeping as she worried about what to do about Zorianthus and Sheldon. And struggled with her complicated feelings about this particular job.

She was never going to get over that Sheldon had killed people. That he'd almost killed Deacon. Especially because he didn't seem to care or want to atone for those murders. And having to protect someone with that kind of ick at their core went against the grain. Big time.

With a groan and a few achy stretches, she made use of Keith's downstairs bathroom while Deacon refolded their beds and readied them to be put away. Sheldon tried to hide under his pillow rather than wake up even though it was well past eight in the morning and Keith had left to tend the sheep two hours earlier.

She still didn't have a plan this morning, other than getting Sheldon away from the pureness of Keith's farm. But since Zorianthus was under a time crunch and couldn't just wait around for her to get bored and go away, she figured the easiest thing to do was return to Sheldon's creepy apartment and hope Zorianthus's patience gave out before hers.

She wasn't a particularly patient person. But the wizard hadn't struck her as very patient either. And she wasn't the one whose body was about to die.

Her body had already done that.

She snorted at her reflection in the mirror, wincing a little at the puffy circles under her eyes as she tried to smooth her hair back into a somewhat neat ponytail. She had fallen into a habit of reminding herself, regularly, that she had died not too long ago. Like poking at a bruise repeatedly as it tried to heal. She should probably stop doing that.

She rinsed her mouth as best she could since she didn't have her toothbrush, then turned the bathroom over to Deacon.

"Gramps left you some coffee in the kitchen," he said to her, kissing her gently on the way past.

"Your great grandfather is the best of all possible people," she said with a sigh. "And I officially adore him."

Deacon's chuckle left a pleasant tingle tightening her tummy as she made her way into the open kitchen for the required and delicious morning ritual that was coffee.

Once she'd had enough caffeine to wake her up and put her in a better mood, she went to Sheldon and nudged his bed. "Up," she said. "We can't impose on Keith anymore."

"You people get up too early," he grunted and pulled his blanket up over his head.

"Only when we're imposing on other people. Get up."

"Bathroom's occupied." Sheldon didn't lower his blanket.

"If Deacon comes out and you don't go directly in, I'm going to have him flip this bed over and dump you out onto the floor."

Sheldon grumbled something under his breath that she ignored, though she was glad Deacon hadn't heard or Sheldon would have already found his ass dumped out of the bed. She left him to his last pouty minutes of sleep, pulled on her leather jacket, and stepped out onto the porch with her steaming cup of coffee.

The morning was cold and brisk. Sunlight rolled gently over the fields as it breached the horizon, but overhead the sky was dim and gray. The soft bleating of sheep, the faint scents of damp soil and grass mixing with the heady scent of her coffee, the sharp kiss of cold air on her cheeks… She was only ever up this early when she had to be. But occasionally, when she was, she really enjoyed the sensation of watching the world wake up.

Deacon came out the door and wrapped his arms around her from behind. She leaned into him, still cradling her coffee mug.

"Sheldon up?"

"He scrambled out of bed when the bathroom door opened. I didn't have to follow through on your threat."

She chuckled.

"I would have been happy to, though."

"We'll head back to his apartment today. Maybe I can get a sense of Zorianthus spying on us and we can…I don't know, plant an idea in his head that makes him come after Sheldon."

"What sort of idea?"

"I don't know. I'm clutching at straws here. Maybe… Oh, maybe we make it seem like we're not going to stay with Sheldon and pretend to leave? Lure Zorianthus in, get him to attack. Then I'll pop out and protect Sheldon."

"Pop out?"

"I don't know." She winced. "From wherever I have to hide before Zorianthus gets there."

"Then what? He already knows he can't get through you. He'll just leave again. Unless you let me kill him."

She shivered a little. He sounded perfectly capable of doing that.

"He's a threat to you, Cary," Deacon murmured against her temple.

"He's tried to kill you. Ridding the world of that evil will not cause me any sleepless nights."

But Deacon wouldn't be killing him out of self defense or in the moment when the wizard was attacking. He'd have planned to murder the man, set a trap for him just so he could kill him. *They* would have done that.

And she wasn't okay with it.

"No," she said, shaking her head when she felt him pull in a breath to respond. "I'm not luring him out just to murder him. That's not the solution."

"Then what is?"

"Argh! I don't know. But not that. Okay. Please. Just… I don't want this particular job of mine to push you into…into doing things the way the bad guys do. Okay? You're the good guy. You're going to stay that way."

He sighed and hugged her a little closer. "What if I'm not the good guy?" he whispered, so quietly she almost didn't hear him.

"You rescue animals for a living," she said firmly. "You are most definitely a good guy."

He huffed out a sound that might have been a chuckle, or might have just been a release of breath. He kissed the top of her head, then stepped back as his great grandfather came into view from around the side of the house. He had a basket full of eggs under his arm.

"I'll whip up some breakfast before you go," he said as he passed them, heading into the house.

"You don't have to," Cary said. "You've done enough." She lifted her mug of coffee, entirely serious about just how much he'd done by having that ready for her.

"Can't let you leave on an empty stomach. Wouldn't be hospitable." He winked at her before disappearing inside. She heard him call out to Sheldon and Sheldon grumble a response.

"Did Sheldon say anything rude to Keith?" Cary said, scowling at the closed door.

"No. Just grumbled about not being able to cook."

"Good. Because if he's rude to your Gramps, I'm gonna drop kick him into next Tuesday."

Deacon gave her a raised-brow look.

She shrugged. "Keith made me coffee. There will be no rudeness to a man that thoughtful. Not on my watch."

Deacon laughed and pulled her in for a kiss, her still warm mug nestled between them.

Breakfast was glorious, and Cary climbed into the car afterward with a full stomach and a much better attitude toward her currently complicated situation. Deacon spent a few extra moments on the porch, saying his goodbyes. The men embraced, a gentle hug without all the back pounding stuff, and Keith gave Deacon's cheek a pat before he left.

When he climbed into the back seat next to Sheldon, she said, "You sure you don't want to stay and visit with him more?"

"We have things to take care of," Deacon said as he buckled his seatbelt. "I'll come back when this is done."

Keith waved to them from his porch as they pulled away from the house, and Cary felt a pang at having to drive away from all this peace and quiet. She knew the instant they left Keith's little bubble of peace, when a sense of potential danger and anxiety settled low in her stomach again.

She sighed. Ah well. Peace, at least in her life, couldn't last forever.

19

The drive back to the city was quiet and uneventful. But by the time they pulled up in front of Sheldon's apartment building, Cary's stomach was tight, and what peace she'd found at Keith's had vanished completely.

Her plan was a horrible plan and there was no getting around that. Even if they did lure Zorianthus out, then what? She refused to let Deacon just murder him. Zorianthus knew he couldn't get around or through her. The wizard would just leave and come back when he could get to Sheldon. He certainly wouldn't waste his magic on her when she was protecting someone because he couldn't risk her absorbing any of it.

And she didn't know how to pretend to hide from the wizard anyway. She couldn't really leave Sheldon defenseless by actually going anywhere. But it wasn't like hiding in a closet would fool someone like Zorianthus.

What she needed was a little help from Jaxer and his super spectacular glamour magic. But she couldn't ask Jaxer for help. Not with her job. Even if this particular job had ties to things she'd done before entering her test year.

Could she ask Eriana? Like Jaxer, she was a faery, and though her primary skill was healing, she was capable of some pretty impressive glamour. Not as impressive as Jaxer's, but still. All the high Fae were capable of it, and Eriana was high Fae. Also, Cary had seen her true self once, the image she normally hid behind glamour. And that moment confirmed for Cary that Eriana's skills with glamour were excellent.

Eriana wasn't her mentor. She hadn't even known her before going into the seventh year test. In fact, she still didn't know her very well. But Cary did know Eriana wasn't officially a Protector mentor yet.

And no one said she couldn't ask a friend for help. She did that all the time. Hell, even her bosses had encouraged it in their way.

She winced a little. She wasn't exactly sure she'd call Eriana a friend, though. They'd fought together in Faery. And Eriana had saved her life, brought her back from the dead. Hard not to like the person who did that for you. But they hadn't really connected in a friendly way since. Cary wasn't sure why, but there was distance between them, distance Eriana insisted on.

Probably because Eriana was a former love of Jaxer's. A great love from what Cary could tell. And, boy, had they screwed things up back in the day—at least two hundred years ago or more. There was still some really interesting tension between them, and Cary maybe delighted too much in watching the soap opera that was their new relationship, whatever it was. That might explain why Eriana didn't warm to her completely. Cary was thrilled Jaxer had a new romantic issue to deal with and seemed to have let go his hopes for her. They were getting back to more of the friendship they'd had before he'd gone and decided he had *feelings* for her. But her delight might not have been helping her friendship prospects with Eriana.

Cary had no idea if the healer could or would help her, but at least she was someone Cary could ask for help without violating any seventh year rules.

Except then Jaxer would find out she was protecting Sheldon.

Given Jaxer's feelings for the former wizard, she wasn't sure that was a great idea. It was hard enough having to worry about protecting

Sheldon from Deacon's anger. She really didn't want to have to protect Sheldon from Deacon *and* Jaxer.

She puffed up her cheeks and let the breath out slowly. This was a really horrible job. She'd had some doozies before, but this one…

They trudged up to Sheldon's bleak and creepy apartment floor as she considered her options, and her horrible plan, and the fact that even if she wanted to ask Eriana for help, she had no idea how to get in touch with the faery. So that wasn't useful.

"What now?" Sheldon said as he flopped back onto his couch, looking as uninterested in "what now" as he'd ever looked.

Cary groaned. She had no idea. "You just sit there and pout or brood or whatever it is you've been doing all this time. Deacon and I need to talk."

She gestured Deacon into the hall, but left the door open so she could hear and see Sheldon. The last thing she needed was him disappearing off somewhere. She couldn't protect him if she didn't know where he was.

She sat on the hallway floor, her back against the doorframe, and Deacon did the same, sitting across from her, leaning against the opposite wall.

"So… My plan doesn't really work," she started. "Not without some sort of glamour magic."

"Angie?"

"Busy with a visiting friend. I don't want to disturb her. Plus, she doesn't do magic like that. And I can't ask Jaxer."

"You've thought of Eriana," he said, not asked.

"And I don't know how to get in touch with her," Cary finished. She raised her brows. "Do you?"

"Why would I?"

"I don't know. You've dealt with her more than I have. I was unconscious for a lot of her earlier time in this realm."

"Don't remind me," Deacon said darkly.

She winced. "Anyway. She also helped get you through Faery when you made that stupid journey to reach me in Ireland." She narrowed her eyes at him. She was still annoyed he'd done that. She'd been fine, and Faery was a very dangerous place for a shifter. They had a tacit agreement not to argue about that night, but still, it seemed relevant now. "How did you get in touch with her then?"

"I got in touch with Jaxer. He brought Eriana along."

Cary watched him closely. He was as relieved as she was that Jaxer had another romantic entanglement to worry about now, though he was doing a much better job of hiding those feelings.

"So to get in touch with her, we'd have to get in touch with Jaxer, and I really really don't want Jaxer to know I have to protect Sheldon. I'm not sure he'd take it any better than you."

"He'd take it worse."

She raised her brows at that. "He wasn't the one almost killed."

"But he was hunting the shifter killer for a month before finally contacting me," Deacon said. "He almost got me killed. Then he lost the woman he loves because of that night. To add insult to injury, the killer got away. Even though he got away with no magic left, Sheldon was still never brought to any kind of justice. Jaxer believes in justice or he wouldn't work for your bosses. He believes. And it wasn't served here. As much as everything else, that pisses him off."

Cary stared at Deacon for a long moment before she could comment. "I don't know why, but I forget that you've known Jaxer for a long time and that you would know that much about him. The fact that you know how he's feeling *now*, after the two of you have been at odds for most of the last year… Yeah, that kind of surprises me."

"He does a terrible job of hiding his scent from me." Deacon shrugged. "I'm not sure if he does it on purpose or just forgets. I know he can hide his scent if he wants to. He just doesn't most of the time. I thought it was because he wanted me to know how he felt about you. But lately… He's still not covering his scent with his glamour. I think he forgets."

"So you're, essentially, spying on his emotions?" Cary asked, lowering her chin.

"Not on purpose. He knows what I am and what that means. Not my fault he doesn't bother to hide anything from me."

She couldn't really argue with that. Although, a part of her was a little envious of Jaxer's ability to disguise his scent. The more time Cary spent with shifters, the more she'd love to have that particular skill.

"I don't want Jaxer to find out about this." She gestured vaguely back to the apartment where they'd left Sheldon. "So I suppose any help from Eriana is out of the question." She sighed. "Which means my vague and horrible plan isn't going to work." Her plan was never going to work. It was a horrible plan. She really really sucked at strategy. She should have studied that more. Probably should study it now, she thought ruefully. If they could keep the world from ending.

"Now what?" she asked, mostly herself. "We just…hang out? Wait for Zorianthus to show up, even knowing he won't."

"He's got a time limit," Deacon said. "Remember that. He doesn't have forever to wait until we get bored and go away."

"But I'll have other people to protect. You still have a job." She whimpered quietly, under her breath. "I really don't want to have to take him into my house."

She pressed her lips together. She still, after all this time, hadn't told Deacon about the glamour on her house. She never told anyone about it—not even Angie, Marianne, and Lucy knew, and they were closer to her than anyone. The less people knew, the better the magic worked. The safer she was when in her own home.

Sheldon could hear them. She didn't dare mention the glamour to Deacon now. She still wasn't sure if she ever would. But she'd used her place before to protect people. Deacon had been with her during one of those jobs. She was rarely called to it, but it was possible.

Unfortunately, it was starting to look like she might have to give in and just bring him into her house to keep him safe. And wow, did she hate that idea. So much she could barely contemplate it.

"We could take him down to my mother's home," Deacon said after a moment.

"Oh no we couldn't. No family involved, remember. Going to Keith's place was more than enough. Besides, there's no magical protection on your mother's house. And that's a shifter refuge. I don't want Sheldon—a shifter *murderer*—anywhere near that place. No. No.

It was bad enough we brought this little shit to your wonderful Gramps."

"I can hear you," Sheldon called.

"I know," Cary called back. Then to Deacon, "No. Not your family's sanctuary. If worse comes to worse, I can bring him to my place, and if the dogs hate him, I'll see if Marianne or Lucy or Angie can take them in for a few days. Frankly, I'd rather send *them* to your mother than Sheldon."

"Still hearing everything," Sheldon muttered from inside.

She didn't bother to respond this time.

"I hate the idea of him in your house on multiple levels," Deacon said.

"Me too. So so much. But it's my job, and if this is going to drag out, if our only option is to wait out Zorianthus, I'll have to do it."

"Let's keep considering other options first," Deacon said.

"In the last twenty-four hours, I've managed to come up with one, and only one, very bad plan that won't work because we don't have any convenient glamour to work with. And probably the stupid wizard just overheard all this anyway, so what I'd intended wouldn't have worked no matter what."

"Are you feeling that threat again?" Deacon asked, sitting up a little straighter. "Like someone is watching?"

Cary frowned. She hadn't been. She just had the creeps being in this building and her nerves were jumping. But because he'd asked, she took a moment to check in and let her senses open, hunting for any potential threat, that sense of someone watching them.

After a moment, she shook her head. "No. Not getting that again. I suppose I've just been assuming Zorianthus will know what we're up to so long as we're here."

"He can't spy on me," Sheldon called. "I have spells in place to prevent that. It's why he hasn't found me before this."

"So you've said. But you wasted your money," she said, "because he can. He was. He likely still is."

"He's not," Sheldon called back. "You're paranoid."

"Around you? Of course I am." She scowled at the wall. "We're going in circles here," she said. "And it's annoying me."

She didn't have any answers. The reprieve at Deacon's great grandfather's hadn't helped. Or well, it had because she'd managed to sleep, even if a little poorly. But the fundamental issues hadn't gone away.

She wanted this job over quickly, and it wasn't that kind of job. And that, in a nutshell, was the entire problem. If Sheldon was a good guy, if she *wanted* to protect him, this wouldn't be nearly as difficult. But she didn't want to be here. She didn't want anything to do with him outside of getting him to tell his former master to back off. To call a truce where they all got on with things and she stopped worrying about Zorianthus trying to kill her.

Except now, there was no hope of that. No easy way out. No coming to an agreement and them all going their separate ways.

No justice either.

She paused with that thought. And she sympathized a lot with Jaxer in that moment. The idea of no justice being served didn't sit well with her at all.

"I'm hungry," Sheldon called from inside.

She scowled back at the apartment. "Then get something to eat. I'm not your mother."

"My mother is a bitch."

"Then she and I have a lot in common."

Deacon's lips twitched.

She raised her brows at him. "Don't laugh."

"Not laughing," he assured.

Right.

She listened to Sheldon get up and stomp heavily across the wooden floor, presumably heading toward the kitchen. With every fiber of her being, she did not want to bring this shit back to her home.

A little tingling started along her spine, a warning that came on so suddenly, she gasped. She scrambled up to her feet, sparing a moment to be irritated when Deacon got up so gracefully and quickly that he was standing next to her before she'd finished straightening.

"What's wrong?" he asked, lowering his voice.

They both took up positions blocking the apartment door. She checked inside. Sheldon was standing just outside the kitchen door, scowling at them. She hunted the inside of the apartment with her senses wide, but the vague sense of danger wasn't coming from in there.

She turned to face the elevator at the end of the hall. The little console over the doors showed the elevator rising from the lobby, approaching their floor. Her sense of unease increased.

Silently, she watched those numbers change, the red glow flickering as the elevator passed each floor.

The number settled on five.

Cary pulled herself up, blocking Sheldon's apartment with her body, keeping Deacon just behind her so she could protect him too.

A ding.

The shiny silver doors opened.

And the new Master vampire of Portland stepped out into the hallway.

Smiling wide enough to show teeth.

2 0

ames was dressed impeccably in a dark black suit and shirt, with a red tie—he'd adopted the clichéd vampire colors since becoming the city's Master—his blond-brown hair still short and neat. His eyes, when they didn't have the jaundiced yellow glow of his vampire nature filling them, were an unremarkable brown. He was tall, lean, pale skinned, and held himself in a perfectly composed, unassuming way.

That was belied by the flash of sharp, pointy canines in his smile.

"Cary," he said in greeting. "What a pleasure to see you again."

"Uh huh," she muttered, moving just a little more in front of Deacon. His very low, almost subsonic growl prickled the hairs on her neck.

So he considered James a potential threat too. Good to know she wasn't the only one.

"You're protecting the old wizard's protégé," James said, cutting to the chase as usual.

"How did you know? Why do you care?" There wasn't much point in prevaricating with a Master vampire, unless of course she wanted to aggravate them. Then she did tend to wander off topic. But only as much as they did. Thing was, aggravating a Master was almost always a bad idea.

"How I know is less interesting than why I care," James said.

"You're flashing your teeth at me with those smiles, James. Are we gonna have an issue?"

He chuckled. A real chuckle, not a practiced one. "I've missed you. It got the best of me."

"Ha! A likely story. Are you a threat right now?"

"Are your powers working?"

"Yup." At least, she hoped they were. She couldn't really tell. If he was a threat, they would be though, so it was a pretty good guess.

"Interesting," James said, tilting his head a little as he stared at her. He shifted his gaze to Deacon. "Good afternoon, Deacon."

Deacon grunted a greeting.

"How is your mother doing? Well, I hope."

"Fine. I'll pass on your well wishes." Deacon's voice was very deep and full of growly leopard.

"Please do." James glanced back at Cary. "You're meeting my stare, by the way. Your powers are working."

"You sound like you're trying to reassure me. Why?"

"So you'll relax a little. I'm always a threat. You'll always be safe around me so long as you have someone else with you."

"Wow. That's a scary and comforting statement all in one go. Why?"

"I like you."

"No, why are you here?"

"The wizard. And his protégé. Have you figured out what the wizard plans?"

"Yup. At least some of it. Do you know his name?"

"I do. But using it calls his attention."

"It does?" She scowled back into the apartment. Sheldon was standing out of James's sight, but on alert, his eyes narrowed and his attention on the conversation, not her. "Did you know that?"

"About using Zorianthus's name?" Sheldon asked, though he didn't look at her when he did. "Yes."

"Well why the hell didn't you tell me? We've been calling his damned attention to us this entire time?"

"I thought you knew. You want to draw him out. Keep using his name and you will."

She huffed, then rolled her eyes and faced James again.

He raised his brows. "I'd assumed you knew."

"Everyone assumes I know everything. Do you know how much there is to learn about all this stuff? How many books I'm *still* trying to get through? It's a lot, okay." She was a little more defensive than usual because she'd just revealed an awful lot of ignorance to both the Master vampire of Portland and her charge, who was also a former-possibly-still-evil pain in her ass. That was just embarrassing.

James dipped his head in a gentle nod of agreement. His attempt at consoling her didn't help.

"What do you want, James?" she asked to get back on topic.

"You show no deference, despite my new position." His comment was quiet and considering, maybe not even something she was meant to hear.

"Since I'm still pretty sure you set me up to overthrow Gabriel, I think we can agree we have a different dynamic than the typical Master vampire/Protector relationship."

"You never showed deference to Gabriel either," he pointed out.

"Well, you know. He was kind of an ass."

James chuckled again. "Ah, Cary. I do so like you."

"Sure, sure. Why are you here?"

"The wizard wants to release Oliver Holland. That would be bad."

"Yup. Though I'm curious why you think so."

"Shall we go inside and be comfortable while we discuss it?"

"No," Cary said at the same time as Sheldon said, "I'm not inviting him in here."

Which showed remarkably good self-preservation instincts from Sheldon.

James shrugged.

"Might as well just tell me why you're here," Cary said. "No point in drawing this out."

"I want you to take a moment first to notice something," James said. He waited, a faint smile curving his lips.

He was no longer showing off his canines. She wasn't sure if that was a good or bad thing. It was always hard to tell with Master vampires. Though, usually if they showed their teeth, that was a bad thing. At least, in her experience it had been.

She stared at him, meeting his gaze because she was protecting people, wondering what he was getting at, what he expected her to notice. The lack of teeth in his smile? The fact that he wasn't trying to force them to invite him inside? That was one of the few pop culture myths about vampires that was actually correct. Couldn't get into a private home without an invitation. Little bit of protection for the poor humans on the prey side of that predator-prey relationship.

A lot of the myths were wrong though, or only had a vague relationship to the truth. Like garlic wasn't any more effective against vampires than it was against shifters. Most of them didn't like the strong smell. But they could tolerate it if they didn't have some sort of allergy. Some even liked garlic—well shifters. Vampires didn't like anything but blood. The crosses and Christian holy objects only worked against vampires who were born during the medieval years in Europe. She still couldn't get anyone to explain that to her. The myth about vampires turning to dust in the daylight always amused her. That'd be handy if it were true. But it wasn't. If it had been James wouldn't be out...

In the middle of the day.

In the daylight.

A Master vampire.

Out in the day.

Her eyes widened and so did James's smile, just a little.

"You're out in the middle of the day," she murmured. "Masters don't do that."

Vampires could go out during the day, but they were light sensitive —she finally noticed the folded up pair of sunglasses in James's lapel pocket—and they lost most of their strength during the day. Many were still strong, but only a little more than an ordinary human, and then only if they were old enough. The youngest ones were as weak if not weaker than humans. Direct sunlight was even worse, even more draining. Though in the Pacific Northwest, direct sunlight was less of an issue, at least in the winter. The oldest ones could still manage a little mesmerism, but it was harder and didn't work as well.

Basically, every advantage a vampire had at night—speed, strength, mesmerism—vanished or weakened in the daylight. Most of them hated being that weak in front of others. They didn't come out during the day because they didn't like how it felt, not because the sunlight killed them.

Master vampires were particularly keen on hiding weakness. Weakness for a Master could mean overthrow and permanent death. They *never* came out in the daylight. Especially those in charge of a hive. They couldn't *afford* to show any weakness. Masters stayed deep inside the hives, deep underground, during daylight hours. Away from the sun, they were still as strong as they were at night. Masters who weren't responsible for a hive also tended to stay in and hidden during daylight hours.

They never came out into the sun. They didn't show this kind of weakness. Not to anyone.

James was out in the middle of the day. At his weakest time.

To talk to her.

"So," she murmured. "This must be pretty serious."

"It is," James said. "Oliver Holland can't be freed into this realm again."

"Why? I mean outside of my own self interest in not getting dead, what will happen if he gets free?"

"His father will return for him. And the planet will burn."

"Ah."

Yeah. That would be bad.

Very very bad.

21

$\mathcal{C}$ary stood, unmoving, in the hallway outside Sheldon's apartment for a solid three minutes coming to grips with the idea that she might have to face Ho'Lud again.

Ho'Lud was a literal god. A demon god, but a god nonetheless. The last time she'd faced him, shifters had died, she'd nearly died, and the only thing that had saved them was poor Buck going full demon dog and dragging Lud back into a demon realm.

She wasn't sure which one. She couldn't exactly ask Buck. But once Lud was back in a demon realm, getting free into this one without loosing all his demon god powers was impossible without a lot of work on another sacrificial acolyte who he could inhabit. The problem with that was that humans didn't last long carrying a powerful demon around inside them. The effort killed the human and banished the demon back to its realm.

If a demon wanted to walk around in this realm all on their own, without a host body, they sacrificed power to do it. The more powerful the demon, the more power they lost. Holland had made that sacrifice. And he was still massively powerful and deadly. Which meant he'd been outrageously powerful before moving into this realm.

Which kind of made sense, since it turned out he was the son of a god.

Still. Holland free in this realm was terrifying enough. His father returning was just…

"Yeah, that would be a very very bad idea," she said.

"Very bad," Deacon murmured.

He'd lost two of his people in that fight. She carried a great deal of guilt over that. She hadn't been able to protect them all, and they'd been there to help her. She did *not* want a repeat of that.

"So," James said, "we're once again on the same side of a difficult situation."

"Once again?" She scowled at him. "You weren't on my side with the Gabriel thing."

"Of course I was," James said. "Your win was my win."

"A set up is not the same thing as being on the same side with someone," she pointed out. "But we don't have time for that argument. What kind of help are you offering here?"

"Sanctuary. For Sheldon. Until his master dies."

Woah. That was… A potentially complicated, but possible solution.

No. No. She couldn't take help from the vampires like this. Not like this.

Could she?

No. The hive was no place for a human with no ability to protect himself. And Sheldon no longer had an ability to protect himself.

Cary had no doubt there was still some underlying tension in the hive. There always was when one Master took over for another. And while technically James hadn't killed Gabriel—even if he'd set him up to be killed—he still hadn't been in charge of the hive long enough to settle all those possible conflicts. Someone loyal to Gabriel, or loyal to themselves, would be plotting James's overthrow even now. It was the way of things in a hive. And that someone, whoever they might be, could use Sheldon as leverage. A pawn in a complicated vampire scheme.

Their machinations were always complicated.

She sighed.

"No," she said. "He'd be in too much danger. I don't care how secure your hold over the hive is now, he'd be defenseless."

"I'm not defenseless," Sheldon said, still safely inside the apartment and behind her protections.

"Against vampires, without all that wizard magic you used to have, yes, yes you are."

"His master pushed Gabriel into a confrontation with you," James said. "And the end result was a dead hive leader. There's no love for the old wizard in the hive. They'll allow the boy to live if it means destroying the wizard."

"I'm not a boy," Sheldon said.

"Sheldon, shut up," Cary said. To James, "It's still too dangerous. He's safer with me." Unfortunately. Back to the same problem.

"We live longer," James pointed out.

"Ha ha. I'm not dead yet." *Yet* being the operative word there.

"I was afraid you'd say that."

"That I'm not dead yet?" She raised her brows.

James chuckled. "Do you have an alternative plan for the boy?"

"I'm not—" Sheldon started.

She interrupted. "Shut. Up." To James, she said, "Don't think I missed how you didn't correct my assumption just there."

His smile flashed just the tips of his canines.

"My plan is to stick with him and ensure he doesn't get dead," Cary said. "That's my plan. If he doesn't get dead, the wizard can't find the Naga city, he can't release Holland, and everyone lives happily ever after. Actually, because of wasting so much time on this quest, the wizard will likely finally die after many centuries, and that's a happy ending too."

"So," James said, letting out a sigh. "He really has been body hopping? I wasn't sure whether to believe that boast or not. It's a complicated and difficult task. The wizards who've tried it usually end up dead, or with a lot of dead bodies around them."

She resisted looking back into the apartment at Sheldon, but it was a close thing. "He body swapped with Sheldon. Practiced enough they could remain in each other's bodies for long periods and only come out when they chose, rather than being dumped out. The wizard is capable. But it takes time to train a new body. And he's apparently wasting that time right now with this Oliver Holland thing." She narrowed her eyes at James. "How did you know what the wizard was after?"

She didn't ask how he knew about Holland's father. She might ask later, but she was pretty sure she knew already. The vampires had spies all around the city, keeping tabs on things. And Lud's impending invasion hadn't been exactly quiet. The demon hunters had had their hands full all over the city while Cary had been working to keep Lud from breaking free into this realm. The vampires would have investigated all that demon activity, and learned the truth from…someone. Maybe even one of the demon hunters if the hunter thought it important the vampire community knew what could happen.

She'd love to know if Gabriel had learned the truth or if it had been James himself. She got the feeling James liked having a lot of information. She wouldn't be surprised to learn he'd been the one to dig out the truth.

But she'd have to satisfy her curiosity about that later. Now, she wanted to know how he'd learned about Zorianthus. That seemed…pertinent.

"He came to us for help first," James said. "He thought he could parlay his last dealings with us, claiming you as a mutual enemy that had to be destroyed. And that only Holland could accomplish that." James shrugged. "Very insulting. Him telling me I'd need a demon's help to kill you."

Cary made a face at that.

James smiled faintly before continuing. "There's a lot the wizard doesn't know. He's unaware of Lud and the impact that would have on our world."

"He doesn't know. But you do? That's…interesting."

"I know most things that happen in this territory. More than Gabriel realized as well."

Which was how James was able to manipulate a situation that eliminated the Portland Master without *him* having to do the killing.

Quite an accomplishment, really. But she wasn't keen on the way he'd used her to stage the coup.

"What did you tell the wizard when he approached you? What did he want you to do for him?"

"He wanted us to help him take over the Naga city. He claimed he could find the entrance—he can't without dying, but he didn't know I knew that."

"How and why do you know that?"

"I learn things. I've lived a long time."

She huffed out an irritated sound. She'd just revealed earlier how much she didn't know and here James went showing off how much he did. Nice.

"Why did you turn him down then? He was proposing to kill himself to find the Naga city entrance, even if he didn't know you knew that part."

"I have no interest in disturbing the Nagas. Or making enemies of them." He added this last very seriously. "And I know releasing Holland will draw his father's attention back to our realm. Can't have that."

"Do you know what Lud wanted with Holland? Because he never sufficiently explained himself to me." Gods weren't as easy to get bad-guy-monologuing as the usual run-of-the-mill bad guys. She'd never learned *why* Ho'Lud wanted his son back.

"No," James said.

Which was a disappointment. Though the fact that he admitted he didn't know something was kind of refreshing.

"I only know it will result in the destruction of this realm," he finished.

"How do you know that?" Maybe he was just guessing. Having a demon god loose in this realm couldn't lead to much else but epic destruction. Still, if James had more information than just obvious guesses, she wanted to hear about them. If he'd admit anything to her.

"That much I learned from former associates of Holland. You might remember them. A triad of witches? I believe they challenged you. Once."

Yeah, she remembered them.

She hadn't been looking forward to meeting them again if they showed up while she wasn't protecting someone. The three witches were incredibly powerful together. But they hadn't been with Holland's army when he'd tried to invade the Naga city.

"I wondered what had happened to them," she said. She frowned at Deacon. "Wow. It's really old enemies week, this week, huh?"

He grunted, a sound she couldn't quite interpret, but he kept his full attention on James. He wasn't looking at James's face, or into his eyes, she noticed. While she was protecting Deacon, he could look into the vampire's eyes and be fine. But he had his attention on the vampire's shoulders. Strategic—watching for a potential movement that would mean attack—or habit—because if Cary wasn't here, he could be manipulated by a powerful vampire's gaze? She wasn't sure which, but filed away the observation for later, when she could ask Deacon without an audience.

She faced James again. "What did the witches tell you?"

"Only what Holland told them. Which wasn't everything. But enough for them to want Holland to succeed."

"Why? What was Holland trying to do with his invasion besides just gain more power?"

"With the power of the Naga city, he could prevent his father from dragging him back to the demon realms. He could fight off his father's attack."

"Wouldn't that be more devastating to this realm than his father just sucking him back into the demon realms?"

"Apparently not," James said. "Holland told the witches that if his father got him back in his control, his father would destroy this realm, turn it to fire and ash, in retribution for Holland having found sanctuary here."

She wasn't completely buying it. And she wasn't sure if James did either. But at least it was more information to fill in some of those gaping holes.

"The witches believed Holland," James said, as if in answer to her unspoken thoughts. "Enough to join forces with him."

"They weren't there in the end, though. If they believed him, why weren't they there for the final invasion?"

"They weren't forthcoming enough to reveal that. Though I suspect, based on what the youngest one let slip, they were commanded to stay away, just in case an alternative plan was required."

"So the witches not being there was…Holland's decision? Wonder what the backup plan was? Probably not Holland being captured by the Nagas."

"No one planned for you," James said.

She couldn't tell from either his tone or his expression whether that was a compliment or an insult so she ignored it. "When did you get all this from the witches? Before or after the wizard approached you?"

And, wow, were there a lot of players involved. This was starting to make her head spin. All of them enemies of hers, too. Even the people technically on her side like James and the person she was trying to protect.

She really should stop making so many enemies.

"Before the wizard came looking for our help," James said.

"Did the witches come to you for help, too?"

"No. But the youngest is…talkative."

Cary waited for more of an explanation, or even a hint as to what he was talking about. James didn't elaborate. She raised her brows. He stared at her without comment.

"Okay fine, don't tell me," she huffed.

His lips twitched but he didn't smile this time. Though she got the feeling it was a close thing based on the way he pursed his mouth.

She rolled her eyes, then took a deep breath and stared at the wall as she sorted through what James had told her. The witch triad—or at least the youngest, talkative one—revealed to James that Holland didn't want his father, a literal demon god, pulling him back to the demon realms, and that if Lud got Holland back, the god would then destroy this realm. Sometime after that, Zorianthus shows up at the vampires' door to ask for help destroying *her* by releasing Holland from the Nagas. He claims he has a way to find the entrance but doesn't realize James knows it's a suicide spell. James didn't know the body hopping option was more than Zorianthus boasting. Zorianthus needs Sheldon's body to complete the spell and maybe to survive even without the spell.

And no one but Zorianthus wanted Holland out of the Nagas' realm because it would bring Ho'Lud back to this one.

"I think I might need some demon hunters soon," she muttered, mostly to herself. The demons weren't actually out yet, but this was starting to get ridiculous. She needed a few more friends and a few less enemies involved. Especially because she still didn't know what Zorianthus wanted from Holland.

"Where do the vampires stand now?" she asked James.

"I'm here. I want the wizard to fail."

"Does he know that? Or does he just think you won't help him?"

"He knows I won't help him."

"But he still assumes I'm a mutual enemy and you won't help me either?"

"He might have been led to that conclusion."

"Led to it, huh?"

James didn't respond.

"Did he tell you he needed Sheldon back? Is that why you're here and offering Sheldon sanctuary?" She raised a silencing hand when she heard Sheldon begin to mutter behind her. He was closer to them now, but still not in a position where James would see him. "And how did you know I'd be here protecting Sheldon?"

That last suddenly struck her as very suspicious.

"The wizard let slip he needed his protégé back and they'd provide the entrance to the city," James said. "I don't think he meant to tell me he didn't have control of his protégé anymore. The last time he approached the vampires, he claimed he wanted you dead to avenge his protégé's stolen magic. Gabriel didn't dig into that very deeply. He didn't really care. He was too interested in you."

"You dug into that more, though?"

"I might have…checked on the situation. So I knew when Sheldon went into hiding from his master."

"Knew they were no longer associates," Cary said.

James nodded faintly.

"So you knew the wizard would have to find Sheldon to make his plan work?"

Another faint nod.

"How did you know I was protecting Sheldon from the wizard? Did the wizard let that slip too?"

"No. He came to us before you started protecting the boy yesterday."

Cary frowned. "So…how did you know I was here with Sheldon? Why come today to offer sanctuary? Why not earlier?"

"The boy's purchased spells were holding. The wizard couldn't find him, though he didn't admit that out loud."

"How did you know, then?"

"His heart rate changed when he mentioned it. He's old and in control of his reactions most of the time, but the body he's in is failing him. He has less control over it than even a few months ago. I didn't realize that was anything but normal human aging. That he's truly been body hopping and his lack of control over this body means more than just…he's getting old in the human way."

That was interesting enough to distract her but she forced herself back to the main topic. Because something else he'd just said worried her. "You said Sheldon's spells *were* holding. His spells aren't anymore? He can be found now?"

She was pretty sure that sense of danger she'd gotten yesterday was Zorianthus, whether he'd been watching them through a scrying bowl or a mundane nanny cam. Either way, when he'd gone to the vampires, he still couldn't find Sheldon, and now it appeared he might be able to. What had changed?

She glared back at Sheldon. "Has my saying the wizard's name aloud broken down the spells you bought? Is that why suddenly everyone knows where you are?"

"How did you find me?" Sheldon asked. "You or that other one, the blond guy, haven't been able to for months. No one has. Suddenly everyone's here."

She ignored his question about how she'd found him. "So your spells have broken."

"No," James said. "They haven't. They're still in place."

Cary frowned, looking between Sheldon and James. How did James know that?

And for that matter, she realized suddenly, how the hell did James know about Sheldon's bought spells? He'd even called the "purchased spells." Had Zorianthus told him? No, he couldn't have. He hadn't admitted to James, at least not out loud, that Sheldon was in hiding. So how the hell did James know about the spells, and how the hell did he find Sheldon if they were still working?

"How did you know there were spells here?" she asked James. "The wizard didn't tell you."

"He did not."

"So how did you know?"

"I had another source of information."

"Who?"

"How did you find him?" James asked, repeating Sheldon's question.

Her bosses had told her, but she wasn't going to say that out loud. Although, it did beg the question, how *had* they found Sheldon? If they'd known the whole time, they'd purposefully kept the information from Jaxer. Jaxer would have already confronted Sheldon if he'd been able to find him. If Liruk and Wisat knew Sheldon's location this entire time, why keep it from Jaxer?

What the hell was going on? What had changed if the spells were still working?

"I had insider information," she said, mimicking the vampire's deflective answer, since she didn't want to reveal any more ignorance than she already had. "What got you here today, James?"

He held her gaze for a moment, and she stared back. She could only do that in Protector mode, and every time it felt a little like a staring contest with Fred to see who was the big dog. Fred always blinked first. She wasn't sure James would.

He did answer her question this time, though. "I was told where to find him. From the witches."

"Wait. What? How? How could they find him through the spells that were keeping the wizard in the dark?"

"The witches said they'd received a vision during another magical working. They didn't deign to tell me what they'd been doing before this vision." His lips flattened but that was the only sign he was annoyed. "In the vision, they claimed to have seen Sheldon, and the wizard. And Holland in this realm. They said all of this centered on this apartment building, and I should seek the boy here."

"Did they see me?" Cary asked, genuinely interested.

James smiled. "If they did, they didn't mention it to me."

"So you didn't know I'd be here?"

"Oh, I knew you'd be here."

"How?"

"Because whenever there's major world-ending trouble brewing in this city these days… There you are."

Cary scowled. "That sounds like an insult," she muttered. "But I don't have time to be offended. What does all this mean to us?"

James chuckled. The sound was silvery and gorgeous in the otherwise creepy hallway, the kind of sound that boded ill for the people hearing it.

"I came here today," James said, "to offer the boy sanctuary. And to see how much you knew of the situation. Understanding your… protective nature—" he smirked, "—I feared you wouldn't let the boy into our care. So I'm here to offer whatever help the vampires can provide. I don't want a war with the Nagas. That will not end well for any of us. I don't want my realm burned down by a demon god. As you might guess, I'm not particularly fond of fire. And since you seem to be at the heart of all these…issues, all the time, I need to help you so that my world remains unharmed."

Her turn to flatten her mouth. "Gee, that's so generous of you."

"It's my job," James said. "As leader of the hive." His gaze settled very solidly on hers. "Just as it's your job. As Protector of this territory."

Well, she couldn't argue with that.

22

Cary debated whether or not to tell James the truth—that she had no plan because the wizard knew too much about her. And the wizard probably knew she was involved now because he'd apparently been spying on them.

Despite Sheldon's spells still working.

But if the spells were still working…

"I still don't know how everyone is finding you here," she said to Sheldon, turning a little to look at him while still keeping James in her peripheral vision. She didn't have to worry too much about that because she knew Deacon was keeping a close eye on the Master vampire. Still, she hated when the bad guys surprised her, even if they couldn't hurt her while doing it.

Sheldon shrugged. "I paid good money for the spells, and the vampire said they're still working. They were designed to hide me here, hide me from anyone seeing me come in and out. Keep the hallway creepy feeling so no mundanes stumble through."

Cary considered *how* Sheldon had been discovered here in the last few days.

Her bosses must have found him with premonitions because that's what they did. She was pretty sure Zorianthus had found a way to scry into the building, though she hadn't asked Sheldon if Zorianthus was capable of that yet. The witches had found him through a vision during spellwork.

"Do your spells prevent people from seeing you through… premonitions? Scrying? Did you think of those things?"

"Wizards and shifters don't scry, so no," Sheldon said, his lip lifting in a slight snarl.

Cary was surprised by the show of emotion. More and more of that was slipping through his hollow façade.

"And you're not a witch, so I didn't think you'd scry," Sheldon said.

"I don't. Good guess. But I have a best friend who can."

Who it never occurred to her to ask to scry for Sheldon. Why hadn't she ever just asked Angie to scry for the little shit? Rookie mistake. Potentially deadly mistake in her seventh year.

She sighed and shook her head. Stupid, stupid oversight.

Deacon's hand settled at the base of her spine, rubbing in gentle circles. Near her ear, for her only, he murmured, "Jaxer didn't think of it either, remember."

She frowned up at him. "How did you know what I was thinking?" That had been too complex for a simple smelled-her-emotions analysis.

"I just realized we might have asked her, too," he whispered.

She let out a long breath. So, she wasn't the only one who hadn't thought of it. And he was right, Jaxer had known Angie longer than Cary had known her, yet he hadn't asked her to look for either Sheldon or the wizard. He must have assumed she couldn't. Angie hadn't volunteered to scry for him, and she'd been offering help, so maybe she couldn't have found Sheldon with her scrying bowl, even if she thought the wizard might have spied on him that way.

Hell, Jaxer might have asked and she told him she couldn't for some reason.

Questions for later.

Argh, so many questions.

But first, she had to save Sheldon from Zorianthus. And now she had the vampires to help her, but she still had no idea what to do or how to draw the wizard out.

She frowned back at James. "Do you know how to get in touch with Zor— With the wizard?" While she wanted to call Zorianthus out, she was hesitant to keep calling his attention without meaning to. Calling him to a specific place on purpose, however…

The very vaguest spark of an idea started to percolate.

"He came to you for help," she said. "Did he leave a way for you to contact him if you changed your minds? Would he come to the hive if you called?"

James's eyes narrowed, just a little. "He would. Even if he finds the entrance to the Naga city, he can hardly sneak in and free Holland without some kind of help. As far as I can tell, he doesn't have that help now."

"You got any trouble with betrayal and manipulation?"

James raised his brows as if offended by the question. "I am a vampire."

She snorted. Fair point. Ability to manipulation was part of their dictionary definition. "To be clear, I'm talking about manipulating and betraying the wizard. Just to be very very clear."

James dipped his head in acknowledgement. She didn't miss the way his lips twitched, though with humor or some other emotion she couldn't tell.

"You have a plan?" Deacon murmured.

"Call the wizard into the hive. Confront him. Get him to go away." She blinked at that last sentence. Ah, the hole in all her plans. How to get the bad guy to just…go away.

She wasn't here to murder anyone, even an old enemy who kept trying to kill her. She didn't want Deacon, or even the vampires for that matter, to kill him. She'd prefer he just went away and died on his own without releasing a demon with a grudge against her.

"You are not pragmatic enough for this world," James said quietly. "Killing the wizard is the only answer to all of these problems."

"Yeah, but I'm not a murder," she said. "I stop people from being murdered. That's my job."

"And by destroying the wizard, you will stop people from being murdered. Sheldon for one. Anyone in Holland's line of sight. Many Nagas who will fight to stop Holland's release. Have you considered what he would do to them and their city if he's freed?"

Cary's gut hurt. The horrible truth in James's words made her ache. Even Deacon defaulted to just killing the wizard.

But there had to be another way. Another answer.

She rubbed a hand over her face. She felt like the "good guy" in a movie who was too stupid to kill the bad guy when they had the chance, and then the bad guy returned and attacked again. Was she being stupid? Was she being too idealistic or…just not pragmatic enough?

But this wasn't the wizard attacking and him getting killed during the fight. She had to keep reminding herself of that. All of these plans involved them setting up a confrontation with the wizard, her arranging for him to be somewhere. And killing him then, that was calculated murder. Not self defense. Not even just being pragmatic. It was cold blooded murder.

It was a step she just wasn't willing to take.

"I'd be a piss poor Protector if I set people up to be murdered," she said to herself as much as to James. "For me, that's not the pragmatic answer. If that's the only help you're offering, I can't accept."

"He wouldn't be the first death you've been responsible for," James said, but quietly and not accusingly. Just a simple truth.

"I know. But someone getting themselves killed because they're attacking innocent people, or—" she swallowed hard, "—or innocent people dying during that fight, those are different things to what we're talking about here. I'm not sure how often I have to keep repeating that, but I will for as long as I have to." For herself as well as the people in her life. "This isn't a spur of the moment battle. There's a line. A line I'm not climbing over."

James sighed, a very audible sound. Done on purpose because he didn't have to breath all that often and certainly didn't have to breath audibly like that. He kept showing her his feelings, in a way not typical for Masters. She had to wonder at that.

"I will kill the wizard if he threatens the hive," James said. "But… I came to offer my help, and if that's not the help you're willing to take, I will accept that. For now. How do you propose talking him out of his nefarious plans?"

"You don't have to be snarky about it," she huffed. "Thank you for agreeing not to murder him in cold blood. I know that goes against your nature."

"Now who's being snarky."

She flashed James a brief smile. Turn about was fair play after all. Her smile dropped away, though, as she considered his question. Same old question. Luring the wizard here for a confrontation, or to the hive… Neither of those plans solved the fundamental problem of getting the wizard to stop his attempts at releasing Holland.

"I suppose we could tell him the truth," she mused. "He wants to release Holland to kill me. That's all revenge." At least as far as they knew. She still thought it had to be more than revenge. But until she could confront Zorianthus, she wasn't going to know the full story. "He's got a pretty healthy sense of revenge to still be at this. But he's also got at least as strong a sense of self-preservation and survival instincts or he wouldn't have been working the body swapping efforts for all these years. He wants to keep living. He doesn't want to die. And if he unleashes Holland, and that in turn brings Lud back to this realm, we all die. No more bodies to swap with. In fact, he's more likely to find his occupied by a demon. Right? So…" She looked up, looked between James and Deacon. "So we tell him the truth."

"You think he'll believe you?" James said. "He hates you and wants you dead so much he's willing to risk releasing a demon to kill you. He will believe you're lying in an effort to stop him."

"But you can confirm I'm telling the truth. Maybe the witches can be there to confirm it. They worked for Holland."

"Be sure to say 'with' instead of 'for' in their presence," James said. "Justina doesn't like the implication that she worked 'for' Holland."

"Which one is Justina?" She'd never gotten any of their names when they'd been trying to rip her apart.

"The leader," James said.

"The red-head? Good to know." She was tempted to ask for the names of the other two but that felt like a distraction from her main point. "If enough people there tell the wizard the same thing—including people that have no interest in protecting *me* and in fact might actively wish to kill me, like the witches, then he might believe us."

"And if he stops trying to find the Nagas and Holland? Then what?"

"Then he can go about his other business, I suppose. So long as it doesn't involve harming innocent people in my territory. Cause I will stop that. But otherwise..." She shrugged. What the wizard did with the rest of his life was only her concern if it involved him hurting people.

Or still trying to kill her. But that was another issue all together.

"You think the boy will be safe then?" James said. "You don't think the wizard will continue to come after him?"

Actually, she was afraid he would. Sheldon wouldn't have gone into hiding if Zorianthus wasn't a threat to him outside of this Oliver Holland thing. But so long as Holland didn't get out of the Naga city, she'd worry about the rest later. The immediate problem, her actual job here, was to protect Sheldon so Zorianthus couldn't free the demon.

"I'll deal with that if it happens," she said. Stalling because she didn't have any better ideas.

James held silent for a long enough moment, she wanted to fidget. She didn't, but it was a close thing.

"Tonight, then," he finally said. "I'll arrange a meeting." His lips twitched. "Midnight?"

She rolled her eyes. "I suppose we'd better. Vampires, a wizard, and a triad of witches all in one place. It'd be an insult to your overly dramatic tendencies to meet at, like, eight or something ordinary like that."

"Precisely," James said with a straight face.

She laughed despite herself. "Midnight at the hive. Do we need an escort? Is there a new entrance I should know about? Is anyone going to try eating us when we arrive?"

"The entrance is the same as your last visit—though slightly redecorated. You won't need a formal escort unless you get lost. And someone might try to eat you, but I'll ensure the hive knows I will frown on that, so hopefully they won't try too hard and get themselves killed."

It sort of annoyed her that she found James charming and likable. She really shouldn't like the Master vampire of Portland. Fear him. Yes. Avoid him. Absolutely, as much as possible. Like him? Somehow that seemed disloyal to her job as Protector of the city.

"Midnight it is, then," she said.

And hopefully an end to this standoff that didn't involve anyone getting dead.

23

The entrance to the hive was a perfectly unremarkable farmhouse outside Portland. The fact that the vampires of the city lived in an area outside of the city had always struck Cary as odd. Why not live *in* the city when that's where they hunted?

She was sure there was some strategic reason for it, something that made sense to the vampires. She might even ask James about it one day. Maybe.

Or maybe not.

They parked next to the farmhouse, but Cary's full attention was drawn to the burnt out remains of what had been a large, red, wooden barn with a peaked roof behind the house. The blackened timbers were little more than deeper shadows in the dark night now. No remaining smell of burnt wood. Or burnt other things. But the visceral memory of those smells came back to her, hitting her harder than she'd expected.

The last time she'd been here, she'd channeled the magic of a not-yet-born goddess and burned down that barn along with a bunch of the vampires that had lived here—including the former Master of the hive.

Six months ago. A long time for her but a blink for vampires who lived for centuries. She was sure she still had enemies here because of that night, vampires who'd been loyal to Gabriel. The fact that they hadn't removed the remains of the barn, left the blackened husk there like some sort of memorial, probably didn't bode well for her either.

She turned back toward Deacon's SUV as he and Sheldon climbed out. And once again shook her head at Sheldon's outfit. He'd insisted on wearing black leather pants and a black turtleneck, as if there was a dress code to meet with vampires. The black emphasized his pallor, though, and the leather pants emphasized how painfully thin he was, and somehow it all looked like he was trying much too hard to look like someone he wasn't.

Maybe this *was* him on some level. Maybe that's why he kept going for leather pants and black colors. Maybe this was who he wanted to be. She couldn't begrudge someone trying to be who they were inside. In fact, she was all for that.

But for some reason, this felt more like dress up. Like Sheldon putting on a costume instead of just expressing who he really was or even who he wanted to be. More like he was dressing up to impress others and to slip into a character he thought others expected of him.

And it only made her feel bad for him. Which she didn't want to do because as far as she knew, he hadn't given up his quest to be evil.

She let out a long breath as Deacon came up next to her, his gaze on the surroundings.

"No escort," he murmured.

"James said we didn't need one. I'm taking this as a good sign." She hoped anyway.

"This is the vampires' hive?" Sheldon said, sounding vastly underwhelmed by his surroundings.

"What were you expecting?" she asked.

"Something more impressive. Something not so…provincial."

It was on the tip of her tongue to point out that not everyone felt the need to dress up like a cliché, but then she remembered the interior of the hive and decided not to comment. Unless James had done some serious redecorating, the hive was substantially more impressive once you entered the house.

Last time she'd been here it was a mix of Ariel's French Aristocracy tastes and Gabriel's minimalist aesthetic. She was actually pretty curious if James had put any of his own personal stamp on the hive yet, or if it still felt like a blending of Ariel and Gabriel's designs. He'd said it was slightly redecorated. Now she wondered just how "slight."

Sheldon gave her a once over as he joined her and Deacon at the front of the SUV. "You should have changed," he muttered. "This is the Master of Portland."

"James just saw me a few hours ago. He knows what I'm wearing already." Which was the same thing she'd been wearing for the last two days, and that was getting old for her, but Sheldon didn't need to know that. "I'm not dressing up to impress him or the hive."

She *had* dressed up a little the first time she'd met Arial and the first time she'd been summoned to meet Gabriel. But in both cases, she'd also had Jaxer there, and he had glamoured her up a better and more impressive look so she hadn't really had to bother too much over what she'd been wearing.

No Jaxer this time, though. No glamour. Just her ordinary clothes. Even more ordinary than her past visits to the hive. But since she wasn't going to leave Sheldon unprotected to go home and change, and since she didn't think she'd impress the vampires with anything from her wardrobe anyway, she just had to accept that she was going into the hive looking like her normal self. With maybe a few more wrinkles in her clothes.

"You didn't have to dress like a cliché," she said to Sheldon, nodding at his leather pants. "Aren't those thinks sticky and hot?"

"Is your jacket sticky and hot?" he shot back.

"Not the same thing." Though she was glad to have her magic Marianne-made jacket with her. Marianne had put a few extra spells on it over the last few months, and one of them was the same wound-sealing magic she'd put into a few of Cary's shirts. Cary hadn't actually had to use that spell yet, but being able to close an open, bleeding wound with the press of material to the injury seemed like a really good idea when walking into the vampire hive.

"If you two are done judging each other's fashion choices, can we go in?" Deacon said, his tone dry. "I'd like to get this over with."

She gave him a disgruntled look that he ignored, then she led the way to the house. She wanted this over with too. Even if she wasn't sure *how* she wanted it all to end.

Just without her or Deacon or Sheldon dead. That would be a good ending.

She had her hand on the ordinary round doorknob on the house's white front door when a throat-clearing stopped her. A familiar throat-clearing. But one she hadn't expected here.

She closed her eyes briefly and let out a breath. "What are you doing here?"

"Why didn't you tell me?" Jaxer asked, his voice quiet, his tone impossible to read.

She looked over her shoulder. He stood a few feet behind them looking his usual self, silk shirt gapping at the throat, his blond hair bright in the faint light from the crescent moon. His angular features were cast in shadows so she couldn't read his mood any better in his expression than she could in his voice.

"If you mean why didn't I tell you I was coming to the hive," she said, "that's because it's a work related thing and you're not supposed to be helping with that this year." Even though he seemed to be around a lot more than she'd been led to believe he would be. So far, that hadn't gotten her into trouble. So far.

"I'm not talking about this." He gestured to their surroundings. "And you know it. I'm talking about him." He nodded at Sheldon without looking at him. "I assume the wizard will be inside."

"Wow, you're good. How did you—" She shook her head. "Never mind." She'd given up trying to get answers for how he knew things. "I didn't tell you about Sheldon because protecting him is an official job, and you can't help with that. And also, I didn't want to have to protect Sheldon from you as well as the wizard. Having to protect him from Deacon is hard enough."

Deacon grunted, his only comment on that.

"You thought you'd have to?" Jaxer asked, still in that unreadable tone.

"Hell yes. You've been after him for months. And I can't blame you for wanting to get some justice where he's concerned. It rubs me wrong that he isn't being punished for the murders he committed, too. But if the wizard gets him, he might be able to use him to find the Naga city and free Oliver Holland, and according to James and the witches that will call Lud back into this realm, and none of us want that, so for the time being, I'm keeping Sheldon safe from the wizard, and we're going to try negotiating an end to all this with the wizard while the vampires serve as moderators, and I know it's all pretty fucked up, but that's my job. And anyway, it's all your fault I'm in this position to begin with, so don't give me any grief."

She had to pull in a deep breath after her rant. A rant that revealed more than she'd wanted to to Jaxer, not the least of which was her discomfort at having tried to hide all this from him.

Jaxer stared at her for a long long moment without speaking. She stared back, proud of herself when she didn't fidget even though she wanted to.

Finally, he said, "You're underdress for this meeting."

Sheldon snorted something under his breath.

Cary rolled her eyes. "I literally just talked to James a few hours ago. He already knows what I'm wearing."

"James came to see you in the daylight?" Jaxer said, his brow lowering.

"I know, right? If he's taking all this that seriously, then it's serious. So, yeah." She stumbled to a stop, not sure if she was glad Jaxer had joined them or pissed that he'd ambushed them right before she had to face the hive of vampires who likely wanted her dead. And the wizard who'd been trying to kill her. And the triad of witches who'd tried to kill her…

A lot of the people who wanted her dead were through that door. Thinking about it that way was a little scary.

"Do you want me to improve your look?" Jaxer asked, walking slowly toward them.

She moved just a little more so she was between him and Sheldon. "You're not going with us. You can't. This is part of my job. In my test year. You can't help."

"You have a test year?" Sheldon asked.

She sighed. She really hated that he'd just learned that. She hated hated this particular job on so many levels.

"I won't help you then," Jaxer said. "But I can have Deacon's back. Vampires love shifter blood."

She blinked at him. Then narrowed her eyes. "That's still helping me." Vampires loved faery blood, too. He was giving her one more person to protect which ensured her powers were working no matter what.

"Not really," he said with one of his absurdly elegant shrugs. "You're on your own. I won't participate in the negotiation or try to harm your charge. I'll just ensure your mate doesn't get himself killed trying to defend your honor or some other irritatingly noble stunt."

Deacon grunted something under his breath she couldn't hear, barely a sound, but to her surprise, he didn't sound annoyed or insulted by Jaxer's comment. If she didn't know better, she'd swear that was an amused grunt.

She wished she spoke "male grunt" better. Or that she had his shifter sense of smell so she could tell what he was feeling.

"Fine," she said with a huff, trying to sound more annoyed than relieved. If she were honest, having Jaxer at her back was reassuring as hell, even with the potential complication of him wanting to kill her charge. It felt right to have both Jaxer and Deacon with her when she faced the stupid wizard. And she wasn't going to argue too hard against it now that Jaxer was here.

"Just don't try anything stupid or noble yourself," she said. "I have enough people to protect already."

She turned back toward the door so he wouldn't see the smile she was trying to suppress, took a deep breath, and opened the farmhouse door.

Time for the Old Enemies Reunion.

24

The interior of the farmhouse had changed dramatically since her last visit. Cary paused on the doorstep for a long moment to take it all in.

James had said he'd done "slight redecorating." These changes did not fall under any definition of the world "slight."

Before, the interior had been a full-on ode to French elegance with a lot of gilt, decorative crown molding, beautifully delicate furniture, muted lighting from wall sconces, and thick blue velvet drapes. The entire thing had been open, too. Just one big foyer, a formal entryway to a palace, any resemblance to an ordinary farmhouse left behind the moment someone stepped through the front door.

Now, the interior of the farmhouse looked like... A farmhouse. A cozy, homey, humans-had-just-stepped-out-and-would-be-back-soon farmhouse.

Where the floors had been marble before, now they were hardwood, stripped and polished to a light, natural color. The walls were painted a soft white and decorated by landscape pastures and posters of the Portland docks. A long rug ran the length of a central hallway, but it was a simple blue with a diamond pattern and looked like something you could order online or pick up at a big box store. Nothing fancy or French about it.

And there were rooms now, with open doors, leading off the narrow hallway. There hadn't been rooms before. Just an open space. Through one door, she spotted a comfortable living room with a huge couch and a flat screen TV hanging on the wall over a low white shelf stuffed with gaming equipment, books, and cable boxes. Another door revealed a large kitchen painted pale green with ordinary white appliances, light wood cabinets, and laminate countertops that were spotless but not particular fancy. Two bedrooms, again simply decorated with furniture that looked modern and inexpensive, and a single, ordinary full bathroom near the back.

All if it just like any other normal, ordinary house.

Ordinary and very human and tidy but also a little worn and lived in. There were some boxes of food stacked on the kitchen counters, a few books scattered across the living room coffee table, two toothbrushes in a plastic cup on the sink in the bathroom.

Cary stood in the middle of the long hallway and spun in a slow circle. She felt like she'd walked into someone's home on accident. Not the Master vampire of Portland's hive entrance. For a split second, she worried she actually had walked into the wrong house and someone was going to step out of the closed door at the far end of the hall and ask them what the hell they were doing there.

But it was midnight and no one was sleeping in any of the beds. The lights were off everywhere except in the hall. And while there were a lot of touches that made the home looked lived in, right down to the boxes of cereal and crackers on the kitchen counter, the house smelled too clean. Not just ordinary clean. A surprising lack-of-smells clean. The kind of clean that took extra special care to ensure there was virtually no scent to the place.

Deacon might pick up something here, but her ordinary human nose smelled nothing but a faint touch of some astringent cleaner, and only barely that. An active human home, even a very clean one, would still smell of…something.

"This is so weird," she murmured as she faced the one closed door at the end of the hallway again—the door that opened onto the elevator leading down into the hive proper. "James said 'slight' redecorating."

"You sure this is the right place," Sheldon said, sounding a little nervous.

"I'm sure," she said, but only because of the burnt remains of the barn behind the house. If not for that, she might convince herself they were in the wrong place. "Can you smell the vampires?" she asked Deacon.

Vampires had a very distinct scent, especially to shifters who could parse out more than just the blood and death and decay that tended to surround vampires. According to Deacon there was no mistaking the scent for anything else that walked around in the world.

"Barely," he said. "And then only in faint whiffs here and there. The scent doesn't permeate the place like it did last time. Whatever James did here, he made sure the hive was almost entirely hidden from detection, casual or otherwise."

"That's..." She raised her brows as she did another spin, taking in the "home" they stood in. "That's impressive."

"Yeah, it is," Deacon said.

"But not surprising," Jaxer said quietly. "Gabriel's death, the chaos that happened here a few months ago... It was enough to draw unwanted attention to the hive if James hadn't acted fast. This is a lot more effective camouflage than either of the former Master's had managed."

"Or wanted," Cary said.

Ariel had been entirely too flamboyant to tolerate this lack of luxury. Her hive had reflected that luxury and opulence, with enough gold, glitter, and marble to make a French king proud. Gabriel had been a minimalist, almost an ascetic. He would have hated the everyday ordinariness and clutter of this place. While he'd kept Ariel's grand entryway, he'd still stripped it back to only the basics. Impressive but spare. And he'd completely redone the hive proper to reflect his minimalist tastes.

Neither of them would have considered pushing the exterior

camouflage of the hive this far off their own aesthetics, even within the bounds of a supposed farmhouse.

James had taken the camouflage all the way. A passerby could look through the front windows now and see a home. A place someone lived and ate actual food and played video games or watched TV. A *human* home.

It was absolutely diabolical and perfect. And Cary was a little more afraid of James now than she'd been before this moment.

James understood the modern world in a way a lot of the ancient Masters didn't, didn't even try. Which made him dangerous in ways other Masters weren't. Dangerous because he could move through the modern world without anyone knowing exactly what he was. A silent, deadly predator hiding in plain sight.

The elevator door opened suddenly, followed by a faint ding. Cary spun to face it, gasping despite herself. The interior of the elevator was empty, waiting like an open maw, brightly lit and clean, simple chrome and laminate wood, less luxurious than on her previous visit. The exterior door had looked like a closet door, but it slid into the wall like an ordinary elevator.

No hint of vampire smell wafted out. Which struck her as an impressive accomplishment, keeping even the elevator from revealing any signs of the hive below.

She let out a breath which fluttered the stray strands of hair on her forehead that had escaped her attempt to smooth them back into her ponytail. Time to face the hive full of people who didn't like her.

She took up a position in front of the others, ensuring she was protecting all three of them as they moved into the elevator and the doors slid silently closed. Last time there'd been manual controls which James had operated on their way down. This time, the interior was like any other modern elevator, but with only two buttons. One with a D for down, the other a U for up.

She glanced at Jaxer. "You okay? All this metal?" His Fae iron allergy wasn't as bad as some, but being inside an elevator was still not a comfortable position for him.

"I'll manage." He smiled faintly.

That would have to do. She pressed the D.

Her heart hammered hard as the elevator bumped slightly and then started moving down.

Taking them into the heart of the vampire hive.

When the door dinged open again, Cary stood firmly in front of Deacon, Sheldon, and Jaxer, and held her breath. She knew nothing was likely to jump out and attack the instant the doors opened. Okay, that might have been dramatic enough for vampires. And yes, she was stepping into the middle of a host of old enemies. Still. She was here because the Master had invited her here to negotiate an end to her current predicament. They were here for a peaceful end to all this. No one would attack.

At least not the moment the elevator doors opened.

But better safe than sorry.

Thankfully, nothing did jump out of the darkness the instant the doors slid silently open. But the darkness after the brightly illuminated interior of the elevator took some getting used to. She stepped from the cage into the hive proper blinking her eyes and taking her time until they adjusted. The elevator door slid closed again, cutting off that extra bright source of light and plunging her into a deeper darkness.

Thanks to protecting three people, her eyes did adapt quickly. She was even able to see better than she'd have been without Protector magic. There was a single overhead, recessed light that gave just enough ambient illumination to allow her human eyes to function— there was only so much magic could do. The light ensured it wasn't so dark she'd need bat echo location or anything. She winced inwardly at her bat-vampire mental reference.

"You good now?" she murmured to Deacon, whose eyesight would also adapt and function perfectly fine in the gloom. He needed even less light than she did.

He nodded. "You?"

"Good. You guys stay behind me and I'll be even better." She took in her surroundings.

They were in the huge, outer corridor, another entryway that opened onto the inner hive. The corridor had very high ceilings and led off in either direction, the shadows too deep for her to see into, but she got the impression of a great deal of distance.

Last time she'd been here, the floor had been stone, with a thin rug to mute sounds. Now it was hardwood, inlaid with a nice diamond pattern, but not particularly remarkable. The concrete walls, left exposed and cold with Gabriel, covered in black silk with Ariel, were now paneled in dark wood, warming the otherwise chilly space. Opposite the elevator, where there had been a giant, steel reinforced oak door, now there was just a dark arch, opening into blackness. A faint shushing sound moved through the corridor, like wind or the movement of water behind the walls.

And, finally, here the distinct, not as unpleasant as it should have been, scent of blood, dust, that weirdly reptilian musk undertone, and just a whiff of decay. The aged smell of...

Vampires.

She wrinkled her nose, grateful her sense of smell wasn't heightened the way her eyesight was by her Protector magic. "Sheldon? Jaxer? You able to see enough to move without tripping?" she asked.

She knew Jaxer's eyesight would adjust. She'd been in the hive with him before. Sheldon was the most human and vulnerable one here, and she wasn't entirely sure he'd realized just how vulnerable he'd be before this moment.

Sheldon barely grunted a response.

"I'm good," Jaxer said, his voice low. "And you look significantly less wrinkled now."

She snorted. "Gee, thanks. What do I look like?" She glanced down, but he'd arranged the glamour so she couldn't see it. She hated that. "Jaxer..."

"You'll be happier not knowing," he said. "But the vampires will be impressed."

"Geezus, what have you put me in?"

"And it better not reveal more of her skin than she's voluntarily showing already," Deacon said, a very distinct growl in his voice.

"Cause that would make me uncomfortable and annoyed," she

finished, in agreement with Deacon. She should be the one to choose how much skin she showed at any point in time. And since she hadn't felt like wearing something revealing and displaying a great deal of skin to *vampires*, she did not want the glamour to do it.

"Don't worry," Jaxer said, "it's nothing like that. Just… Let's say you'd fit in well with a Viking assembly."

She pressed her lips together, not sure whether to laugh or groan. "Do I have a sword?" Because that would make her laugh.

"Not on display. If you need one, I can arrange that, though," Jaxer said. His tone didn't reveal his emotions, but she'd known him long enough to hear the humor. "And don't worry, Deacon, I haven't left you out. Very impressive. I promise."

She had to work not to grin now. To her, Deacon was still wearing jeans and a long-sleeved t-shirt. She liked what he had on now, it showed off his muscles and gave her a little charge if she took the time to admire him, but she would love to know what Jaxer had put him in. She almost asked.

Unfortunately, they didn't have time. They'd been left alone long enough for their eyes to adjust. She didn't want to push her luck by standing around chatting.

"Let's get this over with," she said.

Stepping through the high arch from the corridor into the black cavern beyond was disorienting even without the drama of the giant oak doors swinging open. While the corridor gave the impression of space, she could still see the ceiling there. The main cavern, on the other hand, was so huge the ceiling disappeared into darkness so far overhead, she didn't even get a sense of it. From the outside, the cavern had appeared lightless, but some faint illumination rose once they crossed the threshold. These lights were recessed into the ground, casting strange dancing shadows upward along the walls, further emphasizing the sheer size of the place.

Nothing like this should be underground in Portland. She knew, from asking, it was reinforced and well-built, but it still felt more like a cave than a construction and that always left her worried about collapse.

This area had been the place Gabriel had really put his stamp on the hive, cutting back all Ariel's glint and glamour to a bear aestheticism of emptiness and openness. James had changed all that, but not back to Ariel's Versailles palace drama. This was a new kind of drama. A lot more drama than he'd shown upstairs.

And again, she had to wonder at his definition of the world "slight."

She blinked a few times as her eyes adapted to the uplighting and she was able to take in more of her surroundings. The huge, open, shadowed cavern was now extravagantly laid out like a medieval castle. There were even suits of armor lined up along the walls. Circular metal chandeliers without any candles in them hung from the distant roof, their chains disappearing into the darkness above. Wide stone bricks replaced hardwood and tiled flooring.

At either side of the room, long wooden tables flanked by tall-backed wooden chairs sat in front of the suits of armor. Straw scattered the ground under the tables. Small flickering imitation candles with red "flames" danced down the center of the table alongside rows of pewter goblets.

And in each of the chairs…a vampire. At least forty of them. That she could see.

More than she'd anticipated for this meeting.

She heard the flutter of movement in the shadows overhead, knew there were more up there. But the fact that so many were sitting around tables to watch was intimidating. And she really didn't want to know what they were drinking from those goblets.

A low, almost inaudible hiss filled the huge cavern, and the stink of gathered vampire was strong.

Opposite the arched entrance, on a raised wood and stone dais, in an elaborately carved wooden throne that would make a fantasy author proud, James sat, leaning on one of the huge throne armrests, silently watching them approach. Instead of his usual suit and tie, he wore a long, velvet coat edged with elegantly scrawled threadwork that glittered—Marianne would be impressed—over leather trousers and knee high boots. A golden diadem encrusted with jewels sat low on his brow.

A throne and crown. Even Ariel hadn't worn a crown.

She wasn't sure whether to laugh or dissolve in terror.

Behind the throne hung a huge tapestry, stretching at least twenty or thirty feet in length and the same again in height. It dominated the space behind James, and conveniently, hid anything or anyone that might be standing behind it. There was no movement in the tapestry, not even from a stray breeze. Which didn't tell her much because vampires, when they liked, could stand so still they might as well be dead. Or, well, more dead.

She scowled at the design on the giant tapestry. It looked a lot like one of the real unicorn panels that hung in different museums, but a lot larger and more complete. An imitation?

Or, given they were in a vampire hive, maybe a real one?

"You've been here since he redecorated, haven't you?" she murmured to Jaxer, her "Viking" outfit suddenly making more sense.

"No," he said quietly. "But I've heard stories."

"Leather pants aren't so far off, huh?" Sheldon whispered, sounding too smug.

Cary didn't bother responding. She didn't want to encourage him.

As they approached the throne, the hiss from the surrounding vampires increased, and whispers started, too low for her to hear—for which she was grateful. She didn't want to know what they were saying to her just then. One vampire spit in her direction so, yeah, whatever they were whispering probably wasn't complimentary.

"They don't like you," Sheldon said.

"Nope," she agreed.

"Why are we here, then?" Sheldon asked.

"A neutral place to talk your master out of killing you." Except she really had to stretch the definition of "neutral" to make that sentence work.

To be fair, the vampires didn't like the wizard any more than they liked her, so if being surrounded by mutual enemies could qualify as neutral, this place was actually perfect.

They reached the dais without anyone physically attacking or moving to impeded their progress, which was better than the last time she'd been here.

"So," she said to James, twirling her finger in a gesture to take in their surroundings. "Didn't go for the same plain, ordinary camouflage as upstairs, huh?"

"Well. I couldn't forsake drama entirely, could I? We are vampires after all." He looked her over from head to toe. His gaze, glowing yellow in the faint light, flicked to Jaxer before settling on her again. "You make a fine looking medieval warrior," he said. "A good choice, I think."

She snorted. "Not my idea." She narrowed her eyes at the diadem. "Why medieval? Are you that old?"

Vampires did tend to harken back to the years they'd been human when it came to their personal decorating and clothing tastes. Not all of them, but many liked the drama of earlier eras, and in particular, the eras they'd been born into.

James had always presented himself in such modern clothes, though, she'd forgotten how old he'd have to be to be a Master. The medieval décor hinted at an age that left her a little breathless. Though, if he had been vampire reborn in medieval Europe, it meant he was susceptible to Christian relics like crosses and holy water since those were the only vampires affected by that particular clichéd myth.

Huh. Would he really give that away?

He didn't answer her question, not even with a faint smile, so she was left to wonder.

"The wizard has arrived," he said instead. "And the triad. Shall I have them brought in?"

"Your castle," she said. "Whatever floats your boat."

That flippancy earned her a few snarls from the surrounding vampires but a lip twitch of amusement from James.

Oh good. If she amused him, he was a whole lot less likely to have them all killed.

She hadn't quite realized how terrifying James could be until this moment, though. He made an effort to tread a line between scary and friendly, just scary enough for her powers to work, just friendly enough to relax her fears. He'd done so from the beginning. She'd never trusted him, of course. She'd been leery and aware that he could be a threat. But she often forgot to be bone deep afraid of him.

She was not making that mistake at that moment.

Her thudding heartbeat and rushing adrenaline weren't good in the middle of the hive—the fear and the sound of rushing blood drew vampires like flies—but for her at least, the threat and fear meant she didn't have to worry about her powers. James might have invited her, and the vampires might have to mind their manners, but there was no pretending she and the others weren't in danger down here.

Which was excellent news.

The sounds of movement to the left drew Cary's attention. Huge, rectangular banners unfurled from some place high up near the ceiling, dropping in a dramatic flurry toward the ground and snapping into place. A quick glance confirmed similar banners had dropped on the right side of the hall as well. They were multiple colors—though she couldn't tell what colors in the low light—and bore remarkably realistic-looking coat of arms. Not that she was an expert, but given these were vampires, she had a feeling they could well be authentic. The unicorn tapestry behind the throne fluttered as a breeze moved through the hall.

From the darkness behind the banners to the left, the wizard moved into sight, flanked by two gorgeous vampires. The wizard had stuck to a more ordinary level of drama with an all black outfit that highlighted his pale skin, so much so his head seemed to float in the empty air, which given the medieval surroundings was sort of…appropriate. The vampires flanking him were dressed in leather jackets, pants, and knee high leather boots all of which were covered with pointed metal studs. They wore leather chokers around their necks which were also studded with small metal spikes, and leather head caps arrayed with yet more metal spikes. The combined effect made them look a bit like walking Iron Maidens.

So. No hugs for them.

The wizard glared at her before his gaze snapped to Sheldon and something moved through his pale blue eyes. She couldn't tell if he was happy to see Sheldon, annoyed, angry, or eager. But his eyes narrowed and there was calculation there.

He was as pale as the last time she'd seen him, his silver hair longer and shaggier than she remembered. And he moved a little stiffer now, not so spry and fit as before. The wrinkles around his eyes, mouth, and along his forehead were more pronounced, the skin on his jawline looser.

He looked like he'd aged ten years in a few short months.

And maybe he had. He'd been keeping his stolen body in better shape than it would naturally be in. But Zorianthus's time in that body was definitely running out.

Even thinking his name made her wince now that she knew saying it drew his attention.

And as if thinking his name did just that, he turned back to glaring at her, his eyes snapping with rage, his lips lifting in a snarl.

"You," he said, his voice low and full of menace. "All this is your fault. And I'm going to enjoy killing you."

25

"**W**ell," Cary said as the faint echo from the wizard's words faded in the giant cavern. All the vampires surrounding them fell quiet, waiting. Leaving a silence that made Cary's ears ring. "That's a great way to start a negotiation. Get your position on things right out into the open. No mystery at all. Good. Gives us something to work with." She rolled her eyes and faced James. "This might not have been a good idea."

"Your plan," he reminded her. "I had another."

She pressed her lips together so she wouldn't comment.

"What are you wearing?" the wizard snapped at her.

She frowned down at the jeans, t-shirt, and leather jacket she could see. "I have no idea," she told him honestly. Which, frankly, was her answer even if she'd been able to see what Jaxer's glamour showed the wizard.

"Playing dressup," Zorianthus spat. "All of you, playing like children." He glared at James. "I expected more from you. You're old enough to know better than this."

The wizard scolding the vampires for their drama was pretty ironic, and Cary was a little curious how James would react. His expression didn't change, though. He showed the wizard a blank stare, his eyes

187

glowing yellow, his teeth carefully hidden inside his closed-lipped mouth. The stare was so blank and unrelenting, though, the wizard dropped his first.

From Cary's perspective, since she was used to staring dominance contests with Fred, she'd guess James won that round.

Cary raised her brows at Zorianthus's all black outfit, the black pants, the black turtleneck, all colors that highlighted his pallor.

She shook her head at him. "Someone sporting such a 'serious goth wizard' look in all that black shouldn't cast stones. Scrying or spy equipment?" she asked.

He blinked at her change of subject and stared at her for long moments.

She sighed. "You can't be this slow. You're what, centuries old? Scrying. Or. Spy. Equipment?"

More silence.

"I'm not sure he knows what you're talking about," Deacon murmured.

"What are you talking about?" Jaxer whispered.

"The way this guy was able to spy on Sheldon despite the spells Sheldon bought to hide from him in plain sight."

"Is that what the little shit did?" Jaxer said.

"Hey, I'm right here," Sheldon said.

"And you're still a little shit." Jaxer cursed under his breath. "I should have seen through those spells."

"You haven't been watching his place. You've had other people doing that work." Cary reached back and patted his arm. "It's okay."

There was a grunt she couldn't interpret, but she'd hash this out with him later. They had bigger things to deal with. Like, for example, the wizard looking at them all like they'd lost their collective minds.

"What the hell are you talking about?" the wizard in question said.

Cary frowned at him before shifting her gaze to James. He raised his brows in return, subtly but still enough to indicate a degree of confusion and question she didn't buy even a little bit.

"Where are the witches?" she asked him.

Scrying was a witch skill. Zorianthus might be old, and he probably knew how to scry, and wizards could do it according to Angie.

But it was, predominantly, a witch's skill.

And she should have fucking realized it.

James raised his hand. From the right side of the room, through the unfurled banners, two more vampires dressed in Iron Maiden leather outfits escorted the triad into the main hall.

The three women, together in one place, were just as impressive as the last time Cary had met them.

The least powerful of the three still bore that distinctly California blond-haired, blue-eyed, surfer girl look, her cropped t-shirt and slow slung jeans showing off impressive abs. Instead of the super cool, floor-length black sweater duster she'd worn before, she was now wearing a floor-length black leather coat. Other than that difference, she looked pretty much the same as last time. Young and fresh and smug.

She still looked older than the other two witches, though.

The Black woman had gone from very shortly cropped hair to a completely shaven head, which highlighted her gorgeous angular face and perfectly shaped lips. The last time Cary had seen her, she'd worn a dark pant suit with no shirt under the jacket and impressively spiky high heels, a look Cary associated with supermodels and other chic New York types. This time, she wore black fitted trousers and a thigh-length, black velvet jerkin embroidered with gold thread. Still all elegance and gorgeousness. She looked a few years younger than the blond, maybe in her very early twenties, but her dark eyes were full of a kind of worldly wisdom that belied that youthful exterior.

The most powerful of the three, the leader of the triad—Justina according to James, and wasn't that way too many "J" names in one room—looked the youngest of the three. Barely twenty. Barely old enough to take seriously.

Which was why Cary had taken her very seriously from the beginning.

She had a rich brown skin tone and deep brown-red hair that flowed in long waves down her back. Her hazel green eyes could as easily have been brown in the dim light. She'd dressed in a long black skirt and cropped sweater the first time Cary had met her. Now she wore a loose, flowing, tan skirt and a white poet's shirt that probably made the vampires envious. At least some of the younger ones. She wore flat, strappy sandals that were probably easier to run in than the Black witch's spiky heels. And she moved with an easy confidence that did more to reveal her true power than anything else.

"Sister," Justina greeted, smiling slightly at Cary. "It's been a long time."

"Yeah, I'm pretty sure you know I'm not a witch now, so we can drop the 'sister' stuff. Also, it hasn't been nearly long enough."

The blonde snorted something under her breath.

Cary flashed her a toothy grin. She liked irritating the blonde.

"Holland made a mistake with you," Justina said. "He should have recruited you, not tried to kill you."

"He had better luck trying to kill me." She lifted her hand in a slight shrug. "Obviously."

Justina chuckled. "He can't be allowed back into this realm," she said. "You know that now."

"Tell the wizard that," Cary said. "Because I'm not the one trying to find him and let him out again."

Everyone in the room, including the vampires, turned to stare at Zorianthus.

The wizard glared at the room.

"You know nothing of my plans." He snarled at Cary.

Because apparently, she was the focus of his ire. Which was safer than snarling at vampires, she assumed.

"I know you're looking to release an old enemy of mine as some sort of revenge scenario," she said. "But I also know turning Holland loose into this realm again will be bad."

"Very bad," Justina said.

"What do you know, witch?" Zorianthus sneered at her. "You think your triad brings you so much power. You know nothing of power."

"You're weak." She gestured at him. "Dying. You think I can't see that, brother? You think your age is still hidden? But our master won't heal you."

"You assume I want him for healing?" Zorianthus snorted. "You think I just want revenge?"

"Well," Cary said, "you have tried to kill me, like two or three times at this stage. So, yeah. I think you want revenge. And Holland doesn't like me."

The blonde witch loosed a short burst of laughter at that. She quieted at a look from the Black witch.

Cary ignored them. "But there's more to releasing Holland into this world than just releasing a powerful demon. He's got a dad who will literally burn this realm down to ash to get his son back. He almost did once already. And while revenge might sound lovely to you right now, even you can't survive in a realm that's ash and…well, no longer exists."

She blinked a few times. Wow. That would be bad for not just her realm—and yeah, that was super bad for her realm—but for several other realms all linked to this one. The Nagas needed a link to this realm to survive. Faery needed their links to this realm to feed and recharge the magic that literally made Faery. The Bookstore, whatever it was, was linked to this realm. Would it survive the destruction?

"You're pathetic and small," Zorianthus said. "You know nothing."

She sighed. Looked at James. "Do you understand what he's talking about?"

James raised a brow. "He came to us speaking of revenge."

Zorianthus had the nerve to roll his eyes, despite the vampires on either side of him.

"You want Sheldon back?" Cary asked.

"That's none of your concern."

"You need his body. He told us why you trained him."

The wizard's jaw muscle twitched but it was the only reaction.

"Justina is right, your age is showing. Your current body is dying and if you don't jump soon, you'll die with it."

Still no reply, though his eyes narrowed.

"But…you didn't understand what I meant when I asked scrying or spy equipment." She turned her attention to the triad in time to see the blonde wince and then attempt to hide the reaction.

"Okay," Cary said. "So. You—" she pointed at the witches, "—have been spying on Sheldon through his witchy spells. Did you sell him those spells? Insert a way to look through them?"

The witches stared back without answering.

She was getting a lot of that at the moment.

She turned to Sheldon. "Did you know who sold you the spells?"

"Some old lady," he said dismissively.

She sighed. "Sheldon, you have got to stop with this angry teenage attitude and rudeness. It's not helping your cause with me. Show some respect to the witch who worked with you. Even if the 'old lady' appearance was just a disguise." She faced Justina again.

Justina smiled faintly. "Such a waste," she sighed. "You would have made a magnificent witch."

"Right." Given she couldn't figure out how to release any of the magic she absorbed, she kind of doubted that. "So, you all sold him the spells to hide him from the wizard, but still keep an eye on him." She glared at James. "That's how you knew Sheldon had bought spells to hide."

James stared at her without responding.

More staring without answers.

She faced the witches again. "And then you came to the vampires to warn them they couldn't help the wizard release Holland because of Ho'Lud."

The Black witch hissed something under her breath and made a protective gesture with her hands.

"Wow. That's a serious reaction to just the mention of his name." Obviously, there was more there than she knew. But since she'd faced Ho'Lud already, she wasn't sure it could be any scarier than what she *did* know.

Then she recalled, the demon hunters had just called him Lud. And she'd defaulted to calling him Lud out loud most of the time, too. But not always. "Names," she said quietly to herself. The magical world had a real thing with names. Probably something to do with that. More research for later.

"Anyway." She faced Zorianthus again—speaking of dangerous names—and said, "You want Sheldon because you've trained him for the body swap. He knows you want to kill him off to steal his body. There's something here I'm missing, huh? Something that has all of you concerned with each other and has brought us all here to the vampire hive."

She looked at James. "All of us at the vampire hive."

Her heart thumped a little harder for reasons she couldn't quite place. Something felt wrong. Something felt…inevitable about all this.

But she couldn't find the threads that pulled it all together to make sense.

"I don't get it," Sheldon said aloud, echoing Cary's thoughts. "What do you need a demon for?" he asked Zorianthus. "Why are you wasting time you don't have?"

"The million dollar question," Cary murmured.

Why was Zorianthus so determined to free Holland, while the witches who'd worked *for* Holland were so determined to prevent that, and they'd all gone to the vampires for help in their respective goals, and the vampires—well, James—had come to her. At Sheldon's apartment.

Her bosses had sent her to protect Sheldon. Sheldon was a linchpin in all this. An element that couldn't fall or everything fell apart. But…

But what was the endgame? What was the wizard really after? What were the witches really trying to prevent?

Or were they?

And why the hell were the vampires involved?

"My head hurts," she murmured to Deacon.

He grunted, and Jaxer snorted.

"Bad guys with complicated machinations are a pain in my ass," she said to James.

His lips twitched.

"What's your endgame?" she asked him.

"To facilitate a solution that doesn't result in fire and more vampires burnt," he said without hesitating. "That's my job."

The not-so-subtle reminder that many of the hive had been killed by fire recently—by her—didn't go missed. But since he'd set that up too, she didn't trust his answer now. Even if the answer was the truth. It just wasn't the *full* explanation.

She rubbed her temples. "You know, you all could just say aloud what you're after? Just, you know, communicate. And I can tell you why you won't get whatever it is you want. Then we can all go home and continue with our lives without anyone ending up dead and with the realm still spinning. Easy."

One of the vampires at the tables lining the hall hissed loudly, "Kill them. Kill them all. Let us feed, Master."

A chant started around the room, echoing the demand. "Kill them. Kill them. Kill them. Kill them all. Let us feed. Let us feed." The noise rose as the vampires pounded the tables and stomped the ground in time with their demands.

Cary sighed and shook her head. "No one is feeding on anyone," she snapped, loudly into the cacophony. "Stop that."

To her surprise, the vampires quieted and the chanting faded away into silence.

Uh.

James held her gaze for a long moment, his expression unreadable.

Had she just made a mistake? Because she'd commanded the vampires—accidentally, but still—and they'd actually obeyed. That probably wasn't a good thing in front of the Master.

Oops.

26

$\mathcal{C}$ary felt both Deacon and Jaxer take a step closer to her, angling slightly to face different parts of the hall while still staying behind her so her powers would work.

A breeze of movement flowed through the cavernous room, a shuffling, a repositioning. Followed by silence and stillness. The kind of stillness only vampires could manage.

James continued to stare at her, also motionless and impossible to read.

She stared back but tried to let him see, through body language and the direction of her gaze on his cheek rather than directly meeting his eyes, that she wasn't attempting to challenge his power down here. She didn't want to say anything aloud just then—that would probably be worse than the silence—but she'd have to apologize to him later. She really hadn't meant to step on his toes, and given the way vampires were about these things, the very last thing she needed was to make an enemy of James.

Or at least more than the casual one he was now. Though, she had to admit, it would have been nice if she could have considered him a friend. Having at least *one* of the Big Bads in the city be uninterested in killing her would have been helpful.

Ah well. Too late to take it back now.

"I'd like to get back to the whole no-to-the-dying part of this conversation," she said.

And very obviously dropped her staring contest with James—even if she hadn't been meeting his gaze directly.

She recognized it as a loss and hoped the others did too, that the move would help her position with James.

She faced the witches. "You've known the danger the wizard and his protégé posed long enough to sell protection spells to Sheldon and to spy on him. You've known the wizard would try to free Holland this whole time?"

The blonde witch shuffled her feet and tried to look unconcerned. The Black witch succeeded in looking unconcerned and unreadable, not a single fidget.

Justina smiled. "There's much you don't understand, sister," she said.

Cary laughed, a full-throated cackle. "Well, if that's not the damned truth," she said around her—probably mildly hysterical—laughter. "And since not a single one of you is explaining, which would make my life a *lot* easier, here's what we're going to do."

She pulled in a deep breath. "I don't know what you all are up to. Who's trying to do what, who's trying to prevent what, or why any of you are doing any of this. But since this is where we are, I'm going to say that all of it is now officially over. Sheldon stays safe in my protection. All the machinations stop here. No one frees Holland. No one attracts his father's attention. And no one kills off former protégés for their bodies." She gave Zorianthus a pointed look.

"If you all don't do as I say," she continued, "I will place myself in your way and not budge until you get bored and go home. Trust me. I'm good at that. I would bet on my stubbornness against your impatience every day."

The silence that followed her announcement was deafening.

"Well that got their attention," Jaxer said under his breath. "You might need that sword after all."

"Shut up," she said back, just as quietly.

Zorianthus took a step toward her. When the vampires flanking him didn't stop him, he closed the space between her and him, stopping only when her shields brought him up short.

"You have no idea what you're interfering with. No idea what you've ruined. Again." He glared at her, his voice low and vicious.

"You're right. I don't have any idea, because none of you will explain. You want to tell me, I'm all ears. But I doubt it will change my stance."

"I must reach the demon," Zorianthus said. "I have to reach him before—" He cut himself off, pressing his lips together.

"Do the witches know why?" she asked.

She darted a glance at Justina, but she didn't comment or reveal any emotion. The blonde, however, shifted from one foot to the other. Subtly, but still a definite fidget.

"They know, don't they?" she said. "That's why they're trying to stop you. It's not just about the demon god."

"The demon's father is not my concern," Zorianthus said.

"Did you know about him? Did you know releasing Holland would loose his father onto this realm?" She was genuinely curious.

Zorianthus snarled and leaned closer. "This is bigger than their family squabble."

"Tell that to Holland," she muttered. "Also, I don't think there's much that could be 'bigger' than the destruction of our realm, so yeah, I'm not buying it. Either explain or don't. I'm getting tired of the dance."

He raised a hand, the blue glow of a wizard bolt filling his palm. The snap and sizzle of burning ozone tickled her nostrils.

She grinned. "Throw it. I dare you."

Zorianthus snarled and she could see the debate, the desire.

"You really want to, don't you?" she asked, taunting.

She was safe. Her charges were safe. And she was really tired of this particular enemy lurking in the background of her life.

Her anger rose, and she leaned in closer to the wizard. The gesture forced him backward a step as her shield pushed at him. "Throw it. Go on. Try to kill me now." She dropped her voice to a whisper. "Give me your power. I'll take it all."

A part of her really wanted him to. Wanted him to fire every bit of the magic he had at her. Every last ounce of. Yes, she'd absorb some of it, maybe even a lot. And she'd have to figure out how to release it later without killing anyone. Or herself. But she'd take that risk to end his threat.

To leave him without any magic, any ability to harm this way, she'd take everything he had.

She watched him debate, watched the rage in his pale eyes warring with the knowledge. He knew she'd soak up his power. He knew any strike at her right now was pointless, more dangerous to him than to her. But, oh, how he wanted to kill her. She could see it in the way his jaw muscles flexed, the way his eye twitched, and his lips lifted in a faint snarl.

"Go on," she said. "Do it."

Silence filled the hall, broken only by the sizzle of his bolt and her taunting whispers.

And then the quiet hiss of the vampires again, so faint at first she couldn't pick out the words. It took a moment for her to decipher their murmurs and when she did, she smiled wider.

"Do it. Kill her. Do it. Kill her. Do it. Kill her."

She wondered if they realized they were helping her by pushing the wizard to attack.

James had to know, at least some of it. He knew the attack would be pointless. He didn't stop his vampires, though.

Because he hoped the wizard would kill himself? Or because he wanted the wizard to eliminate her?

She'd have to ask him later.

The wizard's hand shook as he glared at her, the glowing ball of deadly blue energy on his palm vibrated with the movement.

And to her surprise, despite knowing better, he slammed the bolt against her shield. With a scream of outrage that silenced the vampires.

The bolt exploded in a flash of blue light. Cary closed her eyes but too late to protect her night vision. When she opened her eyes again, everything was dancing spots in darkness.

She sighed and waited for her vision to clear. Around her, more hissing and cursing from the vampires. They sounded pretty angry, probably because the flash of exploding light fucked up their vision, too.

She got the impression of the wizard still standing a few feet away and she was pretty sure that was him panting but since everything was still dark and dancing, she wasn't sure. Behind her, Sheldon was murmuring something, and to her right, she thought she heard the witches in conversation. As far as she could tell, James was still silent. She glanced at his thrown, blinking away the spots.

Slowly the room came back into view, the soft lights soothing away the glare of the wizard's attack. When she could see again, she noted James hadn't moved. But the vampire guards who'd been flanking the wizard and the triad had vanished. The vampires from the surrounding tables were all gone as well.

And the witches had formed a protective circle around themselves.

That drew Cary's attention. Hey, she could see the circle. That was different. She couldn't remember seeing Angie's before unless something made the circle flare. But Cary could very clearly see the faint blue line on the floor surrounding the witches and the cone of light that rose from the circle to form a protective barrier over them.

Maybe the danger around them was making the circle's magic bright? Although, what might be a threat to the witches here? Cary couldn't guess.

"Well, that was fun," she said into the silence, turning her attention back to James. "Where'd your people go?"

"Into the tunnels," he said.

"They didn't want to wait around and see if the wizard actually killed me?"

He gestured to the ground, not far from her shield. Some of the straw from under the tables had been strewn across the stone floor. And it was burning.

"Oops," she said and moved a little forward so her shield would put out the fire. The flames hissed and smoked as she moved close to them, the earthy smell of burnt straw surprisingly pleasant, offsetting the pervasive stench of vampire. "That wasn't my fault," she said. "Blame the asshole tossing around wizard bolts."

She shook her head at Zorianthus. "You knew that wouldn't work. Why bother?"

"You absorbed some of the magic," he said. "I know how to kill you, even when you're shielding others. I will kill you."

"Yeah, been there, done that," she said with a huff. "You don't have enough magic to kill me that way. But since you're approaching death fast, do you want to know what it was like? To die. Any of you? Want to know what happens when you die?"

The silence echoed.

James knew, sort of, because vampires technically died and then rose in their new body and form. According to her reading, it was a painful process, the death part, and some didn't rise after because the vampire who'd tried to turn them wasn't strong enough to make the process work. The transition wasn't something they were aware of, if they did rise after, but most retained memories of their death.

She could relate to that more now. She hadn't had to return as a vampire or anything, thankfully. But the moments she remembered before she'd released all the magic she'd absorbed from Faery… Those hadn't been a picnic.

"What happens, sister?" Justina asked, her voice deep and quiet in the mostly silent hall.

"It hurts. And then there's nothing," she said. "Nothing at all."

To be honest, she had no idea what might have happened if she'd stayed dead. She mostly tried not to think about what happened after death. She wasn't religious, so she didn't have a belief system in an afterlife. She'd seen too much in her time as a Protector to believe she had any answers at all, afterlife or not. She'd met gods and demons and evil and good. All right here on this plane of existence, some coming from different realities. As far as she could tell, anything and everything was possible, so she didn't write any of it off. And there was a *lot* she didn't know. Too much actually.

But one thing she did know was that after she'd released all that magic, she didn't remember anything else. She hadn't felt pain, she hadn't heard voices, she hadn't seen a light, she hadn't known anything at all. Just blackness. And nothingness.

And then, some time later, waking up in her bedroom with Deacon at her side.

She stared at Zorianthus. "It's not so bad, really. Dying."

The wizard didn't respond. But then what could he say?

"I'm here to tell you to leave Sheldon alone," she said. "I'm here to negotiate an end to this. All of this. Holland has to stay where he is. Unless you want all existence in this realm to end. I'm harder to kill than I look, and you waste a lot of energy continuing to try, so maybe we just call a truce and put an end to that. We go our separate ways. And neither of us has to deal with the other again." She shrugged. "Unless, of course, you keep trying to commit evil acts inside my territory. In which case, I'll have to stop you. But that's for another time. Right now, we put an end to all this. Because it's only going to get you killed quicker. And I'd rather the world didn't have to end in the process. I kind of like it here."

More silence followed her little monologue. She held Zorianthus's gaze. She still didn't have a clue what this was all about. What the endgame was supposed to be. That was monumentally irritating. But she'd been wanting to put an end to this wizard/Sheldon thing for months. Now was the time. They called a truce. Now.

And she'd stand here all night if that's what it took to finally, finally put an end to all this.

27

Into the quiet waiting, the witches began to chant, low and deep, their murmur in a language Cary didn't know. Although, there was so damned much she didn't know, she sort of expected that kind of thing. They'd used this language the last time they'd attacked her, and she'd tried to focus on it then, tried to decipher it, but she'd been protecting a thirteen-year-old kid who was scared, so she'd mostly focused on keeping him calm.

She had a little more time to study the language now, but it still didn't sound like anything she'd heard before.

"What is that?" she asked Jaxer, gesturing to the spell they were building. "What language? I can't…" She sighed. "Wait, you can't help. That's job related. What a pain in the ass."

Jaxer's chuckle was quiet but a little strained. "If it helps, the language is ancient, and isn't something that shows up in many of the books you've been studying."

"But it's in some of them so I should at least have a clue." She grunted in disgust. "Liruk will never let me live this down."

"You're not worried?" Sheldon asked.

"Wait, you've studied magic." She could ask the former wizard things without violating her test year rules. "Do you know what they're doing? What language that is?"

She turned a little to look at him, and was surprised to see he'd scooted closer to her, standing solidly between Jaxer and Deacon where they flanked her. His eyes were wide and round, the whites showing too distinctly. Sweat beaded along his brow.

"Hey," she said. "What's wrong? It's okay? They can't hurt you while I'm here. Nothing can."

A part of her brain rolled up into a ball of annoyance that she found herself trying to sooth *Sheldon*.

"They're calling power," Sheldon murmured. "A lot of power."

She'd sort of figured that. The last time that power had spun around her like a tornado and she'd been pretty sure it would have ripped her apart if she hadn't been protecting someone.

"Uhm," she glanced at the witches, "who are they trying to kill?"

"They aren't," Sheldon said, his voice strained. "That's not what their spell is about."

"Then…what?"

"No," the wizard snarled. "You can't!" He screamed at the witches. Another bolt formed on his palm, large and snapping with electrical energy.

He threw it before Cary could react, before she could move to protect the witches—argh, protecting more bad guys!—but the triad's circle took the bolt, absorbing it and keeping them safe. Zorianthus threw another bolt, and another, then a strike of lightning.

This last finally brought James from his throne. The lightning hit the triad's shield at the same moment James seemed to materialize next to the wizard. He pulled Zorianthus's arm up before the man could react and snapped his humerus with a shocking ease.

Zorianthus screamed.

Sheldon whimpered.

Cary gasped and gagged at the sight of the wizard's bone sticking out from his skin.

"Ew," she said to James. "Why the hell did you do that?"

James didn't look away from the wizard to answer her. "He goes too far inside *my* hive."

"But…" She glanced at the triad, still chanting and doing… whatever the hell they were doing. "You aren't stopping them?"

James released the wizard, who crumpled to the ground, holding his arm. When Zorianthus cursed up at him, James showed his teeth. "Careful, wizard. You've already violated the rules. One more show of disrespect and I'll rip your throat out."

Cary cringed, not so much at the threat, but at the fact that it crossed her mind James killing Zorianthus would solve a lot of problems. She hated that the thought had occurred to her with such ease, hated more it brought a sense of relief. Allowing James to do the very thing she'd demanded neither Deacon nor Jaxer do, the thing she'd specifically asked James *not* to do, seemed hypocritical. At the very least.

"No ripping throats out," she said to James. Then she relented. "Unless absolutely necessary, like he tries to kill you and you're defending yourself." And because it was his hive, and she'd already stepped on his toes once, and his eyes were very very yellow now, she added, "Please."

James didn't look at her, and there was nothing in his perfect stillness to reveal his reaction to her plea. But he didn't rip Zorianthus's throat out when the wizard cursed at him again, so she counted that as a win.

"What do we do about the witches?" Cary asked the room at large, more interested in James's lack of reaction to their spell than expecting anyone else to answer.

She wasn't disappointed in that.

"Can you…?" Sheldon moved close enough he was practically leaning against her back. "Can you stop them?"

She had no idea. "Depends on what they're doing," she hedged.

With their protective circle up, she actually wasn't sure if she could get through to stop them, if her magic would even work that way since her charges were already safely behind her.

She supposed stopping the triad might protect the hive and so her magic would help her with that.

Ugh. Protecting all the vampires who wanted her dead felt really stupid.

But it was her *job*.

Her inner whine was just as embarrassing as knowing she had to protect people who wanted to kill her.

She edged closer to the triad, a move that put James and the wizard at her back. That made the hair on her neck rise, even though she knew her shields still protected her and her charges. She didn't have to be looking at the bad guys for the magic to work. She just *preferred* they weren't at her back.

"Wait," Sheldon said, grabbing her shoulder. "What are you doing?"

"Trying to stop them," she said, frowning at him. "Just what you asked me to do."

"You said you didn't know if you could," he said. There was real panic in his voice now, real terror.

"Not exactly. Sheldon, what the hell? What are they doing that has you so terrified?"

"They're…" He swallowed visibly. "They're using the body swap spell. They're calling something…someone." His eyes darted around the room as if he were looking for an escape. "They're calling something big. Something that will inhabit them all at once."

"Woah, what?"

"They're using their bond as a triad," Sheldon said, his voice high and squeaky, the panic making him talk faster. "They're making themselves a single body to contain whatever they're calling. Don't you get it? Whatever's about to inhabit them is so powerful it needs all three of their bodies to contain it."

Cary faced the witches again, her eyes wide. Even Ho'Lud, an actual demon god, had only required one human body to enter this realm with his powers still intact. He'd had to carefully bind the human to him, which took time, but he could manage the feat in just that single body.

True, that body would die pretty quickly after taking in the power of a demon god, which limited Ho'Lud's time in this realm. But he'd found a way around that by arranging to have the human's body raised by a necromancer's powers. Or, at least that was the initial plan, which Cary had stopped.

But this… This wasn't the same thing at all.

Was it?

"Are they summoning a demon?" she asked on an awed whisper.

"Shit," Deacon muttered. "I really hate when they summon demons."

"Who?" Jaxer asked.

"Anyone." Deacon sighed, sounding resigned and irritated.

But when Cary glanced at him, his eyes were glowing golden yellow, his leopard near the surface and ready to break out to fight.

She faced the witches again. All three of them were glowing faintly, a white glow that encompassed them like a halo or an aura. Bright and getting brighter. Destroying the shadows.

Zorianthus screamed another denial. Cary turned to see James still standing perfectly still, his back to the witches and the growing light. But Zorianthus had forced himself to his feet. He stumbled a few steps toward the triad before collapsing to his knees again. Sweat covered his face, matted his gray hair to his skull.

"You can't!" Zorianthus shouted. "She'll kill us all. She'll ruin everything. You can't!"

She? She who?

Zorianthus moved his broken arm, almost as if he'd forgotten it was *not* in good shape. He screamed again, high and tight, and fell to his side, cradling his arm.

He met her gaze. "I hate you," he said. "Stop them! You have to stop them."

"I hate you too," she snarled. "Stop them from doing what?"

She turned back to the triad again. The glow had brightened so much she couldn't look directly at them, had to squint her eyes almost closed just to face their general direction.

Their chanting echoed in the huge hall, bouncing off the ceiling, seeming to repeat on itself again and again, creating a dissonance that hurt to hear. She couldn't imagine how James or Deacon with their sharp hearing could stand the noise. It was discordant, disconcerting... like music gone terribly wrong. There didn't seem to be a pattern to it, the words overrunning each other until they weren't like words anymore.

She'd never witnessed a body swap before. She'd seen a god channeled through a human medium. Seen a demon use that medium's body to get a view into this realm. She'd stopped a few attempted body swaps in her time. But she'd never seen one actually happen, never witnessed the results of one entity filling a body not their own while the original occupant went off to inhabit the body left behind.

It was all very icky and gross and she really didn't want to witness it now.

Especially with whatever the witches were calling, since they were changing bodies with something so horrible it terrified one of Cary's biggest enemies, scared him so much he'd asked for *her* help.

This was very very bad.

A sound like the clap of thunder boomed through the cavernous hall. Cary nearly jumped out of her skin, her already stretched nerves shocked by the sudden, loud noise.

Deacon hissed and behind her she heard Zorianthus scream another denial.

She couldn't see the witches through the glow surrounding them anymore. Just a white ball of brightness seen through her fingers, too bright to look at directly.

The thunder clap reverberated off the high ceilings, racing around the room and seeming to grow louder as it bounced off the walls. Cary wasn't sure whether to cover her eyes or ears anymore and it didn't seem to matter.

She heard someone scream again, and for a moment thought it might be her. Only her mouth was pressed together in a tight grimace against the noise and light. She realized the shriek came from all three of the witches, screaming with one voice, the sound piercing and loud enough to join the thunderclap on its bouncing race of echoes around the hall.

Cary was about to join the witches in their screams when the light, the sound, the echoes…everything cut off so abruptly, so unnaturally fast, she thought she might have passed out.

She blinked. No. Not unconscious.

Still seemed to be in her own body, though it took a few moments to ensure she could move her limbs and was still standing. The sudden cessation of sound and sight left her disoriented and wobbly.

But, she thought, not dead. And not knocked out.

And that was always a good thing.

Deacon's hand on her arm, warm and solid even through her jacket, nearly buckled her with the relief. She leaned back into him and his other hand squeezed her shoulder.

"Can you see anything?" she murmured and was grateful to hear her own voice.

"Not yet," he said, also quietly, his voice full of leopard growl. "And my ears hurt."

She nodded. She imagined James hadn't faired much better in the midst of all that noise and light. She didn't bother to call out to him to check, though.

He'd seemed aware of what the witches were calling, what they were doing, and he didn't stop them.

He knew what was about to happen.

Which put him many steps ahead of Cary.

A faint red light rose through the gloom, cutting the darkness back. Cary squinted as her vision returned, staring at the place where she knew the triad had been. She could just see the glow of their protection circle, but fuzzy, as if she were viewing it through fog.

It took her a moment to realize she was actually seeing the circle through fog. A thick, rolling boil of fog which hugged the ground inside the circle. It didn't seem able to spill out, though. Which meant, whatever it was and wherever it came from, the triad's magic contained it inside that space, keeping whatever they'd called separate from this realm.

Which demons lived in places full of fog instead of fire?

Most inhabited realms full of fire and brimstone and lava, just what someone would expect of demons. But there were a few realms that didn't conform to the cliché.

There were a couple full of ice sharp enough to cut like glass and so cold, it sucked the air out of human lungs in an instant. Humans rarely summoned demons from these realms because the human died too quickly if an ice demon actually showed up. Unless very careful, protective circles didn't contain the freezing air for very long and the hapless summoner who hadn't prepared properly ended up frozen to death.

The triad would have hardly called a demon from one of those realms, though. Would they? A body swap, rather than a traditional summoning might prevent everyone from freezing to death—which would be a good thing—but they'd have had to connect with the demon a few times to establish the bonds and spells to make the swap possible. A move that risked icy death.

The fog inside the circle swirled and moved, and what looked like lightning flickered through its depths, flashes of white but without the accompanying clap of thunder. Cary caught the faint scent of something acrid and musty, but not the stench of traditional sulfur, and not the nostril burning whiff of icy air. Not even an electrical smell of lightning.

Had she been wrong assuming they were going to trade bodies with a demon?

What was this?

Shadows moved within the fog, and the triad emerged. Justina in the lead, flanked by the other two. They moved as a unit, each step so well coordinated it was eerie. The white light encircled them still but not so bright Cary couldn't see them. They stood with their backs to each other, Justina facing Cary's direction, but every gesture, every step so simultaneous, a synchronized swim team would have been envious.

Justina's hair floated softly around her face in a breeze Cary couldn't feel.

So… Who spoke first?
And who the hell was inhabiting the triad?
"We are the Angel of Death."
Cary's mouth fell open.
Well. That answered that question.

28

Cary flinched at the voice that emerged simultaneously from the three mouths. It tumbled out slowly, building, like it came from a great distance before coalescing in the room. All three woman moved their mouths at once, the sound seemed to come from all of them. But it was one single voice. And scraped across Cary's ears like nothing she'd experienced before.

She'd met gods. And demons. And powerful beings of myth and legend. She'd even heard the banshee scream.

The Angel of Death was new.

"Hi," she said, because what the hell else did you say to an entity who required three human bodies to contain it and who proclaimed itself the Angel of Death. "So…not a demon then anyway. Right?"

"We are not a demon. We are the Angel."

"Cool, cool." Her voice shook as she spoke, her lips trembled. She tried to clear her throat, but that didn't do much to calm her racing heart or jumping nerves. "And, uh, what brings you here? Long way to come, I imagine. Something important?"

Deacon's hands on her shoulders tightened. She'd almost forgotten she was leaning into him. She should probably straighten away from him, but she couldn't find it in her to do so. His hands on her shoulders were solid and safe and real. And the moment felt too surreal to let go of the one point of reality she could sense.

"We are here to ensure our son does not fall into his father's hands."

"Uh." Okay. So. The Angel had a son. And she didn't want his father to take him. The only father-son problem currently under discussion was… "Oliver Holland?"

"Here that is his name. He is ours. His father will not have him. He is ours."

Holland was the son of a demon god and…the Angel of Death.

Of course he was.

Why not. What else could he possibly be, right? And he hated her and wanted to kill her, so… Sure. She'd made an enemy of the offspring of a demon god and the Angel of Death.

Good year. Good year.

She felt her knees buckle a little and straightened her stance in an attempt to not fall down in front of the terrifying entity she faced. That usually didn't help her position.

"So, uh, you know Holland isn't in this realm, right? I mean, the witches who loan you their bodies, must have told you at some stage."

"He is outside this realm, where his father cannot reach him." The triad, as one, turned their attention to the wizard who was still curled on his side, cradling his broken arm. "You must not retrieve him. He is not yours to claim. He is ours."

The Angel's voice had strengthened, growing louder but still with that echo as if it started a long way away before reaching the room. The sound hurt Cary's ears, but in a way that was hard to describe, like it beat up her brain and that somehow manifested as ear pain. Very very weird.

"I need him," Zorianthus whined. An actual whine. Not a demand, or a hiss, or a snarl. A whine, like a child speaking to a grownup as the grownup denied them a cookie. "I must get to him. I don't have much time left. I need him to complete…everything."

"He refused you for centuries," the Angel said. "He will not relent now."

Cary looked on in fascination. Now that the Angel entity wasn't speaking directly to her, she'd stopped trembling so hard. And the lure of possibly learning what all this was about was irresistible. Like watching a soap opera play out in front of her. Only the stakes were… well, the fate of the world.

"Without him, all this work, all these years…it will fail," Zorianthus continued to whine, pleading now. "If you stop me, if I don't reach him, everything will be lost."

"He failed to secure the power needed to fend off his father," the Angel said. "But his failure put him beyond his father's reach. This cannot be undone. This must be maintained. His father must not have him."

"I won't release him from the Nagas," Zorianthus said, bargaining now. "I can finish this work there."

Wow, the stages of grief playing out in real time. And fast. Cary tried not ping pong her gaze between the two speaking, but boy was it hard.

"They will not allow it. He is their prisoner. He is being punished for his crimes against them."

That didn't sound good.

"And he is content."

Uh? That sounded…wrong.

"He will not return. And he will not help you."

"I can't fail after all these years!" Zorianthus pushed to his feet, stumbled toward the circle. "You don't understand. He didn't understand either. But if I could just explain it to him again, just show him…"

Cary had to bite her tongue to keep from shouting out, "What?! What?!"

Someone had to say aloud what was going on soon or she was going to burst with the curiosity.

And that seemed a super bad idea at that moment.

Her attempt at keeping quiet and out of the way so this could play out were all for nothing, though, when the wizard pointed right at her with his good arm and shouted, "It's her fault. It's all her fault."

"Well, that's rude," Cary said. "I didn't start *any* of this. I'm not even old enough to have started it, since apparently *centuries* are involved. How dare you blame me, you sniveling jackass." And in front of the Angel of Death no less. Zorianthus wanted her dead, this was a hell of a way to arrange it. "I don't even know what's going on. I'm just here to keep you from killing Sheldon. And releasing Holland. And Lud from burning down our realm. And, as a bonus, I was hoping you'd stop trying to murder me. But *none* of this is *my* fault."

"You ruined everything!" Zorianthus screamed and lunged toward her.

Cary just made a face, knowing he wouldn't get through her shields and irritated beyond belief at being blamed for someone else's machinations. Just… Argh. Rude.

She was still mentally grumbling to herself when the wizard started to vibrate. Blood sprayed from his nose and mouth. His eyes bulged from his head. And with a scream that shattered the air, he…

Blew apart. Chunks of human body exploded, flying through the hall like shrapnel.

Ah.

"Well, that was messy," James said into the silence that followed Zorianthus's explosion.

Cary was still blinking at the chunks of body scattered just outside her shield, trying not to throw up as her brain processed the suddenness of what had just happened.

She wasn't making much progress with the processing, though. Her brain was working overtime not to absorb what she'd just seen.

"You could have just let my people feed on him," James said to the triad currently housing the Angel of Death.

"He was not yours," the Angel said.

James sighed audibly. "So you've told me before. Still. It would have been simpler." He glanced around. "And neater."

"You are used to blood," the Angel said.

"What just happened?" Cary murmured, though her throat was so clogged from shock and disgust, she wasn't sure anyone, even Deacon would hear her.

His hands were tight on her shoulders, probably too tight and she'd have bruises later, but she could barely feel around her shock, so she kind of liked that she could at least feel his hold. He grunted something near her ear. She couldn't decipher the grunt, but it told her he'd at least heard her.

Jaxer and Sheldon had both closed in behind her, so that all four of them stood in a tight knot. The physical contact with them all, even Sheldon, felt important in that moment. She'd gone numb, and any breach in that numbness meant she wasn't dead yet.

"Zorianthus has been…causing difficulties for several centuries," James said. "And it was time to eliminate the problem. However, he's cagey. And good at being where our Angel is not. In fact, he's been dodging her for…oh, a very long time."

"By moving to different bodies," Sheldon said, his voice higher than normal, but not shaking.

"Among other things," James said.

"Death comes to all, eventually," the Angel said, her voice moving in and out of sharpness, still rolling toward them from very far away. "We cannot be denied."

Justina's gaze turned toward Cary and all three witches moved, the same gesture, though their gazes were in different directions. Creepy and weird and disorienting, Cary thought with the part of her brain still functioning. It was a little part. Buried under a lot of noisy, screaming hysteria.

"You have danced with us once," the Angel said, "but briefly. You heard the banshee."

"Uh," Cary said. Really, it was the best she could do. There were bloody chunks of body not far from her foot, and it was super hard not to focus on that.

"We would welcome you back into the dance," the Angel said.

"Yeah, no, that's okay. I'm good." Panic made her voice squeak.

Deacon moved even closer, and she heard his soft growl. Oh please don't get any ideas, she thought at him, trying to will him to calm down. She didn't want him to aggravate an entity that could rip a person apart without actually touching them. The Angel had been *inside* a containment circle when she'd destroyed Zorianthus. The circle should have prevented that. Containment circles did that with demons. She had no idea if that process worked on gods that weren't demons. If she survived this, she'd have to add that to her To-Be-Studied list.

But it was pretty universally acknowledged that no matter the entity inside, a containment circle and the protective circles witches drew all served a similar function. To keep what was happening *inside* the circle contained so that it didn't affect the world *outside* the circle. And to keep the world outside of the circle from harming those inside the circle.

This was apparently a rule the Angel of Death didn't have to abide by.

In the less hysterical part of her brain, Cary wondered if she was really an angel or just Death or how that actually worked. Or was it just a title and this wasn't technically Death but just an entity that liked to call itself that. Or a real angel because, theologically speaking, they were related to demons in Christian dogma, which meant that this "angel" could be a sort of demon. She didn't remember the exact real-world relationship from her reading because…well, she hadn't encountered an angel before and kind of thought they didn't exist. This was nothing she'd ever had to face or fight. Not god or demon or dragon or vampire or wizard or anything else even remotely familiar.

There was more shrieking and screaming in her head. All nicely contained inside her skull so it didn't disturb the now eerily quiet hive. That was good.

A ridiculous thought crossed her mind. *This could be worse. She could be a ghost.* And that very nearly drove the shrieking out into the open, accompanied by a she's-gone-insane laugh.

And this entity claimed to be one of Oliver Holland's parents.

Wow. If she'd suspected his parentage was this…terrifying, she'd have been ever so slightly less willing to make an enemy of him. Slightly.

Though, to be fair, she probably would have made an enemy of him no matter what, given the circumstances. Still, she would have taken the whole thing a lot more seriously.

Around the screaming in her head, she said, "Do I get to know what's been happening now, or are we just going to be done here and

I'll leave and take my charges and we'll be fine? It's fine. No problem. No Holland being freed. No more death. It's good." She pressed her lips together to stop rambling.

Shit. She wasn't able to hold a conversation right now. Even if they told her what'd been happening, she probably wouldn't remember. She was having a very hard time not looking at the body chunks scattered across the ground.

And she was also having a very hard time not screaming and running for the elevator.

"The protégé is safe from his master," the Angel said. "But your job is not done, Protector."

Cary whimpered a little. Of course the Angel of Death knew what she was. Of course she did. Because it would be too much to ask that she didn't. That Cary had any secrets at all from *Death*.

Silence followed as Justina's eyes rolled back into her head, revealing only the whites. She stood still, as if she was looking at something inside her skull.

"This is really bad, huh?" Cary murmured to Jaxer.

"Yup," he murmured back.

"Did you know there was an actual Angel of Death? I mean, that's not just a name this entity is claiming, is it? Cause I could deal with that." Maybe. She'd still be on the verge of hysteria now, but it would be less…momentous.

"No. Not just a name. Actual Angel of Death."

There went that hope. "Real angel? Like, religiously speaking?"

"No. Just like Satan isn't the demon of religions. Just another demon. Angels are a species. Like Fae and demons and shapeshifters."

A species she hadn't actually thought existed in real life because she'd never met one and wasn't that a mistake she'd never make again.

"Are you supposed to be teaching me this or are we cheating?" she asked, her gaze still locked on Justina.

"If we die, it won't matter."

"Very helpful."

Her stomach was so tight with fear she could barely breathe. Facing a wraith, which might as well have been a ghost, had nearly broken her brain. Hearing the banshee scream at the same time hadn't helped. She'd only known later the banshee scream had been portending Cary's own death. In the moment she'd heard the scream, she'd just been overwhelmed with general terror.

This...definitely rivaled that. Worse actually. Because, just like ghosts, there wasn't a damned thing you could do to destroy, end, or otherwise eliminate *Death*. It just was. There was no way to fight a ghost, and no way to ultimately win against Death. Even the universe would eventually die one day. At least, that's what Angie had told her. And she trusted Angie's knowledge of these things.

"Is the Angel of Death actually *Death*?" she asked. She was kind of hoping it wasn't. That death was something different and the Angel was just sort of good at doling out death.

Justina's eyes were still rolled back in her head, her head tipped backward along with the other three witches so that they touched at just the tops of their skulls. Cary realized all their eyes were showing just the whites at the moment.

"The Angel is as close as you get in a physical incarnation," Jaxer answered her question. "But not, technically, death death. That's just a process. Not an entity."

"Can this entity be...prevented from doing as she likes?"

"Depends."

"That's not an answer."

"It's the only one I've got. Depends on the situation. And what she's facing."

"But she's not...impossible to defeat, right? She had a son. With a demon. Who is a demon. She's...well, not just a process, right?"

"The Angel is not. The Angel is an entity."

"But?" She could hear it in his voice.

"But this particular angel... She can kill gods."

"Uh."

Yeah, that was all she had. No clever comeback or observation. Her brain just wasn't up to all this.

"Demon gods?" Deacon asked, his first contribution to the conversation.

And a spectacularly relevant one at that.

She straightened. "Are we…are we in the middle of some sort of messy god divorce? Is she trying to kill Lud?"

"Got me," Jaxer said. "The Angel doesn't consult with me on her plans."

"I'll handle the sarcasm, here, thanks," Cary said sourly. "Can she kill a demon god or not?"

"Yes."

Wow. That was…

Interesting.

30

ary was still grappling with the implications of that last revelation, that the Angel of Death could kill Lud, when all three witches—in unison—lifted their heads and Justina refocused on her, her eyes still not quite her own, but at least not rolled back in her skull anymore.

"Our son is no longer beyond the reach of his father. He must also be protected."

"Woah woah woah." Cary raised her hands, palms out. "You aren't... You aren't saying I need to protect *Holland*. Right? Because, yeah, no that's not happening. Protecting Sheldon was bad enough."

"Hey," Sheldon said, his protest weakened by the trembling in his voice.

"Do I have to remind you in this very moment why?" she asked over her shoulder without looking at him.

She felt him shuffle a little but he didn't move away and his grumbling response was too quiet for her to hear. She was sure Deacon did, though, so she'd ask later. Now, she had to focus on this current crisis.

"We have eliminated your greatest enemy." Justina gestured to the scattered body parts Cary was still desperately trying to ignore. "You owe us, Protector."

"Ah, no. I didn't ask for this. And he wasn't my *greatest* enemy. Just one of many." She made a face. That didn't reflect well on her. "And anyway, Oliver Holland is closer to my *greatest* enemy. He wants me dead, too, you know. Why do you think I'm here? To prevent that."

"The protégé can exchange bodies with him," the Angel said.

"No," Sheldon said, his voice quiet. He wasn't denying the Angel so much as revealing his horror at that thought.

On this, Cary and Sheldon could agree. "No," Cary said, her denial firm. "That's not happening. Besides, poor old Sheldon here would be a terrible body for Holland. Holland would hate it." Over her shoulder, she conceded, "Sorry. But you know he would."

"I know. It sucks."

Sympathy for Sheldon still felt wrong, so she refocused on the triad. "Also, Holland would have to…work with Sheldon to make that stick. The process won't work cold. And even if it did, there's no telling what that would do to Sheldon, and my current job is to protect him, so… No. No body swaps."

She paused to consider how Holland had presented himself to the world. An older but fit and attractive English man of great wealth. The wealth hadn't been an illusion. He'd been a freed demon in this world for centuries and had accumulated more than enough wealth to last any ordinary human that many lifetimes. When she paused to think about it, though, she had to wonder how he'd done the "human" look. Illusion? Spell? Demon magic? Taken over a body the way his father had attempted to do to enter this realm?

She'd written off that last possibility after dealing with Lud because the body would have died. Holland was powerful. Really really powerful. No human body would have been able to contain that much demon power for long.

And what Lud had been intending, taking over a human body…it wasn't the same process, the same spells and work that went into what Sheldon and Zorianthus had done. Not even the same end result. What Lud had be intending was a full-on possession. The human didn't swap places and occupy Lud's demon body while the demon walked around in a human body. What the demon god had intended was subsuming the human under its own essence, taking over the body and essentially destroying the human who'd been living inside it.

Classically speaking, it was just straight up demon possession. Only demon possession was a lot harder to accomplish than the movies made it out to be.

What Sheldon and Zorianthus did was an exchange. Two human essences couldn't occupy the same body at once, or so the theory went. So when one entered a new body, the other *had* to go into the old body. A balance. Possession and body swapping on the surface seemed similar, but they weren't in outcome or execution.

So it was only just occurring to her that Holland might be able to body swap. She was certain that wasn't what he'd done to occupy his current look. That was definitely magic of some kind. An illusion to show the world a human façade. But could Holland trade out his demon body and move into a human body the way Sheldon and the old wizard had? *Would* he give up his demon body and all its powers in a swap like that?

And what human would be stupid enough to take over the demon body when it was currently being tortured by the Nagas…and hunted by a demon god?

"Is that what Zorianthus was trying to do?" Cary asked aloud.

"What?" Jaxer murmured.

"Was Zorianthus trying to…body swap with Holland? Was he hoping to take over Holland's body? Cause…yeah, that seems like a really really bad idea."

"He'd have been a demon with a demon's powers," Sheldon pointed out.

"A demon who's currently a prisoner, probably being tortured, and who's demon god father wants to recapture him for nefarious reasons that Holland was so desperate to avoid he needed the Nagas' city and power to prevent it. Of all the possible demon bodies to occupy, Holland's seems like the least…good."

James chuckled at her description. She'd nearly forgotten he was there. Wow. That wasn't wise at all, forgetting about the presence of a Master vampire. Especially one who seemed to know more about all this than she did.

"Zorianthus, for all his centuries of life and study," James said, "didn't always understand much beyond his own needs and driving obsessions. He waved away anything that didn't fit precisely with his plans as something that didn't concern him."

"So… He wanted to body swap with Holland?"

"He intended to offer Holland freedom in exchange for a temporary swapping of bodies, yes," James said. "Zorianthus has spent his life looking for the universal panacea."

"Like an alchemist?" Like the thing Bleak had been searching for?

"In his original incarnation, that's what Zorianthus was. An old school alchemist."

That was a super weird coincidence. "I don't suppose his name back then was Bleak?"

James smiled, a wide, teeth revealing smile that was very disconcerting. "No. He was a contemporary of Bleak's. And he studied Bleak's research. But no… Bleak poisoned himself and died a long time ago."

"Where you around then?" Cary asked, because she couldn't really resist.

James's age was impossible to gage. He had to be old. Very old. But sometimes, like now with that toothy grin, he seemed like a much younger, less controlled vampire. He had to be doing that on purpose. Masters never did anything without a purpose. But what the hell was the point except to keep her on edge?

Or maybe that was the whole point.

If that was the plan, he was doing a damned fine job of it.

He didn't answer, but he didn't drop his smile either. "Zorianthus believed he'd found an easier way to both extend life and gain magic than Bleak's more…poisonous efforts."

"Body swapping," Cary said.

"He learned he could not only take over another body with enough time and the right spells, but that he absorbed their magic too. With ever new body, he built his powers. Developed more and more. Changed into a more powerful human with each permanent swap. Just as Bleak predicted, Zorianthus's cells changed—or I should say the cells of each individual he inhabited changed—combining old with new to create something more. It didn't matter if Zorianthus's protégé had a great deal of magic, though that helped." James flicked a brief glance at Sheldon.

"What about a human without magic?" Cary asked. "Would he body swap with someone like that just to stay alive?"

"Someone with no magic wasn't helpful. And Zorianthus craved power too much to jump to someone who wouldn't contribute some level of power to his own. But he didn't need much from a protégé to increase his magic exponentially with each incarnation. And with each…theft of magic, he became something slightly different than he'd been the incarnation before. Always with an eye to being *more*."

"Would a temporary body swap with a demon have done that for him, even though it would have been temporary?"

"Our son cannot die," the Angel said, entering the conversation with that echoing, deep voice that made Cary's bone's ache a little. "Even I cannot kill him."

Whoa. Wait. That was new. "Because…because you're his parent?"

All three of the witches nodded in unison.

So…

Holland couldn't die.

Not even the Angel of Death could kill him. But she could kill Holland's demon god father.

Cary was starting to get a glimmer of why Ho'Lud might have wanted Holland back.

She tried not to shiver. "Zorianthus thought he could soak up a little of Holland's immortality, is that it?" Not just any demon's immortality. A demon who couldn't be killed even by the Angel of Death. "Did he know? Did Zorianthus know that Holland was different to other demons? That his immortality was different."

Most demons were immortal in the ways humans thought of life and death. But that immortality didn't mean they couldn't be killed.

They just couldn't be killed by humans typically. The best humans could do with most demons was send them packing back to the demon realms, cutting them off from this world and the damage they did here.

But demons *could* be killed. By other demons. By demon gods. By other entities.

At least, most demons could.

"Zorianthus discovered the truth of Holland's imperviousness to death several centuries ago," James said. "Not long after Holland was allowed sanctuary here by the demon hunters."

A demon hunter had told Cary that Holland had been given sanctuary here, but she still found it weird. That seemed…contrary to the demon hunter job description.

"He's been pestering Holland for centuries to allow him a temporary body swap," James said. "Holland has repeatedly denied the wizard's requests."

So that's what the Angel and Zorianthus had been talking about.

"All Zorianthus's human bodies eventually died, no matter what he did," James continued. "And training a new body took time. Every time. Every incarnation he had to spend years finding and then preparing his next body." Another glance at Sheldon. "When you ruined his efforts this time, you…scared him."

"Wait, *I* scared *him*?" That didn't sound right.

"You laid bare all the vulnerabilities and weaknesses in his plans, in his progress over all these centuries. All it took was one tenacious Protector who just happened to be able to absorb magic, and he was on the edge of dying, of losing everything he'd spent hundreds of years developing and accumulating. You proved to him that his supposed 'immortality'…wasn't."

"Not on purpose," she said defensively. "Although I'm not particularly sorry about that."

"He really didn't have any interest in Holland's squabble with his father," James said.

"You told me he didn't even know about Lud," Cary accused. Though why she expected James to be honest with her all the time, she couldn't guess. He was a Master vampire. Subterfuge and outright lying were required for Masters.

"He didn't know Holland's father would destroy this realm," James said, "though he did know about Holland's parentage. But as you heard, he didn't care, or believe. Zorianthus was too focused on his own needs. And he was desperate now. Thanks to you."

"Not really sorry about that," she said. "What made him think Holland would help him now, after denying him all this time?"

"Holland's captivity, and his hate for you."

"Huh?"

James grinned again. Geez, that was disturbing.

James said, "Zorianthus intended to offer Holland both freedom and revenge against you in exchange for finally allowing a temporary body swap. All he wanted was an hour inside Holland's body. Just long enough to take in some of the demon's magic. Long enough to take in his immortality." James shrugged. "Or so the theory goes. Whether it would have even worked…" He glanced around at what remained of the wizard. "We'll never know now."

"It would not have worked as he assumed," the Angel said. "He would have burned."

"With the rest of us when Lud came for Holland?" Cary asked.

"When he entered our son's body. He was human. He would have burned."

Ah. Well. That didn't sound pleasant.

"Wait, you wanted Holland to body swap with Sheldon. That means Sheldon would have burned? Why the hell did you suggest that?" Obviously, the Angel didn't care if Sheldon died or not, but still… It was pretty rude to suggest that option and *not* tell them it would have killed Sheldon.

"Sheldon has no more magic," the Angel said. "It would not be the same for him."

Cary blinked. "So, the only reason Zorianthus would have failed is…because he has magic?"

All three witches nodded in unison again.

Huh.

She shook her head. This was getting complicated. "Still," she said. "Sheldon isn't exchanging bodies with Holland on my watch. That still defeats the purpose of my protecting him, one way or the other."

Because it would mean Holland was back in this realm and that would bring Lud and realm destruction.

But if Ho'Lud reentered this realm normally, the way another demon might, he had to sacrifice a *lot* of power to do it. He couldn't just come back and retake Holland without giving up a lot to get here. That was the entire reason he'd attempted the possession and necromancer thing Cary had stopped.

"He cannot enter this realm without weakening himself," the Angel said, confirming Cary's thoughts as if she'd read her thoughts—which given she was the Angel of Death was entirely possible. But also terrifying. "And if he does that, we will kill him. We are his future, his fate. He cannot avoid us forever. It has been ordained. He will die."

"Unless he reclaims Holland," Cary said. "Because you can't kill Holland."

Ho'Lud wanted to use his son's ability to survive the Angel of Death to keep the Angel from killing him. Now this all made sense. Sort of. In a weird, dysfunctional family sort of way.

"You said Holland is no longer outside of his father's reach in the Naga city," Cary said. "Why? How?"

"The wizard's search brought the location of our son to his father's attention. He monitors this realm, even if he cannot return yet." Justina's head tilted to one side. The movement rippled through the other two like a wave until all three of the witches had their heads tilted. "You did not reveal our son's location to his father. Why?"

"Seemed like a bad idea at the time," she said.

She hadn't really known what Lud wanted with Holland. And really, she'd have preferred to have Lud and Holland well out of her hair. But mostly, she hadn't wanted the demon god to know about the Nagas. She didn't want him anywhere near their city—even if she'd known where the new entrance was, which she didn't. The Nagas were powerful, and perfectly capable of protecting their city and their people. But it seemed unreasonable to ask them to defend their city from an actual demon *god*.

"Can he find the entrance to the city?" Cary asked. "Now that he knows where to look?" This seemed like a very bad bit of news, that Lud knew where Holland was. But if he couldn't find the entrance, he couldn't go smashing in to retrieve his son, and that would be good.

"He is hunting for it now," the Angel said. "And he will find it eventually. This realm has few secrets from the gods."

Shit. How did she warn the Nagas? Maybe they knew already?

"What can I do?" she asked the Angel. This wasn't about protecting Holland, or even Sheldon. An entire city could be at risk if Lud found the Nagas. She had to warn them somehow.

"We will contact an old friend. The demon god must not be allowed to reclaim our son. He must die as has been ordained."

The Angel of Death had friends? Wild. She refocused on the problem at hand. "Okay, I absolutely agree with the first part, but… Just out of curiosity, *why* must he die? I mean, it'd be nice to have one less demon god running around the place, but mostly they ignore my realm, so you know, nothing personal against them. Why does this particular god have to die?"

The triad began to shake, their bodies vibrating, hard enough it looked painful.

Had she said something wrong?

Bright light flashed around the triad, encompassing them fully in a bubble of white. Cary squinted her eyes nearly closed and raised her hand to her face to ward off the glare. The light continued to brighten until it felt like it filled the entire hall.

And then it snapped out, suddenly and completely.

Plunging them back into impenetrable darkness.

31

*C*ary waited out the dancing spots and utter blackness as her vision readjusted. Again.

The pervasive scent of vampires and the grosser smell of ripped apart wizard guts—which she'd been trying really hard to ignore but couldn't now that her vision was compromised and her sense of smell heightened—surround her, making the blackness feel even more oppressive and choking.

"Everyone okay?" she asked into the silence.

A series of grunts from the men at her back answered her. That was reassuring. She gripped Deacon's hand tight when he wove his fingers through hers. From a few yards away, she heard James murmur something too quietly for her to hear, but it confirmed he was still alive.

No sound came from the general direction of the triad.

Cary couldn't see the glow of their magic circle anymore either. Although, to be fair, she couldn't see anything at all yet. But she focused on that general area of the room, blinking against the spots in her vision, and there didn't seem to be any blue light anymore.

She wasn't sure whether to be worried about them or not. Body swapping with the Angel of Death. That just seemed…more complicated than it had to be.

"Why not just channel her?" Cary wondered aloud, her voice low. "Why an actual body swap?" Because that meant the witches had actually been somewhere else during all this, in the Angel's body. Controlling the Angel's body. Whatever the hell the Angel's real body was.

Wow. That had to be strange.

And what did that do to the witches, being in and controlling an Angel's body? An Angel that could met out death so easily.

She blinked harder, squinting her eyes to try and force her night vision back quicker. She had so damned many questions still. Every answer just raised more questions.

It was kind of irritating.

When the faint glow of the ground level lights returned and she could finally see through the gloom, she edged toward the triad, carefully avoiding anything on the ground that looked…lumpy. All three men behind her stuck close, moving with her, which was nice. She hated having to nag them to stick with her so they were all safe.

The three witches laid sprawled on the ground, seemingly unconscious, though it was hard to tell in the dim light. She had to get very close before she could be sure they were breathing, but they were, and their eyes were closed. Cary couldn't see the protection circle anymore. She nudged the place on the ground where she'd last seen it. There was no rebound, and no reaction from her own shields, so it had likely collapsed with the witches.

"You've seen them do this before," she said over her shoulder to James. Then blinked. He wasn't there anymore.

She looked around frantically, only to realize he'd silently returned to the throne and was casually splayed in the huge seat, leaning against the armrest like nothing had just happened and there weren't bits of wizard body all around the hall.

"You need a bell so I can hear when you move," she said.

"That would entirely defeat the dramatic purpose," he said.

She sighed. "Are they going to be okay?"

"Of course. As you've guessed, this wasn't their first exchange with the Angel."

"How long will they be out?"

"Depends. They held the swap for longer than usual. They may be unconscious for a few hours."

Cary glanced back at the witches and let out a long breath. Shame. She would have liked to ask them some more questions. But she didn't want to wait around in the hive. Too many vampires.

"They'll be safe here?" she asked James.

He raised his brows, feigning obvious offense.

She returned the gesture deadpan.

He shrugged. "They'll be safe. We've made previous arrangements for just such circumstances."

"How often have you been around when they do this?"

"A few times. The frequency has increased lately."

"Because of the wizard…Zorianthus." She could freely say his name now that he was dead.

Wow. The wizard who'd been trying to kill her for months was just…dead. Just like that. Without any ceremony or even a real fight.

That was going to take some time to sink in.

Despite the evidence surrounding her, the shock of such a sudden death meant she couldn't quite believe it had happened. Plus, she was trying really hard to ignore the "evidence" around her because it was gross.

"Did they do this while they were working for Holland?" she asked. That added another layer to their participation in helping him find the Naga city. But also, "What do the witches get out of this arrangement?"

"That last you'll have to ask them," James said. "They have been… adamant in keeping that a secret from me."

That told her a lot and nothing at all. Argh, all the questions. But okay. For now.

What they knew was that the Angel said Holland wasn't safe in the Naga city anymore—not that he'd been technically safe before, just out of his father's range, which seemed good for all concerned—and that the Angel was going to talk to an "old friend" about that.

One of the Nagas, maybe? Did that mean the Angel knew where they were? How to get to them? If so, why not warn Holland herself?

Cary shook her head. Later. Save the world first. Pester everyone with questions later.

"Can I leave the witches here safely, without them becoming vampire food?" she asked, again, just to be sure. Not that she wanted to keep protecting bad guys, but bad guys seemed to be all there were about at the moment, and unfortunately several of them needed protecting.

"I give you my word they'll be safe in my care," James said. Very seriously.

And he gave his word. That was both rare and important. At least in the vampire world. Masters rarely did that. Not unless they truly meant it. It was a point of pride from a group that was, generally, from very different eras. Their word, so rarely given, meant something.

"Thank you for that," she said, acknowledging the seriousness of the oath. "Hopefully, we won't see each other again for some time."

James's smiled flashed big again, fully revealing teeth. That was just *so* disconcerting. He knew it, or he wouldn't do it, but still… Whatever game he was playing with her was annoying and she'd be very happy to put an end to it.

"Good luck with saving the world," he said. "Again. If you need our help, my hive is at your disposal. For this particular issue."

"Mm hmm." She wasn't sure whether that was good or not, considering so many of the vampires still wanted her dead. And she never had found out how the vampires ended up in the middle of all this. Their participation was still very suspect. "We'll just see ourselves out. No one's going to attack, right?"

"You'll be safe even if they do."

"Ha. Thanks."

Despite James's dig, though, they made it back out of the farmhouse without encountering any other vampires. She had to guess having the Angel of Death called to the hive didn't go over well with the others—they'd mostly become vampires to *avoid* death.

"Now what?" Sheldon asked as they hovered outside Deacon's SUV.

"Now," Cary said. "I think you're officially safe. So you can go home. Just don't attempt to murder anyone, and we don't have to ever see each other again."

Something she couldn't quite read moved through Sheldon's expression before he reverted to the dead-eyed look of someone not really there inside. "So that's it. I'm useless to you now too."

"You were never use*ful* to me," she said in exasperation. "You were a job, a person I had to—reluctantly—protect to avoid the world ending. Now, thanks to a very abrupt act by the Angel of Death, you can go about your business so long as it doesn't involve doing evil things I have to stop. Anymore. Your value and worth as a human being going forward is up to you."

She wasn't sure why she was so annoyed with him. Why she even felt the need to add that last sentence. She didn't even like him. He was a *murderer*.

But some damned part of her kept feeling sorry for him and wanted him to be and do better, to regret his actions and try to make amends, to *acknowledge* he'd done evil and work to atone. And she was super super irritated by that part of her. He wasn't one of the good guys. He hadn't proved himself one of the good guys. He hadn't even *tried* to atone. And until *he* put in an effort to change, he was still the little shit who'd tried to murder Deacon.

She grunted in annoyance at both herself and Sheldon. "Jaxer met us back at my house. I need to talk with you." She slammed into the car, ignoring the men as she brooded about her stupid feelings and worried about what to do next.

If she had to protect Oliver Holland, after all this, she was going to be so pissed.

32

Cary walked through the door of her house and dropped to her knees to accept doggie hugs and licks and all the dog attention she'd needed for the last forty-eight hours.

"I missed you guys too," she murmured into Buck's thick fur. She pulled back a little and took his face in her hands. "You're feeling okay, right? No fevers? No need to go all big and triple-headed?"

Buck let his tongue loll out and sat on the rug, giving her his Labrador equivalent of a smile. He didn't feel particularly warm, and he was acting like his usual self. That was a huge relief. Good to know the Angel of Death didn't have the same effect on him as Lud.

Marianne rose from the couch, turning the TV off with the remote and dropping the remote onto the coffee table. "They've been just fine," she assured. "We've been having a great visit, talking about all sorts of things. Pickles is a great listener."

"Yeah she is." Cary took Pickles's face in her hands and gave her a squish and a hug. Pickles let out a deep, happy woof.

Fred bounced off her shoulder, then charged Deacon, bouncing off his thigh in a leap that would make his terrier mother proud. Deacon squatted down to give Fred some attention, scratching his stomach when the dog flipped over.

"Why are you up at this hour?" Cary asked Marianne. It had to be at least three in the morning, maybe later. She hadn't actually paid attention to the clocks on the way home. It might even be near sunrise now.

They'd dropped Sheldon off, with very little fanfare and a passing admonishment not to get into trouble, then come straight back to her house in relative silence. She was pretty overwhelmed and exhausted by the night, and she'd lost track of time in all that.

"My assistant is looking after the shop tomorrow, so I have the day off," Marianne said. "The pack and I wanted to stay up late watching scary movies." Marianne waved away Cary's narrow-eyed look. "Don't worry. I covered Fred's eyes when things got too spooky."

Cary snorted. That wasn't why she was worried, but she let the subject go. For now.

"So, everything's good?" Marianne asked. "No one dead that shouldn't be?"

"So far," Cary said. "The wizard is dead, though."

"That's a relief. Who killed him?"

"You took that news better than I'm taking it."

"Why? Isn't it a relief?"

"It was very…sudden, and I'm still in shock," Cary said.

Marianne went with her into the kitchen while Cary made coffee—which she desperately needed because she had to stay up a few more hours, long enough to talk with Jaxer—and Cary told her everything that had happened that night.

Marianne let out a long, low whistle. "Angel of Death. Well, that's… Something."

"Right?" Cary leaned against the counter, cradling her mug and savoring the coffee's rich scent. She could just hear Deacon in the living room quietly talking with the dogs, giving her and Marianne some privacy. She smiled a little when she heard him tell Fred the vampire hive had been redecorated.

The way he was with her little dog pack—despite being a cat!—was one of the many reasons she loved that man.

"Does this mean Holland and his daddy are going to be rejoining us in this realm?" Marianne asked. She waved away an offer of coffee. "I will need to sleep eventually."

"You…managing that? Sleep I mean."

"You're changing the subject."

"I worry."

"You can stop for now. I'm fine and you have bigger things to worry about."

"Nothing's more important than my friends."

Marianne smiled at her, softly. "I think the destruction of the world just might be."

Cary gave in with a shrug. "But only barely. And only because it would mean you'd be destroyed too."

"You are very well suited to your job, you know that?" Marianne said.

"I don't particularly feel like it, but thank you for saying that." She sipped her coffee. "Jaxer should be here soon. We have some things to talk about. I have no idea if Holland and his father and the Angel are going to be a thing. I'm still processing what happened tonight. And not sure I understand any of it."

"Fair enough. You want me to leave before Jaxer arrives? Though it'd be a pity not to gaze upon his beauty."

"Ha! Don't say anything like that to him. He's vain enough as is."

"What's going on with him and Eriana? Any good gossip?"

"He won't tell me. But he gets all jumpy and defensive when I bring her up, so that's a good sign."

Marianne chuckled.

"You don't need to leave. It's too late…or early anyway. But don't feel like you have to stay up either. We'll be quiet so you can sleep."

Marianne waved a hand in the air, and Cary noticed she'd had her nails done recently in a beautiful magenta color, the length longer than she usual got since she spent so much time working with her hands.

"I took a nap this afternoon," Marianne said. "I'm not really tired at the moment. Which was why I was up late watching campy horror movies."

"You sure you're okay?"

"No," Marianne admitted. "But better than I was. And we'll talk all about it after you save the world."

Cary snorted. "I keep having to do that. We'd never have time to talk if we let that get in the way."

"You do have a very demanding job," Marianne conceded. The doorbell sounded…and continued to buzz like someone was holding a finger to it. "And that would be the exquisite but troublesome faery."

Cary laughed as she carried her coffee out to the living room. Deacon had already opened the door for Jaxer.

The two men greeted each other with nods and mumbled hellos that were *almost* friendly. Cary hid her grin in her mug.

"So," she said to Jaxer. "Holland and Lud. Again. And me still in my seventh year. I know I'm not supposed to ask for help, but…what now?"

Jaxer greeted Marianne with a kiss on her cheek that she took as her due, then he flopped onto the couch, sprawling out in a way that took up fully half the space.

Cary shook her head at him and settled onto a chair while Marianne sat on the couch and Deacon took the chair opposite Cary.

"Liruk and Wisat should be here soon," Jaxer said. "This is…a little different to the usual seventh year test for Protectors."

"It is?" Cary leaned forward. "So…not everyone has to face the Angel of Death and demon gods in their test year?"

"Not typically," Jaxer said with a slight shrug.

She couldn't tell if he was kidding or not. And frankly, she didn't want to know.

"I feel like this isn't over, and yet, I did my job. I kept Sheldon safe. The wizard isn't an issue anymore." She shuddered and took another gulp of coffee. "He's not going to free Holland and start the apocalypse now. But… What the Angel said. That Lud knows which realm Holland is in now. That isn't good. It won't be good for the Nagas, and it won't be good for our realm."

"Nope," Jaxer confirmed.

"Helpful. So, what do we do? Or do we do anything? I mean, the

Nagas are magic, they have lots of power, lots of resources. If they're forewarned, they can protect themselves, right?"

"They can. If they get the warning. But remember it takes a lot of time and power to move their connection with this realm. That's why Holland was almost able to invade the city. The move isn't easy. They do it maybe once every century or two, just to avoid anyone finding them, but more often than that and it can seriously drain them."

"They just moved less than a year ago. Can they do that again so soon?"

"I'm not sure. That's not the kind of thing they'd allow an outsider to know."

Cary leaned back in her chair and let out a long breath. The night she'd faced down Holland's army, hoping against hope to give the Nagas the last bit of time they needed... She'd intended to be the wall, the stalling tactic, so they could finish their magic and save their city. But a lot of the night was pretty blurry to her now. She knew what had happened, of course. But it was fuzzy at the edges now, and she sometimes wondered if her memory was accurate.

"Nira's brother, Zakin... Would he meet with us? Somewhere in this realm. So we could warn him all this is going on." Holland had murdered Nira during his attempt to take the city. Her brother Zakin had helped Cary get between Holland's army and the city's entrance so she could do her wall thing. She hadn't seen him since that night, but he was the only one she could think of who might agree to see her.

"Possibly, if we could figure out how to contact him," Jaxer said. "He did say the Nagas would help you if you had need."

She smiled a little. "And then left me no way to get in touch. Which, frankly, I think was pretty clever on their part. But this isn't help I need. I just don't want them caught off guard by Holland's father coming for his son." She paused. "Do you suppose they'd just release Holland back into this realm, to get him out of their city? They can't kill him—which I have to say is a truly terrifying fact to have learned this late in the game."

Marianne grunted in agreement, and Cary lifted her mug to Marianne in a solidarity solute.

"But they could release him," she continued. "Kick him out of their realm. Then Lud would have no reason to bother with them."

"He'd have his son, then, though," Jaxer said. "And he'd destroy this realm. Which would, in turn, destroy the Nagas. Their realm can't survive long cut off from this one. Like Faery, they need the connection."

She knew that. She was just… Hoping for an answer that wasn't the answer she'd been trying not to contemplate. She squeezed her eyes closed very tight.

"I'm gonna have to do it, aren't I?" She couldn't even say it out loud. She didn't want to say it. She didn't want to do it. This should be someone else's job. Someone else's responsibility. Not hers. Why hers?

Wrong place at the wrong fucking time, and now she was forced into protecting all the damned bad guys. It was absolutely infuriating.

And terrifying.

And too awful to say.

But she said it anyway, hoping someone would tell her she was wrong. "I'm going to have to protect Holland from his father." She blinked open her eyes when the silence in the room stretched. "Fuck me. I am, aren't I?"

"Yes," a new voice answered.

Everyone turned to face Liruk and Wisat where they'd materialized into the room, standing near her fireplace.

"Weaver," Wisat greeted Marianne.

Marianne nodded to him. "I'm not leaving," she said.

Wisat smiled. "I wouldn't expect it."

Liruk's lips flattened but she didn't argue the point. "Protector, this is indeed a dire situation. But our realm must be saved."

"Yeah, I know, I know. I just didn't think saving the world would involve so much of me keeping the bad guys from my past safe from… from worse bad guys from my past." She wanted to scream and cry at the same time. Instead, she took another gulp of coffee. "These are the nights—" She glanced at the window. The sky was lightening, a soft gray cloudy morning dawning. "The days," she amended, "when I really hate my job."

No one responded to that.

"How?" She faced Liruk again. "And where? I'm not bringing that demon into my home. I can't get to the Nagas. And—" she raised a hand before Liruk could speak, "—I don't want them any more involved than they have to be. They've dealt with enough because of Holland. I can't ask them to do more."

Wisat and Liruk exchanged a look. Which was never a good sign for Cary.

"We have seen…a darkness spreading over the land," Liruk said, her voice taking on a cadence Cary had never heard before. "A harbinger of death. Wings spreading darkness. And you, Cary Redmond, at the center of it all."

33

"**W**ell. That sucks," Cary said into the silence that followed Liruk's pronouncement.

Even the dogs had gone quiet where they laid under the big living room bay window. She met Deacon's worried gaze across the coffee table. The faint glow of his leopard lit the gold in his eyes.

"Why me?" she asked.

She hated that question. It was a nonsensical question under most circumstances. Why not "you"? But in this particular case, really, why her? She wasn't anyone special. She was just…her. There were a lot more powerful people in the world. A lot more important and significant people in the world. Beings that were much more capable of handling this sort of thing. She was a human woman with the unfortunate tendency to absorb magic and a decent Protector who could channel someone else's magic really well. Outside of that, she just wasn't particularly skilled or knowledgeable. Especially in this world of demons and angels and death.

Why the hell would *she*, of all people, have to be at the center of this darkness?

"Bad luck," Jaxer said.

Cary snorted, her gaze still on Deacon. "The worst," she agreed.

"Cary," Wisat said gently, "this task falls to you. It's part of the test year." He sighed. "Whether we all like it or not."

Was Wisat actually admitting he didn't like this? Well. Maybe she wasn't the only one who thought putting *her* in the center of impending doom was a bad idea.

"So I have to protect Holland," she said, trying unsuccessfully to hide the whine in her voice. "But I can't get to him or the Nagas. Bringing him into this realm will force a confrontation with his father again—one that might destroy this realm, by the way. And Holland would like to kill me. Oh, and he knows how. So… I'm not sure how all this will work."

A huge understatement.

"Wouldn't the demon hunters be better suited to this job?" she asked. "I mean, they deal with demons all the time. At least one of them knows enough about Holland to have had his phone number last fall. Maybe this is something they should be taking care of."

Did she sound desperate? She sounded desperate. She really wanted to pass on this particular responsibility. She didn't want this one. Nothing about it, not one little bit of it, felt right.

But mostly, she didn't feel capable of doing this.

"The hunters will have their hands full when the demon god arrives," Liruk said, still in that deep, rhythmic cadence that was new to Cary. Her eyes were partially closed, not fully, but the lids lowered so that barely any of her crystalline green eyes showed. "They must fight the distractions. They will not be free to focus." She paused. "No. They will not be there. They must be…in other places."

Cary realized suddenly this was Liruk in mid-premonition. This was the work Liruk and Wisat did when she wasn't around, the way they figured out where to send her. They'd never let her see this part before. She wasn't sure if even Jaxer had witnessed the process of them glimpsing the possible futures. And it was both disconcerting and humbling.

"There is one…" Liruk's voice faded a moment, her eyes closing fully. "One near. He may be able to help."

"He? He who?"

The only demon hunter she'd met in person was Aidan, who'd helped her with information when she'd first had to fight Ho'Lud. Aidan had spent the night Cary faced Lud fighting off the demon attacks the god had organized to keep the hunters distraction. According to Angie, and Jaxer, Aidan was a legend among demon hunters.

This seemed the sort of job tailor-made for a legend.

But Aidan was a she. Who was the "he" Liruk was referring to?

"Ah," Marianne said quietly. "Angie is not going to be happy about this."

"What? What don't I know?" Cary said, sitting up straighter.

Angie had links to the demon hunter world that she'd never discussed fully with Cary. In fact, she kept promising to reveal what she could and then somehow managed to avoid the topic. Cary tried not to take it personally. Angie had said some of it was stuff she couldn't talk about. And Cary herself still had one or two secrets she hadn't revealed to her friends—well only the one big one, the glamour on her house, but still, she had kept that to herself—so she didn't feel right pushing Angie to talk about things she didn't want to. But it seemed Marianne did know something more.

"Is this just that she doesn't like dealing with the demon hunters?" Cary asked.

"No. This one is a little more personal." Marianne raised a hand. "And before you get upset, I found out on accident during one of his visits a few years ago. They…aren't supposed to be together."

"Wait. Together as in a couple? Angie has a boyfriend she's never told me about?"

"She doesn't tell anyone about Sebastian," Marianne said. "I only know by accident, and I swore I wouldn't say anything." Marianne made a face. "A promise I just broke, damn it. I hope she'll forgive me."

"How long? Why is it secret? Who is he?"

"I only know he's a demon hunter, and they aren't supposed to be together, and that's it. I don't know anything more."

Cary stared at her wall as the news sank in. Whoa. This was…big.

But also maybe something she'd have to deal with *after* the current crisis.

"Okay," she said after a moment. "So, do we call Angie now and break the news or will this Sebastian guy just show up when the demons start arriving?"

And, oh wow, there were going to be demons arriving, weren't there? Maybe a lot of them. Shit shit shit. She hated having to deal with demons.

She glanced at Buck. He didn't seem to be reacting badly to all this. He was laying with his head on his paws, watching the room, but he seemed pretty relaxed. So that was probably a good sigh. Right?

"We're going to want to give Angie a heads up," Marianne said. "Other demon hunters might start to show up."

"Yeah." She glanced out her window. The sky was significantly lighter now, but still early. "We can call in a few hours. I don't want to wake her up on top of giving her bad news." She faced Wisat and Liruk again. "I have to protect Holland, but you haven't explained *how* yet. How will I even get to him? And for how long? And I'm not bringing him here." She added that last as Wisat opened his mouth to speak. She just wanted that out there again before anyone suggested it. If she couldn't stand to bring Sheldon here, she certainly wasn't going to allow Holland into her home.

And not just because it would piss off her demon dog.

"Holland will come to you," Liruk said, her eyes closed fully now, but there was movement behind her closed lids, like she was dreaming. "Soon. He is…" Her eyes snapped open.

"What? What?" Cary said when Liruk just stared at the space in front of her, not speaking.

Wisat frowned at Liruk too, and then without a word, they both vanished.

"Ah! What the hell?" She looked to Jaxer. "What just happened? What's going on? Where the hell did they go?"

And without even explaining? She was "at the center of a growing darkness" and they just…went away?

If she weren't so damned scared, she'd be infuriated.

"Something must have happened," Jaxer said, frowning at the space where Liruk and Wisat had been. "Something big."

"Like the arrival of a demon god?"

They hadn't done this to her the last time Ho'Lud had appeared on the scene. They'd given her an assignment to protect a necromancer and her brother and then just vanished as usual and let her deal with it all. Including the demon god. They'd left all the protecting and world saving to her without even hinting there might be a demon god involved. She'd never even discovered if they'd known. They rarely talked to her about what they did and didn't know ahead of time.

Something was different now. Something, if possible, bigger. But…what? Why were they telling her more, and letting her see Liruk in mid-premonition, and yet still not telling her a damned thing but that her next job was to protect *another* enemy?

"I have a headache," she said to no one in particular. "Is the world ending now, or can I get in a nap first?" She looked to Jaxer for that answer.

Not that she was likely to sleep. She was exhausted. She'd been away for nearly forty-eight hours. She'd spent most of the night in the vampire hive, talking to the Angel of Death. If there was a time to sleep, this was it. What she really wanted to do was hide in her house and let other people—people who had actual skills they could use— handle all this. She was out of her league. In over her head. And she was going to end up dead.

Worse, she might just get other people killed along with her.

"Sleep, if you can," Jaxer said, still frowning. "I'll go…check on them and see what's happening. We'll figure out how to get you to Holland, or Holland to you, or…whatever soon. The Nagas will have to be consulted, obviously, and that might take time. You should be able to rest." He met her gaze. "You're going to need it."

"You're helping. Someone's going to notice soon."

"Someone can bugger off about it," he said and left without his usual fanfare. He hadn't even bothered to flirt with Marianne on the way out.

This must be really serious.

She met Deacon's gaze across the coffee table. He'd been mostly quiet in all this, but his leopard was near the surface, his eyes glowing yellow. He didn't look any happier than she felt.

"Holland again," she murmured. "And probably Lud."

"We need more help," he said.

"No." She pointed a finger at him. "Last time the leopards helped me with Lud, two of them died. No. No more deaths on my hands." She pulled in a deep breath. "I just need to stand there. Between Holland and Lud. I can do that. The demon hunters will deal with the demon distractions. The Angel will show up and kill Lud. And then… well, maybe Holland won't bother trying to kill me since I kept his father from getting to him."

Wishful thinking? Maybe. But it was at least possible. And since Holland couldn't be killed, really her only hope.

Relying on the gratitude of a demon.

That was a very very bad plan.

34

Deacon sensed the dragon's presence in the backyard while he was still mostly asleep. His instincts brought him fully awake when he realized what he was picking up. Not danger exactly, but the presence of a dragon wasn't something he could sleep through. Careful not to wake Cary, he eased one arm away from her and turned to grab his phone where it lay next to hers on the bedside table. They'd only gone to sleep a few hours ago. Too soon to wake her.

Slowly, he rolled out of bed, untangling himself from her warmth with a regretful sigh. She mumbled something he couldn't understand and burrowed into the spot he'd just left, pulling the blankets up near her face and breathing in deeply. He watched to ensure she settled back to sleep before grabbing his pants off the chair in the corner of her room and quietly padding out.

He gave the dogs a nod where they slept under the bay window in the living room. Buck snuffled and lifted his head. Fred sat up, watching Deacon closely as he headed toward the kitchen. Pickles pulled herself off the floor and ambled behind him. That brought the other two to their feet and they followed as well.

Deacon paused in the mudroom to hand them each a treat from a box Cary kept on a shelf above the coats and padded shirts hanging on a series of pegs for when she wandered out to her backyard. He didn't bother grabbing one of the jackets, though he loved having her scent around him. Beyond the fact that the shirts and coats were too small for him, he didn't need them. Even though the air was chilly enough to raise goosebumps when he opened the back door, his metabolism kicked in and warmed him up immediately.

The dragon sat in the grass, his long, spiked tail wrapped around his hind legs, his head resting on his front legs, the spikes circling the back of his skull flattened to his neck. His golden scales glimmered in the late morning light leaking through a gray cloud cover. His eyes were closed, but they opened as soon as Deacon stepped onto the porch, the multi-faceted red irises seeming to whirl as the dragon focused in on him.

"Is she still asleep?" Rory asked.

Though Deacon knew that voice was in his head, he'd have sworn the dragon spoke aloud, in a voice everyone in the neighborhood might have heard had they been close enough. He'd had to get used to that. It almost felt like an invasion. And yet, somehow, Rory managed it without triggering Deacon's leopard's instincts.

"She's had a long night," he said.

He sat on the porch's top step, a position which put him eye level with the dragon so long as Rory kept his head resting on his front legs. Fred charged into the yard, bounced off Rory's huge shoulder, and then flopped into the grass beside the giant golden beast as if this was a normal day. Buck and Pickles settled onto the porch step on either side of Deacon, relaxed but alert. Buck's scent flavored just a little with wariness. Pickles's carried an element of comfort and familiarity that made him wonder about the relationship between the foo lion and the dragon.

The dragon's scent made his nose twitch—but not in a bad way. The mix of sulfur and ancient animal musk, the very faint hint of heated metal under the surface, was subtle and not unpleasant. It was just so unique, so distinct from anything Deacon encountered on a normal day, he had to refamiliarize himself with it every time he had the honor of meeting Rory.

"The wizard who's been trying to kill her is dead," Rory said.

Didn't ask, Deacon noticed. "How did you know?"

"I have my ways," Rory said with a slight lifting at the corners of his mouth.

It was supposed to be a smile, so Cary had assured him. His leopard saw threat every time.

He held in his instinctive reaction and said, "Do you know the Angel of Death?"

"I've never met her. Not in person anyway." A little huff of smoke puffed from his raised nostrils as he made a sound Deacon assumed was a laugh. "The Angel destroyed the wizard."

"She did. Is that why you're here?"

"I've learned something that's important for Cary to know."

"Her bosses are asking her to protect one of her greatest enemies. A demon who knows how to kill her. Someone who almost killed her once before and has even more reason now to try again. Will what you've learned help her with that?"

"This is Oliver Holland?"

"Turns out he's not just the son of a demon god, but also of the Angel of Death. And he can't be killed. Not even by the Angel. Which is, apparently, why his father wants him back. The Angel intends to kill Lud. Lud means to use his own son to avoid that."

Rory's gaze shifted a little as he took in Deacon's speech, giving the impression of looking away as he thought.

From his position, Deacon could really only see one of Rory's eyes well, but the way his elongated pupil moved in and out like a distorted camera lens was fascinating to watch.

"The last time she faced Holland," Rory said slowly, "was the first time she released a large amount of the magic she'd been absorbing."

"Yes," Deacon said. "And she nearly died."

"Did the Angel reference her death in Faery?"

Deacon blinked at what felt like a change of topic. "Cary's? Yes. She did. Why?"

Rory's pupil whirled in and out again.

"Cary has absorbed Holland's power." Rory's voice sounded far away. "And Lud's. Did she have to protect anyone from the Angel?"

"No. The Angel killed the wizard so fast none of us knew it was happening until it was over. The Angel didn't attempt to kill anyone else, though."

Rory nodded slightly.

For some reason, the gesture struck Deacon as strange in a creature several millennia old. It was a very human way to communicate an affirmative, or in some cultures a negative. Had Rory learned that gesture just to ease communication with humans—and those like himself who were human adjacent—or did dragons naturally nod as part of their physical communication?

It was a strange thing to be thinking about in a moment like this.

"But she absorbed a lot of Holland's magic," Rory said.

"A lot of magic period that night."

"She is unique for someone with her particular ability," Rory said, "because so many of them die early, their bodies overwhelmed by what they take in. Her body has time to adjust, though, time to heal, to adapt to the changes being wrought by the magics she absorbs."

"The magic is…changing her? How?"

"She's less ordinary now than she thinks," Rory said, his tone sounding almost amused in Deacon's head.

Why was any of this amusing? "Will this kill her?"

He was getting tired of that question, tired of the way life kept trying to kill his mate. He couldn't fight it, any more than he could defeat the Angel of Death. But damned if he didn't want to.

"I'm starting to think," Rory said, "this will be her salvation. If she can survive long enough for the changes to…take hold."

"What does that mean?" Deacon asked slowly and with great precision.

"Her body must adapt to the changes. It has managed that so far, because of her Protector shielding. And the healing and slowing of aging… All the things she's been given as part of her job have allowed her body to adapt to things it would not normally have the time to adjust to."

"The magic she absorbs."

"And because of that time, she is changed. She is…" Rory's gaze unfocused and sharpened again. "She's able to do things now that she wasn't before. She could, with training, not just release what she's absorbed. I'm sure now, she could use it. Like other magic wielders. But, with Cary, there's a catch."

Deacon groaned. There was always a catch. Hearing a dragon say "there's a catch"—such a modern phrasing from such an ancient mouth —made it all seem infinitely worse.

"She hasn't trained to this magic. She hasn't grown up with it. And it's not just one kind of magic. It's not a wizard's magic. A witch's. It's not the goblins' magic. The Fae magic. The demon or shadow dragon magic. It's *all* of these things combined into a new mix of…something wholly unique. There's no precedent. No… No training regimen. No way of knowing *how* all of these various magics will combine."

"Which means no one knows how the changes will play out and not even you can train her to them?" Deacon ran a hand over his face. Of course. Of course his beloved mate, who'd always assumed she was just an ordinary woman doing a job she was tricked into, would turn out to be absolutely new, unique…and untrainable.

After getting to know her, he really should have seen the untrainable part coming.

"How does this work in relation to all the mundane things she's protected people from? The knives and bullets and…bombs." He shuddered a little at that memory.

"She doesn't absorb the energy of mundane things," Rory said. "She's not that kind of sponge."

Deacon was pretty sure that was the dragon's attempt at humor, but it was hard to tell, and he wasn't in the mood for figuring it out. "Is there a kind of human who could absorb all that?"

"Not that I've encountered in my multiple millennia on this planet." A very slight lifting of his shoulder, a dragon's gentle shrug. "But I never say never. No one expected Cary to exist either."

That didn't help. But at least it was one less thing he had to worry about.

"Where does this leave us?" he asked, not really expecting an answer.

"In a quandary," Rory said. The spikes around his neck rippled. Fred jumped to his feet, his tail wagging. When the dragon didn't do more, he flopped into the grass again and rested his head on his paws, his tail thumping in the grass. "She will need multiple teachers, a unique curriculum of training if you will."

"But first we have to stop a demon god from reclaiming his demon son who can't be killed and who wants Cary dead. And we have to do it just long enough to allow the Angel of Death to kill the demon god before said god destroys our realm. And then hope the demon son doesn't kill Cary for the fun of it."

"There is that," Rory said. "But if you can manage all that, we will begin Cary's training. I can start certain aspects. Her witch friend, Angie, she can help with other areas." Rory fell silent, his head shifting to one side. "I will need to vet the other instructors. We'll need a wizard and possibly a demon. At the least."

"Her Fae mentor isn't supposed to help her anymore, but we'll need someone who understands Faery magic."

"Yes. Perhaps Herself will help."

"Herself?"

Rory's mouth lifting in that supposed smile that made Deacon's hackles rise. "Danu. She has a mild fascination with your mate that might be useful."

"I'm not sure getting a goddess with an Irish sense of humor is the best idea," Deacon said.

"Your grandmother Belle might be better," Rory allowed with a slight shrug and a chortle that released another small stream of smoke from his raised nostrils.

Deacon sat up a little straighter. "My grandmother?"

"She's very familiar with the ways of Faery. She's not, of course. And her shifter abilities won't really help here. But her Scottish sense of humor might be more…predictable than Danu's."

"My grandmother is familiar with *Fae* magic?"

That was news to him. His grandmother Belle had always been a little different. Mostly the family didn't discuss those differences, so he'd never known the specifics. But Belle was responsible for the magic that kept her own father, his Gramps, in that bubble of peace on his sheep farm. Deacon knew she was capable of some level of magic. He just hadn't realized it had anything to do with the Fae.

"Ah. I see that hasn't passed down through family lore, yet. Well, perhaps her father can explain. I feel I might have stepped on some toes."

"Do you know everything about everything?" Deacon asked. "I'm not being facetious. Do you know…everything?"

"Of course not. No one does. Not even ancient dragons—though there are a few who will claim they do. Watch out for those irritating old buggers." Rory's voice took on a very slight Irish lilt, like his hero Joan, when he said this last. Then his voice changed back to a more formal tone. "But when you've lived through as much as I have, for as long as I have, and pay attention to the human world—at least I pay attention to my corner of it because it's where my home is of course—then you get to hear things, learn things. And I have an excellent memory for faces."

Another pause as Rory's eye whirled and refocused, zeroing in more directly on Deacon. "You share many features with your grandmother, even if you don't have her coloring. Talk to her father. I'm sure she'll work with your mate, if Cary's mentor cannot. Although, I would check with the People and Jaxer. This training falls outside the realms of her Protector job, and her test year. It might not be breaking any rules for Jaxer to train her in Fae magic."

A part of Deacon that still lurked under the surface of the truce he'd come to with Jaxer bristled. He didn't want Jaxer to work with Cary any more than absolutely necessary anymore. He certainly didn't want him training her again.

But… Things had changed. Jaxer's feelings had changed, even though he didn't seem to realize it yet. He was still in love with Cary on some level, but it was…different now. And despite all the personal issues, Deacon knew Jaxer would do everything he could to ensure Cary was safe.

He trusted his grandmother, but the news that she *knew* Fae magic and no one had ever bothered to tell him complicated his feelings on having her train Cary.

He let out a long sigh. All of this was moot if they couldn't stop the demon family fight from destroying their world.

"We will discuss her training after the Holland situation is dealt with," Rory said, as if reading Deacon's mind.

To be honest, Deacon wasn't entirely sure the dragon wasn't reading his thoughts since he projected his voice into Deacon's head.

"Do you want me to tell her all this or should you tell her?" Deacon asked.

"It will be good coming from you. She won't be happy."

Deacon huffed out a breath. "No. She won't."

"Even better for you to tell her then," Rory said.

Again, Deacon couldn't tell if that was supposed to be humor or not. "Does any of this help us with Holland?"

Rory's neck spikes rippled again. "I'm not sure," he said. "But she's absorbed both Lud and Holland's power in the past. And has had time for her cells to adjust to the changes made by those interactions. It's possible she has more defenses against them now."

"Possible. But you don't know."

"There's no way to know. She's unique."

"I really really hate this," Deacon said.

"I'm sorry." The dragon sounded genuinely sympathetic.

"Thanks for the information." He pushed to his feet. "I need to go now, though. If I'm going to tell her all this, I want to get her some donuts first. To help smooth over the shock."

Rory chuckled in Deacon's head, the sound both ancient and knowing. "My hero and I are at your disposal if you require help with the demon situation. We don't usually get involved in fighting those particular kinds of monsters. They're the responsibility of others. But in this case, I think we could make an exception."

"I'll let her know. Thanks for the help."

He watched Rory lift off, taking to the air with a few quick strokes of his wings. Fred raced around the garden barking up at the retreating dragon, even after the giant beast disappeared from sight. Deacon followed Buck and Pickles back into the house, mulling over everything Rory had told him.

Hoping against hope it was good news. Because his gut, and his instincts, kept telling him this was a disaster.

35

Marianne was waiting for him in the kitchen with Pickles already sitting loyally at her feet.

"What did the dragon want?" she asked, her arms crossed over her chest.

"Did we wake you? Sorry."

He studied Marianne closely. She was dressed and looked ready for the day, but there were faint circles darkening under her eyes and a tightness around her mouth. More than the way she looked, though, there was a level of exhaustion in her scent that he'd have a hard time describing to a human. A faint flavor of bitter but not sharp. Smoothly bitter and a bit ashy at the edges. Putting human words to that particular brand of exhaustion wasn't easy, but he knew the feeling, and he picked it up clearly in Marianne's scent.

"You aren't sleeping enough," he said.

Her mouth ticked up in an annoyed look. "You're not supposed to notice those things out loud."

"Sorry," he said again. "We worry."

The annoyance turned to a faint smile. "You're a good man, Deacon. I'm glad she found you. And didn't let that little shit kill you."

"Me too." He leaned against the counter a few feet away. "I know

it's not my business, and that you're not ready. But when you are…
Brandon is a good man, too."

"The bear shifter?" She shook her head. "Cary tell you
everything?"

He shrugged. "Only the things that are allowed."

"I'm not ready."

"We know. He does too."

"How do you know that? Did you talk to him?"

"No. I will if you want me to, but not without your permission."

"Good. Then how can you know he knows anything about me?"

He tapped his nose. "Shifter super sense of smell," he said, using
Cary's phrase. "Brandon has it too."

Marianne let out a soft laugh. "Not sure I want a partner in my life
who can smell what I'm feeling."

"It has its drawbacks. And its advantages."

"You know Brandon?"

"I do. He does some fundraising for us, has volunteered at some of
our shelters."

She nodded. "I'm not ready."

He didn't argue.

"He seems like a nice man, though."

"He is. And he's patient."

She kept nodding, staring at the floor a few feet in front of her.
"I'm not ready," she said again. Then pulled in a deep breath. "And
how did we get onto this topic? I want to know about that dragon. Is
Cary in trouble?"

"Always," he said without hesitance—which was a little horrifying.
"I'd better tell her first, though. And then she can fill you in. But this
absorbing magic thing… She's going to need help."

"Is she dying?"

"No."

"Will it kill her?"

"Not unless she pulls another stunt like she did in Faery." At least
he hoped that was the case.

"That about gave me a heart attack."

"Me too."

Marianne huffed a sound that could have been a laugh except there was too much annoyance in it. "Okay. Well, we're here for her when she needs us."

"Thank you."

Marianne waved that away. "We've got her back. Thank you for having her back, too. I still worry about her getting her ridiculously heroic ass killed, but at least I know you're there to…help."

She held his gaze a moment, nodded, then leaned over and scratched Pickle's behind the ears. "I'll get out of here so you can talk in private."

After she'd collected her overnight bag, he walked her to the front door. She raised her brows at him when he followed her out.

"I need to go get her some donuts for breakfast," he said, closing the door behind him.

"That bad, huh?"

"Let's just say I'm hoping the donuts will soften the blow."

CARY WOKE FEELING GROGGY BUT LESS EXHAUSTED, AND WHEN SHE wandered into the living room, she was greeted by the scents of donuts and coffee wafting from the kitchen.

Either Deacon was being extra special sweet to her—which was entirely possible—or something had happened while she slept and he was trying to soften her up before telling her—also entirely possible.

She decided it was probably both as she entered the kitchen and saw his face. "What's happened? Wait." She raised a hand. "Coffee first. Then you can tell me once I have half a donut in my mouth so I can't gripe."

He chuckled, the lovely sound doing a little to offset her worry.

"Is Marianne awake yet?" she asked as she poured herself a mug of coffee, savoring the rich scent of fresh ground Arabica beans.

"She went home an hour ago," he said. "She thought we'd need privacy to talk."

"You didn't chase her out?"

"Of course not," he said, his brows furrowing as if offended.

She rubbed her fingers over his forehead, smoothing out the creases. "Was she okay?"

"Exhausted still, but probably not just from lack of sleep."

Cary let out a long sigh. "Does she know what prompted you to ply me with donuts?"

"Not the specifics. I wanted to tell you first. Rory was here this morning."

Ah. "Yeah, I definitely need those donuts."

They settled on the couch in the living room, the bag of Boston Creams and coconut flake donuts on the wooden coffee table, and Deacon told her everything Rory had told him.

"So…" She let out a slow breath, her half-eaten Boston Cream mostly forgotten on a napkin on the coffee table. "So I can't just release the power and be done with it. I can't just use it in a simple, lighting-a-bunch-of-candles sort of way and drain it. I need training to use the complicated mix of what I've absorbed, but we don't know how to train me, or what I'll be able to do. And all this magic *has* permanently changed me, but we don't know into what, or what I can do, or how much actual 'magic' I can use. Does that about sum it up?"

"That's Rory's assessment, yes," Deacon said.

She noticed he was being careful with his wording. She couldn't blame him. This was…big. So big she was having trouble grasping it. She felt like she was skirting over the surface of what this really meant, what it really implied. And when the reality of it all finally sank in…

She wasn't sure who she'd be at the other end of that epiphany.

"You're very quiet," Deacon said.

"I'm in shock." She waved a hand in the air, as if dismissing all that. "I'll get over it eventually. I just need… I'm not sure what to think, and it's going to take some time to understand what all this means."

"Nothing immediately. You've managed this long. We can continue on as long as you need until you're ready. Then we'll find you the right teachers. Angie. Rory. Anyone else you might need."

She nodded, though she wasn't really listening. There was too much. She'd known some of this *might* be true, that all the magic she'd been absorbing might be changing her. Bleak's alchemy book, her last conversation with Rory, the pages Sheldon had torn out of the book on her skill… Still, hearing the changes were actually happening, and that they were making her something she hadn't been… She couldn't get her mind around thinking of herself differently. She was still just her. And trying to settle into the idea that she was now more felt like putting on clothes that didn't fit. Too tight here, too loose there. Not the right cut and style at all for her.

But this wasn't something Marianne could fix with needle and thread.

She cleared her throat. "Yeah, I'm gonna need time for this one." She let out a puff of air that was supposed to be a chuckle but failed miserably. "You know, I knew I was unique for a Protector. But that was because I was so fundamentally ordinary. So *not* magical. Now, I have to accept I'm unique in a way that isn't what I'd always assumed about myself. It's a lot."

"It's a lot." He leaned a little closer and cupped her cheek in one large, warm hand. "I'm here. Whatever you need. I've got your back."

The tension that had been holding her upright fled and she melted against him, into his arms, needing the warmth and strength and support in a way she wasn't sure she'd ever needed anything before. His strong arms wrapped around her, and she allowed herself to accept his support. To lean on him a little while she felt so weak and so damned tired. She'd have been embarrassed to need this just a few months ago. Disconcerted that she wanted to find strength in someone else like this. Now…

This was Deacon. And she was safe being vulnerable with him.

She felt the nudge of a wet nose against her leg and glanced down without releasing her hold on Deacon. Fred sat patiently looking up at her, but his gaze kept darting to the half-eaten donut on the coffee table. When she looked at him, his tail thumped rapidly against the floor, the sound muted by the carpet. He let out a little yappy bark, glanced at the donut again, then sat up using his front paws in their little prayer posture to hold his balance.

The absolutely adorable ridiculousness of her dog begging for food while she had an existential crisis was too much. She started to laugh. Too hard for the moment. Maybe a little too desperately. But in that instant, nothing had ever been as funny as Fred angling for a donut while she faced down a massive paradigm shift in who she thought she was.

She pinched off a piece of donut as Fred waved his paws harder, his full attention on the bite of donut in her hand. She indulged him with the treat, and then was instantly surrounded by the other two dogs, hoping for their own bite of donut.

She didn't like to feed them too much refined sugar. Sugar was bad for their teeth, and she was very hesitant to bring either Pickles or Buck to a vet for a teeth cleaning. But just then, it felt so right to share the donuts, to indulge in just a moment of levity with her little pack. Sometimes, Fred had excellent timing.

Her doorbell went off, and continued to ring for longer than necessary. And she laughed harder. Because *of course* Jaxer would show up now.

She was wiping away tears from her eyes as she opened the door for him.

"What's wrong?" he asked, taking her face in his hands and holding her gaze.

She swatted his touch away, but without the usual level of irritation and annoyance. "Rory was here. Deacon talked to him. Did you know, I'm becoming something else all together and all this magic I've been absorbing has changed me permanently, so that I have to learn how to use everything I've absorbed?"

He frowned. Glanced at Deacon. "This requires a lot more explaining."

She snorted and gestured him to the couch. "Settle in, buttercup. It's quite the tale."

He didn't even scowl at her for the epithet, which proved he was as worried about all this as she should probably be. A part of her was worried, but that part was subsumed under her shock and instinctive denial of the facts.

Instead of heading for the couch, though, Jaxer said, "I'll need to get the full story later. We have a problem."

"Of course we do." She jerked her hands into the air. "Of course. Because it wouldn't be my life otherwise. What now? Gabriel back from the dead and starting a vampire war? Lud stomping down the streets of Portland? Holland rapidly approaching and he knows where I live now? Another random god has decided to invade our realm? Faery is on the verge of exploding?"

"Sheldon is missing," Jaxer said.

36

That brought Cary up short. "Wait, what?"

All the mild hysteria and overwhelm got pushed to the side. She could indulge her crisis of identity later. She closed the front door. "How do you know he's missing and hasn't just gone out for groceries or something?"

"He dropped the spells on his floor of the apartment building." Jaxer shrugged and didn't quite meet her gaze when he said, "I asked someone who could detect those spells to watch him after you dropped him off this morning."

"You think I'd be annoyed by that." His body language said he assumed she'd be mad, but she wasn't sure why. She didn't trust Sheldon either. If she had Jaxer's resources, she'd have asked someone to keep an eye on him, too.

"You don't want him hurt," Jaxer said.

"Well, no, unless he does something evil again. Was this person watching him going to hurt him?"

"No. Just watch. Just…make sure he didn't go back to doing evil things now that he doesn't have to hide from Zorianthus."

"Fair enough. And I wish I'd thought of that. I don't know what to make of Sheldon now. I have no idea what he'll do. It was a good plan to watch him. Thank you."

Jaxer's shoulders relaxed, though it was a very subtle shift.

She wasn't sure what to make of Jaxer being worried about her reaction either. Something about it left her feeling mildly uncomfortable. But again, a worry for later.

Deacon rose from the couch to join them at the door. Fred bounced after him, sat at their feet for a split second, then raced back to Buck and Pickles where they were laying under the bay window again.

"He dropped the spells," Deacon said, "I assume your associate went in to check the apartments?"

"Searched the whole floor," Jaxer said. "Every apartment is cleared out, no signs of anyone living there. After my associate called, I went in to make sure there were no glamours hiding anything. There aren't. The place is empty. Even the closets. And we double checked every apartment on that floor."

"This isn't good, is it?" Cary asked, her gaze drawn to Buck for reasons she couldn't pinpoint.

He wasn't acting strangely, like he did the last time Ho'Lud was close to entering this realm, but he wasn't asleep. He was staring at them with his head resting on his forepaws. Pickles wasn't napping either. The dogs knew something. And, boy, did she wish she could ask them what it was. But the only person she knew who could have spoken to them was currently in school, and Cary knew for a fact his mother wouldn't want her interrupting his school day—he needed very little excuse to cut class.

Deacon and Jaxer both followed her gaze.

"Lud isn't here yet," Jaxer said.

Yet. "But Sheldon is missing, and we're still all suitably worried about Holland and his family infighting."

"Maybe Sheldon decided to leave Portland now that his mentor is dead?" Deacon said, though he didn't sound particularly convinced. "Start new?"

"Maybe." She wasn't convinced either. "But why so suddenly, in the early hours of the morning? Why not in a day or two? Did he leave any clues behind?" she asked Jaxer. "A note?" That would be too much to ask, but still, seemed like she should.

"No note. No random things. Every spell has been deactivated."

She frowned a little. "That means the witches can't trace him anymore, doesn't it? They can't spy on him through the spells."

"If he's not using their spells, they aren't likely to know where he's gone."

"He can't find Holland," she said mostly to herself as she worked through the implications of all this. "He would know where Zorianthus lived and kept all his stuff, though. He'd know where to go to get the information Zorianthus had gathered on finding Holland. Zorianthus didn't anticipate being killed last night." She shivered a little. "So he wouldn't have necessarily hidden anything, any more than usual."

"You think Sheldon went there?" Deacon asked.

"No idea. Just thinking aloud. Wouldn't matter if he did, anyway, since we don't know where Zorianthus was holed up."

"If he did, he'd have access to everything Zorianthus gathered and catalogued," Jaxer said. "Including the process of taking over a body permanently. Sheldon was trying that with shifters and failing. But that doesn't mean he isn't still interested in ditching his current body for another."

"He doesn't have the magic to accomplish the swap anymore," she pointed out.

"But maybe Zorianthus knew how to do it without magic," Jaxer said. "He was killed before we knew…anything really. And I doubt the vampires or the triad knew much more."

"Or will share with us if they do," Deacon said.

"So you still think Sheldon wants to try body swapping," Cary said. "Which means he's still got no issue with killing someone." She put her hands on her hips, dipping her head, hoping they were all off base because she'd protected that little shit and kept him from dying, and if he paid her back by returning to killing people, she was going to be so so very angry.

"Where are Wisat and Liruk in all this?" she asked when she

looked up again. "They vanished so suddenly this morning, I assumed they'd have returned by now with news. Or another assignment."

She glanced at the clock on her tv cable box by the fireplace. Four in the afternoon. This time of year, the sun would be up for a few hours still, but the day had moved on while she'd tried to sleep off some of her exhaustion. She kept thinking the conversation with her bosses had been yesterday instead of at dawn that morning.

Geezus, not even twenty-four hours had passed since Zorianthus was killed.

"I haven't been in contact with them either," Jaxer said. "Based on Liruk's premonition and their sudden exit this morning, I assumed they'd be back by now, too."

"None of this is good." She lifted her head to look at both men. "But what do we do about it? Should we try to track Sheldon down?" She focused on Deacon. "Would you be able to follow his scent?"

"Through the city? Doubtful. Too many conflicting things get in the way. Too much time has passed. Scent tracing through a city is hard enough, but with so many hours gone..." He shook his head.

"And we can't trace his magic," she said, again working through all this out loud, "because he doesn't have any to use. The triad likely didn't know where Zorianthus was, or they wouldn't have needed to keep tabs on Sheldon. They could have just spied on Zorianthus himself." She grunted. "But we don't have any clue where Sheldon has gone. For all we know, he moved back in with his parents. None of this may be anything we need to worry about."

"Do you believe that?" Jaxer asked.

"Of course not. My life isn't that convenient." But what now? What was the thing she needed to do at this moment to keep the world from falling apart?

Because she felt it, at the edges of her instincts, that things were about to get a lot worse if she didn't do something soon. But *what* damn it? What could she do?

"Okay," she said, "so the only thing I can think to do is go to Sheldon's apartment and look around." She raised a hand when Jaxer opened his mouth. "I know you did that already and that it's likely a pointless effort. But it's all I've got." She shrugged. "Maybe I'll spot something you didn't consider."

He raised his brows and tucked his chin back.

She scowled at his skeptical expression. "Just... Just meet us there," she said, frustrated because she didn't have answers.

Jaxer left without arguing. Which only confirmed how serious this was. No, Sheldon hadn't just gone back to his parents. Her every instinct said this was trouble.

Because she seemed to be a magnet for Trouble.

37

At Sheldon's apartment, Cary sensed the difference the moment they stepped out of the elevator. The hall no longer had that gloomy feel, that eerie sense that something was going to jump out from behind a closed door and try to kill the person stupid enough to be here. It felt ordinary, if empty. Just a regular apartment floor with apartments needing to be rented. Even the flickering single lightbulb no longer flickered in lone, ominous warning. All of the lights running down the length of the ceiling had fresh bulbs, giving the hall a comfortably bright illumination.

"Scent anything?" she asked Deacon.

Jaxer had been waiting for them when they pulled into the parking lot and both men had stayed at her back as they traveled up in the elevator, assuring she was safe by letting her protect them.

"Nothing out of the ordinary," Deacon said, "but not like before."

"What did it smell like before?"

They crept out into the hallway. The perfectly bland hallway. Now Cary could see the light color on the walls was a sort of pale yellowish cream that desperately needed to be refreshed. The black marble floors were scuffed and dirtier in the brighter lights, like no one had bothered to clean up here for a while. Which was likely true.

"Like wizard magic and blood and something else I couldn't place exactly, but all of that was covered over by 'ordinary.'" He shook his head when she glanced back. "I don't have human words to explain it. The place smelled like an empty building, dust and metal and plaster, which was what it should have smelled like since no one was supposedly living here. But under that smell, I kept getting a…flavor on the back of my tongue. Of burnt ozone and blood. That was the way Sheldon's apartment smelled when he tried to kill me. The smell lingered even after he stopped using wizard magic. And whatever spells the witches gave him didn't completely cover it."

"Wow, your nose can pick out a lot of stuff."

"Super shifter smelling," he agreed with a nod.

She'd have smiled at hearing him use her phrase if she weren't so worried about whatever disaster Sheldon might be causing. "You're not getting the wizard smell anymore?"

"No. Which is strange. Just having Sheldon gone shouldn't be enough to have wiped that smell away. It should have taken some airing out, some time before that left the place."

"Does that mean Sheldon is still here? Or maybe something of his is still here? Or…I don't know. Maybe he just took the spells down and moved to an empty apartment downstairs, off this floor?"

"Let's look around. I'll see if I can pick anything out."

"The apartments are all empty and there's no magic hiding anything," Jaxer said, reiterating his earlier assessment, as he followed them through the first apartment door—which wasn't locked. "My associate has been watching the building and didn't see Sheldon leave, but that's not surprising since the little shit was apparently coming and going under cover of witch spells this whole time."

The growl in Jaxer's voice made Cary's neck tingle. Boy, he did not like Sheldon. Not that she blamed him, but that was a lot of anger for Jaxer.

They searched the first apartment, then covered the rest of the floor. Jaxer was right. No clues. No hints. Nothing but empty apartments that needed cleaning, fresh paint, and new renters. Even Deacon's super sense of smell didn't pick out anything.

Which was, it turned out, really weird. "I should be able to smell him here still. He only left this morning. I might not be able to trace him through the city, but I should still smell him here. Especially in here."

They stood in the middle of the apartment Sheldon had been using. There weren't any more discarded fast food wrappers and take out containers scattered around. The books were all gone. There weren't any clothes in the bedroom. The bed had been stripped. The bathroom was empty but filthy. The kitchen was empty but for a packet of ketchup tucked into the corner of a drawer. Nothing else remained.

Sheldon hadn't bothered to scrub the place. And she had to wonder what he'd done with his stuff. How had he gotten it all out without revealing himself to Jaxer's guard?

There had to be a way. She'd never found out how he came and went without alerting anyone. How he managed to get out of the building without anyone seeing him. She'd assumed it was the witches' spells. But maybe he'd been using something else? Maybe he *had* used multiple transportation spells like the kind Angie had. He'd have laid out a fortune for them, but the money hadn't seemed to be a concern for him.

She huffed and put her hands on her hips. "If he had transportation spells, would you be able to…sense it?" she asked Jaxer. "Would it leave a residue?"

"Depends on the magic used." He frowned as he took in the room. "I'm not sure I would though. The bloody things are so rare, I haven't dealt with them often. Angie would know better."

"Should we call her?" Cary really hated to disturb Angie. Especially since she was apparently spending time with a secret boyfriend. But this was magic—potentially—and that was her realm of expertise. Plus, apparently the boyfriend was a demon hunter, and given they were trying to avoid demons… Well, having them both nearby seemed useful.

"Even if we know he used a transportation spell," Jaxer said, "Angie won't be able to tell us where it took him. They don't work that way."

"Damn." Though it did mean she wouldn't have to bother Angie immediately.

"What next?" She'd hoped the building would give them clues. And maybe it had, but she didn't know how to interpret them. The fact that Sheldon's "smell" had gone so completely was strange. That meant something.

She just didn't know what it meant yet.

"Maybe we should go to The Bookstore," she said. "It's one of the few places we know he goes regularly." She turned in a slow circle. "He took all his books with him, wherever the hell he went," she muttered, mostly to herself. "He hasn't abandoned all that learning." She shrugged as she faced the men. "Worth a try, right?"

Jaxer nodded, but didn't look at her, his gaze focused on the floor a few feet away as if he were thinking and not really listening.

"What?" she asked him.

"Nothing. The Bookstore is a good idea. We'll try that next. I'll meet you there."

She stared at him, waiting him out, sure he wasn't saying something. Her patience didn't last long, though. "You might as well say what you're thinking out loud or I'll just nag. I'm as good at that as Liruk and Wisat."

She was still curious what had happened to them and would have a *lot* of questions for them when they showed up again. But right now, they had to find Sheldon, and for some reason, Jaxer's expression made her nervous.

Jaxer ran a hand over his hair, his frown deepening. "I'm thinking about what you said about Sheldon having transportation spells. Buying even one of those is expensive. They aren't easy to make, only a very few witches can construct them, and each one costs a lot in both the time it takes the witch as well as the money required to buy them. Sheldon would have to have access to a lot of money for that."

"His parents seem to have a lot," she said. "At least that's the impression I got from him."

"Maybe. Or maybe he's done something else."

"Like what?"

"Something simpler."

"An invisibility spell?" She shook her head. "You would have thought of that. You would have seen through it."

He nodded absently, still deep in thought. "I'd see through most illusions. But…"

"What? What don't I know?" Besides a lot.

"It's a very old spell, and I hadn't considered it because no one uses it anymore. If it fails suddenly…"

"Stop stalling at just tell me. You're driving me nuts."

"I need to go into Sheldon's old apartment. The one he was in originally."

Before she could comment, he was out the door.

Cary muttered irritated expletives as she followed him, Deacon close on her heels. Jaxer hurried into the apartment Sheldon had originally called home. They'd searched the place already. There hadn't appeared to be anything unusual. Nothing of Sheldon's left behind to give them a clue.

Still, Jaxer seemed intent as he walked the perimeter of the living room, searching for something along the walls, pausing several moments at each window, pressing his hand against the glass panes.

The apartment looked a lot different than it had the first time she'd been there to rescue a black cat. The living room was stripped back to a lumpy brown couch and a wooden stand against the opposite wall that could have held a TV. No rugs or side tables or any signs of personality. None of what remained was the furniture Sheldon had originally had in this place. The kitchen was bare and a layer of dust had built up on the counters and appliances. There were dusty brown curtains hung on the windows, but they were pulled to the side letting in the late afternoon light.

Jaxer's frown deepened and he hurried to the bedroom, still without explaining.

Cary grumbled under her breath and followed.

The bedroom was entirely different, too. At some point, Sheldon had removed the chains covering the light fixture, and all of the leather and animal print had been stripped away. The room still had a gaudy red carpet, but that was the only lingering sign that Sheldon had lived here. Even the bed was different, smaller, with a bare mattress on a metal frame. And the magic headboard that Deacon had been chained to when she'd found him had been replaced by a rickety wooden thing that looked like even she could break it without much effort.

Jaxer circled the room, checking walls and window panes again. Then he hurried into the bathroom.

"You have any idea what he's looking for?" Cary asked Deacon as they followed.

"Nope."

The bathroom wasn't big enough to accommodate all of them, so Cary and Deacon stood in the doorway, watching Jaxer run his fingers lightly over the walls.

"You gonna tell us what you're looking for?" she asked. "Or just keep caressing the walls?"

Jaxer didn't rise to her bait. He frowned at the mirror over the sink. Stared at it hard. He pressed his hand to the glass and cursed.

"What?" she snapped.

"I can't find anything," he said. "There's nothing here."

"We knew that already. What the hell are you looking for?"

"A gate." He faced her. "It's… It's basically a doorway between two different locations."

"Like a wormhole?"

"Only made and maintained with magic."

"Why doesn't everyone have one of those?" That seemed like the kind of thing that could be very useful.

"They take a lot of magic and work to set up, and are unpredictable in their stability. They can last for years or break down suddenly in moments. That's why no one uses them. Even if they can be established and they hold, it's impossible to tell when they'll collapse. And if you're trying to walk through one when it does, you die. So no one bothers. There are other ways to get around."

"You thought maybe Sheldon had one of those?"

He shrugged, his gaze skimming around the bathroom. "It was a thought. A shot in the dark, I guess." He waved them away from the doorway. "Let's get to The Bookstore." He started toward them but paused when Cary didn't move.

"You've been searching the walls, but also window panes and mirrors," she said. "The gate needs an anchor?"

"Twin mirrors are best. Those links last longest. But finding two mirrors made at the same time and separated… Trickier in modern mass manufacturing times. So walls, windows, doorways, anything can be used. Most of those are just less stable."

They'd searched the closets in this apartment already. There hadn't been any mirrors in any of them. In fact, the only mirror in the place was this one in the bathroom over the sink.

Cary gave the bathroom door a look, then gestured Jaxer out of the way and stepped inside. "You ever closed the door in here to check behind it?" she asked even as she swung the door closed.

And revealed the full-length mirror carefully hung on the back.

"Uh," Jaxer said on a sigh.

Deacon, still outside the bathroom, said, "You found something?"

"Possibly." Cary opened the door enough for him to step in.

The three of them had to cram together inside the small space, wedged between the sink cabinet and the showers' stall door. But they managed with Deacon turned sideways and Cary leaning into him as she closed the door again, revealing the hanging mirror.

It was a lot more elaborate than anything else left in the apartment, but it didn't fit with Sheldon's previous style of leather and chains either. The mirror was a six-foot by two-foot rectangle of smoky white glass, like Venetian glass, pretty but opaque. Making it useless as an actual mirror. The frame around the glass was an elaborate golden scroll of baroque glory the former Master vampire Ariel would have loved. Cary risked touching the frame. It was solid and felt to the touch like wood instead of metal, so she assumed the gold was decorative paint. Still the glitter of it, the elaborate luxury of it, was impressive.

"Should I touch the glass, or is that going to be one of those too-stupid-to-live moves?" she asked as her fingers hovered over the foggy white face of the mirror.

"You're in Protector mode," Jaxer said. "It should be fine."

"Should be?" Deacon said, his voice a low grumble.

"And are we sure I'm even in Protector mode?" she asked.

Yes, she was standing in front of them to keep them safe from any potential danger. But since there wasn't any danger around right at that moment that she could tell, and since she wasn't getting any tingling along her spine to indicate trouble, she was pretty sure she was her ordinary self just then.

She frowned a little as she moved her fingers within a breath of the glass without actually touching it. A little zip of energy, like a few bugs landing on her fingertips, tickled her hand. Not quite like a static electric shock, but these particular tingles, mild though they were, were becoming very very familiar to her—now that she knew what to look for.

"Magic," she murmured. "Definitely magic."

"You're absorbing some," Deacon said.

He put his hands on her shoulders and eased her back from the mirror, closer into his chest. There wasn't enough room for him to really pull her away from the mirror. She just had to stretch another few inches and she'd still easily reach the glass. But the gesture made his point.

She lowered her arm. "Okay, so we know there's magic in that glass because I got some tingles. Which meant the magic was… moving out at me when I got close. Not exactly thrown at me, but not passively just sitting there either, or I wouldn't have felt anything." Unless literally surrounded by magic, like in Faery which was made of magic, she only felt those tingles when she was hit by magic, when it was thrown at her. She could walk past an active magic spell, and if it wasn't shooting magic at her, she wouldn't notice. "Reaching out sounds like too active a word for what I just felt, but it's the best I've got. I had to practically touch it first, though."

She looked to Jaxer. "Is this a gate? Is this what you were looking for?"

Rather than answer, he eased closer to the glass. The change in position forced her tighter against Deacon, and there were a few annoyed grunts as they rearranged themselves so Jaxer could study the mirror.

"No glamour on it," he said under his breath. "Definitely magic." Before Cary knew what he was going to do, he stuck his finger onto the pane.

Through the pane.

Cary reached for him, to jerk him away from the mirror, but before she could, the smoky face of the mirror changed, swirling into to a crystalline translucence. So clear it was almost like the glass was no longer there. The only way she could tell there was still a surface there was because a slight shimmer distorted the view beyond.

The view beyond that shimmer caught her breath.

A dark room lined with shelves stacked with leather books, vials, and canisters filled with things she couldn't—and in a few cases didn't want to—identify. Thick half-melted candles stuck inside metal trays. A few skulls. A stuffed crow which she had to look at twice to make sure it was stuffed and not a living animal. A long wooden bench overflowing with a collection of tubes, pipes, graduated cylinders, and vials in metal racks to give any chemistry class a run for its money. A Bunsen burner on low—that couldn't be safe!—and something in a vaguely greenish hue bubbling gently in the base of a rounded glass beaker. The only illumination came from flickering candles—again that struck Cary as a serious fire hazard—and the Bunsen burner's low blue flame.

She couldn't smell anything or hear anything from beyond the glass, but the view was enough. The room looked like something straight out of a bad B movie about alchemists and wizards.

"Well, that's…a little obvious," she said. "But also probably what we've been looking for."

"Zorianthus's lab?" Deacon asked.

"Likely," Jaxer said. "And also Sheldon's 'back door' out of the building."

"But he's been in hiding from Zorianthus," Cary pointed out, in what she thought was a calm and reasonable, and not condescending at all, manner. "He would hardly keep a gateway between himself and his former mentor open, nevertheless *use* it, if he didn't want Zorianthus to find him."

"It's possible it's only a one way gate," Jaxer said, frowning slightly.

"Yeah, but then he couldn't use it to get back into the building, and you'd have seen him coming *in* more often."

"Could Sheldon…lock it?" Deacon asked. "Use it only when he was sure the wizard wasn't around?"

"We'll have to ask Sheldon," Jaxer said. He hadn't looked away from the space beyond the mirror and his finger was still sticking in the glass, holding the gateway open.

"We're going through?" Cary asked, hoping her panic wasn't too obvious. Jaxer said these things were unpredictable and could collapse easily, killing anyone in mid-movement between locations. She wasn't keen on being killed by a magic mirror. That just seemed…well, kind of ridiculous, honestly, after all she'd been through.

"Stay here," Jaxer said. "I'll check it out first and make sure it's safe."

She let out a sound that was sort of snort, sort of laugh, filled with a lot of incredulity. "I'm the Protector, faery. If we're going, I'll go first so I can protect you guys." She shoved him, pushing and jostling until she was standing between the two men and the mirror again.

The minute Jaxer removed his finger from the glass, the pane smoked up again, blocking any view of the room beyond.

"This is a bad idea," Deacon said under his breath.

"Yup," she agreed as she stuck her hand into the mirror, gasping a little when she didn't meet any resistance. She very nearly fell forward through the gateway, but caught herself and remained on this side long enough to study the lab a moment longer.

She reached back and took hold of Deacon's hand. With a deep breath, she said, "Gird your loans, fellas."

Then she ducked into the mirror.

3 8

The disorientation and stumbling-into-a-new-location experience that Cary had been expecting…didn't happen. Her heartbeat pounded hard, like she'd run a marathon, because worry that the gateway would collapse had her wound up into a panic. But the practical transition between Sheldon's old bathroom and the laboratory felt no more complicated than stepping from outside to inside, or walking through an open doorway.

It only took that amount of time as well. No time pauses or stutters that made the transition feel like it took longer than moving from one room to another in a house.

"That was really weird," she murmured aloud. "For not being particularly weird."

She released Deacon's hand only when she was sure he and Jaxer were with her. Then she took in her surroundings.

The mirror, from this side, looked decidedly different. Still the same smoked glass obscuring the view beyond. But that was the only similarity. This side of the gateway, the mirror was a small circle of glass about the size of a basketball, surrounded by a black plastic frame that looked like something you could buy at a box store or a pharmacy. The cheapness of the frame actually highlighted the uniqueness of the glass, but the overall effect was a lot less impressive than the giant pane hanging in Sheldon's old bathroom.

She couldn't even imagine how they'd all fit through that small circle, what that might have looked like from this side. Probably really weird.

"How the hell are we getting back through that thing?" she asked.

"Getting back isn't the problem," Jaxer said. "I can find us a way back through Faery if needs be. Getting here, finding this…" His eyes were narrowed to slits as he took in the lab, his lips pressed together in a straight line. "This is what we've needed."

"We, huh?" She followed his gaze, taking in the rest of the lab.

It looked as it had through the gateway mirror. But now she could smell the place—a mixture of chemicals that made her nose twitch, an undertone of sulfur, and a whiff of formaldehyde that made her want to gag. And she could hear everything from the bubbling of the liquid in the beaker on the table, to the pop and sizzle of the candles, to the faint buzz of the Bunsen burner.

She looked around for a light so they could blow out the candles. "Should we turn off the burner? Lit candles and a burner going indefinitely seems like a recipe for fire. We know the wizard isn't coming back to turn them all off himself."

"Not sure messing with anything in here is a good idea," Deacon said. His voice had that growly quality that came when his leopard rose to the surface.

She faced him and realized his eyes were glowing, the yellow luminous in the dim lighting.

"Wow, you okay? What's going on? Why are you on the verge of shifting?"

"Something about this place…" He shook his head. "Has my hackles up."

"Yeah it does." She scanned their surroundings again, looking for what had put him so on edge. "What are you smelling under all the chemistry lab stench?"

"Blood," he said. "And adrenaline flavored with fear."

"Yeah, that's not good. Recent?"

He shook his head. "Imbedded in the place. I'm not smelling anything from the last few days. But sacrifice and suffering have happened here. More than once."

"This is one of those times I do *not* envy your sense of smell."

His answering grunt sounded more like a cat hiss.

She carefully moved deeper into the room, to the table holding the percolating beaker. "Someone stand behind me," she said. Deacon joined her without asking questions, in that flash of speed that blurred his movements. "Stand there and let me protect you while I turn this off. Just in case the green stuff explodes."

"I hate when you take explosions," he said, putting his hands on her shoulders but remaining firmly behind her.

"Good thing I haven't had to do that very often over the years." She did have a moment's pause to wonder if this explosion would release any magic she might absorb. She didn't want to guess what the wizard had been doing here, what sort of experiment he'd left behind before going to the vampires last night. But she was pretty sure it wouldn't be just run-of-the-mill chemistry experiments and that magic was involved somewhere.

She frowned at Jaxer, across the room, studying the shelves without touching anything. "You should get over here too," she said. "This explodes, there's no telling how far it'll go, or what it'll do."

"It could just not explode," he said, but he did move closer so he was also standing behind her.

"That would be lovely," she said. "I will be delighted if it doesn't explode. But no point in being careless."

She'd hated chemistry in college. It had been a necessary course for her biology degree. More than one term of chemistry actually. And the theory classes hadn't been bad, though she'd had trouble staying awake in one of the huge classes because the professor's lectures were profoundly monotone. But the labs had been stressful events every week. She kept expecting to burn the place down, or accidentally kill everyone by mixing the wrong things together. She'd never been so absolutely delighted to get finished with a collage requirement as finishing those couple of chemistry classes.

She gave the burner and the apparatus above it a close look, then wincing and turning her head away a little, she flicked the burner off. The little blue flame winked out without fanfare. The liquid in the beaker stopped bubbling almost instantly. A puff of green steam rose from the liquid to swirl around the inside of the beaker, but it didn't leak out of the rubber stopper so that felt fortunate. She was pretty sure her Protector magic protected against aerial poisons, but she'd rather not have to smell that steam any more clearly, even if it didn't kill them.

Some of the steam rose up through the tubbing inserted into the rubber stopper. She watched the climb of that green smoke as it wound through the tubbing, cringing in anticipation of disaster. But the smoke reached a point halfway through a section of circular loops in the tubes, then fell back to the beaker, almost like it was being sucked back into the liquid.

She held her breath, waiting for something bad to happen. Let out her breath when nothing except a gross but unidentifiable stench from the beaker reached her. Her nose twitched and she tried to suck in her nostrils so she didn't have to smell whatever had been brewing.

"I don't envy the person who has to clean this place up," she said.

And then the beaker exploded in a flash of green light and thick, viscus goop. The goop hit her shield along with shards of glass and sizzled like acid. She hurriedly took a few steps back as the goop slid to the ground, burning black holes in the dark, scarred wood.

"Huh," she murmured.

"Probably shouldn't touch that," Jaxer said.

Deacon muttered something rude and Cary tried not to laugh. But she did agree with Jaxer that it would be better not to touch the sizzling goop. In unison, they all moved backward another few feet, giving the smoking mess a wide berth.

She winced as more of the floor melted beneath the goop. "Wonder what that was supposed to be?"

"Probably better not knowing," Deacon said.

"So long as no one considered drinking it," she muttered and started a circuit of the outer edges of the room.

Deacon stuck with her while Jaxer moved off to the opposite side of the lab to investigate more shelves, these full of books and bottles she hadn't seen through the mirror from Sheldon's bathroom.

The shelves she searched didn't provide a lot of clues as to where Sheldon was, but they did give her a rather scary insight into what his former master had been studying. A lot of anatomy, chemistry, and medical text books which might not have seemed strange except she knew that Zorianthus had spent years perfecting body swapping and somehow his study of anatomy seemed creepy. There were books about alchemy—of course—and she even spotted another book by Bleak, though not the first volume that had been missing from The Bookstore—she was still very curious where that book had gone.

There were jars filled with eyeballs, and two with actual brains, and others with squishy things she didn't look at too closely, all carrying the distinctive scent of formaldehyde and alcohol. Between the chemical scents and the book dust, the place made her sneeze. Twice.

"You handling the smells okay?" she asked Deacon as she eased a book off a shelf. This one was on the principles of wizardry and anatomy. The book sent a little shock of electricity up her arm, so she hurriedly replaced it.

"Managing," Deacon said. "Could be worse."

"Sure." If they were at a waste management plant or walking through a sewer. "Find anything interesting?" He was looking over her head on the higher shelves, but he hadn't reached up to touch anything yet and she really couldn't blame him.

"A lot of stuff on herbs, and a rat in a jar."

"Yuck on the rat." She paused. "It's dead, right?"

"'Fraid so."

"Okay. Still yuck." She was an animal person but rats were not her favorite things in the animal kingdom. "Books on herbs seems more of a witch thing, though."

"Haven't actually discussed wizardry studies with a wizard before, so I wouldn't know," Deacon said.

To be fair, she hadn't discussed any of this with a wizard either. But she had with a witch. And herbs were definitely more in the witches' realm. Wizard potions tended to involve chemical reagents and the like. Witches used herbs from a cultivated garden. To an outsider, this stuff seemed to overlap, but Cary had learned the hard way not to suggest such a thing to a practicing witch.

"You find anything interesting?" she called to Jaxer. She had a vague idea that they should be looking for the book or papers that Zorianthus was going to use to find the Naga city entrance. That spell probably shouldn't be lying around the place for anyone to stumble across. Jaxer, or her bosses, would probably have a better place to store it. Out of harm's way.

She also sort of hoped they'd find a diary or writings to tell her what Zorianthus had been planning with all this. He wanted some of Holland's immortality. He wanted a body swap with Holland and hoped he'd pull in some of Holland's demon essence and bring that back to his own body, a way to extend his life indefinitely without the body swapping. But the Angel of Death had made clear that wouldn't have worked. Did Zorianthus know? Had Holland warned him it wouldn't work?

Did Holland know?

Holland didn't seem the type to let a human nag him about something off and on for centuries without killing the source of the nagging. Or even telling Zorianthus the flaw in his plan. She could see why Holland would refuse a body swap even if he didn't know it would kill Zorianthus—Zorianthus could kill off his own body and that would kill Holland. Or so the theory went. But with a demon... No telling what the end result would have actually been. Especially with a demon like Holland. And since Zorianthus wouldn't have been able to survive being inside Holland's body, the whole thing seemed pointless. Unless Zorianthus hadn't known and neither had Holland. But what either of them knew or didn't know was impossible to learn unless Zorianthus wrote it all down.

She was curious enough to want to find those writings if they existed.

Jaxer didn't answer her, so she turned away from a jar of what looked like bats' wings—poor bats!—to check on him. He was across the room, looking through some loose sheets of paper.

"What did you find?" she called and started toward him.

A strange shimmer of something out of the corner of her eye brought her up short. A bit of something metal stuck out from underneath a dark sheet, which covered most of whatever it was, and there seemed to be colors or lights moving over the metal that had nothing to do with the still flickering candles scattered around the lab.

She changed directions to investigate, Deacon sticking close to her side.

She reached for the sheet, frowning, a strange sense of unease curling in her stomach.

"This is weird," Jaxer said. "These pages look like they came from the book about people like you, Cary. The one Renee has in The Bookstore's back room. That can't be right. It would mean someone ripped them out of that book, and Renee would be outraged if someone had damaged one of her books. But I've never seen mention of your particular ability anywhere else, especially not in loose pages."

The sense of unease in Cary's stomach turned to full blown horror. She jerked the sheet down, revealing an elaborately scrolling brass headboard with runes swirling over the surface, melting in and out, impossible to read.

The headboard Deacon had been chained to in Sheldon's apartment when Cary had come to rescue him.

Deacon cursed as Cary swung to face Jaxer. "This isn't Zorianthus's lab. It's—"

Sheldon stepped out from the shadows behind a shelf, moving slowly into view.

"Mine."

ary slowly turned toward Sheldon, facing him fully. He was still dressed in the clothing he'd worn to the vampires' hive, black leather pants, a black silk shirt. His hair was mussed and there was a small cut on his cheekbone now that hadn't been there the night before. His eyes were wide, his face, if possible, even paler than he'd been before, and the dark circles under his eyes looked like bruises.

There was a wariness to him as he hovered far enough away to make it obvious he'd put the laboratory table between himself and the rest of them.

Since the last time they'd all be in the same place together she'd been protecting Sheldon, his wariness now would have put her on alert that something was wrong even if his disappearance hadn't.

"How did you find this place?" he asked.

"You left your gate mirror behind," she said.

"You came looking for me sooner than I thought you would. I was just about to smash the gateway."

"What's going on, Sheldon?"

He didn't answer at first, just stared at her, his eyes too wide.

"Talk to me. What's happening?"

"I… I thought about what you said, outside the hive."

"What did I say?" That seemed like years ago when it wasn't even twenty-four hours yet. Wow, a lot had happened.

"You said my worth and value as a human being were up to me now."

"It is. It always has been up to you. Your choices to make."

"Good or evil?"

She shrugged. "That's one choice. You've been on the wrong side of that one in the past."

"You think I'll go back to doing bad things."

"You haven't given me any reason to think otherwise."

His gaze finally flicked away from hers, resting on the floor on the opposite side of the table from where he stood. "You probably shouldn't have turned off that burner."

"I'd apologize for the mess, but you left a fire burning unattended. That's dangerous. Also, you haven't told me if you're moving onto the good side of the spectrum or sticking with evil yet, so I'm not really sorry I disrupted whatever you were brewing."

"The witchcraft… It isn't working for me. I can't… I can't get the hang of it. I'm not a witch."

She wasn't sure how to respond so she held her tongue. She could feel Deacon at her back, his big body tightly coiled. If she looked at him, she'd probably see his eyes glowing. But she didn't dare look away from Sheldon. She did, however, remain standing firmly between Sheldon and Deacon, just in case.

Though who she was protecting from whom, she still wasn't entirely sure.

From her peripheral vision, she noticed Jaxer moving just slightly, facing Sheldon more fully, but not otherwise getting closer to her. She wanted to motion him over so she could include him in her protective magic. But she didn't want to draw Sheldon's attention to him. So far, the former wizard hadn't glanced at Jaxer. The longer Sheldon kept his attention on her, the better.

Her heartbeat thudded harder as she waited for him to continue. The not knowing, the worry about what he was doing, sent her adrenaline spiking. And the longer he remained quiet, the more her nerves stretched.

Finally, he pulled in a breath and looked away from the burnt section of floor. "I was attempting to brew a cleansing potion, from one of the books on witchcraft. But the witches do things so differently. I tried to adapt it to what I know." He made a face at the hole in the floor. "I guess that didn't work."

"Not for cleaning anyway. Though it probably would have made a hell of a chemical weapon."

Sheldon's slight wince gave her a very small nugget of hope to cling to. Maybe he wasn't returning to evil. Maybe he intended to change. A cleansing potion—even disastrously executed—didn't sound like the efforts of a person trying to commit murder again.

Or maybe he was just lying about the spells intended purpose.

She didn't relax her stance in front of Deacon. "If you had a gateway between this place and your old apartment this whole time, why didn't Zorianthus use it to find you?"

"He didn't know about it," Sheldon said. "I found the mirrors and kept them hidden from him. He knew where my apartment was, even though he never went there, but not my lab. Wizards don't let other wizards into their labs."

That was interesting to know. "How did you find his papers, then, the ones that let you know he'd intended to kill you?"

Another wince. "I found his lab. He never realized... Well, he might have realized after I went into hiding. But I've known where his private laboratory was for the last year."

"Can you take us there?"

"No."

"Why?"

"I just destroyed it."

Jaxer curse quietly under his breath. Sheldon finally looked at him.

"There's nothing there that can hurt anyone anymore," Sheldon told him. "If someone had found all of his research, all of his spells, they could have done a lot of damage."

"But we could have ensured that didn't happen," Jaxer said.

"Too late now."

Sheldon's tone was so matter-of-fact, but his eyes were still wide. The unemotional tone didn't match his expression anymore. He didn't look dead inside. But for all that, she still couldn't read him or judge what he might be thinking.

"How did you get to his lab from here? And back again?" Cary asked. Because she hadn't heard a door open before he made his presence known. So either he'd been in the lab the entire time, or he'd crept in from some exit. Deacon hadn't noticed him, though, hadn't scented him before he spoke up. Which meant Sheldon hadn't been in the room. Or he'd found a way to disguise himself from a shifter's sense of smell.

Given he'd killed shifters in the past, that might be a possibility. And it might explain the lack of "wizard smell" at the apartment building.

"Car," he answered her question. "I have one, you know."

"That you keep here," she guessed. She was extremely curious where "here" was, but she'd have to figure that out later because first she needed to know, "Why did you run, Sheldon? Why clear out the apartment and disappear?"

"Zorianthus isn't a threat now. I didn't need to hide there anymore. And I do need to do something with my life. Witchcraft isn't the answer. I can't make it work right. I'm a wizard, even without my magic."

She nodded, still wary. She couldn't read him, but something about his wide eyes worried her. Something in the way he held himself. Something was wrong here. But what?

"The Angel said I could body swap with Oliver Holland and survive, that you could keep Holland safe that way."

"I don't recall her saying that last part." At least not in those words. The Angel had implied it. And her bosses had pretty much confirmed she was going to have to protect Holland from his father. But she didn't want to encourage Sheldon in his current thinking.

"I don't have the magic for it, but I could work the spell still, even without magic, so long as someone else supplied the magic."

"Like…who?"

"The triad. They could help me."

"Uhm, I'm not so sure that's a good idea." For some reason, the thought of them helping Sheldon set off all Cary's alarm bells. Like a gong on impending doom. "Why don't we wait for more information from the Nagas? I'm sure we'll hear something soon. We wouldn't want to jump in to anything yet. Maybe we can… I don't know. Negotiate Holland's release, and I'll protect him, and the Angel can kill his father and…" And she could hope to survive all that but at least Sheldon wouldn't be involved.

"If the Nagas won't release him? If they're willing to face his father rather than give up their prisoner?"

"Well, then maybe I join the Nagas again, and I'll protect the city while they keep Lud occupied with their magic until the Angel shows up and kills him."

She was making that all sound pretty simple. But it wouldn't be. If it had been a simple thing for the Angel to arrive and kill Lud the moment he entered this realm, she would have shown up the last time he did. He'd broken the circle and sacrificed power to step into this realm when his plan to occupy a reanimated corpse fell through. He'd been in this realm for a little bit, in a weakened state—which as she recalled was still terrifying and powerful—and there'd been no Angel of Death arriving to off him. So she had no faith that any of this would be simple.

But the last thing they needed was for Sheldon to do something rash and make it all infinitely worse.

"If the demon is in my body, his father won't sense him right away. His father won't know to invade this realm yet."

"We can't be sure of that." They couldn't be sure of anything.

"Actually," Sheldon said, "I can."

He straightened his shoulders, let out a long breath. His wide-eyed stare eased. He leaned his head to one side, then the other, and she heard the popping sound across the lab.

"Sheldon," Cary said. "Don't do it. Whatever you're about to do. Don't do it."

He met her gaze. And smiled. "Too late."

His body jerked and his head dropped back, the neck muscles tightening, tendons standing out, his jaw clenched so tight his teeth audible cracked together.

Cary took a step toward him, not thinking, intent on stopping whatever was happening. Deacon grabbed her shoulders, holding her back. Instinctively, she wanted to fight his hold, she wanted to get to Sheldon and... She didn't know. She didn't know what she'd do.

The not knowing kept her rooted in place, horrified as Sheldon's long, thin frame jerked first to one side, then the next, and then crumbled against the wooden table. His fall scattered the glass and tube apparatus, sending flasks and beakers to shatter against the floor.

The sound of crashing glass quieted, leaving a deep silence behind.

Cary tugged at Deacon's hold again, but he didn't release her.

"Wait," he murmured, so quietly she was sure only she heard.

Across the room, Jaxer had also stilled, watching the former wizard like he expected him to explode.

Given what had happened to his former mentor, the idea that Sheldon might explode didn't seem as ridiculous as it might have a few days ago. Which sent Cary's panic skyrocketing.

"Sheldon?" She made to move toward him again, but Deacon still held her back. She started to turn, started to shake him off, but stopped short when Sheldon groaned and pushed up from the table.

For a long moment, he stared down at his hands, pressed against the table. Cary held her breath, waiting for him to say something, do something.

But her impatience got the better of her. She sucked in a shallow breath and said, "Sheldon? You okay?"

He looked up from the table and met her gaze. His once brown eyes now glowed faintly red. When he smiled, the expression wasn't anything she'd ever seen on Sheldon's face.

But it was familiar.

"Well. Ms. Redmond," he said in a voice not Sheldon's.

The faint English accent. The cadence. That voice had never come out of that face. But that hardly mattered. She'd know that voice anywhere.

Her heartbeat kicked into triple time and she gasped despite herself, lurching backward into Deacon, who caught her closer, keeping her upright when she might have tripped in her hurry to put distance between herself and Sheldon.

Who wasn't Sheldon anymore.

"Fancy seeing you again," Oliver Holland said.

40

*P*anic tightened Cary's throat, made breathing difficult, her heart hammering so hard she could feel it painfully against her ribs. She started to see spots dancing at the edge of her vision and had to gulp in air in quick, desperate swallows to keep from passing out.

"How?" she gasped past the panic.

"My triad," Holland said as he pushed away from the table and took in his surroundings.

He even moved like himself, despite being in a completely different body. There wasn't the awkwardness she would have expected, the adjustment to a shape and form he wasn't used to. The demon just took over Sheldon's shell and moved it around like he belonged in that lanky frame.

"You've kept your leopard," Holland said, his tone managing a degree of condescension that would have set Cary's teeth on edge if she weren't so terrified. "How sweet."

"Uh huh." She wanted to say more, ask questions, do…something. But she couldn't drag herself away from Deacon. He was behind her, which meant he was probably safe. But Holland knew what she was, knew how to kill her. He could simply ignore Deacon and Jaxer and focus on her if he wanted her to die.

Jaxer!

She looked toward him, frantic for him to be closer so she could protect him if Holland decided killing everyone might be fun. To her surprise, he wasn't there.

She blinked. Frowned.

What the hell? Where had he gone? Had he left?

That didn't feel right. But since she didn't want to call Holland's attention to the fact that there'd been someone else in the room who was no longer there, she turned back to the demon.

"What now?" she asked, surprised her voice came out loud enough to be heard.

"Oh, this is just a little test," Holland said. "Don't worry. I'll release the child soon. I don't think he's happy in my body anyway."

"Why not? Is he okay?"

Holland faced her again. "You met the Angel."

"How is Sheldon? Is he okay?"

"What did you think of her? I know you didn't get the full effect since she had to use the triad, but she's impressive, don't you think?"

"Sure. Impressive." And terrifying. "You haven't answered my question about Sheldon."

"Why so worried?" He paused, frowning slightly as if searching his memory. Then he looked at her closer. "He tried to kill your leopard, and yet you worry about him." He tsked and it was such an Oliver Holland sound, Cary could practically see the demon's human face instead of Sheldon's. "That compassion. It's going to get you killed."

She resisted the urge to add "again" to his statement. The less Holland knew about anything to do with her last few months, the better. "How do you know he tried to kill Deacon?"

"Well, body swapping is an interesting practice, Ms. Redmond. Really you should try it one day. Very different, occupying a stranger's body when they're not there. I've done both, you know. Proper possessions where the former occupant is subsumed under my will, and this…" He gestured at Sheldon's frame.

"Uh huh."

"The funny thing is, memories are left in the bones and blood, even when the…essence has left."

"Does that mean Sheldon's picking up your memories now?" That sounded horrifying.

"The ones he can comprehend that live in the form he's occupying. Yes. Although, *that's* something I wouldn't recommend."

Cary's stomach rolled.

"Such a waste. Such potential the child had. But you…" His tone lightened from mournful to playful scolding. "Ms. Redmond. Keeping secrets from me. Absorbed all the magic we threw at you, and you didn't die. I'm impressed."

"I can tell."

He chuckled, the sound like a series of cuts from a thin razor across her back. "I've missed you."

"The feelings not mutual."

"Now I'm hurt."

"Right." She swallowed, trying to wet her dry throat. "I met your father."

Holland's casual perusal of the lab stilled and he faced her, the red glow in his eyes brightening. "Yes. And yet, you're still alive."

"It was a close thing."

He titled his head to one side, his gaze narrowed. "Why didn't you tell him where he could find me?"

"I didn't want the Nagas to get hurt."

"Didn't care if he killed me?"

"Not even a little bit."

He chuckled again. "You didn't understand what that would have meant. You still don't."

"I'm getting a better idea. Though a full explanation from someone in the know would be great so I don't have to keep guessing."

"Oh, I'll explain soon enough. But not now. This is just a brief visit. I can't stay in this body very long. I've probably killed it as is."

"No." She started forward again, only to have Deacon's iron grip keep her in place. "Let him come back to his own body. Don't kill him."

"I have to know. Why do you care? He tried to kill your mate. He killed other shifters. Why should you worry about him dying?"

"I…" She didn't know why she cared. Sheldon still hadn't done anything to make up for his past behavior. He hadn't said he wanted to do or be better. And he had just invited one of her biggest enemies into his body, letting the demon face her without warning her first. She couldn't explain why she didn't want Sheldon dead to herself, nonetheless Holland. Especially in that moment.

The best she could do was, "Don't kill him. Just…don't kill him."

Holland glanced up at the ceiling, as if considering something. "I'll be free of my captors soon," he said. "When they've released me, I'll be back. We have some things to discuss." He met her gaze again. "And I wonder, will you protect *me* this time? To avoid the destruction of your world?"

"If I have to, I will."

"Even though I'd love to kill you. Might kill you once my father is…taken care of."

"Even though."

"Even knowing there's no way to kill me? That you won't be able to save yourself. That I can't die."

"Even though," she repeated.

"You, Ms. Redmond, are a fascinating creature." He smiled, slow and dangerous. "And I look forward to our next meeting."

"Wait…"

He closed his eyes and collapsed into a heap on the floor.

41

ary froze for an instant, the reality of what had just happened shutting off her ability to think or act. Part of her was aware of the lab around her, the smells of chemicals and formaldehyde, the flickering, uneven light of candle flames, the press of Deacon at her back. But most of her was numb from shock.

And then fear for Sheldon gripped her, choking her.

She rushed to his side. Deacon let her go this time. She dropped onto her knees beside Sheldon's body and pressed her fingers against his neck, feeling for a pulse even as she watched his chest for signs he was breathing. In the back of her mind, every horror movie she'd ever seen leapt up to scream at her not to get too close, not until she was sure Holland was gone, to move away quickly before his eyes popped open and he grabbed her. But the logic didn't stop her pressing a hand against Sheldon's chest, looking for a heartbeat, hoping to feel some kind of movement.

Deacon knelt beside her. "He's breathing, but barely. It's Sheldon again."

She blinked up at him. "How can you tell?"

"I can hear his breath, and I smelled when he returned and Holland left."

"That's why you let me go to him." She nodded, realizing Deacon wouldn't have released her if he'd been afraid of that horror movie scenario—the bad guy tricking her close by pretending to faint. Having a mate with such an excellent sense of smell really did come in handy.

"What the hell happened to Jaxer?" she asked as she leaned over Sheldon, putting her cheek near his mouth, trying to feel his breath. She couldn't feel anything for a long moment and then a very very faint puff of air.

"I'm here," Jaxer said, startling her. "I thought I'd better get help. Just in case."

The Fae healer Eriana stepped out from behind Jaxer and knelt beside Sheldon as well. Cary hadn't seen Eriana in a while. Not since Ireland. The healer continued to show herself as a relatively ordinary human woman, pleasant-looking but not particularly head-turning, her brown hair cut short and spiky around her angular, pale face, her jeans and t-shirt casually boxy on her wide-shouldered frame.

She nodded Cary to one side, then stretched Sheldon out so he lay flat on his back. "What happened?" she asked, her voice low. She'd adapted her accent so it was more American than either Irish or English now, but there was still a little hint of lilt in her sentences.

"He traded bodies with a demon," Cary said. "Not long, but… The demon said the exchange might kill him."

Eriana put her hands over Sheldon's chest.

His rib bones stood out against the material of his black silk shirt, which for some reason made Cary's heart hurt. She couldn't see any movement. "Is he breathing?"

"Barely," Eriana said. She closed her eyes and her hands began to glow pale purple.

Cary hadn't seen Eriana heal before. She'd been the object of her healing. Eriana had brought Cary back from the dead with her power. But Cary had never witnessed the process. Her fascination was tempered by worry, though.

She stood so she was out of the healer's way, taking a few steps closer to the table, careful to avoid the broken glass littering the floor.

"Thank you for going to get her," she murmured to Jaxer, keeping her voice low so she didn't distract Eriana. "But why?"

"Sheldon couldn't change bodies with a demon and not suffer for it. I didn't want him to die."

That startled her into looking at him. "You've wanted him dead for months."

"I've wanted justice for months. I've wanted him punished for his crimes. But you don't want him dead. And I'm willing to acquiesce to your instincts on this, so long as, eventually, justice is served." Jaxer met her gaze, his expression serious and solemn. "Your job was to keep him alive. I won't let you think you've failed. Not when I can do something to help. So, for now, we keep Sheldon alive. If we can. And the rest... We'll have time for that later."

She let out a breath, long and slow, as some tension in her shoulders eased. "You're not supposed to be helping me."

He shrugged, his expression lightening just a little. "Technically, I'm not. Eriana is."

She'd take the technicality. "Holland will be back. He said he'd be free of the Nagas soon. We need to warn them somehow."

"They've been warned."

"They have? By who?"

"The Angel."

When he didn't continue, Cary shoved him a little. "Explain or I'm going to scream."

"Don't. You'll distract Eriana."

She nudged him again and made a face. He flashed her a quick smile before growing serious again.

"Eriana was with Liruk and Wisat when I reached her. We didn't have time for a long talk obviously, but they said the Angel warned the Nagas not to resist Holland's release."

"They agreed?"

"Again, I haven't gotten the full story yet. No time. But that was the impression I got from Wisat. Liruk didn't say anything. She just looked annoyed."

"Yeah, well, that's normal for Liruk." But another worry loosened in Cary's gut. She'd been afraid Holland would kill to escape. If the Nagas let him go, they'd be safe at least. "What happens when he's released?" she asked, not expecting anyone to have answers. It was a rhetorical question.

She wasn't disappointed. Both men remained quiet as all three of them stared at Eriana working on Sheldon. Silence filled the lab, broken only by the occasional spit and putter of one of the candles. The healing seemed to take a very long time, though Cary's sense of time was twisted and distorted at this stage. How long had they been in the lab before Sheldon found them? How long was Holland in his body?

How much damage had been done?

As if in answer to that unspoken question, Eriana murmured, "He has a lot of internal injuries. Like he's been…cooked on the inside."

Gross. Cary pressed a hand to her stomach, nearly doubling over. She wanted to throw up.

Oh… She started and looked up at Deacon in horror. He could probably *smell* that. Oh god. She gripped his hand, tightening her hold when his fingers flexed hard against hers.

"Can you help?" Cary said after swallowing hard to force down bile.

Eriana didn't answer immediately. Her eyes were closed, her glowing hands moving over Sheldon's chest in a slow sweep, back and forth from collar to hip and up again. "It'll take more than one session to repair all the damage," she finally said, her voice quiet and deep. "Getting the worst of it fixed. He'll live."

Cary's knees wobbled. She held tighter to Deacon as a mix of emotions she couldn't fully identify washed through her. Some of it was relief. But that was mixed with anger. And confusion. And strangely, a sense of betrayal.

That last she'd have to examine once she could think again. When she didn't have the stench of the lab in her nose and the horror of having faced Holland again destroying her logic.

"We'll take him back to his old apartment," Jaxer said. "He can recover there and Eriana will know where to find him for future sessions."

"Will he stay?" Not that Jaxer had any great insight into Sheldon's thinking. She wasn't sure what she expected him to say.

"He'll stay put if he wants to live," Jaxer said.

Cary didn't respond. There was more in Jaxer's comment than just an answer to her question. But she didn't have the capacity to deal with it in that moment.

Another long silence descended as they waited on Eriana. Cary's nerves stretched tight but she held still and remained quiet. Finally, after what felt like an hour, Eriana sat up, the glow in and around her hands died away, and she pulled in a deep breath.

"That's all for now," she said, her voice scratchy and quiet with exhaustion. She wobbled a little as she stood, but when Jaxer moved toward her she waved him away. "He'll recover, live, but there is some damage that… He won't be quite the same. Ever again."

"Geezus," Cary murmured.

Eriana was a miracle worker. She'd brought Cary back from the dead and fixed most of the damage done by all the magic Cary had absorbed. Of course, some of that recovery effort had been helped by the fact that Cary healed faster than a normal human since becoming a Protector. Still, that wouldn't have been enough on its own, wasn't enough on its own. Eriana had literally kept Cary from dying and repaired her injuries at a deep, cellular level.

Cary could only imagine what kind of damage the demon had done to Sheldon's body that it wasn't something Eriana could fix completely.

"He'll need to sleep for a while," Eriana continued. "I've put him in a…a kind of magical coma to help with the healing."

"Thank you," Cary said, letting a long sigh out, puffing up her cheeks. "We should get him back to the apartment."

Deacon lifted Sheldon with a surprising amount of gentleness, and they went back through the mirror into his old apartment, moving through one at a time to accommodate the tiny bathroom.

The unmade bed groaned as Deacon laid Sheldon down. Cary scanned the room. Sheldon had emptied it. There weren't any blankets or sheets or pillows. The place was barebones and ready for new renters. She hadn't seen any blankets or pillows in his lab either. Whatever he'd done with his living stuff, he hadn't stacked it there.

"I'll go home and get some spare pillows and sheets and things," she said as Deacon straightened away from Sheldon's prone body. "If he's got to sleep for a while to heal, we shouldn't just leave him like that." She gestured at the bare mattress. She frowned at Jaxer. "Are you okay staying here? Watching him until I get back?"

"I brought Eriana to heal him," Jaxer said dryly. "I'm not going to hurt the little shit now."

She made a face. "That's not what I meant. We need to talk to Wisat and Liruk."

"I'll monitor the young man until you return," Eriana said. "He may need additional assistance anyway."

"Thank you." Cary wanted to say more but didn't know what to say at this stage because exhaustion was chasing her adrenaline rush, and now she was just tired. So she repeated, "Thank you."

Eriana tipped her chin up in a brief nod of acknowledgment.

"I'll meet you at your place," Jaxer said. He glanced down at Sheldon's prone form. "I don't know what motivated him to do such a stupid thing, but I hope he survives so I can ask."

"Yeah," Cary murmured. "Me, too."

THE DOGS GREETED HER THE INSTANT SHE WALKED THROUGH THE DOOR and the comfort of dog hugs was soothing. Her soul hurt. And she knew this wasn't done yet. Holland would be back. And she'd have to deal with him, because once he was free in this realm, Lud *would* return eventually. But for now, for a little while anyway, she'd breathe and recover and rest so she could face the next fight.

She explained the situation to the dogs as she got them treats from the mudroom, because Lud's return had implications for Buck, and she didn't want any of them caught unawares.

Fred took the news with philosophical ease, banging his tail on the floor when he sat up to encourage the speedy issuing of the treats.

Pickles let out a low woof, which Cary took as acknowledgement that things were gonna get weird soon. And Buck nudged her leg a few times before sitting and waiting for his dog biscuit. She wasn't sure what Buck was trying to tell her. She just hoped the return of the demon god didn't set off his demon dog side again. He'd recovered just fine, but still…

By the time she'd finished with the dogs, Jaxer had arrived and was sitting in one of her living room chairs, quietly talking with Deacon. They both looked up when she walked in.

"Dogs settled?" Deacon asked.

"And brought up to date on the situation. I think they'll be fine. I hope."

"We have some time," Jaxer said. "Time before Holland reenters this realm. Time to…marshal the troops."

"And hope it helps. This is one hell of a way to spend the last few months of my test year. Just saying."

Jaxer snorted a very inelegant laugh.

She flopped onto the couch next to Deacon and rubbed her hands over her face. "I've gotta tell you, I'm not looking forward to this. Not even a little bit." She dropped her hands to her lap. "What now?"

"Now, we wait," Jaxer said. "The pieces are in motion. It's just a matter of time."

"I hate waiting," she said, "but in this particular case, I'm good with a break. I'm gonna need to prepare for this. And talk to Angie and her demon hunter boyfriend we're not supposed to know about. And maybe find out what the vampires are doing in all this."

"But not tonight," Deacon said. "Tonight, you eat and you rest. It's been a hell of a day."

She snorted. "Yeah it has."

Because she figured he needed to know, she told Jaxer then about everything Rory had told Deacon. The consequences of the way she absorbed magic, the way she'd probably have to release it by using it, wasn't something she could keep to herself given the confrontation to come.

"I don't know what it all means in the grand scheme of things," she said when she'd finished. "But I'm gonna need teachers from a bunch of different magic disciplines. Including someone who can teach me how to use Faery magic."

Jaxer stared at the coffee table, his brows lowered. "We'll have to update Wisat and Liruk. This has…implications."

"It does." Though she still wasn't sure what those implications were. She hadn't had time to even process the information herself yet.

"We'll take care of it," Jaxer said, facing her, his expression relaxing. "We'll get it all sorted."

"Okay." Since she needed the reassurance, even if she didn't fully buy it, she let herself be comforted.

"For now," Jaxer said, "we'll look after Sheldon and pass the word to all our contacts about what's coming. This isn't going to be a small thing. Not just a test of your abilities as a Protector. This is a lot."

She snorted. "An understatement of epic proportions." She considered Jaxer a moment. "Does this mean I get help? From you, from everyone?"

Since Jaxer had *been* helping her, even if he could justify it as helping someone else, she was pretty sure they'd already wrecked any adherence to the test year rules. But that was also something she'd have to worry about later. First, she had to survive the upcoming confrontation. Then she'd worry about whether or not she'd failed her test year.

Frankly, if she survived and the people she loved survived, she'd consider that winning no matter what happened with the test.

"I'm here," Jaxer said. "Whether it violates rules or not. This isn't a normal Seventh Year. The rules be damned."

"Thanks," she said. "And thanks again for getting Eriana even though you can't stand Sheldon."

"Well, I have a feeling the little shit has more to play in this."

"So, not just worried about me being upset then?" She tried to smile to make light of her statement, but she was so drained it didn't really work.

"More worried about your feelings than Sheldon, if that helps."

His joke fell flat too, but she made an attempt at a smile again.

"I'm going to need dinner and sleep soon. Let me get the linens for Sheldon."

She got a spare pillow from her guest bedroom and some sheets and a summer blanket from the hall closet, stuff she wouldn't need back. She had very mixed feelings about Sheldon still, even if she didn't want him dead, and she wasn't sure she was going to want these sheets returned.

By the time she got back to the living room, Jaxer was standing near the door, talking quietly with Deacon again.

"You're leaving?" she asked Jaxer. "Will you meet us at Sheldon's?"

"I'll take the sheets to his place." He held out his hands for her pile. "You need time to rest. Been a few shocks today. You won't be any good to us strung out from everything that's happened."

She handed over the sheets and gave him a sideways look. "You just want time alone with Eriana, don't you?"

His scowl was instant and helped her gloomy mood a lot. "Just get some rest, smart ass. You've got a job to do soon."

She chuckled. "Give Eriana our best. Thank her for me again."

"Uh huh." He bundled the sheets and pillow under his arm and then gave her a more serious, gentle look. Then he leaned in and kissed her on top of her head, something he hadn't done in months.

To her utter surprise, Deacon didn't growl at the gesture.

"Rest," Jaxer said, touching his fingers to her cheek. He turned and clapped Deacon on the shoulder, holding his gaze for a long moment. "We live to fight another day."

When Jaxer had gone, Deacon pulled her close, holding her in a quiet hug for a long time.

"We're gonna get through this, right?" she asked, knowing he couldn't be any more certain than she could, but also needing the comfort, even if it was a lie.

"We're going to get through this," he said. "And we won't be alone in the fight. We'll have help."

Part of her wanted to refuse the help because she didn't want people to get hurt. The bigger part of her knew this wasn't anything she could do on her own. A demon god was coming. Again. And his demon son who couldn't be killed was about to be her new charge. The Angel of Death lurked in the background of all this. And there were a lot of enemies to confront in her future.

But for now, for this moment, for this night, while she had Deacon's strong arms wrapped around her and everyone she loved was, in this moment, safe and secure, she'd pretend everything would be just fine. None of the good guys would die. The bad guys would get their comeuppance. And the world would keep turning. All would be well.

She hoped.

THANK YOU

Thank you for reading The Trouble with Wizards and Old Enemies. I hope you enjoyed it. I realize this is more of a cliffhanger than I usually put into these books, and for that I'm sorry! I hate cliffhangers most of the time. But this turned out to be too big a story to fit into one book. I do promise not to make you wait long for the next book, though. Book Seven is written and will release in May of 2022, so depending on when you're reading this, you'll have it soon, or it's already out. And until then, we live to fight another day!

For an excerpt from the next book in the Cary Redmond series, The Trouble with Death and Demon Gods, keep reading.

For readers who'd like to keep up on new releases and news, and maybe get in on the occasional free read, you can join my newsletter at https://bit.ly/KatSimonsNewsletter. The newsletter goes out once a month, and new subscribers get an exclusive, free short story when joining—but the short story is from my Tiger Shifter paranormal romance series and was originally written for an erotic romance anthology. The story is…hot. You have been warned. If you'd prefer, you can always check for news and updates at my website at https://www.katsimons.com, or follow my author page at your favorite vendors. Thanks for reading!

THE TROUBLE WITH DEATH AND DEMON GODS

A CARY REDMOND NOVEL

EXCERPT

1

Cary pulled herself off the hard, navy blue mat, groaning only a little bit, and straightened her shoulders. The lovely scent of frankincense sticks burning by a small statue of the Buddha near the front desk of the dojo didn't completely hide Cary's sweat stink, but she'd take it. At least she wasn't bleeding.

"I'm not sure this is working," she said to her best-friend-current-torture-master, and her bear shifter training partner.

"This is only the third time you've trained with Brandon," Lucy said in her little girl's voice, putting her hands on her hips. "Give the process time."

Lucy Evans-Nakada was, physically, not what you might expect of a multi-blackbelt holding martial arts expert. She was a petit red-head, with brown eyes, pale skin, freckles across her nose, and a high-pitched, sweet voice that made her sound like a little girl. But she'd been training in martial arts since the age of two, including time spent in Japan studying under masters, and she could kick the ass of grown men—more than one at a time—without breaking a sweat.

She owned the dojo they were training in and had been teaching for years. And because she was one of Cary's best friends in the whole world, she tortured Cary here on a regular basis. To be fair, Cary was trying to get better at the self-defense stuff. Her job as a magical Protector just kept getting more and more complicated, and knowing how to at least not freeze in the face of danger if her powers weren't working seemed like a really good idea.

Although, freezing in the face of danger was *precisely* the instinct that made her a good Protector. Get between bad guys and good guys and then just…stand there. The magic she channeled from her bosses rose up and shielded both her and the good guy. And all was right with the world.

At least in theory.

"You got up quicker than usual," Brandon said. "That's a marked improvement over the last two sessions."

She grunted in response.

Brandon Hawthorn was, physically, everything you might imagine a bear shifter to look like. Huge at six-foot-nine, at least, thickly-muscled, and when he didn't smile, pretty intimidating. He kept his dark hair cut very close to his head and was clean shaven, showing off a granite jawline any model might envy. His dark complexion was smooth, and his brown eyes hooded and hard to read. Until you looked directly at him. Then suddenly you spotted the sweet, gentle man lurking behind the large scary façade.

Being a bear shifter, however, meant he was faster and stronger than Cary. By a lot. And since he'd been training more diligently with Lucy for a lot longer than Cary, he was also a better martial artist.

The first time they'd sparred—at Lucy's insistence—Cary had spent most of her session flat out on her back, staring up at the dojo's ceiling tiles. He was right about her getting up quicker now. But she had a feeling that was because he was pulling his punches.

"Are you two taking it easy on me?" she asked. "You're feeling sorry for me, aren't you?"

"Not…exactly," Lucy said, though she wouldn't meet Cary's gaze.

"Right." Cary huffed and straightened her training gi with a little more oomph than absolutely necessary.

"It's mostly distraction," Brandon said, his deep voice gentle. "Not pity."

"You hate waiting," Lucy said.

Well, that was true enough. And she'd been waiting for two weeks. Which was starting to make her a little...difficult. Deacon would say that nicer, but he was her mate so he had to. But difficult was a good word for her snapping, brittle, irritable mood. Taking that mood out on her friends was unacceptable, though.

"I haven't been making your life miserable, have I?" she asked, now feeling worse than when they'd been tossing her onto her ass for the last hour. "Have I been grumping too much?"

"Not too much," Lucy assured. "Just enough. I'd be grumping, too. It's not like you're just waiting on a package or a repairman or something. Waiting to stop the end of the world must be extremely frustrating."

More truth. Cary pressed a hand to her stomach to stop the jumping nerves—the real reason for her irritability she was sure. Waiting for the world-ending confrontation between a demon god, the Angel of Death, and their demon offspring who, coincidentally, hated and wanted to kill Cary was not exactly a fun experience.

Waiting for that confrontation without any signs of it actually happening was a whole lot worse.

If she was going to face—and maybe have to actually protect—one of her most deadly enemies, it'd be nice to just get it over with.

But no. That would be simple. And Cary's life never seemed to follow the simple path.

She let out another groan and sat on the mat, dropping abruptly enough both Lucy and Brandon took a step forward as if to catch her. She snorted. "I'm not fainting. I'm just tired. More emotionally, though, you know."

Lucy also dropped into a cross-legged seat on the mat. "Makes sense."

Brandon settled on his knees. "I get that."

She hadn't actual meant to unload the whole thing in front of Brandon, but it had just come spilling out during their last training session because she'd been too distracted to even attempt paying attention. He'd tossed her around the dojo like a ragdoll for all of ten minutes before Lucy called a halt and demanded an explanation for Cary's lack of effort. The whole thing just…spilled out.

Fortunately, according to Deacon, Brandon was a really good guy and could be trusted with the information. At least the parts of the story Cary had admitted to. Brandon was a professional fundraiser, and Deacon had worked with him in the past on fundraisers for Deacon's family business—they ran animal rescue shelters around the country, which was, of course, the reason she'd fallen in love with him because how was she supposed to resist that? It didn't hurt that he was a gorgeous, sexy leopard shifter who smelled like heaven and brought her donuts regularly. But the animal rescue job had really pushed his appeal over the top in Cary's mind.

The fact that her mate said she could trust Brandon had probably been the reason Cary had let go with all her pent-up anxiety.

"How's Sheldon doing?" Lucy asked quietly.

Ah, there was another thing that had her stretched too thin. The not quite twenty-year-old wizard who had at one point tried to kill Deacon, Cary had accidentally drained all his powers, his former master had tried to kill Cary for it—more than once—and now, maybe, possibly, Sheldon was no longer evil. But she wasn't sure about that, which only complicated things. Sheldon had most definitely been a bad guy. And he'd never really apologized or worked to atone for the evil—and murder—he'd committed before being drained of all his wizard magic. So he wasn't a good guy for sure.

Cary had been forced to protect him as part of her last job which was the job that had gotten her into the waiting-on-the-world-ending-confrontation position she was in now. And because, for reasons Cary still couldn't grasp, he'd done something monumentally stupid and possibly suicidal, Sheldon had spent the last two weeks in a coma with his insides…well, not in good shape.

"He's hanging in there," she answered Lucy's question. "Thanks to Eriana's healing efforts."

Eriana was a Fae healer and a Protector mentor-in-training— although Cary wasn't supposed to know that last part—and she had a very complicated past, and current, relationship with Cary's own former mentor Jaxer, also a Fae. Unfortunately, Cary hadn't been able to enjoy that drama because she'd had too much drama of her own.

"Has he woken up since…everything?" Lucy asked.

"No. Eriana isn't letting him. He's still got too much healing to do. But she says he's mending, so I suppose that's something."

"How's Deacon handling the whole Sheldon thing?"

"With a lot more…kindness than I would have expected."

The little shit had tried to kill Deacon. Cary had *met* Deacon because she'd had to save him from Sheldon and his nefarious plan to steal Deacon's body. There was no reason in the world, not even a little bit, for Deacon to have any concern at all for whether the former wizard healed or not. Yet he checked regularly with Eriana on Sheldon's progress, and had even been to see Sheldon in person once. She wasn't sure if he did all that for her sake—because Sheldon was so young, Cary's feelings about him were very very complicated—or if he did that for his own piece of mind. But the fact that Deacon hadn't ripped Sheldon's throat out yet was a miracle, and the fact that he seemed genuinely concerned that Sheldon *not* die was even more amazing.

"Your mate is a good man," Brandon said quietly. "Even when he doesn't think he is."

"You've known him a while?" She'd never talked to Brandon about Deacon, and only really once to Deacon about Brandon. She'd be interested to put the two men in the same room to see for herself how they got along.

But that was mostly because Brandon had eyes on one of her other best friends and Cary wanted to make sure that situation was a potential good thing and not a potential bad thing. Deacon getting a good super shifter sniff of Brandon would give him all the information Cary needed in regards to Brandon's feelings for Marianne. Brandon—being a shifter himself—would know that and likely only let Deacon get close enough to judge his motives if his motives were good.

And since thinking about Marianne—and her healing heart—and Brandon was a lot less tormenting than considering the fact that one of her old demon enemies was, even now, on his way to Portland for this world-ending confrontation with his *parents*, Cary decided getting to know her sparring partner a little better was a good idea.

Or, it would have been a good idea if they'd gotten the chance to actually have a conversation.

Unfortunately, any hope of discussion was cut off when Deacon stalked into the dojo, looking entirely too serious.

Cary came to her feet instantly. "What's wrong? What's happened?"

"Sheldon is awake," Deacon said. "Eriana and Jaxer are with him. He's asking for you."

Shit. But also maybe good? Given the look on Deacon's face, she wasn't sure what to hope for. "I'll change. Give me two minutes." To Lucy and Brandon, "Thanks for the session. And for the not-pity distraction. I appreciate it."

"Call if you need us," Lucy said, giving her a brief hug.

Cary hurried back to the locker room to put on her street clothes, anxiety clawing at her gut.

～

Don't miss
The Trouble with Death and Demon Gods!
Out May 2022

BOOKS BY KAT SIMONS

THE CARY REDMOND SERIES

1 – The Trouble Black Cats and Demons

2 – The Trouble with Ghouls and Serial Killers

3 – The Trouble with Leopard Queens and Shifter Wars

4 – The Trouble with Baby Gods and Vampires

5 – The Trouble with Magic and Faery Curses

6 – The Trouble with Wizards and Old Enemies

7 – The Trouble with Death and Demon Gods

COMING May 2022

CARY REDMOND SHORT STORIES

When Cary Met Jaxer

When Cary Met Pickles

When Cary Met Angie

When Cary Met Lucy

When Cary Met Marianne

Cary and Deacon (Try to) Go On A Date

Date Night Take Two

Third Date's the Charm

Cary vs the Goblin King

Dinner with the Jones

Cary and the Cursed Jack-o-Lantern

Cary and the Demon Witch

Cary Goes to Hawaii

Cary Holidays

Cary and Dragons and Goblins

When Cary Met the Good Guys (Collection 1)

Dates, Dinners, and Other Disasters (Collection 2)

Romancing the Leopard: A Tiger Shifters-Cary Redmond Crossover Novel

TIGER SHIFTERS SERIES

1 – Once Upon a Tiger

2 – Along Came a Tiger

3 – Here There Be Tigers

4 – Her Tiger To Take

5 – To Tempt a Tiger

6 – Down Will Come Tiger

7 – To Catch a Tiger

8 – What a Tiger Wants

9 – Taming Her Tiger

Tiger Shifters Series Vol 1 (Books 1 - 3)

Tiger Shifters Series Vol 2 (Books 4 - 6)

MORE BOOKS BY KAT SIMONS

DEMON WITCH SERIES

Moonlit Strange (short story)

1 – Bone Lantern Witch

JOAN OF KERRY SERIES

1 – Joan of Kerry: Joan and the Abhartach

2 – Joan and the Leprechaun

HAUNTS AND HOWLS COLLECTIONS

Haunts and Howls and Guardian Spells

ABOUT THE AUTHOR

Kat Simons earned her Ph.D. in animal behavior, working with animals as diverse as dolphins and deer. She brought her experience and knowledge of biology to her paranormal romance and urban fantasy fiction, where she delights in taking nature and turning it on its ear. Her Tiger Shifters series combines romance and the otherworldly with heart-pounding action adventure. Her latest urban fantasy romance series follows the adventures of Protector Cary Redmond as she tries to manage her personal life while saving the world. A lot.

For something a little different, Kat also publishes fantasy romance, science fiction romance, and the occasional hockey romance under the name Isabo Kelly (https://www.isabokelly.com).

After traveling the world, Kat now lives in New York City with her family. She is a stay-at-home mom and a full time writer.s

For more on Kat and her future books:
Website: https://www.katsimons.com
Newsletter: https://bit.ly/KatSimonsNewsletter
Facebook Page: https://www.facebook.com/KatSimonsAuthor

www.ingramcontent.com/pod-product-compliance
Lightning Source LLC
Chambersburg PA
CBHW060902190726
48286CB00002B/335